COBBLESTONE

B.M. GRIESE

Love Clones Publishing
www.lcpublishing.net

Printed in the **United States** of America

First Printing, 2014

ISBN: 978-0692277454

Publishers:
Love Clones Publishing
Chicago, IL 60604
www.lcpublishing.net

Editor:
YM Editing Service
Yttebmartin417@gmail.com

To order additional copies of Cobblestone email B.M. Griese at bmgriese@gmail.com

DEDICATION

To my mother who is my rock, you have spent long grueling hours trying to teach me how to read and write even though it proved to be very difficult with my dyslexia; you are the reason why I am where I am today.

To my nephew who works hard every day through his challenges and comes out on top. You are not afraid of any trial. To my sister who spends extra hours to help her son, no matter the situation or what is going on, she is there for him, working with him so he can be the best he can be. You are amazing and I love you all very much.

ACKNOWLEDGMENTS

To God, the true writer behind my hand, without you and your strength I would never have written this book. Lord you have granted me the strength and patience to fight to learn to read and write. You've given me people in my life, like my mother, to help me through all of my challenges.

To all the mothers and fathers who have put in long extra hours to help their children accomplish more, without you there wouldn't be so many amazing people in the world.

To anyone with a learning disability or handicap that makes you feel different from everyone else, you are special, smart and I admire you. Unless someone experiences the hardships that you have gone through they will never know the strength you have. You are truly amazing and a wonderful gift from God.

No matter who you are, you are truly amazing. God made us each unique with wonderful gifts and challenges because only he knows what we can handle.

CHAPTER 1

She looked out of her hotel window as the rain pelted relentlessly against the windowpanes. It was eight thirty on a Monday spring morning in Washington, where she was looking to make her new home. Cobblestone, Washington had a population of three hundred people; make that three hundred and one when she makes her transition. "How am I going to deal with the rain?" she asked the lonely air around her. Ever since she found her, now ex-boyfriend in her bed with her so-called best friend, she felt alone, betrayed and couldn't trust anyone; that was a year ago.

Cristina was your average twenty-five year old woman. She was five foot, five inches in height, long brown hair and deep chocolate brown eyes. To top it off, she had a perfect hourglass figure that many people considered fat since her hips had her in a size eight, not the socially acceptable size six or smaller.

She pulled on a pair of jeans, a black long-sleeved t-shirt and her gray Bart Simpson "Represent" hoodie. "You'll have to do with this rain," she said, as she took in her appearance in the full-length mirror in the bathroom. She pulled on a pair of black boots, grabbed her purse and car keys and headed to the little coffee shop around the corner after ensuring the little plastic key card was in her pocket. She was meeting realtor, Jackie Blake, to discuss a few properties in the area for sale, hoping to find the perfect one quickly.

With the low population and the fact that it was now eight-fifty in the morning, there was practically no traffic, so Cristina was able to pull into a parking space right in front of the coffee shop, Blake Coffee and Tea. It was raining even harder when she quickly climbed out of her car and made a beeline to the awning of the coffee shop before clicking the button on her keys to lock her car.

As soon as she opened the door to the coffee shop, she was assaulted by the wonderful smell of coffee, not that she drank it herself, but she did appreciate the smell. "Good morning, welcome to Blake Coffee and Tea, can I get you anything?" a young man asked from behind the counter. He was tall, thin, young and very easy on the eyes.

"Can I have a large iced black sweet tea and, um," she paused checking out the muffins, "A banana nut muffin?"

"Sure thing; that will be three fifty please," She passed him her card. He swiped the card then passed it back to her with the receipt and the muffin before leaving to work on her tea. She sat at a little table in the corner of the shop and pulled out her phone to check the news. *"Nothing new has happened in the world since yesterday,"* she thought. As she nibbled on her muffin Cristina took in the little coffee shop. It was a simple little place, the walls were baby blue, you know Tar Heels blue and the floors were done in a simple black tile. There were about eight small round tables scattered around the room in silver and black with two matching chairs at each table. It was a cute little place, and very clean.

"Here you go miss," the young man said as he placed the cup in front of her.

"Thank you," she replied with a small smile. She could not remember the last time she really smiled, or even really laughed for that matter. Her heart was broken, and it seemed everyone she ever allowed into her heart caused her pain or left her. Halfway through her muffin, the door opened and a lady dressed in a dark navy blue suit came in shaking off the rain. "Sam, get me a coffee please." She turned and walked towards Cristina. "Cristina, I presume? I'm Jackie." Cristina stood and extended her hand for the customary handshake.

"You would be correct. How are you doing today Jackie?" Cristina asked as they shook hands and Jackie took a seat in front of her. Jackie was a pretty little thing, brown hair pulled into a tight bun at the nap of her neck, light make-up, which Cristina was sure she didn't need. She had a happy smile and the little lines around her eyes and mouth told Cristina that Jackie smiled a lot and laughed often.

"Well, I'm good, would be better if the rain would let up." Jackie glanced out the window next to them; the rain was falling so hard it was hopping off the ground for a second fall. The water was rushing into the street drains like little rivers throughout the parking area.

"Does it rain a lot here?" Cristina knew the answer, but she was hoping for a different one.

"We have a few dry days, but really, rain is inevitable here. So tell me, what brings you to Cobblestone?" Jackie leaned back in her chair and looked as if she was appraising Cristina. Cristina sipped her tea before responding.

"Well, I have always wanted to live on the west coast, but I'm not a fan of the heat," she simply said. She was intently avoiding the real reason, she wanted away from all of the reminders of her old life, away from the men who hurt her and the friends that laughed in her face. "Plus, I was told that Cobblestone was a quiet town and in need of a librarian soon."

"Well, we do need someone to run our little library since Mrs. Smith is retiring next month, but surely you didn't come all the way from Florida for a little job like that?" *"What? Are you seeing right through me or something?"*

Cristina thought.

"Well, I needed a change, I sold my house in Florida, and I'm ready to take it easy for a while," Cristina replied, she wasn't going to spill her crazy little life to a woman she just met.

"You don't look old enough to "Take it easy" you seem like a fun loving young lady," Jackie replied leaning forward in her chair raising an eyebrow that looked to have been plucked to within an inch of its life to create the perfect shape.

"Well, thank you. I'm young yes, but as my mother once told me, "My dear you have an old soul", so even though I'm twenty-five, I have grown up faster than my peers, plus, some things should stay where they are." She smiled at Jackie hoping that would end the interrogation. She didn't want to remember the year of bad luck, the cheating boyfriend and the back stabbing best friend. These were just the small things that began to tear at her life and what made her heart hard as a rock was a different matter altogether. The young man brought Jackie a large coffee and she smiled at him but didn't say anything.

"I can completely understand that. Sam is my son and this is his coffee shop. We moved here from San Francisco, I needed a change and Sam was just a baby when his father passed with cancer. I couldn't handle living in the city any longer and all of the hustle and bustle the city life required; so I moved us here when he was five and we love the area."

"Wow, I'm sorry about your loss."

"I loved him deeply, but I've moved on, he still has a place in my heart, but I no longer grieve over him and I'm finally seeing someone after all these years. You see Sam's father and I were high school sweethearts and we married at eighteen. Sam was born nine months later and my poor late husband was diagnosed with brain cancer just two weeks after Sam was born and died three months later." She smiled up at her son as he cleaned behind the counter. "I'm sorry for laying my little life on the table when we've just met. Sam tells me I really need to keep our story for at least the second meeting." Jackie laughed and Cristina joined in with a light laugh herself.

"It's ok, and really refreshing. I haven't come across many people who are open like you are," Cristina responded and took a long drag of her tea, letting the cool liquid calm her nerves.

"So, as far as houses go, we don't have many for sale, but I'm sure the ones we do have, you'll love. The first one I want you to look at is my favorite; it has three bedrooms, two and a half baths, an amazing master bedroom and it sits on a large parcel of land that goes back to the forest area. The nearest neighbor is about a mile, since you wanted seclusion." Jackie pulled out the listing and showed it to her. It was a cobblestone house, which went perfect with the name of the town.

"Wow, that looks perfect, when can we see it?" she asked eagerly. She wanted out of the hotel, and her things brought from the holding location at the storage facility two towns over. What she really wanted was a fresh start and to live a simple calm life.

"We can go now if you like. This home is move-in ready and all of the utilities are on and with one call they can be in your name should you want it. You said you're paying everything out right, so this should be a quick process."

"Sounds perfect. If you don't mind I would love to check the place out." Cristina stood, tossed her muffin wrapper into the trashcan behind her.

"Ok, follow me," Jackie smiled and stood. Cristina followed Jackie as she departed the little coffee shop with a wave to Sam who was still cleaning. They got in their cars and Cristina followed Jackie onto the main road and headed north. Ten minutes later and around a few twists and turns they reached a driveway and turned off. The driveway was newly paved with a beautiful brick boarder and trees on both sides.

The house was a stunning cobblestone two-story with an Irish appeal. Cristina fell in love almost immediately. The house looked like it was part of a fairy tale; there was a two car garage off to the back of the house, but the trees were near the home, yet spaced to allow for grass to grow and for children to run and play. Children, the thought put an ache in her heart, she really wanted children, but at the rate she was going it would never happen. There was a subtle front porch with an arched roof and a swing. They parked in front of the house and got out, lucky for them the rain seemed to take a break.

"Let's check around the house while the rain has stopped, shall we?" Jackie asked as she approached Cristina.

"Sounds good." She knew she didn't want to sound eager about the house, but she really wanted it, without seeing any other house, she was in love with this one. As they walked around Cristina could hear subtle sounds of rushing water. When they made their way to the back of the house she was stunned. A stream flowed by the back of the house surrounded by beautiful rocks, which matched the house perfectly. The water flowed down from the east into a large pond, great for cool swims, and then moved on to the west. It was magnificent. Nearby were two trees that appeared to have been planted just for a hammock. Off the back of the house was a screened in porch with a large sitting area. Cristina was in love.

*****

"Dang it Jeff, what is the deal with this place?" Luke called as he sat his tea cup down on his best friend's kitchen table. He was visiting for a few weeks to help out with his friend's construction business, but the rain was really getting him down. He grew up in the area, but he had moved to Los Angeles five years before, enjoying the sunshine, laid back city life and all the girls wearing practically nothing.

"Luke, you know it rains like cats and dogs here when you accepted my plea for help. You can handle it for a few weeks then you can go back to California, where the people are crazy and never seem to sit still for more than five minutes," Jeff teased as he entered the kitchen. Jeff was his best friend, but sometimes he wished he would rethink that friendship. Jeff was tall, with dark hair and blue eyes like Luke so everyone thought they were family when they were in school.

"When's the first job Jeff?" Luke asked. The inevitable would be for them to have to work out in the rain *"might as well get it over with,"* he thought. Luke knew Jeff was always building something, but being in the rain all the time wasn't really his cup of tea anymore.

"We have a meeting with Jackie Blake out at the old Patterson place. Remember the one with the cobblestone house, we're doing an inspection for a possible buyer, she just called me. She told me "get ready, this buyer is eager to get going," so let's hit the road Luke, it's already a quarter to ten."

"Oh, great. Inspections, the joy," Luke said sarcastically. Luke actually didn't mind dealing with inspections since they were mostly done inside, and Luke was just along for the ride. He didn't know much about inspections nor was he qualified to do them; he was a Jack of all trades, but the muscle part was more his style.

"Luke, you're going to kill yourself with all the running you do before you turn twenty-seven if you keep this up. Inspections take time, yes, but it's easy work. Who knows this new buyer could be a beautiful young lady, shoot, maybe the girl for me." Jeff elbowed Luke in the ribs. As much as he cared for his best friend, Jeff was too obnoxious to keep a woman longer than a month, if he was able to snag one since he was also pretty shy; an odd mix.

"Alright, let's get this over with." Luke pulled on his heavy jacket and they piled into Jeff's pickup truck. Lucky for Jeff, he didn't live far from the Patterson property, so five minutes later they were pulling in beside a blue Subaru Forester and a black Ford Escape. The house still looked as amazing as he remembered from his teen years. He had even dreamed of owning this place once upon a time, but after his fiancé slept with the whole football team, he left Cobblestone and moved to LA, vowing to only return to see his best friend, but it had been years.

"Ready?" Jeff asked as he killed the engine.

"As I'll ever be." The rain had stopped so they headed inside to look for Jackie. Jeff had his tool belt on and his check list and everything he needed to do his job. Luke was just there for the ride. They found Jackie in the dining area with a young woman with a hidden shape under a large hoodie, but even from behind he could tell she was in shape. As they approached the young lady turned around and his heart skipped a beat, she was remarkably beautiful. Her heart shaped face, pouty lips, and Hershey Kiss eyes made him crave chocolate like he never craved before, not to mention her very tan skin.

"Jeff, thank you so much for coming on such short notice, this is Cristina, and she's hoping you'll give the go ahead so she can make this place her home." Jackie stood and shook Jeff's hand, then Cristina extended hers. Jackie was just as Luke remembered her, but he never knew she went into real estate. He knew her son was the local coffee shop owner which had quickly turned into the local teen hang out.

"My pleasure Jackie, nice meeting you Cristina. This here is my best friend Luke, he just came in yesterday to help out with a few construction jobs I have going on." Luke reached out his hand and shook Jackie's then Cristina's hand. The moment he clasped her hand a warm heat zapped through him, something he had never felt before, and he could feel his pulse quicken.

"Nice to meet you Luke." Cristina smiled.

"Pleasure is all mine," he said without thinking but the smile on her face caused dimples to present themselves and her cheeks flushed red.

"Well, um, shall we get started?" Jeff said breaking up the awkward silence and causing them to release their hands. The moment he let go of her hand he felt a cold shiver run through him, like she was his warmth and he just let it go. Odd, he thought. He smiled at Cristina and Jackie as he followed Jeff around the house while he inspected this and that. It all seemed to be in perfect order and most everything had been replaced in the last three years, according to the website Jeff was checking on his phone, which is pretty good for a house for sale. "Dude, what was that in the dining room?" Jeff asked while he was checking out the master bedroom.

"What are you talking about?" Luke was trying to avoid the question, he knew what he meant, he just didn't want to think about it.

"Dude, come on, you lit up like a Christmas tree when you saw her face down there, almost looked like something else may have lit up too." Jeff laughed, Luke knew what he meant, but it wasn't like beautiful women gave him an instant hard on or anything. He wasn't like that; Luke could appreciate a woman's beauty without instantly thinking about taking her to bed.

"Shut up Jeff, your head is always in the gutter." Luke punched him in the shoulder. Cristina was beautiful, he'll give him that, but surely that was it. It wasn't love at first sight, he doesn't even believe in that any longer, not after Lilly, but he will admit she seemed like someone he wanted to get know. He would wait to see if their paths crossed again.

"Whatever dude, but I think she was taken by you as well, I know you saw that smile. She's a very attractive young woman; unique in her look, and that hoodie, I mean, that was awesome, a chick that likes the Simpsons is a win in my book." Jeff laughed and headed toward the hall.

"Dude any woman who gives you a second look is a win in your book, you almost done?" Luke said as he followed Jeff into the hall.

"Yeah man, I'm done."

"Alright then, stop wasting the ladies' time downstairs and let's get out of their hair, I'm sure Cristina is dying to know she can buy the place without any repairs, which is odd mind you. What are they selling this place for?"

"Actually, she's getting it for a steal, two hundred even; the place is really worth over three with all the land that comes with it. No one really knows why the place went up for sale so fast and why so low, but no one before now has wanted to buy it, fishy if you ask me. Something has to be wrong here, but we just aren't seeing it."

"Do we tell her that, I mean, shouldn't we tell her something seems off, that everything is far too perfect for comfort?"

"Nah man, maybe this is fit for her. She looked like she's dealt with a lot in her life already, she didn't look too happy even with the prospect of buying such a great house. Maybe this is just a good omen for her to start fresh," Jeff said thoughtfully. Luke had to admit that even though Jeff was a kidder, he did see more than the average person when it came to people.

"Maybe you're right, ok let's give her the good news." They headed down stairs and found Jackie and Cristina out back on the enclosed porch, the rain had begun again, but it was calmer then it was earlier, a nice mist instead of a torrential downpour.

"Jackie, Cristina," Jeff said as he stepped out on the porch interrupting the two ladies talking. "I have great news for you Cristina, everything is perfect. Actually it's too perfect, but maybe it's a good omen for you to have a fresh start." Jeff actually told her it was odd. *"Damn man, I like you even more now"* he thought, reassessing his earlier thought to reconsider Jeff a friend. Cristina smiled, but no dimples, just a subtle smile. If she was ecstatic she was not showing it, the smile he saw earlier was much brighter, so he knew she could smile better than that. Something happened before she decided to move here to make that smile hard to get, yet he got it upon the first meeting. Luke knew from that moment that he wanted to see that smile again, even if it was just as a friend.

"That is great news," Jackie said giving Jeff a good hand shake. "Thank you for doing this on short notice. You'll email me the report so we can have it for the final paperwork?" she asked him.

"Yes, ma'am I sure will. You'll have it by the end of the day," Jeff said as he turned and made his way out the door. The time for making a move on Cristina was suddenly closing in. Luke reached for a card with his cell phone number on it and handed it to her.

"If you need help moving your things in, give me a call," Luke said quickly as she took his card and smiled that small smile.

"Wow, thank you. I may take you up on that offer," she said. Luke nodded to her then turned and headed for the truck.

"Man, you got it bad, what took you so long?" Jeff asked as Luke closed his door to the truck and Jeff turned the engine on.

"Man, I was giving her my card so if she needs help moving in."

"Man, you like her."

"Dude, you don't know anything, I was being nice. Did you see anyone with her that might be able to move a dresser?" Luke asked harshly.

"Come on, we've been friends for years, you find her attractive." Jeff gave him a dubious look. "But I think you're right in the moving help situation."

"Who wouldn't, she looks great, but I'm not looking to start any relationship here in the God forsaken wetlands," Luke snapped back. After that, they drove in silence and headed to another site.

*****

Jeff Parker sat at his desk working on the current Bed and Breakfast plan that was coming together faster than he thought was possible. Running a hand through his hair he stood to grab a cup of coffee trying to block out the pain in his chest. Everything revolved around his work; he was always working on one project or another. Ever since the accident in high school, he couldn't handle sitting still for too long, the images that invaded his head always brought him to tears.

"Are you excited about the dance?" Jeff put the car in reverse as he left the restaurant.

"Yeah, I can't wait," Sara smiled sweetly at him, her green eyes shining in the lights of the parking lot.

"Have you decided what colors we're going with?" Jeff asked knowing she wanted him to coordinate with her dress. As a cheerleader everything had to be perfect down to the perfect color.

"I was thinking dark blue, you look amazing in blue." She smiled at him and he laughed. She sure did love him in blue and even though he was always picked on for doing everything she wanted of him, getting called whipped was nothing compared to the loneliness he would feel without her.

"We could do green since you look amazing in green," he added, she did look wonderful in green, her eyes were always bright with the color.

"I had considered that, but for Prom, I want everyone to know what a hunk of a stud-muffin I get to go with," she

laughed as he pulled to a light.

"I love you," he said softly as the light turned green.

"Love you too." She smiled at him the instant he saw the oncoming lights and before the vehicle hit them square on the passenger side. The last thing he could remember was the glass breaking, squealing of tires and the shrill cry of Sara before everything went black.

Jeff took a deep breath and dropped into his chair in front of his computer to send Jackie the inspection report. After filling out all the necessary documentation and checking permits on everything, he sent the inspection report off along with his bill.

"Hey Jeff, what are you working?" Luke entered his office with a smile on his face and Jeff couldn't help but roll his eyes at his best friend. Luke had come out to help him with a few projects, but once he showed up he didn't really need his help after all.

"Just sent off the inspection report to Jackie and went over a few details of the Bed and Breakfast we're working on, other than that, nothing. You?" Jeff crossed his arms across his chest and swayed in his chair back and forth as Luke took a seat on the other side of the office. His foreman, Rick, was heading up the construction site that day and he was free to relax a little bit.

"Nothing," Luke smiled.

"So, I was thinking..."

"Oh no, Jeff thinking, yikes." Luke laughed and Jeff rolled his eyes again.

"How would you like to become my business partner and move back here?" Jeff asked. He was sick of living alone and the new addition to the town looked like someone fit for his best bud.

"Can I think about it?" Luke asked leaning his elbows on his knees.

"Yeah sure. When is your lease up at the apartment?" Jeff asked wondering how long he would have to wait for an answer.

"This month, I have to sign a new lease in two weeks," Luke said simply. The man was bright and honest and like his brother for all intents and purposes.

"Ok, well, let me know." Jeff smiled crossing his fingers that his friend would move home finally after five years of being in California. Jeff needed his buddy back.

*****

"Emily," Alan yelled her name again from the bedroom. She was working on dinner and he kept interrupting her. Her heart was heavy as she quickly walked to the bedroom to see what he needed this time.

"Yes." Emily smiled weakly at him where he sat on the floor behind a pile of socks and her heart fell, she knew what was coming.

"You're incompetent," Alan scolded her and she closed herself off for the onslaught, waiting for the first blow to come, knowing it would be painful.

"Sorry, I know I am," Emily agreed with a smooth lie. She had been lying since she was a girl about one thing or another. Alan stood and walked toward her and her heart began to race. The anger was clear in his eyes and she never understood how such a sweet handsome man could have so much anger, so much pain. The slap fell across her face so hard she collided with the door frame as the tears sprang to her eyes.

"You're going to learn if I have to beat it into you like your father had to," Alan yelled before grabbing her by the head of hair and dragging her back to her feet for yet another slap.

"Please," Emily begged, her face was searing in pain and the tears coursed down her face betraying her. She fought to keep herself in control because the tears always made him hit her harder. He shoved her to the ground and kicked her in the hip and she winced.

"Sort these socks, and make sure you do it correctly this time," Alan spat. "And get my dinner on the table." Alan pulled the bedroom door closed with a slam and she let herself sob into the socks as she gently held her cheek that was no doubt red and swollen and would need a good cover of make-up before school the following day. *Why do I still go through this? God, what have I done to warrant this in my life?* Emily climbed to her feet, wiped her tears away and headed back to the kitchen knowing full well God had forgotten about her and was enjoying his little joke of her pain. *I go to church every day, yet you won't save me from these animals who have controlled my life for twenty-eight years so far.*

CHAPTER 2

Cristina lay awake that night, excited over buying the house and thinking about Luke; he was a remarkably handsome man. Bright blue eyes, dark military cut hair and she could tell he was built like a brick house even under the jacket he wore. His smile was breathtaking and his teeth were a perfect white and straight. He seemed very nice and the fact that he offered to help her move in was just perfect, since she couldn't lift her couch on her own. "Oh get over yourself Cris, he's bound to be a player like the rest of them," she said out loud then rolled over trying to find a comfortable position to sleep. The hotel bed was a little lumpy and the blanket smelled of bleach. Finding a semi-comfortable position Cristina fell fitfully to sleep.

Running through the property was exhilarating. The trees and the sounds of the birds singing were relaxing for her morning run. She was running the full perimeter of her land; when she felt the hair on the back of her neck stand on end and her heart began to race. Something was wrong. She picked up her speed hoping to make it back to her house before whatever was out there got her. With the house in sight she pushed herself faster, she could hear the foot falls behind her gaining on her; with a glance behind her she saw a wolf making an advance on her. She screamed as she tripped over a tree root. She tried to pull herself back up to run before the wolf made its advance, but she was too late. The wolf pounced and she screamed.

She bolted upright in bed, her heart racing and sweat covered her skin. "What a dream." She rolled out of bed and made her way to the shower. Glancing in the mirror she noticed that she had dark circles around her eyes and she looked pale even with her tan. She always had an easy time tanning, her mother, who had been raped, figured her birth father was of either Native American or Latin American decent. Unfortunately, all her mother remembered of the man was the powerful odor of alcohol and strong hands gripping her.

Cristina shook herself and climbed into the warm shower to let the heat of the water relax the taut muscles in her shoulders and neck. As the water cascaded down her body she couldn't help but think about Luke's blue eyes, the brightest blue she had ever seen, and she felt as if they could see right into her soul. She shook herself again and finished her shower. After she dried off she flipped on the radio for a distraction as she got dressed. "Think positive Cris, today you're going to be moving into your new house," she told herself as she brushed her hair and pulled it into a high pony tail. Pulling on a pair of jeans and a t-shirt she glanced out the window to see an overcast sky with a little sunshine, but no rain. She had called the ABF moving company the night before and had a delivery time frame from nine to eleven.

Putting all of her things into her suitcase she was packed and ready to check out. After one more check of the room she decided to call her friend Ray, the only friend who seemed genuinely concerned for her. They had been friends since before school and she felt he was more like a brother than anything else. They were remarkably close friends and he was the only person other than her mother that never hurt her.

"Hello," Ray answered the phone.

"Hey Ray, just wanted to let you know I bought a house yesterday so I'm checking out of the hotel this morning."

"Wow that was fast, I thought for sure it would take you a few more days."

"Nah, they had this house on some acreage surrounded by forest, it took my breath away when I saw it, and it was in perfect condition, practically everything in it was replaced in the last three years."

"Wow that is great; I can't wait to see pictures."

"I'll be sure and email you some once I get the internet turned on and moved in."

"I can't wait. Wish I could be there to help you move in."

"Miss you to Ray, well I better run, I have to check out, grab food and head out to the house before nine for my scheduled drop off between nine and eleven."

"Have fun, and see if you can get some help, don't try and move everything yourself this time," Ray reminded her. She almost fell down a flight of stairs when Ray had shown up that day. She had packed quickly when she sold her house, she couldn't get out of Florida fast enough. Her mother had passed and there was nothing keeping her tied to that place any longer..

"Will do Ray. Have a great day, talk to you soon."

"Later." They hung up and with one last look over of the room she headed to checkout. She loaded her suitcase into her car and headed to the little coffee shop for tea and a few muffins for breakfast, then made her way to the house. The sun was shining by the time she rounded the bend to the house, and pulled into the garage with the remote Jackie had given her. Honestly, she was surprised everything happened so fast, now she held the deed to the house and was the proud owner.

Walking through her new house she opened all of the blinds and checked all the rooms one more time, then opened the closets and windows to get fresh air circulating through the house. Everything was so perfect, the birds were singing as the large ABF moving truck rounded the corner with her storage cube and began to unload it placing it in the driveway.

"Ms. Williams?" the driver asked when she came out the door.

"That would be me."

"Sign here please." She signed and they left. So much for small talk or bribing them to help. She unlocked the unit and forgot how packed it was. After thirty minutes of pulling boxes out and setting them in the living room she gave up; she pulled out her cell phone and Luke's card. She needed help, she couldn't do this on her own. She dialed his number and let it ring.

"This is Luke," he answered; his voice sent a shiver down her spine.

"Luke, this is Cristina we met yesterday, sorry to bother you."

"Hey, it's ok. What's up?" he said happily.

"I actually just got my moving cube, and I could use some help if you know of a few guys who would be willing. I can order pizza and drinks and feed them. I just know I can't do this on my own." She knew she sounded desperate, but she didn't care.

"Yeah, sure I'll see what I can pull together. How soon?"

"As soon as possible," she laughed weakly.

"Ok, sounds good," he laughed back. "How much can you lift, I mean, sorry about that."

"Hey, it's all good. My friend Ray and I moved all the furniture so, I can manage." She actually laughed. After she had attempted to carry the mattress to the curb in the first place and almost fell down the stairs, Ray helped move everything else.

"Ok, let me see what I can pull together."

"Thank you."

"Not a problem, see you shortly." Then he hung up. He was coming and that made her feel better. *"Wow Cris, lighten up."* She moved more boxes into the designated rooms as she waited, at least they wouldn't have so much to do when help arrived.

*****

Luke couldn't believe she actually called. Getting his head on straight, he pulled on a pair of jeans, a t-shirt and his boots. The sun was making a rare appearance today and since Jeff was off at a sight an hour away, he hadn't needed his help so he was lying around his house bored to tears. He made a few phone calls with no luck on getting more help, sighing he pulled on his jacket and headed for his truck tossing in a case of water Jeff had sitting in his garage, if they used it, he'd replace it.

Five minutes later he was rounding the corner to Cristina's house, it was a sight with the sun shining down upon the house. It was like something out of a fairy tale, some story his mother read to him when he was a child. To the left he saw the large unsightly moving cube, he sighed, what had he gotten himself into? He was too nice for his own good sometimes.

He jumped out of his truck just as Cristina stepped out of

the house in jeans and a fitted black t-shirt. She looked mouthwatering with her hips and perfect hour glass shape, and he decided he was glad he was a nice guy.

"You look plum tuckered out already," he called to her as she paused on the porch. Her hair was a bit of a mess and as he got closer he could see sweet beads glistening on her cheeks and forehead.

"Ha, yeah I was trying to get as many boxes in before anyone showed up, so there wouldn't be as much work," she replied as they made their way to the cube. She didn't want anyone to have to do more than necessary, she was a hard worker and apparently hated having to ask for help, something Luke liked about her.

"Wow, you know how to make a man feel weak," he laughed. "So I made a few calls but everyone was working so you have me."

"You'll do," she smiled then they laughed.

"I'll do, ok we will see if you'll do." They laughed harder and he loved the sound of her laughter. Her dimples were mini craters in her cheeks and she looked amazing. "Shall we get started before the weather changes on us?" he asked and headed inside the cube.

They pulled out her bed set and took it to the master bedroom along with the matching dressers. Followed by the office desk, shelves and filing cabinets, spare bed and dresser, dining room table and chairs along with her mother's china cabinet. Then finally, the living room couch and tables, then her TV stand. Once the last box was placed in the correct room it started to pour outside.

Luke watched as Cristina ran to the cube and closed it up. When she ran back the rain was pouring so hard she was soaked when she reached the porch. "Man, the weather around here really does change at the drop of a hat," she said as she pulled her shirt out from her thin waist and wrung the water out. She looked so hot, Luke had to look away.

"Shall we get your furniture put together?" Luke asked her. Her face registered shock that he offered to help put everything together.

"You don't have to stay for that," she said.

"Nah, I know you can handle it, but I'm sure you don't want to spend all day putting furniture together, besides, two people will make short order of getting this place livable." She smiled at him, apparently he'd said the right thing.

"Sounds good." She looked at her watch. "Wow, shall I order us some pizza?"

"Sounds good to me. What do you like on your pizza?" Luke asked her.

"Oh I'm a "Meat me" person," she laughed.

"Girl after my heart, I mean I love the meat lover's pizza." Luke tried to reclaim his "whatever" stance, but she smiled a bright smile and he no longer cared that he slipped up.

"Ok, I'll order and we can work on the bed frame, it's a pain to put together," she laughed. He watched as she walked into the kitchen and ordered the pizza and drinks. She headed for the garage and a moment later she had donned a pink t-shirt ridding herself of the wet one. Pink looked amazing on her. "Pizza is ordered, hope you like Dr. Pepper," she said then turned and headed for the stairs.

"Love it!" He called after her and raced her to the stairs, winning with ease. She laughed behind him as he bounded up the stairs to her room. Oh how he wished she would invite him to stay. *"Wow man, get your thoughts together,"* he thought. He hadn't been in a real relationship since Lilly, but something about Cristina made him long for that closeness again. "I win," he said as she entered the room just behind him.

"You have longer legs, that's not fair," she replied with a laugh.

"So where did you move from?" Luke asked as she moved the head board where she wanted it.

"Well, I moved from Miami. Got sick of the hustle and bustle of the city and all the back stabbing people who were in my life." She clamped her lips shut like she didn't mean to give too much away, but it slipped out.

"Well, I surely can understand leaving all the back stabbers behind, that's why I moved to LA, not that I'm a fan of city life, but I needed a break from here."

"Mind if I ask who?"

"Ha, well my ex-fiancé slept with the whole football team at our college."

"Wow that sucks."

"How about you?" he asked as she turned and faced the large bay window.

"I found my boyfriend in my bed with my best friend."

"Damn girl, not this bed I hope."

"Nah, I bought a new one. I saw this set in a store a few days before and I thought it was a nice collection so I bought it after everything happened." She walked back to the bed and pulled on the bed post and hooked in the bed slate, which interlaced with cross beams so Luke leaned down and popped his side into place. They moved to the foot board and popped it into place. With a little readjustment, the bed sat against the wall. They uncovered the mattress and box spring and put them in place. Cristina positioned one nightstand where she wanted it and Luke did the same on the other side.

"I love the dark Cherry wood of this set, very classy and goes great with this house." Luke admired her furniture choices. Nothing he saw so far was super feminine, but a nice mix. All he'd had in his apartment in LA was a futon, a coffee table and a desk.

"I love Cherry wood, the dark gloss of it just draws me in," she replied. They arranged her dresser just in time for the doorbell to ring. "Food's here." They headed down stairs and Cristina opened the door to a young man holding flowers, better yet, a large vase of red roses, looked like two dozen to Luke.

"Ms. Williams."

"Yes."

"These are for you."

"Wow, who are they from?"

"Not sure ma'am. Please sign here." She signed and accepted the flowers and the young man left. Luke followed her into the kitchen where she placed the roses on the kitchen island and pulled out the little card.

"Oh. Um."

"What's wrong?"

"Nothing, the card just says welcome to your new home, no name or anything. How odd."

"You seem generally concerned, what's up." She brushed him off with a wave, but he knew something was off.

"Nothing, just no one has my address yet, well except for a handful of people here." The doorbell rang again. "That must be the pizza." She went for the door, but Luke beat her there. And it was the pizza boy. Luke slipped the pizza boy a twenty before Cristina could get her wallet out. "Hey, food was my treat for you helping me," she protested.

"You got me out of the house, and I never let a lady pay for food." He smiled and the young man ran to his car.

"Pain," She laughed, "Fine, thank you for lunch."

"Back at you and you're welcome." He laughed back at her. She pulled up a barstool to the island then moved the roses to the counter. Luke sat the pizza and two bottles of Dr. Pepper on the counter and pulled up a seat.

"So Luke, what do you do?"

"Ah, well, I'm a Jack of all trades really. Mostly I work in construction, but right now I'm in between jobs, that's why I'm here with Jeff helping him out."

"Sounds fun," she replied biting off a piece of pizza right from the box.

"What about you?" He asked doing the same. The pizza tasted wonderful to him, the hamburger, ham, bacon and pepperoni was a perfect blend.

"Well, I'm a history major, and I have bachelor's degrees in Psychology, Business and Marketing." She took another bite, chewed and swallowed. "But really, I love reading and being around books."

"Wow, so what are you going to do here?"

"I'm taking over for the Librarian."

"Wow, way to take charge and be around what you love," Luke replied. She didn't look the librarian type, but after seeing Roberta for years, he realized they didn't really have a look.

"I wanted to slow down. I had my associate's degree in Psychology when I graduated high school, and I plowed right through the rest, completed all three in three years. I was working at the university when I met my ex, and I could only handle it a year after so I found this little place and just decided to up and leave after my mother passed." She began to eat, perfectly ending the conversation.

After they finished eating Luke helped with arranging the rest of her furniture, setting up her computer and entertainment center with her surprisingly large flat screen. Luke noticed the array of movies he helped unload onto the shelves and the different television collections she had. Around four in the evening they were done, and Luke was headed back to Jeff's.

*****

Jeff worked all morning hammering away on the Bed and Breakfast. With each nail he tried to drive out his haunting dream and the tears that came unannounced when he woke that morning.

"Jeff," Sara whispered in the dark somewhere he couldn't see, he hurt everywhere and he didn't understand why. *"Baby, don't leave me."*

"I won't leave you," Jeff said weakly, his voice sounded

wrong, off somehow, like he was in a tunnel.

"You're leaving me," Sara cried and she sounded as if she was in the distance.

"I love you, I won't leave you," Jeff cried out trying to reach for her but his arms were pinned by an unknown force.

"I love you too, please stay with me." Sara begged and he could feel a bolt of searing pain shoot through his chest like an electric shock one hundred times more powerful than anything he had ever felt before. "Don't leave me," Sara cried, he tried to reach for her again as the zap of electricity flamed through him and light began to pool around him. He could feel the rain hitting his face and could hear other voices and excitement as he opened his eyes unwillingly to beg whoever was shocking him to stop.

Jeff swallowed the tears that threatened to spill over; he couldn't look weak to his men, each working hard to get the Bed and Breakfast finished in record time.

*****

Emily sat and smiled at her class as they worked on their art projects for their parents. Her face wasn't as red and swollen as she thought it would be, and the make-up was an easy cover for the day. Alan had cooled off after she got dinner on the table and fixed the socks. She smiled at how he kissed her and apologized for hitting her and begged her to stop angering him so he wouldn't have to punish her.

"Ms. Hensley." Little Aiden smiled up at her with his bright blue eyes and mischievous smile.

"Yes Aiden."

"Caelin took my crayons," he pouted and she glanced up to see Caelin smiling at her with her chocolate brown eyes twinkling in innocence, but she knew better.

"Caelin, give Aiden back his crayons," she said sternly and watched as Caelin's small face paled as she placed the crayons back on Aiden's desk before she dropped her head in her arms and began to cry. Emily let the girl cry, knowing full well sometimes, they just need to cry; just like her. "Aiden, go back to your desk," she instructed and watched as he stuck his tongue out at the unknowing little girl.

"I'm so sorry baby, please, please don't make me angry." Alan pulled her close and kissed her gently on the cheek he slapped.

"I'm sorry," she said weakly. He was such a gentle man when she didn't upset him. She needed to remember to do everything he said and how he said it, and she wouldn't feel so much pain.

"Why do you do this to me?"

"I'm sorry, I don't know what I was thinking." She felt helpless but she knew she should have mated the socks more carefully. She needed to focus more on each task she was given and she would be fine, she didn't want to let him down.

Emily couldn't help but remember the night before, like so many others, she should have tried harder and not rush through things she knew would upset him. She took a deep breath and worked on grading the spelling tests from that morning.

CHAPTER 3

After Luke left, Cristina unpacked her kitchen, bathrooms, and finished working on the living room. She had already had the cable turned on so she decided to take a break and she settled into the couch to relax a bit. She had already locked her doors and closed all of her windows on the first floor. As the night crept up on her in her own little world out in the middle of nowhere, she felt oddly at peace with being alone. She figured the roses were from Jackie and not from the odd stalker she had back in Miami, whom she hadn't seen anything from for a few months.

Taking a seat she couldn't help but let her mind wonder and Luke seemed to be the focus of her conjecturing mind; he was like an annoying fly that wouldn't leave her alone. He was funny and she was able to mostly relax around him. He was sweet and very good looking and burned just like she was, a small thought formed that maybe they could make something of the situation. She knew she was getting ahead of herself so she focused on the television show in front of her, which was currently a rerun of Buffy The Vampire Slayer.

After flipping through the channels and finding nothing on, she resolved to head upstairs and work on her room a little before taking a shower and going to bed. Cristina had finished hanging up all of her clothes when her doorbell rang. "Who could that be?" she said to herself as she headed downstairs. She glanced at her watch and noticed it was just seven in the evening, but it was pitch black outside.

After checking the peep hole she found Luke standing at her door, *"well how odd,"* she thought and opened the door.

"Sorry to disturb you, but I realized half way home that you wouldn't have anything in the house for dinner, so I wanted to see if you would accept my offer of taking you to a great little Italian restaurant in town?"

"Wow, um, that was really nice of you. I would love to, let me change first?" She replied, he was in jeans, a clean shirt and a leather jacket. "Please come in." She stepped aside and he entered taking in what she had accomplished since he'd left.

"I see you've been busy."

"I hate living out of boxes. I'll be right back. Please make yourself at home." She didn't mean it to sound like she was begging for him to stay, but damn he looked good in her house. She watched as he sauntered over to the couch as she closed the door. "I'll be just a minute." She quickly made her escape and headed for her room. She pulled on a clean pair of jeans, a teal V-neck t-shirt and her leather jacket. She ran her hair brush through her hair and pulled it back up into a neat ponytail and slipped her feet into a pair of boots. Grabbing her purse off the bed she headed back to the living room, but froze just at the door when she saw Luke standing casually and totally at ease by her picture window. He turned and smiled at her, then she realized he could see her in the window. *"Idiot,"* she scolded herself. "I'm ready."

"That was really fast. Didn't even have time to get tired and have a seat." He smiled and opened her front door wide.

"After you, I have to lock up." She smiled and he walked out the door. She felt completely safe with him and she was not sure she could trust her feelings, but for now, she was going to enjoy the break. She pulled the door closed and locked up, turning she smiled at Luke who was smiling down at her.

"Ready?" he asked. She nodded at him and he motioned for her to go first. He opened the passenger door for her and helped her in since it was a bit off the ground. As she watched Luke walk around the front of the truck she noticed how clean the truck was. The seats were big and plush cream leather. Large console in the center, the perfect workman's truck, tons of compartments.

"I love your truck, it's very clean," she blurted out once he was seated.

"Ah, well I like to keep it clean, but really I just cleaned it out last night, I still had some junk from traveling," he laughed. They fastened their seatbelts, Luke started the truck and the radio kicked on, a country song rang through the speakers. "Sorry, I like country music."

"It's all good, I like country too, I'm pretty eclectic as far as my music is concerned," Cristina responded. Luke put the truck in gear and headed down her drive to the main road, through town to a small little restaurant called "Little Italy" and behind the words was the shape of Italy. Luke pulled into a spot and quickly killed the engine, jumped out of the truck and came around to open her door. She couldn't help but smile at the chivalry he still presented, when she thought for sure it was dead. Luke reached his hand out for support as she climbed out of the truck. When her hand clasped in his she felt a warm surge run through her body. "Thank you," she said to him once her feet hit the concrete, his smile was warm and reassuring that she was in good hands.

They entered the little place and Cristina fell in love immediately, everything was done in the country colors red, white and green, with images of the land everywhere, dim lighting made it feel more relaxing and romantic, which sent a surge through her since she was with Luke, the most amazingly handsome man she had ever laid eyes on. *"Snap out of it Cristina, he offered to bring you to dinner because he's nice,"* Cristina berated herself.

"Table for two?" the young waitress asked as they approached her podium. She was a small thin, blond with lots of make-up and her hair was pulled into a mass of curls on the top of her head. She was looking at Luke like he was an aged bottle of wine and she was an alcoholic; Cristina felt like an outsider, *"What if they had dated, or could they be dating? She's looking at him like she's in love with him."*

"Yes, please," Luke responded, Cristina just smiled. They followed her to a round table in the corner of the restaurant and she laid menus on the table in front of them.

"Linda will be your waitress, she'll be with you in a moment." They thanked her and she sauntered off to assist a couple that had walked through the door.

"This place is so nice, if the food is as good as this place looks I'll be one happy woman," she commented to Luke as she opened her menu. She already knew what she wanted, chicken parmesan, her favorite dish of all time. The last time she had it was at an Olive Garden with Ray and that was last year for her birthday.

"I have always loved eating here, and the food is wonderful and hearty portions too, you may have leftovers." He smiled and winked at her, he apparently didn't remember her putting away half the pizza today, she had a great appetite but ran a few miles every day to keep her figure, granted she hasn't had to work that hard luckily, but still she won't be young forever.

"Well I'm pretty hungry actually, who knows, you may have the leftovers," she laughed back. Just then the waitress came and took their orders, they both ordered chicken parmesan, extra sauce and bread sticks, with Dr. Pepper.

"So, what do you do in your free time?" Luke asked leaning back in his chair. She couldn't help but admire his good looks, granted she knew looks weren't everything. But he was like a wonderful piece of art she couldn't get enough of. To top it off, he smelled amazing, a scent she couldn't place but knew she would have to ask what cologne he wore.

"Well, I enjoy reading, hiking, and watching sports on TV, shoot, live is even better. I run a few miles most every day, but since I moved here I haven't had a chance with the rain," she replied.

"Sporty and smart." He smiled, oh how she loved that smile.

"So what about you?" She asked placing her elbows on the table and leaning on her hands.

"Ah, well, like I said before I'm a Jack of all trades, but I love sports and I run every day myself. Running in the rain is so much fun, or maybe I'm just used to it. Running in Cali, is like running in a sauna," he laughed. "I'm considering moving back here to work with Jeff full time, he asked if I would partner with him since I'm so good." He winked at her. "I think he was buttering me up since he's been so busy, he really needs help and I hate Cali."

 "Well, if it's what you want then you should do it. I have learned through the years, never do anything for someone else's happiness it will only bring you down; plus it's a lot of work," she said matter-of-factly.

"Wow, I know about the boyfriend and the backstabbing best friend, but what brought that lesson on?" Luke asked leaning forward, placing his elbows on the table and resting his chin on his hands.

"Well, I worked really hard in school because my mother didn't want me to worry about who my father was and she feared I might turn out like him; as if that could happen. My mom expected me to become the top historian in the state and then get my forensics degree so I could work with the FBI and meet the president, she had real high hopes for me. My friends wanted me to help them all the time without ever helping me, and everyone around me thought I would fail as a human because of how I was conceived and they blamed my mother for being a poor piece of work who asked for what she got. No one ever thought about the fact that my mother never asked to be raped, never asked to have a child at eighteen and right out of high school and no one ever thought that they should try and help out." She fought back the angry tears that threatened to make themselves known.

"Wow," Luke replied quietly.

"I'm sorry. Life has made me distrust and not really believe a lot of good is left in humanity, it's something I'm working on and seeing as to how you've so far been nothing but good. I guess after mom died, everything went downhill from there," she shrugged. She knew she had given away too much of herself and she would never get it back, maybe Luke won't mind, maybe he will look over the little outburst.

Before he could respond their dinner arrived looking mighty tasty and distracting to her. "Mind if I say a quick prayer?" she asked Luke.

"Not a problem at all." He smiled at her. They bowed their heads and Cristina began her quiet prayer.

"Dear heavenly father, we want to thank you for this food, may it be for the nourishment of our bodies. Thank you for Luke and all the help he has been today and for bringing me to dinner; in your precious name, Amen."

They ate mostly in silence with a little talk about the weather and how great it was that it held off long enough for them to get everything into the house. Cristina told him how fast she was getting everything put together and Luke told her about his many odd jobs. Cristina couldn't help but worry about what her little rant did to impact her impression on Luke, she hoped she still had a chance at having a friend in the area.

*****

Luke was enjoying his time with Cristina, he couldn't get over how easy it was to get her to open up to him, and now he understood her a little better. Now if he could get the walls to come crumbling down, like Jericho, he would be happy. He really enjoyed talking to her and spending time with her, it didn't make sense to him, and maybe he had been single for too long.

"So, do you think you might stay awhile?" Luke inquired. *"Please stay,"* Luke thought. *"Man get a hold of yourself."*

"Since I just bought a house and land, I do believe I'm here for the long haul. Why?" Cristina replied while she forked another piece of chicken into her mouth, that beautiful mouth.

"I was just making conversation, that's all." Luke quickly responded then stuffed a fork full of pasta into his mouth. The taste of the marinara momentarily reminded Luke to take it slow with her. No matter the hurt in his heart, he had to give her a chance; surely not every woman was as secretive and vindictive as Lilly was all those years ago.

They sat in silence while they finished their meals. People buzzed around them in conversation, but Luke could only see Cristina. It was like they were in a bubble in their own little world, an odd feeling for Luke, one he had never experienced with any other woman before, not even Lilly.

"Are you ready for dessert?" the waitress asked. She was a pretty thing with red hair pulled into a tight pony tail and a pale face with a dash of make-up. He looked over to Cristina and her dinner was polished off to his amazement.

"I'm fine thank you," Cristina replied in a quiet voice, her face held a thoughtful expression. *"What was she thinking?"* Luke thought. She looked sullen and withdrawn, maybe he'd already messed up, maybe he was too pushy. He knew women were confusing and none were ever the same as far as how they responded differently to things, but this was crazy, or maybe she was just tired.

"Are you sure?" Luke asked and she just nodded. "I'm fine as well thank you," Luke told the waitress and she scurried off to the next table. "Is everything alright?" Luke asked Cristina in a small non-threatening voice.

"I'm fine. Dinner was amazing, thank you for thinking of me this evening. I'll have to come back here again, such a wonderful little place," Cristina replied, less herself and more calculated in her response. She was officially closed to him this evening, their friendly conversation vanished into thin air, but he would try another day.

"Not a problem, it was a joy to talk with you more today." The waitress quietly brought the check to Luke and he slipped his card to her without even glancing at the check. The waitress turned to run his card while he studied Cristina, the most beautiful woman sitting in front of him, yet for the life of him he couldn't figure out what he had done to close her off to conversation so quickly.

The waitress brought back his card and the receipt for him

to sign, with the added tip he signed his name and tucked his copy and card in his wallet. With a final sip of her Dr. Pepper Cristina stood and pulled her jacket on, informing Luke she was ready to go. Not to make a big deal about anything he stood and donned his jacket and pushed in his chair. He had noticed the dark circles under her eyes from earlier were getting darker, so he figured she was just tired.

He held the door open for her to exit the restaurant then again with the truck. Her only words were thank you, which was great, but she was brooding over something and it bothered him. What had he said? What was she thinking, that was the main question asked by men everywhere when it came to their women. He left the radio on as he drove her home; he tried to make conversation with her a few times but her short responses left him hanging.

He pulled around to the front of her house and hopped out to open her door but by the time he got around she was already hopping out of the truck, quick escape apparently. "Thank you for dinner and all of your help today." She smiled, but not the time stopping, dimple creating smile he enjoyed so much.

"It was my pleasure," he smiled back at her. She closed the door to his truck and headed straight for her door, unlocking it quickly and escaping inside after a quick wave good bye. *"Wow, I really did something wrong here,"* Luke thought. After another moment of looking at her closed door he hopped back in his truck and headed back to Jeff's.

The rain had started up again as he pulled in front of Jeff's house and parked. He killed the engine and thought about the conversation they had at dinner but he couldn't figure out what he had said that was wrong, sure he knew he was stupid for asking if she was going to stay a while after her buying a house, but surely that wasn't it. Clambering out of his truck he headed inside.

"Hey man, where have you been?" Jeff called from his easy chair as Luke entered the house dropping his keys in the bowl on the counter next to the door in the kitchen. Jeff's house was a good size with an open concept living room, kitchen and dining area.

"Other than helping Cristina with moving her stuff into her house and then taking her to dinner this evening, nothing much," Luke responded after pulling a Keystone beer out of the fridge and settling himself into the couch.

"Man you got it bad," Jeff chided. He looked completely at peace in his t-shirt and basketball shorts chugging on his beer. Jeff still looked like he was seventeen with his soft pale skin and his five o'clock shadow whereas Luke looked more his age.

"Nah man, just being nice. Not sure if I'll see her again." Luke shrugged and focused on the large flat screen.

"Dude, you sound down, what the hell happened?" Jeff insisted. Jeff always knew when something was bothering Luke, they had been friends forever, so he should.

"Nah man. We were having a great time at dinner and then I asked if she was looking to stick around for a while like an idiot then after that she pretty much shut down, not even room for idle chit-chat," Luke responded. He didn't want to sound like a little girl nor like he cared but both rang true in his words. He liked her, he couldn't help it. She was different, yet he felt like he already knew her. Maybe it was his Native American heritage that ran thin in his veins, or maybe he was just feeling lust after the beautiful girl; he was aiming for the lust since that was a viable feeling.

"That sucks man. She's attractive isn't she? The vibe I got

off of her though, she's more like a brick of ice." Jeff shrugged and focused on the flat screen. Jeff knew when to hush, but those words irked him to no end, Jeff shouldn't have made such a harsh comment. He didn't even know the woman.

"Dude, she's not made of ice, she's nice, funny, and quite brilliant," Luke hissed then jumped to his feet and made his way to his room.

"Sorry man. Didn't mean it like that," Jeff called after him.

Luke closed the door behind him as he settled onto the bed. Slamming back the rest of his beer, Luke pulled off his boots and trudged off his jeans, then plopped back on the bed. Cristina was a mystery to him, yet he experienced pretty much the same thing. Luke knew girls were softer than men, but it was as if she put her life in a box and she's now just living out some sort of play she read. Acting like everything is fine, never sorting things out or letting anyone get close to her. Luke knew he was thinking too much into the situation, especially since they just met, but he liked her.

Giving up the idea of getting his restless mind to try and sleep, Luke pulled on a pair of shorts and slipped into his sneakers and headed back to the living room. "Going for a run," he told Jeff as he pulled the front door open.

"Really, you just drank a beer, is that such a good idea," Jeff asked his eyebrows pinched together, his usual concerned face.

"I have my cell and it was just one, I'll be fine, if I'm not back in an hour come looking for me," Luke responded and out the door he went. After a quick stretch he took off down the road. In a small town like Cobblestone, there wasn't much traffic after nine at night, so he wouldn't have to worry about getting hit by a car. With each house he passed with the porch light on, he couldn't stop thinking about Cristina and how she quickly zipped into her house and closed the door on him. Focusing on the task at hand, he pushed himself harder trying to outrun the image in his head, instead he focused on a conversation he had had with his mother so many years ago.

"Luke honey, what's bothering you?" his mom asked. She was a small woman with long dark brown hair and bright blue eyes. He leaned and kissed her on the cheek where she sat at the table peeling potatoes for dinner.

"Nah mom, it's nothing," Luke responded plopping into the chair in front of her after grabbing a glass of her amazing sweet tea.

"Is it Lilly?" His mom always knew with him, she read him like an open book.

"Yeah."

"What happened son?" She put the knife down on the table and studied him closely.

"Ah mom, it's nothing." He got up to leave the room.

"Luke, you sit that behind right back down in that chair and you talk to your momma," she scolded, and he was quick to obey. His mom was everything to him and the only family he had left, and even though he was in college he always listened to her.

"Well, she's mad because I forgot that I was supposed to meet her for lunch today and instead was out shooting hoops with Jeff. He's still having a hard time after his mom passed, so to let off some steam he wanted to play a little."

"That poor child. Go on, what did Lilly say when you

explained."

"She told me that I should have called her or texted to let her know. Then she got all huffy and stormed off. Mom we are supposed to get married next year, why is it I keep feeling like I'm going to fail her somehow or that no matter what I do I'm always making her mad?" Luke dropped his head in his hands. He loved Lilly but he felt like he was drowning every day. He heard his mother get up then she wrapped her arms around his shoulders and leaned into his ear.

"Something your grandma always told me, follow your heart dear child. If something or someone is making you feel like you can't breathe, then maybe you need to reconsider." Luke wanted to protest that he loved Lilly, that he could breathe even though he really couldn't, his mom stopped his protest.

"Son, I know you feel like you love Lilly deep in your heart and she's a fine young lady. But you both are so young and she's very head strong. Jeff is your best friend and he's grieving something awful, she should be able to understand that." She kissed his forehead. "But remember, we women are a different race from you men, we are soft flowers in a field blowing in the wind trying to capture the heart of a good man. Most of us struggle to make sure we are good enough for a fine man like you, Luke dear."

She took a deep shaky breath, "Give her time, maybe she thinks you just didn't want to see her today but didn't want to hurt her feeling, which in turn did anyway. Give her tonight, then tomorrow take her a rose and make it up to her. You both will be heading back to college in a month, you'll work it out if it's meant to be. Now off with ya, I need to finish dinner." She settled back in her chair and started working on the potatoes again.

"Thanks mom. You're the greatest. I love you." He kissed her cheek.

"I love you too, son."

A few tears dripped down his cheeks as he ran down Main Street. He quickly dashed them away, before he came upon anyone left in the streets. His mom was a wise woman, one he would never forget, he only wished she was here to talk to him about Cristina. Resolving to give it time, he made his way back towards Jeff's to hit the shower and get some sleep, Wednesday was going to be a long day.

*****

Jeff sat watching the game Nuggets versus the Jazz but he wasn't really watching the game, he couldn't focus on anything. He had already downed four Keystone beers and was just thinking long and hard about his life and why things turned out the way they had. The idea that he could have died in that car accident really tore at his heart. *Could I have stayed with Sara forever? Could I have saved her?* Jeff had been utterly depressed since his senior year and for the life of him he didn't understand how many more years he would go that depressed.

Every woman he came across, the words never came to mind and he sat stock-still, frozen like an idiot. He wouldn't find a woman at the rate he was going and he was already twenty-seven. Jeff downed his fifth beer and got up to retrieve another one. It has been a long day and he needed to sleep to get more done the next day. He'd already eaten his dinner of leftover steak and potatoes. Luke was off somewhere doing dinner. Ever since his best friend met the Cristina Williams woman, he was like a new man. Jeff wanted to feel that way, wanted to find a woman who would change his world completely.

*****

"Damn it Emily," Alan yelled as she tripped over her feet

and fell into the kitchen spilling his glass of water everywhere.

"Sorry, sorry," Emily cried thanking her lucky stars it was just water.

"You need to watch where you're going," Alan yelled louder getting to his feet.

"It was the lip from the kitchen to the living room. I called the office to report the problem, they said they would be here this week to fix it." Emily quickly supplied him with a reason for her clumsiness; her foot got hung on the lip and she could feel the blood pooling in her sock as she knelt on the floor with Alan hovering over her.

Alan slipped off his belt and Emily quickly tucked her face in her arms and huddled to the floor just as the first blow fell across her back in a loud nauseating clap. Alan hit her five more times, each blow harder than the last. "Next. Time. You. Will. Watch. Where you're walking," Alan said through clenched teeth.

When he finally stopped hitting her with his belt she crawled away to the bedroom still clutching the glass that had contained the water for the man she kept trying to please. She put some oils in the bath and ran the water as warm as she could stand it, stripped out of her clothes and looked in the mirror to see the damage on her back. The crisscrosses of the swelling red belt marks made her cry, he hadn't hit her as many times as before, but each hit was stronger and filled full of hate and anger. *I don't know how much more I can take of this. I can't do anything right. Maybe I should take my life and be done with it.* She eased herself into the warm water and winced again as the sting of the oils penetrated the welts on her tender back.

CHAPTER 4

Cristina woke with a jolt when her alarm rang through the room to remind her it was time to get up. It had been a restless night reliving her dinner with Luke; she closed herself off quickly with the thought of getting close to him. She remembered the confusion she saw on his face and it hurt her like stabbing herself in the gut with a dull blade. She couldn't figure out why it hurt her so much to see the pain on his face but it did. With a huff she rolled over, turned the alarm off and climbed out of bed.

Heading for the bathroom to take care of a few things and brush her teeth she glanced out the window to find a gray morning, but still dry. Quick in her movements, she was in her running clothes and out the door in ten minutes. Doing a few stretches to loosen her taut muscles she focused on the birds singing in the trees, the branches crunching together from the wind blowing them into a harmonious dance. Setting off around her property she tried to focus on the beauty of the moss covered tree basins, the soft feel of the ground as she sloshed her way into the wooded area. Jackie had informed her that her neighboring properties had a simple fence around theirs so she would know her property line when she went exploring.

The forest was decently thick, but still she made easy work with her run, jumping over a few down logs and under low hanging branches. Everything was beautiful, but she couldn't stop her thoughts from traveling back to the blue eyes of Luke. They were bright blue, like a perfect spring clear morning. She felt completely safe when she was looking into those blue eyes, yet she felt like he could see her deepest darkest secrets as well. How could she tell Luke she liked him after just meeting? She felt like she could tell him anything yet that nagging feeling about trust kept her at bay.

She was sure one day she would need to tell someone about the feelings she kept having, the fear that crept up on her while she dreamed, the nagging feeling that she's always being watched which she knew was pure paranoia. *"Who sent the roses?"* she thought. How could anyone know her address after just purchasing the house the day before? Who would send two dozen roses and not sign the card? Far too many questions about the roses for her to think about now, maybe it was Jackie and in her rush she forgot to note the card. But Cristina knew that the roses would come, she had gotten two dozen red roses often and at odd moments, but she never knew who they were from.

She came upon a small stream and ran right through it not caring about the chill of the water that soaked her shoes, she kept heading north and angled herself east to make a large circle when she came across an odd rock formation. Trees were down all around the area but the rocks reminded her of the ones crafted into her house. Taking note of the location she ran past the area with a sense of loss as she passed the area and made her way back south towards her house. She decided she would do a little history on the area, maybe her house set on tribal land long forgotten, surely not, surely someone would have kept the land from coming into commoner's hands. Cristina thought more about the rocks and decided that maybe they were left over from when the house was built and dumped out of the way for use later. *"Who knows why some people do what they do,"* she thought.

When she got back to her house she glanced at the clock and had a moment of panic as she realized she was gone longer than she had intended to be, she had to leave in twenty minutes if she wanted to get tea and something to eat and be at the library before nine. Quickly jumping into the shower she was washed and dried in ten minutes, a record for her. Pulling her wet hair into a bun, she dabbed on a little mascara and lip gloss, not being a fan of make-up. She pulled on a pair of black slacks, and a navy blue blouse finishing the look off with a black suit jacket and her 3-inch black dress boots. With a glance in her full length mirror, she approved of the simple look and headed for her purse and out the garage door.

Waiting for her tea at the coffee shop Cristina quickly called Ray to give him a heads up.

"Good morning," Ray answered brightly.

"Good morning, did you get the pictures I sent you of the house?" she asked. Last night she took a few quick photos of the inside and sent them with her new address to Ray.

"I did and I was just looking them over. That house is truly amazing, and it seems like a perfect fit for someone just as amazing yourself," Ray commented.

"Oh Ray, you're a flatterer," Cristina teased playfully. "You know I'm starting at the library today?"

"Yeah, miss librarian, don't forget to get a pair of reading glasses." He teased her about the customary librarian look since she told him she got the job.

"Oh you. I have to run, talk to you later Ray."

"Looking forward to it Cris." They hung up and she took her tea and muffin to her car and made her way two more blocks to the library. She thought for a small town the library would be tiny; she was sorely mistaken when she came upon the large building that had a magnificent sign that read "Library of Cobblestone". "Wow," she said to herself. She polished off her muffin and tea, pulled herself together and headed inside, leaving her little Subaru parked underneath a tree near the entrance. Trees lined the sidewalk and it had begun to sprinkle just as she entered the library. She was greeted with beautiful bright paintings; the vast majority were of various Native American scenes.

The walls were painted in a simple cream and the carpet was a dark green. For as luscious as the landscape was outside, there were almost as many plants inside. The smell of books wafted through the air with a hint of cologne and sweet perfumes. Cristina felt completely at ease, especially since she spent a lot of her time in a library growing up. She made her way to the large desk in front of her where an older lady sat reading a book.

"Good morning," Cristina said as she approached her.

"Good morning dear, how may I help you?" she asked. She was a very thin lady with plenty of wrinkles but had a bright smile and a young look in her eyes. Cristina noticed a simple gold band around her ring finger, the wrinkles of her hand made it look as if she never took the ring off, *"How sweet,"* Cristina thought.

"My name Is Cristina Williams, I'm looking for Roberta Smith," Cristina responded.

"Well, that's me Ms. Williams. You're early, that is perfect. Please come with me and I'll show you around," Mrs. Smith said and stood to walk around the large round desk. Roberta Smith was about five feet four when she stood, wearing a pair of jeans and a simple blouse. "You're a little too dressed up dear, tomorrow I want to see you a little more relaxed, after all we want the younger crowd in here," Roberta chided her as she came to stand in front of her.

"Will do ma'am," Cristina smiled at her and they both laughed. It was a merry sound in the Library, one that never would have been allowed in the ones she visited back home.

"We have a few rules here. First, be comfortable. Second, let them have some fun now not too rowdy, but a little giggle or low laugh here and there is alright. We want people to enjoy reading and coming here, but not so much so that some get out of hand and disrupt others trying to study. Third, all books must be checked out of course, and each person has to present a library card. We are open six days a week from 9am to 9pm, closed on Sundays, we are closed all federal holidays. Everything is pretty simple around here."

"Sounds easy enough to remember."

"Sure is. Now you'll be working with Jill Taylor and Jessica Mills. Jill started here last year and Jessica has been here for a while, she will be your main partner. We have a position open but we are still looking for someone to fill that spot. As the main boss here, you really don't have to do much other than schedules, random appearances during off hours and ensure everyone gets paid. We get new books in every month and we cycle out old ones every other month. A lot of the time we just tag the old books with a red sticker so if someone wants the book instead of checking it out we take it out of the system as they come around. That system is pretty slow, but works pretty well, you can change it if you like." Roberta smiled at Cristina.

"How long will you stick around after all of this?" Cristina asked her, she knew the job wouldn't be too difficult, but still she might have questions.

"Oh honey, I ain't going nowhere. You'll be taking over for me, then I'll be on part time, getting old you know." She laughed and entered into an office with two large mahogany desks, windows on the opposite side of the door and bookcases on either side stocked full of binders. Both desks housed a computer and comfortable looking rolling chairs. On one desk, which made Cristina pause, was a large vase full of red roses, a lot like the one she got at her house the day before but with a beautiful blue glass vase. "By the way dear, those flowers came for you this morning, sure are beautiful." Hesitantly, Cristina moved to the flowers and pulled out the card.

Cris, Congrats on the new job, may it be everything you hoped for.

-Ray

Taking a steady breath Cristina was relieved that it was just Ray. "They're from my friend Ray back in Miami," she told Roberta when she saw her staring at her expectantly.

"Well, isn't that just sweet. Will he be moving here with you?"

"Oh no, we're just friends, have been since we were little. He's more like a brother to me, only family I have really," Cristina responded sadly. Roberta took note and started going over payroll and other office needs and how everything got ordered.

*****

Jeff paced quickly back and forth in his work trailer, the rain was falling pretty good and they were waiting for it to ease off to work more on the outside. Most everyone was inside working on the few odds and ends that needed to be tended to. The knock on his trailer door brought him to a stop. "Yeah."

"Hey Jeff, my wife has gone into labor," John said with a big smile on his face. It was his first child and it was a boy, Jeff was excited for him even though he wished it was him getting the news of his wife going into labor.

"Go, yeah, I'll tell Craig he needs to slip in," Jeff said thinking about the new guy. He was withdrawn and kept to himself. Jeff often wondered what had caused the scar that ran across the left side of his face. For someone only eighteen, Jeff felt the kid needed to relax but he was working his way through medical school and off for a few weeks.

"Thanks man," John said and ran out to his trailer. Jeff made arrangements with his crew and was pleased as the rain eased off, but he still needed an extra pair of hands.

"Hey Luke."

"Yeah man," Luke said sleepily.

"Can you come down to the site? One of the crewman's wives just went into labor and he had to leave," Jeff explained. He didn't really need the help but Luke had a way of distracting him and that is what he needed at this point in time.

"Yeah, sure. I'm on my way," Luke said and hung up the phone. Jeff settled into his chair to make a few phone calls about the supplies he ordered along with settling the details of the next project.

*****

The drive to Bellingham was a little longer then Luke would have liked, and the rain was pelting heavily on his windshield. Jeff had called him earlier and asked if he could come out and help since one of his worker's wives went into labor not five minutes after he showed up for work. They were building a Bed and Breakfast for a newlywed couple. Traffic was light since it was just reaching ten in the morning and most everyone was where they needed to be. Luke was in a sour mood after not getting enough sleep the night before, he had tossed and turned all night. Even after the revelation of giving Cristina time and not pushing her, it was hard for him not to want to be near her. Every fiber in his being yearned to be close to her, to hear her sweet voice, and look upon that beautiful angelic face.

"Get a grip man," Luke yelled and hammered his fist on the steering wheel of his truck. He flipped on the radio and cranked it up, when he heard ACDC playing. Drumming his thumbs along with the music he focused on the road in front of him. Twenty minutes later he was pulling in next to Jeff's truck and hopping out, thanking God for the rain taking a break. Trudging through the mud to the office trailer where Jeff would surely be, he tripped over a large rock that was hidden in the mud, and he face planted, all sprawled out like an infant learning to crawl. *"Really,"* Luke thought as he pulled himself up to his knees and sat back on his heels. His arms, legs, chest and face were caked in mud and Luke knew he looked a sight.

"Wow, you really know how to start the day off right," Jeff laughed, snapped a picture then handed him a towel to clean off his face.

"Really man," Luke rolled his eyes and stood. "You wouldn't happen to have a change of clothes in that trailer would you?" Luke asked rubbing the towel down his arms.

"Yep, even got a shower," Jeff continued to laugh as Luke followed him into the trailer. Just as Luke entered the trailer, Jeff turned to face him and snapped another picture of his muddy mess. "I'm so keeping that for the album," Jeff laughed.

"Man, really," Luke grunted as he trudged to the bathroom.

"Yep, you know the drill, you got me in a few interesting pictures if you don't remember," Jeff laughed back. "I'll get you some clothes and set 'em in the bathroom in a sec."

"Thanks man."

"Well, hurry up, we have lots of work to do." Jeff laughed and Luke shook his head and closed the door. Glancing at himself in the mirror he had to laugh, he sure was a sight. Streaks of mud on his face, his hair was covered and his neck had this odd tan going on. Flipping on the water he quickly stripped and washed himself in short order. The door opened then quickly closed, Jeff he assumed, dropping off the clothes. Toweling off, Luke stepped out of the shower and Jeff snapped another picture of him.

"Dude really, you going to use that later or something?" Luke reached for the camera, lucky for him his member was covered by the towel when he stepped out of the shower. "Something I should know about you before we room together for longer than two weeks?" Luke chided.

"Nah man, figure I would give it to Cristina." He laughed then darted out of the room pulling the door closed as he went. Luke knew Jeff would do it too, but he hoped he waited until she asked at least, granted she might find it funny, but it was a little too soon. Luke pulled on a t-shirt and the jeans Jeff left him, which were a size too big, but they would work. He put on his socks since they didn't have mud on them, then rinsed his boots off in the shower and slipped them back on.

Leaving the little bathroom Luke found Jeff sitting behind his desk drawing up plans. "What are you working on there?" Luke asked gazing over Jeff's shoulder. The design was hand drawn and immaculate.

"Just something I have been playing around with, my

dream home," Jeff shrugged then dropped his pencil.

"Looks good man, you're going to have one happy wife someday," Luke replied looking closer at the plans.

"Yeah, if I ever meet that perfect someone. Let's get to work shall we?" Jeff said as he rose to his feet, the sad look on his face was hard for Luke to take. Remembering back in high school his longtime girlfriend was killed in a car crash and Jeff hadn't been the same since, either he was still grieving- which he always would, or he hasn't met the right person, only time will tell.

"Yes let's. I didn't drive all this way to just play in the mud," Luke said lightening the mood. They left the trailer and started working on the interior. The Bed and Breakfast had three stories with only two rooms on the third floor, each with a bathroom. The second floor held four bedrooms, also with separate bathrooms. The first floor had a good sized kitchen, large dining room and living room with two bedrooms also with separate bathrooms, and off the living room was a double bathroom. The bones were all you could see at this stage of construction, but the roof was on and the exterior walls were in place, the studs were visible but would be covered in short order.

Starting on the kitchen they finished up the walls, since all the electrical had been done the week before and started installing the cabinets. The kitchen had windows every two feet on the exterior walls for natural lighting per owner's request. Along the ceiling was a flexed monorail lighting system so that the owners could adjust the lights how they felt best. Lights would be installed under each cabinet for enhanced lighting for work spaces and a single drop light over the sink for optimum performance. A large island in the center would allow for more work space and a few stools for guests to sit and visit.

Laying tile was a pain on the back and knees, but since everyone else had started working on the dining area Luke was left alone with his thoughts. While laying the grout, tile, and spacers to keep them even his mind began to wonder to Cristina's beautiful smile, and her chocolate eyes. He could see the sadness in her eyes but he could tell she was strong and would never let on that she was sad; he remembered those days. Thinking about the roses she got yesterday and the look on her face made him uneasy; she didn't seem to like them or maybe didn't like who they came from. Luke really hoped she wasn't in some sort of trouble, she seemed far too sweet to be in trouble or have done something to put her on someone's radar. Granted that story about her mother and how she came to be, had him worried, maybe the guy had been watching her all these years and would try something. Luke really hoped not and he knew that it was highly unlikely, perhaps just a random incident. Who keeps track of that sort of thing, though Luke knew many convicts who had kept track, they were usually in the local paper.

Before Luke knew it he had tiled the whole kitchen and was now leaning on his heels in the living room that would be done in wood before the day was done. Jeff had many hands on this project so the Bed and Breakfast would be up and running in just under a month from start of the project. Luke knew how efficient Jeff was at planning everything out, knew that no matter what happened, Jeff had a contingency plan in place and Luke would be in good hands partnering with him. Jeff was the brain and Luke saw himself as the brawn, as crazy as that sounded. Luke was very smart, but Jeff was scary smart, but he never did show it except in his work.

"Damn man, looks good. What do you think of the colors? The wife really wanted blue throughout the kitchen," Jeff asked coming right up behind him.

"I really like it, the speckles of blue are not daunting, it really plays up the area and will complement the paint we are going to do tomorrow," Luke replied, pulling himself to his feet to really look at the floor from Jeff's vantage point. The center of the intersection of the two entries had a starburst pattern which really set it off, the floor looked more like one of the quilts his mother used to make.

"By the way, it's quitting time, you missed the lunch call, what were you thinking about?" Jeff asked him concerned and the thought of missing lunch brought a rumble to Luke's stomach that he was surprised he hadn't noticed.

"Cristina. Let's get some dinner," Luke turned and left Jeff standing gaping at him.

"Dude, what's up with you and this chick, this is not like you," Jeff said running up beside him.

"I have no idea, I can't stop thinking about her. Maybe I'm worried about a pretty young thing living out by herself," Luke shrugged him off.

"When was the last time you got laid?" Jeff bluntly asked.

"Really dude, before I left LA," Luke stopped dead in his tracks and replied. Jeff looked him square in the eye.

"Tell me about that little honey."

"Ain't much to tell. She was a coworker, we both got plastered and ended up at my place since the bar we went to was just down the street from me. She came on to me, and that was that. The next morning she left a note telling me she had a good time, but it would never happen again since she was with someone," Luke spilled his guts. That night was not the highlight of his life, he didn't care much for one night stands, but it was done and over with now.

"That sucks man, do you even remember it?" Jeff laughed.

"Sure, wasn't anything to write home about, more like two drunks fumbling around, sad really." Luke walked to the trailer to grab his clothes, which he had stuffed into a plastic bag earlier.

"Wanna take one truck since you'll be here tomorrow?"

"Sure." They piled into Luke's truck after kicking off the caked on mud while standing next to the truck chatting.

"So, what is up with you and Cristina, really?" Jeff asked as Luke pulled onto the main road headed back to town.

"Nothing, really. I helped her move her stuff in yesterday then took her to dinner. After dinner everything went cold, like frigid cold," Luke replied angrily.

"What do you mean?" Luke could feel Jeff's prying eyes focused on him.

"I don't know what happened, she just went cold on me. Even idle chit-chat didn't even work. She just shut down."

"Maybe she plays on our side of the field? Or she was just tired," Jeff suggested.

"Nah man, she was burned by an ex-boyfriend and a best friend, she plays the same game, but she was hurt; I get that, but damn."

"What do you mean?"

"She came home one day and found her boyfriend in bed with her best friend." Luke glanced at Jeff and saw that he was looking at him intently.

"That really sucks. You two are pretty much in the same non-trusting boat huh."

"I guess we are, but I know she's not like Lilly. Don't ask me how I know, I just feel it deep inside that she's nothing like her."

"Remember women are like china, fragile with every turn and word. You just need to give her time. You're a great guy, your momma raised you right, after your dad passed. She would be proud of you if she was here today," Jeff said softly.

"Thanks man," Luke replied as he turned into Red Robin, pushing the memories of his parents to the furthest parts of his mind. He wanted to focus on eating, not getting sentimental.

*****

Emily sat quietly reading "A Fall of Water" the fourth book in the Elemental series and she was in love with the characters and the love and relationships described within. Tears streamed down her face leaving hot wet streaks as she thought about how different her life was in comparison to those in the story books. *Lord, why do you challenge me so?* Emily let her head fall in her hands knowing full well that Alan was visiting family and wouldn't be home until late that night, a relief.

Emily dried her eyes and set to work on her dinner to ensure everything was cleaned up and placed perfectly in its place so that Alan wouldn't come home in a fit of anger, even though she was sure he would either way. Her phone rang just as she was loading the last dish in the dishwasher and she took a deep breath and answered.

"Hello."

"Hey girl how are you doing?" Jackie asked with a soft, pleasant tone.

"Alone tonight," Emily replied plopping into her chair. "How are you?"

"Not bad. We need to get together and hang out soon," Jackie said. She was her only and best friend, though they were separated by several years, they got along exceptionally well.

"Good, when are you going to leave him?" she asked angered. Jackie had been begging her to leave Alan but she just couldn't.

"I can't. He loves me," Emily tried to reassure her friend as well as herself.

"Sure he does, he just knows that no matter what he does, you'll stay with him," Jackie said infuriated. Emily could understand where her friend was coming from, but it was different for her, she wasn't meant to have the happily ever after with the picturesque family.

"Jackie, I have to go." Emily hung up the phone without listening to another word from her friend and burst into a fit of tears once more. Emily jumped up and flipped on her CD player and pressed play on her Skillet CD. With each word of the songs that played Emily fought her tears and tried to find hope through everything, to find her voice to stand up to Alan and tell him how she felt, but she knew in the end it wouldn't happen. She wished there was a song of how she felt inside, she hated her life and everything around her. Every Sunday she went to church and never felt right with her life. She was growing sick of all the pain.

"I'm so sick of it!" Emily cried out loud and dropped to the floor in tears.

CHAPTER 5

Taking her run through the woods became a habit for Cristina. She loved the feel of the mossy ground beneath her feet. The crisp morning air woke her senses as the light sprinkle of the morning rain cooled her off. Making her full circuit, she came across the pile of cobblestone rock formation and with a closer look she could tell it was some kind of large grave. Taking a pause she walked carefully closer to the rock formation. A large gray wolf walked out in front of her, lowering its head with a light growl.

Knowing she would not be fast enough to outrun the wolf, her smarts were gone. She bolted back in the direction she came from, pushing herself harder with each foot fall. She could hear the wolf gaining on her without looking back. Seeing the house in the distance she pushed herself harder, she was almost there, she could make it. Swiping the rain out of her eyes as she ran, she tripped over a root and the wolf was on top of her. Rolling trying to knock it off her back it jumped on her chest and growled at her with such ferocity that tears streamed down her face. The wolf pulled back, opened its mouth and lunged for her…

Bolting up out of bed Cristina clenched her chest, her heart racing as if her dream was real. She was covered in a layer of sweat, her hair plastered in a very unattractive way to her forehead. "Get a grip Cris, it was just a dream," Cristina said to herself. The light was just shining outside her window and it wasn't even six thirty in the morning yet. Clambering out of bed she fell sprawled out on the floor because her sheet was wrapped around her feet. "Idiot." She slammed her hand down on the floor. She pulled her feet loose from the sheet and walked to her bathroom. She splashed water on her face, took care of a few needs, brushed her teeth and pulled on her running clothes.

It was Sunday morning and she didn't have to work. After three weeks she had taken over for Roberta completely and was feeling pretty good about herself. So, to relieve herself of the dream she decided she would take a run into town instead of around her property that morning. Zipping her phone into her shorts pocket she headed for the front door to slip on her sneakers and lock the house up. When she set off down her driveway the sky was clear of clouds, so she felt pretty good that she would make it back before the rain began.

Instead of thinking through the dream like her Psych training taught her to do, she thought about Luke. Three weeks and he hadn't contacted her. *"Maybe he's giving me space?"* she thought logically. *"Or maybe he thinks you're nuts after your little rant about your past. Stupid woman, should have kept your mouth shut,"* she berated herself. She couldn't help but feel lost and confused, she didn't want to care about him, but something pulled at her every time she remembered his amazing blue eyes. She started to call him over a dozen times in the past three weeks but could never complete the call. The fear of rejection constantly at the forefront of her mind.

She replayed the conversation with Tom after she found him with Linda. *You just aren't what I need, you don't do anything for me. I'm sorry but the idea of you no longer gets me where it should. Linda is a beautiful woman unlike yourself and she knows how to pleasure a man. Cristina, you're a very bright woman, but you have no man sense. Sorry you found us, but better now than later.*

Cristina wiped away a stray tear, she didn't want to cry over the worthless piece of crap anymore, yet he was her first and she thought she loved him, thought he loved her, but she wasn't good enough for him, she wasn't good enough for anyone. She had boyfriends throughout high school and college, but Tom was who she had been attracted to, even Ray tried to be more than a friend but after a long conversation with him, he lay off and they were even closer friends.

Making her way onto Main Street she was glad she only lived two miles from town, otherwise that trip would have been harder then she thought. As she ran down the road she saw a few others running as well, this seemed like a pretty fit town from what she had seen so far. Turning to run down a street she circled around a large tree and face planted into a large muscular chest. "Oh my God, I'm so sorry, I should have been looking where I was going." She was pulling herself back and looked up to see Luke. "Luke."

"Good morning, you sure know how to wake a man up," Luke laughed. She took a good look at him in his black basketball shorts that hung to his knees and his white tank top. He looked like a perfect model for basketball. His hair glistened with a hint of sweat but his face was glossy and his arms had a nice shine as well. "What are you doing all the way out here?" he asked her.

"I needed a change of scenery," she responded while trying to catch her breath. He was a breath of fresh air himself and she absorbed every inch of his face, sad that her memory hadn't done him justice.

"You live like two, three miles from here, did you drive into town?" he asked.

"No, I ran here. I like to run. I run a lot actually. Every morning I usually run around the perimeter of my property but, I uh, needed a change of pace and to give my ankles a break from all the roots," she told him. She knew she looked a sight and she could feel her pony tail not sitting quite straight any longer.

"Wow, how many miles did you plan on running today?" He looked at her inquisitively. *"Man you're so hot!"* she thought.

"Just a few, I have a few things to run off. How about you?" She asked putting the ball back in his court.

"I run anywhere between five to ten miles a day. Relaxes me, usually that is. Want to run together, I can take you on my usual route, which includes a very nice park," he asked, actually looking hopeful. Hopeful for her to refuse or accept she didn't know, but she wasn't done running and the idea of learning where the park was, was a good idea.

"Sure, that, um, sounds great," she accepted. His bright smile told her the positive answer she gave was just what he had wanted to hear.

"Well, let's get going then." He laughed and took off back in the direction she had come. After only a moment of hesitation she caught up with him. His long legs making him move a bit faster than she was used to going, but she wouldn't let him see her struggle with his pace, not that it was too much work for her.

It was easy running with him, neither one used a music player but the evenness of their breaths made a nice sound with the added drums of their foot falls. They had created their own music and she was relaxed. She hadn't realized that her pace on the way to town was more like she was running from something, now she felt calm inside, safe even. She felt safe running with this man next to her, she smiled to herself.

"Smiling, that's a good sign," Luke said interrupting her silent reveling.

"I love running," she lied coolly.

"Sure," he responded, sounding as if he knew she was lying but wasn't going to question her. He just smiled and focused on the sidewalk in front of him. He turned to the right and she found herself closing in on a very beautiful park. Trees were on both sides of the side walk with benches and a large pond to the north. The park was definitely a relaxing place to run through. They passed a few other runners with waves as they proceeded onward.

Luke started to move a little faster causing her to move quicker in response. She was actually starting to get tired at his pace. Just when she thought she couldn't run anymore she tripped over a lip of the sidewalk that was lifted and she scraped her knees and palms and almost caught her face in the process. "Shit," she blurted after the impact.

"Oh my God. Are you alright," Luke asked running to her side pulling her to her feet. Lucky for her a bench was close by. He helped her to sit and dropped in front of her to look at her scrapes.

"I'll be ok. Can't believe I tripped, I never trip," she said, scolding herself for being an idiot while in the presence of such a sweet and great looking guy. Luke pulled off his shirt and Cristina's breath hitched as she took in his sculpted chest, he really was sexier than should have been legal. He used his shirt to lightly wipe away the debris from her knees and dabbed the blood that had started to skate down her shins. Reaching for her hands he repeated the process but they weren't that bad. "Thank you." She finally found the words that were lodged in her throat.

"I think you'll be just fine, but let's head back to Jeff's and get you bandaged up." When he finished that statement it began to rain. "Then I can give you a lift home." He grasped her elbow and helped her up. She was already getting sore from the fall and the rain was making her cold.

*****

Jeff sat in church and listened to Pastor Reynolds speak of forgiveness and hope. "Matthew 6:14-15: For if you forgive men when they sin against you, your heavenly father will also forgive you. But if you don't forgive men their sins, your father will not forgive your sins. Ladies and gentlemen, it is not simple to find forgiveness deep in your hearts but if you can find the strength then do so. Not only will it make your heavenly father smile but your heart will be lighter in regards to letting it go. Cast your pain unto the Lord and let him shelter you from the storm and the pain." Jeff smiled as he thought about those words.

Jeff listened closely to everything the man said before him, soaking up the wonderful lightness he always felt when he got up and went to church. Jeff glanced to the aisle next to him to where Jackie and Emily Hensley sat listening to the sermon. Emily was a pretty thing, brown wavy hair and brown eyes and a sad smile. Jeff wanted to talk with her so bad, but she was dating someone and wouldn't even look his way.

*****

Emily sat and listened to the sermon; she couldn't help but wish she was at home. Church didn't hold her like it used to when she was younger, she wasn't feeling any hope of a better future or God intervening and getting her out of the situation she was in. *Surely, if this is not the life I'm meant to endure he would give me a sign; help me out of it somehow.* Emily risked a glance to her right to the handsome young man Jackie kept trying to get her to talk to. His dark brown hair was a little shaggy giving him a rough look, but his bright blue eyes spoke volumes and the sadness she could see there did cry to her, but she was scared.

The young man's name was Jeffrey Parker and he was in construction and Alan's cousin Rick was one of his employees. He was nice and always smiled sweetly at her but Alan would know if she reciprocated at all. Emily took a deep breath and focused on Pastor Reynolds as he continued to prattle on and on about forgiveness and hope, all of which she couldn't see herself doing, not with the life she had, not after everything.

*****

Helping Cristina to her feet was simple, she was tiny and when she winced something called to him deep in his heart, he hated that she tripped. Hated that she was now in pain because he picked up the pace without thinking about the fact she might not be used to running that fast, or the fact that she had already run from her home. He placed his arm around her waist, glad she wasn't super short, in which case he would just carry her.

"Thank you Luke," she said softly as she limped along.

"Not a problem Cristina, sorry I wasn't thinking about the path," Luke admitted.

"I wasn't paying attention myself. I've been running over roots for three weeks, I should have been looking where I was running, I was distracted." She laughed and looked down.

"What was distracting you?" Luke asked, hoping it was him.

"The scenery, it's so beautiful here," she responded. Hiding the disappointment on his face he commented quickly.

"It sure is, I love this park. My mother and I used to walk around here every day," he said sadly.

"When did she pass?" Cristina asked her limping getting worse, he was sure the cold air and the rain wasn't helping matters much. Since they were not far from Jeff's house, he bent and in one easy movement lifted her into his arms. "Hey, I can walk," she protested, squishing her face a little. Luke thought it was the cutest look and he tried not to smile or laugh, but he couldn't help it.

"Sorry, it's easier on my back this way," he laughed. "But my mom passed away five years ago today. That's why I was out running so early," he said sadly.

"I'm sorry. I understand your pain," she replied leaning her head against his shoulder. He loved the feel of her in his arms, she fit perfectly.

"I know. It was why I moved to LA, well the main reason anyway," he told her looking down at her beautiful face. She was even more beautiful from his current vantage point.

"I see you decided to stay here," she said.

"Yeah, I went back two weeks ago and moved everything out here and closed out my condo there. It feels good to be back." He wasn't going to admit that he wanted to be close to her so he could get to know her better.

"Glad you stayed," she paused. "I mean are you glad you stayed?" She was glad he stayed or had she really misspoke. He felt completely happy now that she'd said that, unless it really was a wrong choice of words.

"I'm very glad I stayed." He smiled down at her then leaned to sit her on her feet. He had reached the door of Jeff's house much faster than he wanted. He unlocked the door and stepped out of the way to let her go in first. He watched as she stopped in the entry and attempted to slip off her shoes but failed in an awkward way. Leaning down he put his arm around her waist and she immediately wrapped her arm around his neck. He lifted each foot pulling off her shoes but didn't release her.

Standing, he kicked off his shoes then motioned for her to head to the living room. "Have a seat, I'll be right back." She obeyed and he headed for the bathroom to collect some bandages and antiseptic. *"What is wrong with me?"* he thought as he realized he almost pulled her lips to his. Grabbing a washcloth, he soaked it in warm water then had a better thought.

Walking back to the living room he found Cristina still sitting and shivering; he knew his better idea was perfect. "Hey want to take a shower to warm up, I can give you a pair of shorts and a shirt to put on after." She looked at him for a second and he swore he thought the look on her face was because she thought he was inviting her to shower with him. Not that it hadn't crossed his mind, but it was far too soon for that. "I figure I could grab one in Jeff's room and get warm myself," he quickly added.

"Um, sure, that sounds great." She said her teeth chattering from the cold. She stood and slowly walked to Luke and he led her to the small bathroom, pulling a fresh towel down for her. He quickly zipped into his room and pulled out the shortest shorts he had with a draw string and a t-shirt, there was nothing small about the shirt but it was dry. He went back to the bathroom and she was turning the water on. He placed the clothes on the sink. "Thank you," she said as he was pulling the door closed.

"My pleasure," he replied, pulling the door closed behind him.

He made his way to Jeff's room and jumped in the shower, in double time he was clean and warm. He pulled on a pair of jeans and a shirt and went back to his room noting that her shower was still on, he put on his deodorant and sprayed himself with his favorite cologne, His Story from Avon. His mother had loved the smell on his father and bought it for him, now that's all he wears.

Coming out of his room the bathroom door opened and Cristina appeared in the doorway. She looked like a kid in his shorts which hung to her knees and his t-shirt which would have looked that long if she hadn't twisted it to the side and put a knot in it, smart cookie she was. "Go have a seat on the couch and I'll doctor you up." He smiled at her and she nodded and obeyed. She had gotten very shy since the shoe deal. He collected the bandages and headed to the living room finding her seated on the couch like he had instructed. She looked completely at ease sitting in his shared home with Jeff.

Dropping down on his knees sitting on the heels of his feet, he sprayed the antiseptic on her knees and put the bandages on. Reaching for her hands she willingly passed them to her. They didn't look too bad now that she was showered and they were cleaned out. He sprayed the antiseptic on them and put Band-Aids over them. "Now that you're patched up, can I get you a drink?" he asked still on his knees. He had placed his hands gently on her thighs.

"Sure, I'm feeling a little parched now." She smiled at him, not her normal I-Am-Hiding-My-Soul-From-You smile but more of a shy smile, one he looked forward to seeing more of.

"I have water, orange juice, Dr. Pepper, or I could make you a stiff drink." He smiled and winked at her.

"Stiff sounds good but I'll settle for orange juice, if that's alright." She smiled at him and he pulled himself to his feet and walked to the kitchen. He had the perfect solution, he would make her a screwdriver, since it was orange juice and stiff. Smiling at himself he made quick work making it more juice then anything, but enough vodka to ease the tense set of her shoulders.

"Here you go," he winked at her and she took a sip.

"Sneaky with the vodka. Thanks." She smiled up at him and he settled into the recliner next to where she sat on the couch. He watched as she eased herself deeper into the large plush leather couch. "This couch is so comfortable," she commented giving him a look that almost took his breath away. She had cocked her head to the side and her smile brought her dimples halfway out. She looked absolutely stunning, even in his large clothes.

"Love the color on your toes," he said absentmindedly. He watched as she looked down and curled her toes under her feet hiding them. "Why are you hiding them?" he asked curiously.

"I, um, hate my feet," she answered and took a bigger drink of her screwdriver.

"Oh stop now, you have cute feet," he told her and he meant it.

"You're just being nice, so thank you." Being nice, what him, no way.

"Hey, can I make you some breakfast?" He asked her, trying to change the subject.

"No, but thank you. I probably should be heading home, I don't want to impose and I have a few things to finish up." She finished off her drink and slowly stood. Before Luke could respond she was in the kitchen rinsing her glass and placing it in the dishwasher.

"You're not imposing," Luke said scrambling to his feet to block her exit from the kitchen.

"Still, I, um. I think I should be heading back. Walking will relax the muscles in my knees so I can get back to running tomorrow," she said and she snaked around him like a scared rabbit.

"At least, let me drive you. It's still raining off and on and you wouldn't want to catch pneumonia, " Luke insisted. She chewed on that a moment then agreed. The woman was stubborn he thought. "Thank you," he said then slipped his shoes on. She already had hers on and her clothes under her arm. He didn't remember her having them when she left the bathroom, but he had been a little distracted.

He held the door open to his truck, without hesitation he lifted her inside, her arms reflexively wrapping around his neck. His face was now inches from hers, no longer able to restrain himself, he brought his lips to hers. Her lips were so soft and she responded instantly. He grazed his tongue over the part in her lips and she granted him access. Their tongues did a dance of pure want, desire, need as he held her in his arms, her feet off the ground. She smelled of his body wash and honey and her tongue tasted of vodka and orange juice.

He sat her in his truck and reluctantly pulled his mouth from hers, forehead to forehead he caught his breath. She was becoming part of him and when she pulled away it would feel like he was being ripped in half, but he knew it was way too soon for this interaction and he would reap that pain later.

Collecting himself, he closed the door and walked to his side, shaking himself for being so brazen in kissing her, but oh she was sweet, oh so sweet. He would remember her taste and the feel of her in his arms even if he never got to hold her again. Then he remembered he had to help her out of his truck he got all excited, all over again. He drove her to her house and pulled as close to her as he could. Hopping out of the truck he ran around to open her door but she was moved much faster, he missed his chance to help her down.

"Thank you for the run, bandages, drink and the ride home," she said casually.

"Anytime," he replied as she made her way to her front door, opened it and with a wave and a small smile she closed the door. Just like that. He knew she was going to shut down after that kiss and he could kick himself for it, but it was too great of a kiss to regret. Closing the passenger door he ran around and hopped back into his truck to head home. "Women, are so confusing," he said out loud as his tires hit the main road.

The rain had started to pelt on his windshield as he made it into town and back to Jeff's just as Jeff was pulling into the driveway from church.

CHAPTER 6

Leaning against her door she listened as Luke drove away. She reached up and touched her lips still a little swollen from his amazing kiss. She was on fire while she was in his arms and he was kissing her, now she felt like she stepped inside a freezer. Rubbing her arms up and down she realized she was still wearing his clothes. She would have to face him again, she knew that, but she needed a little time to wrap her scattered thoughts around what she was feeling.

Pulling herself up she realized she was super hungry. Kicking off her shoes she headed for the kitchen to make her some breakfast. "Why am I so stupid?" she asked herself. He kissed her, which had to mean that he liked her, or he was taking advantage of her. "No, I won't think that way, he likes me and I just pushed him away." She was talking to herself, she was in bad shape, so she picked up the phone and called him.

"Hello."

"Luke I'm so sorry, I, I..." then she hung up, losing her nerve. At least she said she was sorry, she knew he would be confused about what she was sorry about, but she couldn't explain to him when she didn't really know herself. She flipped the phone on the counter and made her way up to her room. She would change and get his clothes in the wash, but she could smell him on her, a smell that would surely haunt her dreams that night.

Pulling on a long shirt, not bothering with shorts she folded his clothes and set them on her bed. Pulling on a pair of socks she heard a crash from downstairs. She was frozen in place, but realized her phone was down stairs she made a run for it, her knees aching with the action. She entered the kitchen and stopped in her tracks, a rock had been thrown through her window and sat on her island and there was a piece of paper attached. She glanced outside but didn't see anyone. Slipping on a pair of clean gloves from under her sink that she used for cleaning she carefully unwrapped the note from the rock with shaky hands.

Cristina,

You've wrecked me, how could you do this to me? We had something so special. I love you, yet you do this to me. You left me hanging when I needed you so. I wanted to tell you how much you meant to me, and you left me hanging. The rock through your window is how my heart feels right now, shattered. -

No name was written on the note, but she thought it was Luke, who else could it have been. She heard him leave, how did he get back there so fast she thought. She couldn't explain it to herself how a man who had driven away could have come back, scribbled a note, tied it to a rock then throw it through her kitchen window which was in the back of the house then leave again. She couldn't figure it out, but she knew he had done it, "Who else had I ignored, or pushed away?" she mused out loud. Granted, he didn't seem like the kind, he seemed so nice and sweet, but her fears took over and instead of thinking of him as innocent she already thought the worst.

Maybe she was losing her mind, maybe it was someone else. She thought it couldn't be someone else, no one else was close to her, she hadn't left anyone else hanging like that, hadn't closed anyone out since Tom, now Luke. Of course she had broken up with a few boys in high school, but that was a while ago.

Pulling out the broom she started sweeping up the broken

glass and placed the rock and letter in a zip lock bag and placed it in the pantry for later review. How could she have been so stupid to let herself get close to him, she knew she was falling for the man, but now, she just didn't know. Collecting her phone she called him.

"Hello," he answered.

"Sorry Luke, I'm really am. My phone dropped the signal. But I really am sorry. I'll bring your clothes when I get them washed. Have a good day," she said and she hung up. She wasn't leaving him room for conversation and she knew that was not kind of her, but the rock through the window was far too much, and she couldn't handle explanations right now. Finding a piece of cardboard and packing tape she patched the hole in her window. Then started working on her food once more as tears streamed down her face, she was scared but didn't want to be, didn't want to think about everything happening again here in this peaceful place as it had in Florida, only Cristina knew it was worse now, she just didn't understand why.

Giving up on the idea of a warm meal she settled with cereal and an action movie on her flat screen. Watching Die Hard with Bruce Willis was a great distraction to her crazy thoughts. Continuing on she watched Die Harder, Die Hard with a Vengeance then finished the night off with A Good Day to Die Hard. With only eating once she was ready for bed and her tear swollen eyes ready for rest.

Making sure all her doors were locked she made her way to her room and without turning on any lights she crawled straight into bed after sliding a chair in front of her door. The normal comfort her bed usually brought her, brought nothing but anguish that night as she cried herself to sleep, which she hadn't done since Tom.

Sad Blue eyes looked down on her as he shook his head and

walked away from her. She tried to run after him but her feet felt like they were stuck in a tar pit. As he disappeared from her view she started running after him finding the will to move her feet. She ran in the direction he had left only to find herself running through the wooded area of her land.

Pushing herself faster she tripped and found herself at the base of the odd rock pile surrounded by ferns, moss and fallen trees. Pulling herself to her feet she looked around to see Luke walk around a tree, she blinked and in his place was a large gray wolf. The wolf growled at her and she took off running towards her home. Pushing herself harder, faster she was almost to the door when she tripped over a root and face planted in the dirt. Looking down at herself as she pulled herself up she found her hands and knees bleeding, and grass was concrete. Hearing the growl behind her she tried to get to her feet but the wolf was on her in a flash. The wolf opened its mouth and reared back barely missing her arm as she raised it to protect herself. The wolf nipped at her arm then lunged for her throat.

Cristina bolted upright clutching her chest, her heart racing with her alarm blaring beside her. "One more night like that and I'm going to scream." Ever since she moved into town and came across that odd rock formation she'd had nightmares every night, now Luke was a part of them. "Geez," she said as she slammed her hand down on the snooze button on her alarm with more force than she intended and felt the warm ooze on her palm. She quickly clambered out of bed making sure not to get blood anywhere. She went straight to the bathroom, rinsed the blood off her hand and took a shower.

Coming back out of the bathroom she flipped the alarm to off. Dressing in a pair of jeans and a light blue sweater she made her way to work. Today she would work with Roberta and she was determined to ask her if she knew anything about her property. Grabbing her purse she checked the makeshift window fix and finding everything how it should be, she grabbed her purse and left for work.

"Good morning Roberta, how are you this morning?" she asked as she approached the older lady.

"Right as rain. You look like hell if I do say so myself," she replied.

"I didn't sleep well, I keep having nightmares, ever since I moved here."

"Ah, then the tales just might be true," Roberta laughed.

"Let's take a seat in the office and you can explain that statement." They headed to the office and since the staff always showed up a half hour later they had plenty of time to talk. "Ok, talk to me goose," Cristina said as she planted herself in a chair.

"The legend says a princess of a long lost tribe will come and unite her people with the Lummi Tribe."

"Huh," Cristina asked.

"Legend says, many years ago a small tribe was traveling south from Canada in hopes of warmer and greener land. They had made homestead roughly around where your property line is. The Lummi tribe had been helping them out with planting and medicines since the tribe was so small. A few months after they had settled in they had gotten sick, some type of fever. A shaman would travel and check on them every few days, most of the time he helped bury the dead. On the last trip the Shaman had found the mother of an infant son had perished from the fever, but the son was healthy and perfect."

"Wow."

"There is more. The shaman buried the mother, tore down the village and burned what was left to keep the fever from spreading. The Shaman had set up a tent for two weeks with the infant child to ensure he was not sick before bringing the child to a barren mother of his tribe. The tribe took the son in and raised him. That son married and each generation was blessed with one son. Legend says that they were waiting for a daughter to be born so she could marry a male descendant of the Lummi tribe and join the tribes as one. Once the daughter was born and of age she would come back to the land of her people, find her mate and marry him. When she consummated her marriage with her new husband her family would be able to move on to their next life. Until then, their sprits remained in the small village where they once lived."

"Wow, do you know the name of the decimated tribe?" Cristina asked leaning against her desk. She couldn't believe the story that she was told, but it was an amazing story nevertheless.

"Nah, the name of the tribe was never known, they may not have had a name, they were fans of the wolf totems, the child had a small one as a toy according to the stories."

"Do you really believe that?" She asked her.

"Of course, you see the Lummi are my people and this story was passed down through each generation. Our people will not rest easy until both tribes are joined."

"How come the male child who married into the Lummi tribe didn't, you know, seal the deal."

"A male brings the female to his tribe, but a female joins the other tribe, joining the two people to make them one."

"I guess that makes sense, when a female marries

nowadays, she takes on the male's last name, takes on his family as her own."

"Precisely."

"And you think this person is me?"

"You moved here from Florida, you're not sure why, but this place feels like home to you. Have you dreamed of wolves by any chance?" Cristina leaned back in her chair like someone had thrown ice water in her face. "I thought so. The stories tell how the Shaman dreamt of wolves while he was staying near the site of a small tribe to ensure the baby was healthy. He dreamed of how the princess would come and join their people, freeing them to move on."

"Wow that is some story. Maybe I wanted a good deal of distance between me and where I came from. Maybe I fell in love with the house and just had to have it, and maybe I'm having dreams of wolves because I take runs through the land around my house," Cristina responded solidly. She wasn't about to tell her about the odd rock formation that sort of confirmed the tales, for all she knew it was just a rock pile long forgotten.

"Maybe," Roberta smiled. "Let's get to work." She smiled at Cristina and left the office. Cristina had a lot to think about but she highly doubted she was Native American, although she would love it if she was, learning her family history would be so much easier then.

*****

Luke went to work with Jeff that morning and he couldn't keep his mind off of Cristina, her lips pressed to his and how perfectly they fit together. The odd phone calls after he dropped her off and was at Jeff's left him confused. "Why are you still brooding man?" Jeff interrupted his thinking as they painted the final room in the Bed and Breakfast.

"Not brooding, just tired," Luke answered, dipping his brush into the paint and starting on the window frame.

"You're so," Jeff said as he felt a spatter of something wet hit the back of his neck. Reaching his free hand back he felt the white paint Jeff had thrown at him.

"I can't believe you did that," Luke yelled and whacked Jeff with his paint brush leaving a white streak of paint in its wake.

"Really," Jeff said then tried to hit him in the face but Luke was faster than Jeff and he only got his chest. Luke got Jeff in the chest and dumped his brush into the paint and went back to painting.

"Ok, fine, I'll talk, can it wait until we get done here first?" Luke asked before Jeff could nail him with paint again. Jeff nodded and focused back on his painting the neighboring window frame.

Two hours later they were cleaning up and making a final pass. Tomorrow Jeff would be come out to inspect everything and give the happy couple a walk through. As Luke walked through the rooms to make sure everything was collected he was pleased with the way everything came together. The room was painted white, which wouldn't have been his pick, but the contrast of the wooden floors and chair rail really came together.

"Hey Jeff," Luke called from the third floor.

"What's up man," Jeff asked as he entered the room Luke was in.

"Look at that," Luke said pointing out the window at the crest of the woods. He saw a few baby wolves playing in the grass area.

"That's pretty cute, reminds me of us when we were younger and our dads sitting by letting us beat each other up then listening to our moms yell at them," Jeff said laughing, then he slugged Luke's arm.

"Yeah, fun times, but thought I would share. We ready to go?" Luke asked picking up the paint bucket and the tool bucket.

"Sure thing, I'm famished," Jeff replied heading for the door.

"You need a wife," Luke joked. "You're wasting away to nothing," Luke chided Jeff.

"Have to find a woman first, but maybe I can nab Cristina since she's single and attractive," Jeff said, then ran out of the room away from Luke's evil glare.

"Man, really. I'm staking claim," Luke blurted after Jeff.

"I know man, just kidding." Jeff laughed as they made their way down the stairs. Jeff pulled the front door closed and locked up as Luke dumped the tools and paint into the back of Jeff's truck.

"Shall we hit the local IHOP?" Luke asked Jeff as they climbed into the truck.

"Why would we hit it? I'm sure they'll feed us man?" Jeff laughed.

"Really dude, do you have to take everything literally?" Luke snapped back, rolling his eyes at his best friend.

"Nah, man just love your reaction," Jeff replied laughing. He popped the truck in gear and headed to the main road.

They reached the IHOP two minutes later, headed in and took a seat. The place was packed for a Monday, but the wait staff was on the ball.

"What can I get you fine men this evening?" a young lady asked as she brought them glasses of water. She was tall, thin, and cute by most standards.

"I'll have a coke," Jeff answered with a big flirty smile.

"Water is fine for me thanks." Luke smiled back but he was glad to see the young lady was eyeing his best friend.

"Okey dokey, I'll be right back with your coke." She winked at him and sauntered off. Jeff watched her backside as she left.

"Well, she was cute wasn't she?" Jeff asked smiling at Luke.

"Dude, you know as well as I do that past that smile you gave her, the only thing you'll be able to say is what you're going to eat," Luke chided.

"Spoil sport," Jeff laughed. "I know, I really need to stop being shy with women, but they're a scary bunch. Happy one second then biting your head off the next. Biting your head off one second then loving on you the next. They are like tornados, you never know where they will hit next," Jeff said drinking up his water.

"Point well made Jeff, point well made," Luke replied looking thoughtfully at his water. Cristina was that way, well not biting his head off or anything, but the mood shifts were like sudden shifts of the Tectonic Plates causing earth quakes, each with a different magnitude.

The waitress brought Jeff a coke and slipped him a piece of paper. Without looking at it, Jeff slipped it into his pocket with a smile. "What can I get y'all to eat?" she asked them.

"I'll have the breakfast sampler please." Jeff responded with a bright award winning smile for the waitress. She blushed and wrote down his order.

"How would you like your eggs?" she asked him.

"Over easy please." Jeff replied.

"And for you sir?" she asked Luke.

"Can I get the Smokehouse combo, with scrambled eggs and add a few slices of bacon to that please," Luke replied passing her his menu. She wrote down his order, took both menus and was on her way.

"She gave me her phone number." Jeff said quietly leaning towards Luke.

"Very nice man, you gonna call her?" Luke asked.

"Well, yeah I'll, maybe, I'll take her out on a date," Jeff said leaning back in the booth.

"Yeah, she'll probably be jail bait for you man, she doesn't even look eighteen yet," Luke responded back. She really didn't look old enough to be working but the make-up made her look older.

"Yeah, you're probably right. But maybe, we'll see," Jeff replied, he looked thoughtful again, and a little sad, but Luke knew he had to be honest with his friend or he may end up in more trouble than it was worth.

They talked about the Bed and Breakfast, then moved to discuss the plan for the hotel they would be starting. Their food came and went rather fast. As they went for the truck Luke saw a piece of paper under the wiper on his side so he plucked it off and hopped in the truck.

Opening the paper to see what it was he saw a hand written message.

Luke,

Stay away. There is no reason why you should come by.

"*What the hell?*" Luke thought, who could have put the note on Jeff's truck, how did they even know it was Jeff's truck, and how did they know where they were. Luke folded the note and stuck it in his pocket.

"What was that about Luke," Jeff asked starting the engine. Luke hadn't even noticed that Jeff had gotten in.

"Nothing just a random note. No big deal. I don't know about you but I'm ready for a shower and to crash for the night." Luke laughed and turned on the radio. He would think more on the note later, try and process what it meant and who placed it there.

*****

Jeff drove quietly wondering about the pensive look on his friends face and not really listening to the radio. The note the waitress gave him was burning a hole in his pocket but he knew he would never call her, he was terrified of women and didn't want to get hurt. He liked Emily, he wasn't sure why he liked her since she never even looked him in the eye, but he was drawn to her.

"Why do you look so puzzled?" Luke interrupted his thinking.

"Oh, nothing really, processing the plans for the hotel we will be starting soon," Jeff said quickly pulling a believable lie right out of thin air.

"Sure, so are you going to call that lovely waitress?" Luke

asked jokingly.

"Nah," Jeff replied absentmindedly.

"Want me to call her for you and set up the date? You really need to get a girlfriend man." Luke encouraged him like he always had when it came to relationships. Jeff was a jokester and when it came to Luke they were always catching each other in odd forms of distress or sneaking pictures in different forms of undress to tease each other later.

"Nah man, it's all good," Jeff said softly. He wanted to go out, have a good time, but for the life of him he just couldn't. The idea of Sara disapproving of any of his dates or him sitting there comparing each girl to Sara was not fair to the other women.

"Alright, if you change your mind just let me know," Luke laughed and cranked up the radio and a Skillet song blared through his speakers with the words of Monster. They were lost in the song, the loud music with the screaming and drums and it was heaven to his thoughts.

*****

"Emily, honey," Alan called from the bedroom as she was putting away the last dish. She walked swiftly to the room and found him sitting on the edge of the bed wearing only his boxers and holding a large bouquet of roses; she couldn't help but smile.

"Hi." She replied shyly wondering where he was going with the flowers and the sweet smile. Her face still hurt from the night before along with the welts on her back.

"Come sit," he commanded with a soft pleasant voice and she instantly complied. He wrapped am arm around her waist and pulled her close to his side. "I'm so sorry about

91

the way I reacted yesterday after you returned home from church," Alan said softly. For once Emily was starting to feel the lies in his voice but she didn't dare to challenge him. Instead she listened closely, fearing a change in the atmosphere should she object to anything he had to say.

"It's alright baby." She smiled softly at him. He kissed her softly on the lips before pulling away and looking at her again.

"I over reacted. I know you love church and honestly it helps your mood when you go, I hate it when you're crabby and moody," Alan said harshly. "Either way, I need to remember you're so weak and you need guidance as well as discipline." Emily had to restrain her emotions before they gave way to her anger to the man next to her. She wanted nothing more than to go a whole night without feeling some sort of pain that she would have to conceal for her young classmates the next day.

"It's alright," she smiled softly at him.

"Let me love you," Alan said softly and pulled her to the bed with him. Emily wished fervently that he could make love or could love her even a little bit, maybe then he would restrain his fists or reign in his anger a little before lashing out at her.

CHAPTER 7

Scrambling out of bed Cristina rushed to jump in the shower. She had twenty minutes to get to work and she wouldn't be able to grab breakfast. She had fallen in love with Sam's banana nut muffins and Black tea. Not bothering with washing her hair, she dried off and put her hair into a tight bun, pulled on a pair of jeans and a blue sweater. She hadn't seen or heard from Luke in a week, and since it was Friday, she was almost ready to call and give him a piece of her mind about the window.

Ignoring her nagging thoughts she grabbed her jacket, purse and headed for the stairs. Turning she heard her phone ringing which was still connected to the charger on her nightstand. "Damn," she said running for it.

"Hello," she answered unplugging the phone and heading for the stairs once more.

"Hey girl, did I wake you or catch you at a bad time?" It was Ray. She felt like a bad friend because she had not spoken to him in a few days.

"Running late for work, but I can talk on the way, what's up." She knew she shouldn't talk on the phone and drive, but she was in one of those moods.

"Hey, call me after work, no talking and driving ok," Ray said as she slid her feet into her shoes and climbed into her car.

"You sure?" She asked pressing the garage door button so it would open and starting her car.

"Yeah, have a good day at work, and call me after," Ray said.

"Will do. Have a great day," she said, backing the car out the driveway.

"Will try, bye," he said and hung up. She missed him like crazy. If he hadn't been so straight, she would be calling him her best girlfriend. As it was, he was straight and her best male friend, but she could still talk to him about different things. She was just afraid to talk about the rock or the random, unsigned roses that kept showing up every week at work, all the same and never signed. They would just say have a great week. She was really starting to hate roses, even though they were her mother's favorite flower.

The drive to work was quick and she made it right at nine and already had a few people waiting on her to open. Roberta would be in an hour later to give her a break, but Cristina just wanted to crawl back to bed. She smiled at the people waiting, unlocked the doors and let them in. She took a deep breath and followed them inside and got right to work.

*****

Frustrated, Luke jumped out of bed, he was late for work and his alarm never went off and Jeff had told him the night before that he would be leaving earlier to pick up supplies. Glancing at the clock he noticed it was flashing on and off as if the power had went out in the middle of the night. "Damn." He checked his phone, which was still off. Last night some unknown number kept calling him and hanging up, so giving up he just shut his phone off so he could get some sleep. Turning his phone on he jumped in the shower to wake up.

Last night he tossed and turned thinking about Cristina and how she freaked out about the kiss Sunday and had called to say she was sorry but hung up before he could say it was ok. Then not ten minutes later she called back, but she sounded off, scared even, but apologized again then hung up before he could ask what was wrong. Wrapping a towel around him he shaved quickly and pulled on his work clothes and gave Jeff a call.

"You're alive," Jeff said when he answered.

"Yeah man, sorry about that, the power went off so my alarm never went off."

"I had tried calling you several times but your phone went straight to voice mail, why was it off?"

"Some crank caller was blowing up my phone last night and I couldn't get any sleep so I turned it off figuring the alarm would wake me. I'm on my way in, I have to make a quick stop but I'll be there ASAP."

"No problem man. Get here when you get here," Jeff said reassuringly.

"Will do." They hung up and Luke went to the coffee maker and grabbed a cup of what was left from Jeff's make this morning. Grabbing his keys, slipping on his boots, he opened the door and froze. His truck was where it was supposed to be, but glass was all around it. "Damn it," Luke said pulling the door closed behind him with a slam. "Shit," he said as he got closer, he saw paint was plastered on the inside of his truck. Flipping his phone open he called the local police department.

"Cobblestone Police department, this is Jess how can I assist you?" a woman said over the receiver.

"This is Luke Black over at 4267 West Main. Someone has busted all the windows in my truck and there's paint inside."

"Luke we'll send a patrolman over, don't touch anything."

"Thank you ma'am." He disconnected the call and dialed Jeff again.

"What's up man, one of us has to work," Jeff kidded.

"Man, someone busted all the windows in my truck and paint is on the inside, what did my truck look like when you left this morning?" Luke asked.

"It was fine, damn man that sucks, you call the cops?"

"Yeah, they are sending a patrolman over now."

"Don't worry about coming in man, take care of what you need to. We'll talk when I get home."

"Thanks man."

"What are friends for." Hanging up, Luke was furious. Who could do this to his truck, why would someone do this to his truck. He was nice to everyone, helped out as often as he could. He had wanted to go see Cristina, but a call would have to do for now.

"Hello."

"Cristina, it's Luke."

"Oh, um. How can I help you Luke."

"I wanted to tell you it was ok how you shut down Sunday, I never should have kissed you without a few more dates. After I left that night I felt awful, I drove back to Jeff's and we had a chat. I should have called before now, but Jeff's been keeping me busy, and I wanted to give you some space."

"What about the rock Luke, like really. You had to be pissed to do that." Cristina sounded angry, but a rock, Luke was confused.

"What rock? What are you talking about?" Luke asked.

"The rock and note that was thrown through my kitchen window. Luke, I don't have time for this, I'm at work. If you want to get mad at me because of something I did or didn't do, talk to me about it, don't resort to breaking my window, it was very immature." With that she hung up. Luke wanted to call her back to get more information but he was too stunned to do so. He never threw a rock through her kitchen window, he left in his truck, why would she think he had done it? Now his windows were busted in his truck. He wanted more time to process the information, but the patrolman was headed his way.

Watching as the small, round pudgy man got out of his car and strolled towards Luke, the guy looked familiar but he couldn't place him.

"Luke, how have you been son?" Pete asked.

"Good I guess, well except for my truck," Luke responded looking at the officer questioningly.

"Ah, you don't remember me. My name is Pete; I was friends with your father before he passed. So what happened here?"

"I was hoping you could tell me. I wake up late and find this for breakfast," Luke motioned towards his truck.

"When did you get home last night?"

"I have been parked here since last night at nine p.m."

"Where was Jeff at this morning?" Pete asked.

"He left earlier this morning to pick up supplies for the hotel he started this morning."

"And he didn't say anything or see anything wrong with your truck when he left?" Skepticism written all over his face.

"No, I called him after I called you and he said the truck was fine." Pete nodded and approached the truck.

"See this?" he pointed to the driver's side, where Luke hadn't bothered to look. A large blue paint spatter with a dent was on the door. "Looks like someone was using semi frozen paintballs and your truck was target practice."

"What, why would someone do this?" Luke stammered. His truck was paid off, his pride and joy.

"Luke, sometimes people don't need a reason, other times it's a girl," Pete said and Luke's breath caught in his throat.

"You mean this could be about a girl or a girl could have done this?" Luke finally asked getting over the initial shock.

"I would say it's about a girl, the shots are too precise. Not to get sexist or anything, but I don't know many females who can shoot this good. Besides, most women will shoot out one, maybe two windows, and give up thinking their point has been proven, but a man would want to make it hard to come back from this."

"So we're assuming this is a male and it's because of a girl. Who are you dating these days Luke?" Pete asked.

"No one sir, I mean there is a girl I would like to date, but she's a hard fish to catch sir."

"Who might she be?"

"Cristina Williams, she just bought the Patterson place."

"Oh that pretty young thing." Just then his radio dinged.

"Hang on Luke," Pete said then turned and walked to his car. He pulled out his radio. "This is Pete."

"Pete we have another vandalized car over at the Library, a Ms. Williams." Pete looked right at Luke and they knew it was connected.

"Details Jess."

"All the windows were shot out, blue paint over most of the car."

"Ok, I'm with Luke, tell her not to touch anything and I'll be right over."

"Yes sir."

"Looks like we found the link," Pete said to Luke. "Roger, yeah get the kit and head over to Luke's to get the truck checked out and bring the plastic to keep the rain out. Then get to the library, we have a twofer today."

"Yes sir."

"Want to ride with me over to the Library?" Pete asked Luke.

"Yes sir," Luke said and he hopped in the front seat of the patrol car and they headed over to Cristina. She was pacing back and forth by her car wearing fitted jeans and a blue sweater, she looked good enough to eat, at least to Luke she did.

"Ms. Williams. What do you know?" Pete asked her as he pulled up next to her.

"I don't know, I drove to work and everything was fine this morning. I came out to grab my phone charger about five minutes ago and this is what I find." Cristina was in tears and it tore at Luke's heart, he didn't want to see her like that. He climbed out of the police car and walked around to her.

"Mine too Cristina, I woke up late and walked out of Jeff's house and my truck windows were all busted in." He reached for her but she stepped away.

"You sure you didn't do your truck to cover up mine?" she said with anger clear in her voice.

"Hold up you two, what are you talking about Cristina?" Pete looked from Luke to Cristina.

"Ask him, Sunday he throws a rock through my kitchen window and now this." She waves at her car. Luke could tell she was upset but he didn't do it and for the life of him he couldn't see why she would think he had.

"Back the truck up miss, what broken kitchen window? We had no reports of that Sunday," Pete said.

"That's because I didn't bother with it. I thought it would be the end of the situation." She was crying harder now, her breaths were raspy and her shoulders were heaving with her breaths.

"Details about the kitchen window," Pete persisted.

"Sunday morning after Luke dropped me off I went upstairs to change out of his clothes when a rock was thrown through the kitchen window with a note. It wasn't ten minutes after Luke left. It didn't make sense that he would throw something through the window since I heard him drive off, but the note that was attached was a tell-tale sign that he had."

"What did the note say?" Pete asked.

"It said *Cristina,*

You've wrecked me, how could you do this to me? We had something so special. I love you, yet you do this to me. You left me hanging when I needed you so. I wanted to tell you how much you meant to me, and you left me hanging. The rock through your window is how my heart feels right now, shattered. – But no name was written on it," Cristina replied and Luke just stared at her dumbfounded.

"Well, Luke what do you have to say to that?" Pete looked at him.

"I didn't throw the rock, and I sure didn't write the note. I dropped her off and went straight back to Jeff's, he will tell you as much. Took me about ten minutes or less to get home as it is." He turned to Cristina. "I don't know what my feelings for you are but I would never do anything to hurt you or bring those tears to your eyes, please believe me," he pleaded with her. She didn't hesitate another second as she went to him. His arms wrapped protectively around her.

"I'm sorry, I always think the worst of people. I'm so sorry, I thought it was you Luke," she sobbed into his chest.

"It's ok, I understand, if it makes you feel any better, when Pete and I were looking at possibilities I thought it was you." She looked up at him, her eyes red from crying and her face just looked shocked.

"You did?" her eyebrows pinched together.

"Yep, I think the worst sometimes as well."

"Well, now we know it wasn't either of you, it seems we are dealing with someone who thinks he's in love with you Cristina. We will need the rock and note, did you touch it at all?" Pete asked her.

"No, I used new rubber gloves I use to clean with and then I placed them inside a Ziploc bag and put them in the pantry." She turned and looked at Pete, but Luke didn't let her away from him. The protective instinct inside him was set free and he wasn't going to let anyone hurt her.

"Ok, let me drive you both over to your house so I can retrieve that evidence. Roger will be by to take care of the car. Once he gives the go ahead you can contact your insurance to see about getting the repairs done," Pete said and motioned for them to get in the patrol car.

*****

Emily sat in the principal's office and waited patiently for the older woman to make an appearance. One of her students had been out all week without a call or form of notification and Emily was worried about the little girl. "Ms. Greely." Emily stood as the small woman entered the office. Ms. Greely had her silver hair pulled into a bun and her green eyes peeked sadly through her thick glasses.

"Emily, I have sad news." Ms. Greely stopped and leaned her small behind against the front of her desk.

"What?" Emily asked. She knew the worst was coming but didn't want to acknowledge it.

"Sally Moore took a terrible tumble down a set of stairs while her parents were outside."

"Oh my God," Emily began to cry. "Is she alright?"

"No, she broke her neck. The school will be holding a ceremony for her after school and the funeral is tomorrow at three. Her parents have requested for you not to attend because it would break their hearts again since you were her favorite teacher," Ms. Greely said coldly. Emily knew the real reason and so did Ms. Greely. They had beaten the poor girl as often as Alan had beaten her.

"Ok." Emily stood, rained in her emotions and put on a calm, cool and collected expression to inform her students of the sad news of their fellow classmate.

*****

Jeff hit the nail a little too hard and bent it over in an unusable shape. *How could I not have seen the paint on the truck? Was it there when I left? No, it looked fine, I would have noticed a mess like that if it had happened before I left this morning.*

"Boss, you alright?" Rick asked him with raised eyebrows.

"Yeah, just got a lot on my mind," Jeff said quickly. "Take over for me? I think a break will be good," Jeff asked.

"Yeah sure man, take your time," Rick replied and Jeff hastily walked to his trailer running a hand through his rugged shaggy hair. Everything was happening all at once and he was getting Luke to move in with him and become his partner, now the truck gets doused in paint and Jeff was at a loss, things like that didn't happen in their small little town.

Jeff slammed the trailer door closed and locked it before dropping to his knees. The dreams were back full force, he wasn't sleeping and now his best friend was the target of some vandal. *Lord, please help me understand this. Life was so simple before Luke came back. Should I not have asked him to come home or is this the life we are in for? I need your help Lord, give me the guidance to understand what I need to do.*

CHAPTER 8

Wrapped in Luke's arms Cristina felt safe, but the pain of thinking it was him was crushing her. Every so often she felt Luke press his lips to her hair and one hand rubbed up and down her back. "Never should have assumed you did all this Luke, I heard you drive away," Cristina whispered.

"It's ok. You had a shock and the note only made sense with what I did." He pulled her tighter against his chest, and if she didn't know better she would think he was trying to assure her she was safe. She felt safe and she felt her heart softening towards this man she was clinging to but, she knew he would break her heart. He was too good to be true, at least so far.

"Cristina, I suggest you grab a bag with some things and stay in town," Pete said as he entered the living room where they waited. She didn't want to leave her home just because of a little scare, she wasn't going to.

"I think I'll be alright here. I have a shot gun in the coat closet and I'm a pretty good shot. I also have a pistol in my bedside table for good measure." She smiled at the officer.

"Well, I can't force you, but I think you're being stubborn about this," Pete rebuked.

"My mother always told me I was stubborn, but I won't run scared. Whoever this is has only damaged property, there is no reason to assume he or she will resort to bodily harm," she replied.

"Well, with all due respect, there have been many crazies out there who start out like this then turn to violence. Listen to reason woman." Pete was getting angry. She knew she should be worried, but it was her home and if something was going to happen to it because she was there she didn't want anyone else's home to be harmed because of her.

"Cristina," Luke said her name softly. "How about I stay in the guest room until this all blows over."

"No, I don't need a babysitter and I won't put you out," she refused. She wanted him there because she needed him but she wasn't going to have him stay because he felt compelled to protect her. Her logic was not working for her at the moment but she wasn't going to have a babysitter and she sure wasn't going to put anyone out.

"Cristina, Luke should stay here or I can have a deputy sitting in a car out front while you're home if that's what you want, but as a man raised right, I wouldn't be able to sleep at night knowing you're out here alone with some crazy person who thinks they're in love with you," Pete insisted.

"Ok, ok I understand, but I don't want anyone sitting out in a car all night or all day for me."

"Then I'll have Jeff bring me a bag when he gets off work," Luke said, cutting her off and pulling her into his vast strong chest. It was taking everything she had not to plant her face right into his chest and breathe in his amazing scent and brand it to memory.

"But Luke, this person has already targeted your truck."

"The lady has a point Luke. Maybe distance from each other would be a good thing," Pete agreed.

"No, I'll stay. I was in security at one point, I think I can handle a little harassment, and this way if we are targets then maybe he will be caught unaware and mess up."

"Ah, also a good point," Pete said looking thoughtful. "At least let me give you a lift to the rental car place so you'll have a vehicle." She nodded and with Luke in tow, they followed Pete back to his car. She slid into the back seat and Luke climbed in beside her and pulled her once more into his arms. She rested her head on his shoulder, feeling completely calm with everything, well not about the rock and her car, her beautiful car.

Pete drove them to the local rent-a-car and she insisted she would cover the car. She had already called her insurance agent and they gave her the go-ahead. She was now sporting a black Ford Escape. Pete left them at the rental car place and told them he would be in touch and he was having their vehicles towed to their garage for further inspection. "Shall we head to your place to get your things?" Cristina asked.

"Sounds like a plan," Luke responded settling into the passenger seat. "This is a change," Luke said more upbeat then he had been all day.

"What do you mean by that?" Cristina was super confused but he looked so good sitting next to her. She turned her whole body to look at him while she was still sitting in the parking spot.

"I was meaning you driving and my riding along." He laughed and it was an amazing sound, one Cristina would love to listen to all day. Then her stomach growled in protest of not eating anything all day. "Maybe we should grab lunch first?" Luke suggested as he smiled at her.

"Where to?" she asked him, she really was hungry and really wanted a distraction from the day's events.

"You drive, I'll direct," Luke said. Apparently it was a secret.

"Ok," she pulled out of the parking lot, turned left on his direction, made a right and then got on the highway. Five minutes later she was exiting at a Mexican restaurant.

"I hope you like Mexican," Luke smiled at her as she pulled in to a parking spot.

"I love it, but you might not like me later," she laughed and killed the engine. The little place was done in orange stucco with bright multi-colored curtains on the windows. The sign read 'La Casa Fiesta' with a green pepper wearing a sombrero. The parking lot was already filling up as they made their way to the door. Luke opened the door for her as she pressed the lock button on the SUV and entered. Along the walls were small tiles of different colored scenes, Latin music played lightly in the background. The lighting was muted, they approached the hostess table and a little brunette approached them, her name tag read Lucinda.

"Two for you. Oh Luke, how are you doing?" Little Miss Lucinda batted her eyes at him and smiled sweetly, while flirting with him and something in Cristina snapped.

"Yes two," Cristina said interrupting the little eye ogling Lucinda was doing to Luke.

"Hello Lucinda. Can we sit in the garage?" Luke replied.

"Sure Luke, would you like to be near the fire place?"

"Please" he said and Luke wrapped his arm around Cristina's waist calming her down a bit as they followed Lucinda to the appointed location. The garage, as they called it, was a room with two garage doors and in the corner was a nice gas fireplace. Luke pulled out a chair and motioned for her to sit. And she did so. He was such a gentleman and Cristina couldn't help but remember that Tom had never done that for her, nor had he opened a door for her or offered to buy her dinner, they had always split the check.

"Thank you," she said when he sat down in front of her and Lucinda had departed.

"For what?" He looked confused, which made her like him even more. He looked as if everything he was doing was normal behavior, and maybe for him it was.

"For pulling out my chair for me, that was very nice of you."

"Oh, habit I guess, I would have done it at the restaurant the other night but you moved too fast for me to do so." He smiled at her. "My father taught me when I was little, treat every woman how you want your mother to be treated." He smiled but the sadness showed in his eyes.

"Your father is a wise man," Cristina said. She couldn't remember if he had passed or if it was just his mother; she was so overwhelmed with everything, her head felt like it was spinning.

"He was a wise man." Luke paused. "He was killed in action on a detail over in Africa when I was ten."

"That is so sad, I'm so sorry."

"He was a great man. Mom was told that he fought to stay alive but the bullets passed through a few vital points and the last thing he told the solider next to him was, "tell my wife and son I love them." And then he was gone." She watched as Luke's eyes reddened and watered. Just when she thought he would shed a tear he started laughing, a defense mechanism she thought.

"Wow," was all she could say. She couldn't laugh with him because it was sad, but she couldn't be mad at him either because after her mother passed she did the same thing to keep from crying when she spoke with people. Eventually the tears stopped coming the more she spoke about it, but still left a sadness in her heart.

"My mom passed shortly after everything happened with my ex, the doctors say it was from a broken heart. And I'm inclined to agree. She fought and tried to be happy for me but I could tell she was getting weak. I think when Lilly broke my heart it broke the last bit of will power she had. She and my dad were soul mates, now they are together." He said softly. Before she could say anything the waitress appeared, she was tall and blond and quite pretty. Cristina couldn't help but wonder if all the blonds moved to Washington.

"Good afternoon y'all, my name is Beth and I'll be taking care of ya' today," she said in a heavy southern accent. "Can I start y'all off with something to drink?"

"I would love a Dr. Pepper," Cristina said quickly.

"The same please," Luke responded.

"Sure. I'll be right back with those drinks." Beth scurried off towards the kitchen.

"How did your mom pass?" Luke asked.

"Two years ago she was diagnosed with a tumor in her brain. The mass grew at a rapid rate and within six months she had passed one late night. That was around the same time when I really fell in love. Or so I thought, with Tom." Cristina hung her head. It was hard to think about her mom passing, but at least she remembered to think about the happy memories versus the sad times before she went on to heaven.

*****

Luke was engrossed by the woman in front of him. She was beautiful, vulnerable and now she trusted him once again, or at least she seemed to be trying to. He told her about his parents hoping to open a door or even a small window, and it seemed to have worked.

"You've been through a lot," he said.

"So have you, more so I would say," Cristina responded.

"How about this, we have both been through a lot, just different stuff." He smiled at her.

"Ok." Her smile was small. He had to think of something funny to tell her.

"Hey you know that Wednesday after I helped you move into your place?" Luke asked.

"Yeah." She looked confused.

"Jeff called me to work that day. I was walking toward the trailer to get the heads up and I tripped over a rock and went face first in the mud." Luke laughed and Cristina covered her mouth with her hand but with crinkles around her eyes, he knew she was smiling brightly at the image that had to have popped in to her pretty little head.

"Oh my goodness, that had to have been a sight."

"Well, Jeff got a picture, but I was covered with mud." He laughed again.

"That's far too funny, I so, want to see that picture." She was laughing hard now. His plan at distraction was a success.

"I'll have Jeff show it to you. We have an album of all the stupid stuff we have done over the years."

"Sounds like fun. You two have been friends for a while haven't you?" she asked, back to seriousness again.

"Yeah, since we started school," Luke said.

"That is awesome. My friend Ray and I have been friends since school started pretty much. We were two outcasts so we automatically bonded and we were a force to be reckoned with. We are like brother and sister really," Cristina said absentmindedly.

"Are you sure he sees it that way?" Luke asked. He knew any man who was friends with her had to have other feeling for her, well, unless they played on her team that is.

"Oh yeah. We are good buddies. What's good to have here?" she asked, subject change.

"I usually have the beef enchiladas with the green chili, big fan over here," he said then chuckled. The smile on her face was purely amazing. She was becoming something to him, and fast too. He wasn't sure what it was, but he really hoped she would let him find out. His mother always told him he would know when he found the one, but of course he was holding back because she was giving him so many road blocks he couldn't keep up.

"That actually sounds pretty good, usually I have a taco salad. Sad huh?" she laughed.

"Nah, simple yes, but still tasty. I have this Frito salad that is just wonderful, I'll have to make it for you sometime," Luke said... conversation, food for the heart.

"I love Fritos," she replied placing her elbows on the table and leaning on her hands. She was opening up. *"Don't ask anything serious,"* Luke reminded himself.

"So, other than running until you hit the ground. What else

do you do for fun?" Luke asked.

"Well, I enjoy hiking, good books, and I love going to the movies. My mother taught me how to quilt and knit while I was young and I still enjoy that in my free time."

"You quilt, really."

"Yeah, I have quilted since I was ten, mostly baby quilts though. I have made the occasional handbag or shirt. But nothing too serious," she replied nonchalantly.

"That's pretty cool. My mom quilted a lot, every time she heard about someone having a new baby she made them a quilt. The town loved her," he said absentmindedly.

"That's pretty cool," she said, her mood shifting.

"What kind of movies do you like?" he asked.

"All kinds, I enjoy the classic chick flicks, but I love action movies, big fan of Die Hard, The Expendables and The Fast and The Furious. I love old movies with John Wayne and I enjoy newer movies and sad to say, I even enjoy the Twilight Saga, but I find the books are far better and I think a few of the characters they chose to play the main roles could have been portrayed by better individuals."

"Wow, I know some of those films." He smiled at her. "Do you always nit-pick on movies," he chided her.

"No, just the ones that they've created from books that I've read. I like the Harry Potter series, but I won't read the books because I think the movies will be wasted on me after that. I have read the Twilight Saga and fell in love with the characters before they came out with the movies," she replied guarded.

"I was only picking, frankly I nit-pick some moves as well.

Especially the ones that are supposed to have good graphics and blood scenes, but you can tell when it's fake. Or when there are continuity errors. I can't remember the movie but there was a part in a movie, set in the gladiator times with a scene where a gladiator had a wrist watch."

"Ok, good. I do that too." She smiled and the waitress appeared with their drinks super late.

"I'm so sorry, I'm the only one here, our other two waitresses called in sick, so I'm working all the tables today." Beth looked beat. He had been so engrossed with Cristina he hadn't even noticed all the people around them. Taking notice, the noise reached his ears and he felt sorry for her.

"It's alright, we are in no rush," Luke responded with a warm smile for her.

"Are y'all ready to order?" Beth asked, pen at the ready. Luke motioned for Cristina to go ahead.

"I'll have whatever you're having," she responded by putting the ball back in his court.

"Ok, I guess we will have your two spicy beef enchiladas with the green chili."

"Rice and beans?" Beth asked.

"Just rice for me," Luke said then looked at Cristina.

"Same." She smiled sweetly at him.

"Ok, I'll get these orders in for ya'. Flag me down if I can get you anything else." Beth smiled and scurried on her way.

"So, did you play any sports in school?" Luke asked her.

"No, but I enjoy most of them. I love running the most, I

really like volleyball and basketball. I enjoy watching football and ice hockey, but baseball has to be live for me to watch it and usually I get bored." She laughed.

"No problem there, what do you think of golf?" he asked. He didn't find it a sport but he had to admit it did take some skill and precision to place a tiny ball in a little hole, but polo was kind of the same way.

"Eh, fun to play, but frankly, not a sport, and it's really a rich man's game," she replied gulping down her Dr. Pepper. He was falling hard for this girl, she was so down to earth and on his level. Thinking about her made his heart jump in response to everything she said. He was engrossed and falling hard.

"I'll agree with you on that" he smiled at her. Beth brought their dinner and they ate in silence, but he couldn't help watching how she devoured her food. He loved the fact that she had a hearty appetite, he hated when girls picked at their food. He knew he needed to get his thoughts under control, but with her sweet smell permeating the air around him and her beautiful face in front of him, she made it really hard to ignore.

He paid for their lunch and they made their way to Jeff's so he could grab his clothes. Taking note that his truck was no longer in front of the house he ushered Cristina inside while he gathered his things. He couldn't stand to leave her out in the car even if she didn't have some crazy stalker after her. With her near him, he felt whole, he could feel the life inside of him like he hadn't felt since his mother passed away. He grabbed a duffle bag and stuffed in some clothes and his shaving kit and he was ready to go. He was about to close his bedroom door when he remembered his cologne sitting on his dresser. Grabbing it he tossed it into his bag and headed for the living room. Finally he and Cristina headed back to her house for the night.

She showed him to a room that was right across from hers and the only other room with a bed. If they left the doors open, they could see each other from their beds, he wasn't about to bring that up, maybe she slept with her door open, if he could get lucky, which he highly doubted. He placed his duffle on the bed and turned to find her staring at him.

"Wanna go for a run?" she asked after a moment.

"Sure but maybe we should wait a little bit since we just ate a big lunch." He looked at her and hoped that his pleading eyes would give him a pass for now.

"Good point. Want to watch a movie?" Perfect he thought.

"Sure, pick out whatever you want to watch. I'll be down in a minute; I'm going to use the little boy's room." He smiled at her and her face reddened and she left the room. He wondered if by chance she liked him as much as he was starting to like her, but he doubted that he would find out any time soon. He went to the bathroom, used it, washed his hands, checked himself in the mirror and then mentally slapped himself for being such a girl.

He headed to the living room to find Cristina relaxed on the couch and the movie ready to play. He settled himself into the opposite side of the couch and she pressed play. Smokey and the Bandit started in the opening credits. They watched and laughed at the same parts. Instead of taking a run, they watched the complete collection of Smokey and the Bandit and called it quits for the night.

*****

Jeff sat on the couch watching reruns of CSI: Miami drinking on his sixth Keystone. A commercial came on and Jeff dropped onto the floor and began to do pushups. The sweat began to ripple over his skin and he kept pumping them out hoping the process would wear his body out enough for him to sleep. Flipping over, he began crunches followed by planks and pull-ups on the pull-up bar in the hall. Jeff could feel his body tiring so he clicked off the TV, locked the doors, and jumped in the shower.

Jeff pulled on his boxers and climbed into bed, flipped on his side lamp and rolled over trying to get comfortable by letting the darkness take over.

"Jeff, I love you." Sara smiled at him, her brown hair shimmering in the sunshine as they sat on the picnic blanket eating their lunch she prepared for them.

"I love you too." Jeff smiled at her and took a bite of the fried chicken she brought.

"Friday, we're still going to dinner, right?" Sara asked sipping on her sweet tea.

"Yeah, why do you ask?" Jeff replied wiping his mouth and pulling himself into a sitting position.

"Just wondering, I remember you saying something about a double date with Lilly and Luke, and I wasn't sure if that was this week or next week," Sara said softly.

"Next week, if that's still alright," Jeff smiled at her just as the sun glinted off her cell phone and shined right into her beautiful green eyes.

"Don't leave me," Sara said sternly.

"Baby, I won't leave you," Jeff replied confused by her sudden change in mood.

"You're leaving me, please stay with me," Sara begged as the sky darkened and lightning struck.

"I won't leave you," Jeff said again. "I love you."

"I love you too, please stay with me," Sara cried out as the rain fell harshly onto their skin sending shivers down his spine. "Stay with me," Sara begged as she began to drift further away from him. He reached out his hands, trying to grab her hand but her crying, shuddering small frame kept drifting from him. "You left me," She sobbed and drifted further away from him.

*****

Emily sat in the emergency room with her left wrist cradled in her right hand. She had come home late from school and Alan had been in a fit of rage because dinner wasn't on the table when he got home. The ceremony for her student lasted two hours as each of the teachers comforted the students.

"Where is dinner?" Alan slammed the door of the apartment as she busied herself with making the spaghetti and hamburger meat. She had hoped she would have had it finished before he returned home.

"Almost done. I'm so sorry, we were holding a ceremony for one of our students." Emily began to cry again, not only from the anger she could see in his eyes but the sadness she felt for her student.

"I don't give a damn. I want my dinner on the table when I get home," Alan yelled, walked over to her, grabbed her left wrist and twisted it so hard she heard the snap before she felt the radiating pain. She screamed and dropped to the floor. "Next time, you'll have dinner on the table," Alan said coldly and left the kitchen and she cradled her wrist in her hand. The pain was so great the tears poured down her face as her wrist began to swell quickly.

"Ms. Hensley, the doctor will see you now." Emily stood and followed the nurse to the exam room. They had already completed the x-rays, but she already knew her wrist was broken, it had been broken once before. Emily took a seat on the small medical bed rattling the paper as she settled in. "Dr. Townsend will be her shortly." The nurse smiled and pulled the door closed behind her. Emily sat patiently looking around the sparsely decorated room. The walls were white, stark and void of any color. To her right was a stack of magazines with bright smiles and comments of weight loss and births of beautiful babies.

"Emily, I'm Dr. Townsend, how are you feeling?" The doctor was tall and handsome, his face held a light, yet concerned smile and his brown eyes twinkled in the florescent lights of the room.

"Could be better," Emily said softly trying to look anywhere but at the handsome man before her.

"Want to tell me what happened?" Dr. Townsend asked taking a seat on a small round black rolling stool.

"I tripped and fell catching myself," Emily lied coolly, it had been the lie her mother had used when she was a little girl.

"If that is how you want to have it noted, but I'll tell you, the break is one of a forced fast twist and not concurrent with your falling story," he said sadly. "I'll need to set your wrist and then wrap it tightly with a splint and ace bandage while we work to get the swelling down before putting on a hard cast, ok." Emily nodded and braced herself for the searing pain surely to follow as the doctor prepared to set her wrist.

CHAPTER 9

Cristina turned off the television while Luke checked all the locks and the kitchen window. Cristina couldn't help the swell in her heart for the man that gave up his comforts to stay in her home so she was comfortable and safe. Turning off all the lights as they headed for the stairs she could feel Luke's presence behind her and she was tempted to invite him to bed, but she wasn't easy or that type, besides she wasn't sure if he even liked her that way.

"If you need anything please help yourself," Cristina turned to Luke as she stood in the doorway of her room.

"Thank you. Sleep well, I'm a pretty light sleeper and this door will be open so I can hear anything." Luke smiled at her and she wanted to run her hand over the five o'clock shadow on his face, but she resisted.

"Thanks again for staying here. I'll give you a lift to work in the morning if you want, you work Saturdays correct?"

"Normally yes, but Jeff gave me this weekend off. Do you have to work?"

"I do," she replied, it was the rare Saturday she did have to work.

"Are you sure you want to go to work?" Luke asked concerned.

"Of course, just because some loon is out there I still have to work," Cristina said with a little more sarcasm than she intended. She wasn't playing off the fact that some lunatic was after her of all people, and she was mad as hell at the crazy person interrupting their lives.

"I understand, trust me I do. But if this really is a stalker, then he knows your every move, what if he's waiting to do something crazy, like, I don't know, kidnap you?" Luke sounded just as angry now.

"I know," she said quieter and crossing her arms in front of her.

"Hey."

"Yeah."

"Everything is going to be ok." Luke crossed the hall placing his large warm hands on her shoulders and looked her in the eyes with that concerned look he had donned a lot that day. "I promise everything will end up ok in the end." Luke gently squeezed her shoulders, but even though the contact sent shivers down her spine it was nothing more than a friendly gesture.

"I know. Thank you again Luke. Sleep well." She looked up at him fighting the tears that were threatening to escape, she smiled at him and he released her and walked to his door.

"Good night Cristina. Sleep well yourself." Luke smiled at her then entered his room without a second glance back. She watched for a moment as he dug in his duffle bag but then turned and closed her bedroom door. Flopping on her bed she stared up at the ceiling, looked at the odd swirled pattern while seeing little pictures the harder she looked.

She wanted to get the note from her stalker out of her head, the fact her car was trashed, and the fact that she had no idea who could possibly be doing this to her. Thinking back to the man across the hall she smiled. Cristina found that Luke was so sweet and if he turned out to be the crazed stalker, who knows, maybe she would still... no she knew that would never work, and knew in her heart that it couldn't be Luke, why would it be? Besides she had been getting the roses off and on for a year or so now, and she had just met Luke.

Grunting she got out of bed and jumped in the shower, taking more time then she normally would, letting the hot water relax the tight muscles in her neck and shoulders. Drying off she pulled on her night gown then brushed out her long hair letting it hang down her back as she climbed into bed. Glancing to her nightstand she saw that it was one thirty in the morning and she needed a drink, a stiff one. Creeping to the door she saw Luke's light was out so she lightly padded her way to the kitchen. Pulling a wine glass from the cabinet she filled it with her favorite strawberry wine and headed back to her room.

"Everything ok?" Luke asked from his room without turning on a light.

"Sorry, I needed a drink. Everything's fine. Good night." Cristina quickly responded hoping he couldn't see her in her very simple night gown. She hadn't thought the sleepwear out all the way.

"Alright. Good night." With that she went back to her room closing the door with a deep breath. She was glad that she had thought to turn off her bedroom light before she left, since his door was open. She was not thinking straight and she threw back the wine like it was water and crawled into bed.

Letting the small amount of alcohol from the wine take over, she let her mind drift through the day. She focused on the wonderful lunch with Luke, and was starting to feel bad about letting him buy once more and deciding that she would pay from then on. Thinking about the time frame for the car damage for both of their cars, she felt it was way too odd that the unknown person would know what Luke was driving. Then again she knew who ever it was had seen him kiss her and saw his truck as well. So whoever it was had followed her Sunday when she went for a run. She shivered at that thought since she now lived on the outskirts of town. Rolling over to her side she began to count sheep, since her thoughts were keeping her awake, and at this rate she would never get to sleep. Finally she felt the heaviness of her eyes and she drifted to sleep.

Strapping on her shoes and pulling the door closed behind her, she stretched and started off around her property line just like every morning. Yet another dry gray morning, it was perfect to run. Feeling the light breeze brush her skin like silk she smiled and pushed herself faster. The stress of the past few days pumping through her veins, helped push her onward. Her breathing was even from years of running. She glanced beside her and found Luke keeping pace with her and he smiled at her. He was as stunning as ever, even in his running shorts and t-shirt he looked good enough to eat. She pushed herself faster dodging downed trees and low branches.

Looking to find Luke had disappeared she felt a sudden surge of fear when she heard another set of foot falls not far behind her. She glanced back but couldn't make out the figure's face. She pushed herself faster and found herself in the library and the figure was still after her, but she was faster. Running through the exit to the east of the library she was out the door in seconds running as hard as she could to get away.

Looking behind her she found that she was gaining distance from him but she tripped over the large rock formation she has seen on her land. The large gray wolf was on top of her before she knew it. The advancing figure had distracted the wolf long enough for her to make a run for it. She pushed herself faster towards the refuge of her home. Glancing back she found the wolf and figure approaching her. She pushed herself even harder. Seeing Luke at her back door with his back to her, she screamed to him, but he didn't turn around. She tripped and the figure was on top of her holding her down as the wolf started to nip at her.

"Cristina. Wake up, it's just a dream." She could hear Luke's voice from behind her but her focus was on the nipping wolf and the person on top of her. She felt Luke's strong arms wrap around her and pull her to his chest and the wolf kept nipping and the figure tried pulling her from Luke's grasp. "Cristina, wake up. Come on, wake up," Luke said.

"Come on Cristina, it's just a nightmare," Luke said again gently shaking her. She opened her eyes and he was staring at her with wide worried eyes.

"Luke?" she all but cried his name.

"Yeah, it's me." Luke brushed her hair from her face and smiled weakly at her. Without hesitation he crawled into bed with her and pulled her back to his front and pulled the covers over both of them. She would have protested, but secretly she had wanted that to begin with. Still thinking on her dream she focused on his breathing as it quickly became low and even. It didn't take long for her breathing to match his.

The sun was warm on her face as she laid in the rare sunshine in Washington. Looking beside her she found Luke smiling at her. He was wearing a pair of blue jean shorts and a blue shirt which played up his eyes so wonderfully. She smiled back at him then closed her eyes again. "Cristina. You're so beautiful," a soft voice said. She knew that voice but it was too light to be Luke's normal baritone voice. She opened her eyes to find a man but she couldn't see his face, just his blue eyes glistening in the sun. She couldn't help the smile she gave him. She didn't feel threatened, but she had a side thought as to where Luke had vanished to.

"Thank you."

"Always my love. How's our baby doing?" She rubbed her large mid-section with affection and smiled at him.

"Just fine," she smiled and kept rubbing her belly. The man leaned in and kissed her sweetly.

Jerking awake she found herself wrapped in Luke's arms; at least she remembered how that happened. But during sleep she had managed to roll onto his shoulder with his arms still securely wrapped around her like a vice. Trying not to move any more she breathed in his scent to command it to memory. She noticed that his sculpted chest was bare; he had a few chest hairs but perfect in every way. He was too good to be true, but she felt so warm and safe in his arms, she actually let herself hope that one day the situation would be different, and they would both want to be wrapped in each other's arms as they slept.

*****

Waking from a wonderful dream, Luke felt Cristina stir in his arms, but he didn't move and he quickly closed his eyes again. He wanted to see how she reacted to waking to him. She had been so scared that night that tears had been streaming down her cheeks; he felt them when he brushed her hair out of her face. He was enjoying the feel of her warm body curled with his and he felt odd with the surge of protectiveness for the woman in his arms.

Feeling her lightly pull out of his arms he opened his eyes but released her. He turned and smiled at her bed head. She still looked like the most beautiful woman he had ever seen. "Good morning," Luke said softly and he watched as her cheeks rapidly flushed from a sleepy pale to a bright red.

"Morning," Cristina said sleepily.

"How did you sleep?" Luke asked pulling himself into a seated position and leaning against her headboard.

"Not bad." She smiled and tried to quickly tame her wild hair. She crawled out of bed jerking her night gown down quickly. She smiled and scampered to the bathroom. Feeling the need to be gone when she came out he quickly crawled out of bed and went to his room to dress quickly. Pulling on a pair of jeans and a t-shirt he headed for the bathroom to brush his teeth and shave.

When he exited the bathroom he heard Cristina downstairs and the smell of bacon wafted through the air. Grabbing his jacket he headed downstairs and found Cristina dressed in a pair of jeans and a black blouse. Her hair was pulled up into a bun and she looked completely at ease in the kitchen.

"Good morning," Luke said. "Can I help with anything?"

"You can pull the orange juice out of the fridge and grab glasses and plates from the cabinet," she replied, pointing to the cabinets he needed.

"Sounds good." He went to work setting the table. He was finished just in time for her to put breakfast on the table. "This looks wonderful Cristina. She'd cooked bacon, eggs, hash browns and pancakes.

"I didn't know what you liked," she smiled and bowed her head. They said grace over the meal and she flipped a pancake and bacon onto her plate.

"Well, it all looks wonderful and I'll be glad to eat it. Shall I get the syrup?" he asked her.

"Oh, yes, it's um, in the pantry." She pointed to the pantry, which he already knew where it was but he didn't saying anything. He got up and retrieved the Log Cabin syrup from the fourth shelf and sat it on the table. Dropping eggs, bacon and hash browns on his plate he started to scarf the wonderful tasting food down. They ate in silence, not bringing up the sleeping situation which Luke was happy about. He didn't want to push her, nor did he want her to think he was taking advantage of her either. He liked her, but he didn't want her to jump in his arms because she was afraid. He wanted her to jump in his arms because she wanted to be there.

Once they had completed breakfast he cleared the table before she finished off her orange juice. "You didn't have to do that, Luke." Cristina protested but didn't move.

"You made breakfast, I clean up." He smiled as he placed the last dish into the dishwasher.

"I think I got the short end of that deal," she laughed, "You got the easy job." Her smile was award winning, at least to him. He smiled back at her and they locked up the house and headed for the car.

"Are you sure you want to do this?" Luke asked as he buckled himself in. He had decided to hang out at the library and get some reading done, on what he didn't know, but he would do something.

"Yes, you know you don't need to stay home, I can take you to work. Jeff did send me directions."

"Do you want me to go to work today Cristina?" Luke asked her.

"Well, I think we should keep up appearances for now, really I'll be just fine." She insisted and Luke knew his unknown plan just evaporated into thin air.

"Ok, do you have a good handle on where you're going then?" Luke asked, giving in to the woman next to him.

"Yep, I'm good." She smiled and headed for the main road and in the right direction.

"Well, good I can go back to sleep then," Luke said then shrugged down into the seat, crossed his arms and closed his eyes. Cristina reached over and wacked him lightly on the shoulder.

"If I have to be awake for this ride, so do you mister," she said as he sat back up in his seat and laughed. She flipped on the radio and ACDC came on from the preprogrammed station. They listened to the various rock songs that came on as she drove. Luke kept glancing over at her and thoroughly enjoyed the view. She was comfortable behind the wheel; she would have to be after driving from Florida.

She pulled in smoothly next to Jeff's truck and put the SUV in park. "Have a good day," she said simply.

"You as well. If I asked you to do something would you do it?" Luke asked.

"Depends on what it is." She looked at him with a-don't-be-ridiculous look.

"Would you stay inside the library until Jeff drops me off later?" Luke almost pleaded but he didn't want to sound controlling or needy. He really just wanted her safe.

"I'll do the best I can." She smiled at him and that statement was all he could ask for at this time. She wasn't his and if he commanded her to stay or begged her to, she may never be his.

"That's all I can ask for I guess." He smiled lightly and climbed out of the car. Before closing the door he leaned through the door. "Drive safe please and keep a watch out. If you need me just call." She nodded and he closed the door. He watched as she backed out of the parking area and headed back to town.

"Hey man, how are you doing? I didn't think you would be here today," Jeff said patting him on the shoulder.

"Doing alright, you? And Cristina insisted, " Luke asked and turned his attention from the tail lights of Cristina's car.

"Not bad. How is she holding up?" Jeff asked as they headed for the trailer to look at the plans for the hotel.

"She seems to be doing just fine until she falls asleep. But let's not talk about that, let's get to work."

The foundation had already been poured the week before and today they would be setting up all the beams and praying the rain would hold off. Jeff has the perfect system down and this was the tenth hotel he put up in the last ten months. Luke couldn't help but be proud of his best friend's ability to keep on task and get the job done in the allotted timeframe. By lunch time the main floor was set up and the second would be going up after they ate.

"Thanks for bringing extra, man. This is an awesome sandwich." Luke picked at Jeff. Jeff couldn't cook and if it weren't for lunch meat and bread the man would starve to death.

"Not a problem as long as you stop dissing the sandwich maker. And I sort of figured she would bring you by anyway." Jeff elbowed Luke hard enough in the ribs to make him wince. They were quick to eat and everyone got started. No chit-chat and no goofing off, which was Jeff's motto. Luke worked as hard as Jeff and sometimes harder. Luke hated to do anything halfway. The goal was to get all the bones in place today so they could get the skin on before the rain did damage to the wood. Last week while the foundation was being poured the team treated the wood as best as they could so it could withstand the rain they were destined to get that week. Spring was the worst for rain.

Six hours later, later than they had hoped, the bones were all in place and plastic was nailed down for the weekend where the roof would be. The day was done, and Luke was dead on his feet. "Ready to head to the library?" Jeff asked as he locked up the trailer and spun his keys around his pointer finger.

"You bet. Hey you want to come to dinner with us tonight?" Luke asked as they walked to Jeff's black Pick-up.

"Sounds good to me. You know I'm always down for some good food. Where at?" Jeff replied slipping into the driver seat and starting the engine.

"Well, I was thinking about Dave's Diner. I could use some home cooked food without the cleanup," Luke answered strapping his seat belt on. Dave's Diner was a route 66 set up, with plates, pictures and mini juke boxes on all the tables. He had tried to make it as cool as possible with small tire coasters and old looking decorations and a paint job.

"Sounds wonderful to me," Jeff answered and headed for town. Luke pulled out his phone and texted Cristina: *Do you mind if Jeff joins us for dinner?* he typed. Three seconds later his phone pings.

Sure, where do you want to eat? I can meet you there: She

sent. Luke knew she would insist on meeting them there so he texted her, the name of the place and the address. *Ok I'll meet you there.* That was it, nice and easy. Luke worried for the remainder of the drive that she would be there, safe and sound.

"Man, you with me over there?" Jeff interrupted his worrying.

"Yeah, sorry man. What were you saying?" Luke replied coming to the here and now.

"I was asking what you and Cristina are like as a couple."

"No, we are not a couple. I wouldn't mind it, but she's holding back."

"The best things in life come after some really good patience," Jeff informed him.

"Yeah man, but it sucks sometimes," Luke replied and stared out the window as the rain ran across the windshield making the passing trees green and brown blurs.

"I feel ya. I wish I had a girl to take up some of my time; even if she wasn't ready to be mine, yet," Jeff glanced and smiled at Luke.

"I wish you had a girl too, and then you wouldn't be all up in my business," Luke chided.

"I'm living vicariously through you man. But hey, she'll come around. You're a great guy, and not trying to be girly or anything, but if I was a chick I would date you," Jeff laughed.

"Um, thanks man. I think," Luke said sarcastically back. He didn't like the idea of Jeff wanting to date him, girl or not. Jeff finally made it to "Dave's Diner" and pulled into a spot.

Before Jeff could get the truck turned off, Luke had his seatbelt off and was walking into the restaurant to see that Cristina was safe.

"Hey Luke, over here." He heard Cristina call to him and relief washed over him. He didn't know why he wanted her safe or if it was just good guy instincts, but he didn't care anymore. He walked over to where she was sitting, which was in the corner next to the windows. "Where's Jeff?" she asked, glancing behind him. Luke turned towards the door but Jeff was not behind him.

"Guess he's still in the truck." Just when he finished talking Jeff came walking up to him and thumped him on the back.

"Ok I'm here, the party can start now," Jeff said pulling up a seat right next to Cristina. An overwhelming feeling of jealousy stirred in him when Jeff leaned into Cristina and bumped shoulders with her like they were old friends.

"What do you call a plum and an apricot?" Jeff asked Cristina. She looked at him and smiled.

"I plum-forgot." She laughed.

"Good one Cristina," Jeff laughed with her.

Jeff went on telling little stupid jokes and the waitress finally came over, took their drink orders and meal orders.

"Strumming my pain with his fingers, singing my life with his words, killing me softly with his song, killing me softly.... with his song, telling my whole life with his words, killing me softly..." Cristina sang softly as she gazed out the window.

"What are you singing over there Cristina?" Luke asked and watched as her face turned red.

"Oh sorry, it's the song on the radio," she replied and he listened closer and sure enough.

"Hey Cris, so you like, have a stalker now? That's pretty hip, you're a hot commodity it seems," Jeff poked fun at her.

"Yeah, hot, that's me," Cristina replied, but she didn't look too thrilled.

"Didn't mean that as it sounded. But you're a total babe, if I may be so bold. You have my man here all twisted up in knots."

"Jeff, really. Man. Geez." Luke kicked him under the table.

"Ouch. Just being real man. She should know she at least has one good guy crushing after her."

"Jeff. Don't make me take you out back," Luke said harshly. All the while Cristina had either a pleased or embarrassed look on her face.

"Luke," Cristina smirked at him, the corners of her mouth fighting to turn into a smile.

"Yes."

"Thanks," she said then to make matters worse for him she started laughing. Saved by the meatloaf! The waitress appeared and brought their food. Silence ensued as they devoured their meals. Luke kept glancing at Cristina and caught her looking at him a few times. Luke knew she either liked him, or was now worried about staying in the house with him. He would find out later.

"Well, I better head home. See you two in the morning, you're coming to church aren't you?" Jeff said dropping a twenty in front of Luke to help with the meal.

"Sure, I'd love to," Cristina replied and Luke nodded.

"See you in the morning Jeff. Nice chatting with you." Cristina smiled at him. Jeff nodded and headed for the door. The waitress appeared and Luke gave her the cash for the bill and stood.

"Ready?" Luke asked Cristina.

"Yep." She smiled brightly at him, yep she liked him and Luke was doing a jumping air fist pump in his head. He held the door open for her then ran to open the drivers' side and got in. On the drive home they talked about how much she loves her job. "Reading all day. Can't get any better than that," she told him. He told her about how much work they got done at the hotel and how fast everything was coming together. By the time they reached her house she was already yawning and making her way to her room for some shut eye.

"Sleep well," Luke told her.

"Yeah, you too," she said then closed her door quietly. Luke pulled his clothes together, jumped in the shower and hit the sack. He hadn't slept well the night before and now he was plum tuckered out.

*****

Jeff sat in his truck so long he began to fall asleep. Dinner with Luke and Cristina was fun and he could easily see the blossoming relationship forming between them and knew Luke was already head over heels for Cristina. Jeff was jealous of his best friend, and he felt horrible for that. Luke had had a hard enough time with losing his mother and his cheating fiancé who had the gall to continue to wear the engagement ring Luke had given her.

Jeff leaned his head back into the headrest and closed his

eyes just as the calm before sleep took him to a dark sad place. *"You came back,"* Sara smiled at him. *She was wearing a long white gown, her hair fell around her shoulders and her green eyes looked brighter than ever before.*

"I'll always come back to you," Jeff said softly with a smile.

"No you won't," Sara replied sadly. *"But it's almost your time."*

"My time for what?" Jeff asked confused.

"To find love again," Sara said with a sad smile.

"I love you," Jeff argued.

"I know and I you. We will be together one day, not now, I understand that now." Sara smiled brightly. *"Don't let fear keep you from your love,"* Sara said as she drifted away, Jeff tried to follow her but he was stuck where he stood, helpless. Tears streamed down his face as he watched Sara smile and wave to him as she drifted further away.

Jolting awake, Jeff wiped the tears that had fallen from his eyes and clambered out of his truck stiffly and made his way inside to shower and crawl into bed.

*****

Emily sat on the couch with her wrist elevated, she hoped and prayed Alan would come home in a better mood, the doctor wanted to see her Tuesday to put a hard cast on her wrist so it would heal properly. The night before Alan hadn't said one word to her when he dropped her off at the ER or when he picked her up, but he also didn't raise another hand to her. They rode in silence back to the apartment and she went straight to bed while he fiddled around in the living room with something, she didn't know what.

Emily sipped her water and took another pain pill the doctor had prescribed and she let her head settle against the couch.

"Daddy please don't," Emily cried as her father lifted her small frame in the air and hit her with the belt over and over.

"You little brat, one day you'll learn," her father yelled at her, strike after strike. Her brother and sister huddled in the corner of the living room watching in horror with each pass of the belt. She could feel her shoulder twist painfully with each blow.

"Please daddy, I'm sorry," Emily cried, her small pitiful voice not making a difference to the beast of a man she was forced to call father. He threw her across the room and she slid a little as her body collided with the hard tile floor. Her brother grabbed her arm and pulled her into their small huddle and tried to comfort her.

"You three get out of my sight," her father yelled and they quickly scrambled to their feet and made a bee line out of the living room and up the stairs to their shared room.

Emily jolted awake when she heard the door close softly. "Hey baby, how are you feeling?" Alan asked softly as he kicked off his shoes.

"Oh no, I didn't mean to fall asleep. I'll have dinner done soon." She lurched up and her head began to spin as she fell back on the couch with a plop.

"No worries baby, I know the medication is strong. I brought food from La Casa Fiesta, I know it's your favorite place to eat." Alan smiled kindly and took a seat next to her on the couch and set the food out on the table.

"Thank you," she said softly as he pulled out her meal and removed the lid to her enchiladas.

"You're welcome. Eat up then I'll help you with a bath and we can get some rest." Alan smiled at her and a confusion of emotions coursed through her body. *Where is Alan and what have you done with him, never mind I like this Alan better.*

CHAPTER 10

Cristina woke Monday morning to a pounding headache. She and Luke spent Sunday at her place after church, they had gone for a run around her place, she even showed him the rock formation and he had the same "dumping" idea as she had. Luke had made her his Frito Salad for dinner, which she loved and they had a few glasses of wine, far more than she was used to having. But Cristina couldn't help but to smile up at the ceiling thinking about the conversation they had last night.

"So, this is Frito salad, the Thousand Island dressing might be a little strong, it has been a while since I have made this," Luke said giving her a taste of the spoon he was mixing. Luke was wearing his fitted jeans that hugged him in that oh so appetizing way, and a blue t-shirt that fought to cover his muscular chest, and the color made his eyes even brighter.

"Wow, that's pretty good," Cristina informed him.

"Ok so now, take a seat and let's eat," Luke said bringing the bowl to the table. They said grace, and piled the salad onto their plates.

"Ok, so, you like me huh?" Cristina asked. She had already had three glasses of wine, trying to relax.

"Um, well, you know. A bit."

"Really? Well, shoot I like you too." She smiled at him and forked a bit of salad into her mouth, she couldn't believe how brazen she was getting with the wine.

"Ok, so we like each other. What was the strangest date you've been on?" Luke asked and Cristina wasn't sure how to answer him.

"Well, let's see, the strangest would have to be with Michael. He was a freshman boyfriend in high school, he had this thing with worms. So he had taken me fishing, which would have been great, if it had been real fishing, but he called it worm fishing. Being a girl, I thought he was talking about going fishing with worms." She took a drink of her wine. *"So when he came to pick me up he was wearing a water suite and we went worm hunting. And he insisted on giving each worm a name. Like who does that? Needless to say that was the last date for that odd ball,"* she replied and took another bite of salad. *"How about you?"*

"Well, there was this chick I had just met in LA. She was cute, bright green eyes, black hair, legs that went to the sky. She told me her name was Candy and that she was a student at the university. I was game, I was going through a rough spot, not looking for anything long term, just a few fun nights," Luke said and smiled at her, she just rolled her eyes at him. *"Anyway, the first date we went on, she took me to this tattoo parlor and wanted to get matching tattoos"*

"That's not so odd," Cristina told him, *"Well other than the first date, deal."*

"That and the tattoos were of her parents. Like really." Luke laughed and she was enjoying the light banter.

"Wow, she was wacked out of her head."

"You can say that again."

"What's the stupidest thing you've done?" she asked him.

"Oh, well, that...hmm," he took a pause to think. *"Depends on what you mean by stupid. Jeff and I have streaked through town after painting ourselves green, yelling we were aliens. There was the time that I snuck into the school pool and went skinny dipping, and was caught on camera by a*

fellow student who posted the video on the school news feed. She was expelled for it."

"Oh my goodness," she laughed.

"There was another time, Jeff and I ran on stage at the senior graduation our freshman year wearing costumes. We mooned everyone and then ran off stage while being chased by the football coach. We were never caught for that one, but our parents knew. There are a few other things, but I think that's all I'm going to tell you for now, your turn." Luke laughed and motioned for her to go.

"Well, um, hmm. I drove from Florida to Washington, by myself."

"That's it?"

"I haven't had much of a life. I mean Ray and I were book worms, we were boring. But there was this time I was in gym class my freshman year. I had sort of befriended this small girl, her name was Sam. Well, we were doing a basketball intramural and this preppy chick decided to get rough with Sam. Now you have to imagine that the preppy girl was about a foot and half taller than Sam. Anyway, the preppy girl really started picking on Sam and I snapped. After gym class I went into the locker room and the preppy girl was harassing Sam again, so I grabbed this chick and slammed her into the locker room mirror." Cristina lowered her head, she didn't like what she had done, but the preppy girl never messed with Sam again, nor did anyone else for that matter, at least not around Cristina.

"Ok, note to self, don't piss you off. Did the girl leave Sam alone?" Luke asked.

"She sure did, and no one else messed with her after that either, at least not around me. I got a reputation after that,

*that I was nuts and when I would walk down the hall
everyone would part. I didn't have a great experience in high
school."*

*"If they saw you now, they would be like, "Damn, she's fine,
who is she, really is that Cristina Williams? Wow, life has
treated her well, unlike all of us slobs," Luke said and it
made Cristina laugh. He didn't understand that high school
really wasn't that simple as being left alone after that
incident, but she wasn't going to spill anything else.*

Cristina stopped reliving last night and jumped in the
shower and downed a few Advil to relieve the pounding in
her head. She pulled her hair into a pony tail, donned on a
jean skirt, black blouse, and brushed her teeth. She heard
her phone ringing in the other room and she ran for it.

"Hello."

"Hey Cris, how's everything going?" Ray asked her and she
had a moment of panic.

"Hey, um, don't freak out ok," she t told him.

"Well, too late for that, now what's going on?" Ray asked as
his concerned voice penetrated the air waves.

"I have a stalker."

"Another one?" Ray had known about all the odd roses she
was sent over the last year and the odd little notes.

"Or the same one."

"Wow, did you finally go to the police?" he asked.

"Yeah, had to. This person threw a rock through my kitchen
window then almost a week later trashed my car and
Luke's."

"You still with this Luke fellow?" He asked.

"Yeah, he's staying with me."

"Wow, girl, that was fast," Ray said and Cristina rolled her eyes at the phone.

"Not in the same room you dope. He's staying here while we figure everything out."

"Ok, do the police have any leads on this guy?"

"Not yet, still in the works. Nothing happened over the weekend, so we'll see."

"Do you like him?" Ray asked and she was momentarily confused.

"The stalker?" Cristina almost shrieked.

"No dinga-ling, Luke."

"Oh, yeah. I'm really starting to. Wish you could meet him."

"Hey, I'm looking to get some time off here soon so I can come for a visit."

"Oh Ray, that would be so great, but give it some time ok, I wouldn't want you to become a target or anything ok. Please."

"I'll only agree if you promise to keep me in the loop."

"Will do. Thanks."

"Not a problem. Hey, hang in there ok."

"Will do my best, I do have to head off to work. Talk soon ok."

"Yep, try and stop me," Ray laughed.

"Sounds good. Bye Ray."

"Bye." After hanging up the phone she headed down stairs where she could hear Luke already clinking around in the kitchen.

*****

Luke was making Cristina breakfast. He woke up before his alarm, was in and out of the shower before she had gotten to hers. When he was dressed he heard her phone ringing then heard her talking to Ray. Luke was feeling a little jealous of the relationship she had with Ray, but he knew it was unreasonable for him to feel that way.

Pulling out the griddle he started making pancakes. He had learned that, that was her favorite breakfast. He was almost done when she padded down into the kitchen, she looked amazing in her jean skirt and black top, and Luke had noticed that she loved black.

"Morning," Luke said happily to her.

"Morning," she replied pulling out plates and glasses. "Thanks for making breakfast," she said.

"Not a problem. How did you sleep?" Luke asked flipping a pancake into the air.

"Not bad, but this morning I have a pounding headache."

"I do too, did you know we polished off two bottles of wine last night?" he asked and she laughed.

"Wow; that explains it," she said shaking her head.

"Yep. Here you go," Luke said flipping a few pancakes on her plate and adding a few to his own.

"These taste great, so much better than mine," she said

taking a bite. He didn't want to admit to her that it was hard for him to swallow her pancakes; they were usually dry or under cooked. They polished off breakfast and Cristina dropped him at work and left him standing at the site of the hotel they were still working on. Luke had wanted to kiss her again, but held himself back. They were getting to know each other, and he was enjoying each moment of it.

"Jeff," Luke called as he entered the trailer where he was sure to find his friend. He found Jeff sitting behind his desk working more on his dream house.

"Morning Luke. How was yesterday?" Jeff greeted him, dropping his pencil on the desk and standing.

"It was great, we had some pretty good conversation, and the night ended well."

"Have you two kissed anymore?" Jeff asked nosily.

"No, I think it might be too soon to be that close, especially with everything that is going on," Luke said with a shrug. He had wanted to kiss her again, but figured now was not the best time for them to get that close, not with her dealing with a stalker. That had to be way too much on her poor little shoulders right now. "Shall we get to work?"

"Sure enough, back to business then," Jeff said and they headed out side with the crew that was already hard at work.

Eight hours later they had gotten the walls up to seal the place up from the rain. Jeff drove him to Cristina's since last night she insisted that she would be fine driving home by herself. Luke waved good bye to Jeff and headed inside. Finding Cristina in the kitchen, wearing her "Kiss the Cook" apron. He leaned down and kissed her cheek but the reaction was not what he had expected, she just gave him a small smile.

"Go wash up, dinner will be done in five minutes," she instructed stirring pasta. Luke scurried upstairs to shower and change before dinner. He was back at the table, already set, within five minutes.

"Smells wonderful, Cristina," Luke said as she placed a bowl of spaghetti in front of him.

"Just pasta, nothing too hard," Cristina replied, calculated response again, Luke wondered what he had done to bring that one, again.

"How was your day?" Luke asked her after they prayed over the meal.

"It was fine. Yours?" she asked.

"Not bad, we got a lot done."

"Good deal," she responded and dug into her pasta.

They finished dinner with very little conversation, but Luke knew something else was bothering her, but she wasn't talking. They watched a few episodes of NCIS before going to bed.

"Have a good sleep," Luke said as he stepped into his room.

"You as well," she replied with a small smile then closed her door. Luke flipped off his bedroom light and flopped onto the bed trying to figure out what he did wrong; coming up with nothing, he rolled over and went to sleep.

*****

It was Tuesday morning and Emily sat in the waiting room once more to get her cast off before she headed to school.

Alan had been super sweet to her, buying her roses every day, making dinner or bringing dinner home and hadn't raised his voice to her since he broke her wrist. He was currently waiting in the car for her to get done so he could take her to work.

"Ms. Hensley, Dr. Townsend will see you now." The small nurse interrupted her happy memories and she stood and followed the nurse to the exam room once more where Dr. Townsend was already waiting.

"What color cast would you like? I have, red, pink, light and dark blue, white, or black."

"Light blue would be pretty," Emily replied softly as she took a seat on the paper covered exam bed.

"Light blue it is then." He smiled at her and deftly removed the ace wrap and splint and began to work on her hard cast. He placed gauze around her wrist gently, followed by the damp light blue tented plaster, wrapping the stripes around gently and through her thumb making her wrist completely immobile. "We will let that dry for a few minutes and I'll be right back," Dr. Townsend said softly, rose to his feet and was out the door in a graceful fashion.

*****

Jeff sat across the aisle from Jackie and Emily at church and he couldn't help but notice the cast on Emily's arm. Anger spurred within him and it left him uneasy. He had no idea what caused her to have that cast but the idea of her being in pain angered him. The service went quickly and as they rose he was quick to approach Jackie.

"How are you doing today Jeffrey?" Jackie smiled kindly at him.

"Not too bad and yourself?" Jeff replied finding it easy to

converse with the older woman. "How are you today Emily?"

"I'm ok," Emily said softly but wouldn't look him in the eye.

"What happened to your wrist?" Jeff asked, wondering where his nerve was coming from.

"I fell," Emily said simply before turning and walking away from them. Jeff caught the eye roll of Jackie and was going to inquire about it when he was interrupted by Joy, a small frail little old woman who had been going to that church since Jeff could remember.

"Little Jeffrey, all grown up. Where is your mother dear?" Joy asked in a shaky voice as she stood with her walker.

"Mom died several years ago Joy," Jeff said sadly.

"Oh, of course she did dear. So sorry to hear about that, she was such a fiery young thing." Jay rambled on as Jackie retreated to follow after Emily. Jeff spoke kindly to the older woman and walked her to a seat so they could chat while she sat. She was so small, her gray hair thinning on her head, the veins in her arms easily visible against her pale skin but her bright blue eyes still shined with knowledge. Jeff loved this little old woman and often thought of her as his grandmother, for all intents and purposes.

CHAPTER 11

It had been three weeks since the vehicle incident, the nightmare and cuddling situation, and three weeks since her and Luke were close. Almost as many weeks had passed since they'd had dinner with Jeff, and she and Luke actually talked about anything more than the weather. Sure, they went for a run every morning, had dinner every night and she made breakfast most every morning, but that was just it. "I think I pushed him away," Cristina murmured to herself.

"What was that?" Luke asked catching her talking to herself.

"Just thinking out loud is all, pancakes?" She smiled at him and the look of confusion was a tell-tale sign that he didn't believe her, but this was not the time for that conversation.

"Sure," he said and started setting the table. His hair was nice and wet from the shower. His jeans and black t-shirt looked amazingly sexy on him. Cristina gave herself a little shake to focus on putting the pancakes on the table and getting the orange juice.

"Sorry, it's been three weeks and I never even thought to ask if you prefer coffee in the morning," Cristina asked as she dropped the orange juice on the table with a little more force than was necessary.

"Actually, it does sound strange, but I'm more of a tea person myself." He smiled shyly at her.

"Oh, so am I." She smiled and poured the juice. They liked tea, enjoyed a good morning run and had hearty appetites. Cristina couldn't help but notice everything that they had in common, but she figured that it was too good to last. "So, it's been three weeks since anything happened. I think whoever it was has given up and moved on to someone else," Cristina finally said. She had wanted to put some space between them for a while, but was too scared to put it into action.

"It has," Luke said looking at her with a questioning expression as he plopped a few pancakes on his plate.

"Well, I figure you're probably good to go back home. No need to worry about little ol' me anymore. I'm sure you miss hanging with Jeff all the time, and I'm sure I'm cramping your style," Cristina said and started eating her pancakes. For the longest moment Luke didn't move, didn't respond.

"If that's what you want, then I'll head back to Jeff's after work today, but I think you should think about it a little more. Who knows, this person may be waiting for me to leave," Luke said, but the look on his face told Cristina he wasn't happy about it and she knew she should consider his words. She was falling for Luke, but she wasn't sure if it was due to the close proximity, or true feelings, she was confused.

"Sorry, I just hate being a burden to anyone, besides, nothing seems to be happening," Cristina said quietly.

"You're not a burden Cristina," Luke said and the look on his face told her she shouldn't be thinking that about herself. She knew she shouldn't have said what she was thinking, but around Luke, her lips started talking before her brain stopped her.

"Sorry, it's just, I know it is not easy for you to be here, and it's not really conducive to our relationship or our life styles, maybe a little break will bring us to where we should be." Laying it out was the best practice. She liked him, really liked him, but having him here under her roof was confusing and she needed to make sure they had something before they ended up in bed together and she knew for sure that's what she wanted. Well, she wanted to be in bed with him the night they spent together was the most restful sleep she had gotten. But, that could've simply been because she knew she wasn't alone, not for whose arms she was in. She was confused and she needed some space from him to sort things out.

"It's ok. I understand," Luke simply said then went back to eating. It was quiet the remainder of breakfast, during clean up and the drive to the hotel site. Cristina made note of the dark gray clouds above, but hoped the rain would hold off until Luke's crew was ready to go home.

"Have a good day, I'll text you ok, let you know when I get home and stuff," Cristina told him as he climbed out of her new Subaru Forester.

"Thanks, I appreciate that; and have a good day yourself, please stay safe," he replied then closed the door and walked off. Not a second glance, not even a smile. She knew he was brooding. "Damn it," she said to herself. She was messing the relationship up one side and down the other. She backed the car up and headed back to town to go to work. Roberta was off that day and she would be alone, not to mention the group of students scheduled to come in.

Tears began to stream down her face as she realized just how much she'd made a mistake, but she wasn't going to back down, at least not right now. She did need the space, she really needed to figure out what was between them and she prayed it was more than a friendship or a brotherly love. She decided that when she got settled at work she would text Luke and see how he felt about going to dinner and a movie, an actual date. That made her smile; dating was a good option if he was for it.

Pulling into her parking spot she looked around and found that she was alone, perfectly safe. She hurried to the front door and unlocked it. Settling into her desk at the entry she pulled out her phone and texted Luke.

I'm sorry how I acted this morning, but how would you feel about a dinner and a movie, my treat. She waited and waited. Giving up she placed her phone on the desk and fired up her computer as a few older ladies came in for the morning book club. She smiled at the ladies as her phone pinged with a new message.

You don't have to feel bad about this morning and you don't have to ask and pay for a dinner and movie to make up for it. "*Stubborn man,*" she thought and replied back.

You're stubborn, you know that? I was asking you on a date, a real one, not one that happens so we have something to do since we are staying together, a date. She hit send and waited again. "*Men!*" she thought and slammed the phone down with more force than necessary. Five minutes later her phone pinged.

"*Oh.*" A simple message from a complex male, how funny," she whispered. Then her phone pinged again.

You pick, but my treat. She smiled at her phone, they were going to argue over who paid.

My treat, I asked you. ;)

You're killing me. ;)

Back at you bub.

Bub, really? My treat, please.

Yes bub, and no. You've bought enough. I asked, my treat, you pick I pay.

You're killing me, but ok. Name the time and I'll pick the place.

Friday 7pm

Perfect. I'll think on the place. Now I have to get to work, you're distracting me. ;)

Ok, see you Friday then. ☺

Smiling and completely giddy she set to reading her book which was incidentally, Men Are From Mars And Women Are From Venus. She couldn't focus on her book for long as a rush of young people came rowdily into the Library and she had to shush them. The teens quieted down and she still couldn't get back to her book, she was thinking about Luke. She would have a week before she would see him. It was Monday morning and she wouldn't see him until Friday evening.

"Pardon me Cristina, can you help me find, Pride and Prejudice, along with a few books on the Native American wars?" a young lady asked and Cristina set to helping the young girl out. She used all her focus on finding the books and offering piecemeal advice for a paper the girl was writing.

At five o'clock Jill came in to relieve her, wearing a jean skirt, Mary-Jane's and a blue blouse. All the blue was really playing up her vibrant blue eyes. "Have a good night Cristina," Julie said as she settled into the seat that Cristina had just vacated.

"You as well," Cristina replied and headed out the door. The rain had started coming down hard as she ran to her car. She started her car and slowly made her way home. The rain was coming down so hard it made it hard for her to see where she was going, but lucky for her she knew the town like the back of her hand; not that that was difficult with such a small town, and there wasn't much traffic. Pressing the garage door opener she found it wasn't working so she pulled in front of her house and decided to text Luke so he wouldn't worry about her. *Made it home, my garage door seems to be broken, know any good repair men? And the rain is coming down so hard I can't even see my front porch and I'm parked as close to it as I can. Hope y'all are done for the day. I'm looking forward to Friday :)* She pressed send with a smile.

Gathering her things she made a break for it and ran to her door. She heard a noise behind her but before she could turn around, strong arms wrapped around her and a cloth covered her nose and mouth. As panic rose within her, darkness crept in.

*****

Luke felt the vibration of his phone as he climbed into Jeff's truck. They had intended to work a few more hours and finish up the hotel, but the rain was falling so hard, they called it quits. Luke reached into his pocket and pulled out his phone and saw there was a message from Cristina. He smiled as he opened the message; *made it home, my garage door seems to be broken, know any good repair men? And the rain is coming down so hard I can't even see my front porch and I'm parked as close to it as I can. Hope y'all are done for the day. I'm looking forward to Friday :)*

He smiled and replied: *glad you made it home safely, I can fix the door for you. Let me know when you want me to come by. If you need anything let me know. ;) Looking forward to Friday as well.* Hitting send he watched as Jeff ran around the truck and climbed inside soaking wet.

"It's raining cats, dogs, elephants and the whole zoo out there," Jeff said as he started the truck to get the heater on.

"Sure is," Luke said, waiting on the reply from Cristina, she normally responded pretty quickly, but he had to realize that maybe she was doing something or changing out of wet clothes.

"Back to Cristina's?" Jeff asked pulling on to the main road.

"Nope, I have my duffle in the back seat, going home tonight."

"Wow, here I thought you were going to move in with her."

"No man, but we are going on a date on Friday. I guess she needed a little space, but she wants to date or go on a date."

"Dude, that's a step in the right direction, maybe you won't be so gloomy," Jeff chided.

"Maybe, we'll see." Luke laughed and glanced at his phone again and still, nothing from her. *"Chill Luke, I'm sure she just busy with something,"* Luke told himself and tucked the phone in his pocket.

"Since you're not going to Cristina's, lets hit the pizza place; I'm dying for pizza and beer," Jeff said as he made his way slowly into town. It was hard to see where they were going and even though Luke really wanted to crash for the night, he had to admit beer and pizza sounded really good to him.

"Sounds good to me, Bob's has the best pizza and beer in town," Luke replied. Sadly, Bob's was the only bar that served beer and pizza, but no need to bring it up, and Luke was hoping Jeff wouldn't want to travel to a neighboring town for pizza and beer, like he normally did.

Fifteen minutes later they were pulling into the parking lot of Bob's. The place was packed and the rain had eased up a bit, but was still coming down pretty hard, so they made a run for it. Jeff locked his truck with his remote once they reached the covering of the awning, which was worse for wear, but still kept the rain off for the most part. Bob's was a bar, looked like one, smelled like one, but Bob, the owner, really tried to go for the sport's bar theme. The dim lighting helped people see the flat screens that were peppered around on the walls, large posters were scattered around where there weren't windows, and the windows were tinted.

Jeff sat at an open table next to the window and was waving down the waitress. "Can we get two fat tires, and large meat lovers," Jeff said then looked at Luke for approval. Luke nodded and the waitress set off to put in the order. Luke pulled out his phone again, but still no message from Cristina. He couldn't help it, he was officially worried. Talking himself out of borrowing Jeff's keys and heading to her house he focused on the flat screen, which had a commercial playing for Bob's Bar. It was a local channel, which covered the news for the surrounding areas.

"Hey, what's up? You seem distracted," Jeff interrupted his thoughts, even though he was focused strictly on the TV and the funny commercial.

"Sorry man, I'm distracted. I'm so used to having Cristina text me back pretty quick, but she hasn't responded since she sent me her text that she was home," Luke finally said.

"Maybe she's taking a long warm soak in her bath tub; you know girls love bubble baths," Jeff informed him and Luke felt like an idiot, it had been raining hard and she couldn't use the garage door, so maybe she was warming up in a bath. "If she doesn't respond by the time we are ready to go, we'll head over there. Deal?" Jeff said, and that made Luke relax.

"Sure," Luke smiled.

"Now stop being a girl and relax," Jeff kicked him under the table and laughed. Luke kicked him back and the waitress came with their beers and Luke was quick to throw his back. He had needed the drink and it tasted pretty good at the moment.

"So, who have you got your sights set on this week Jeff?" Luke asked getting back into the groove of fellowship.

"Well, there is this one chick, she goes to our church. Her name is Emily. She's tall; maybe about five eight, long wavy brown hair and brown eyes, and has this amazing smile. But," Jeff paused.

"But what?" Luke asked.

"But, she won't even look at me," Jeff almost pouted.

"Well man, you have to do something to get her attention, maybe say good morning to her?" Luke laughed. He knew his friend was shy when it came to women.

"Yeah, I know," Jeff said taking a long swig of his beer. The waitress appeared with the large meat lover's pizza and Jeff was quick to snatch up a piece and start eating. The waitress brought a pitcher of beer and Luke refilled his now empty glass. They always ate when they drank, and always split a pitcher, that was their limit. After they finished off the beer they would drink a few glasses of water and stay a while watching whatever game was on to make sure they were good to drive home.

Three hours and a Broncos and 49ers game later Luke was checking his phone for a message from Cristina, still nothing.

"We'll go by and check," Jeff told him. Luke nodded and stood. He had already settled their ticket an hour ago and he was ready to make sure all was well with Cristina. The rain had stopped when they had stepped outside the bar. It was dark and almost nine at night. Luke knew she went to bed reasonably early but she was good about checking her phone since she was always in contact with her friend Ray. "Let's get this over with lover boy." Jeff elbowed Luke in the ribs then ran to his truck so Luke couldn't retaliate.

Jeff drove a little faster than normal, so they were pulling onto Cristina's drive within seven minutes versus the usual ten. As they came around the bend Luke was relieved to see her car, but every light in the house was out. "She always leaves the front porch light on when she goes to bed," Luke said as he jumped out of the car and pulled on his work gloves and then pulled out the house key she had given him.

"Don't go in Luke," Jeff said as Luke rounded the front of the truck. "Let me call Pete first." Jeff was already dialing his phone.

"Sure, yeah. Good idea." Luke paced back and forth next to Jeff's truck when Pete came flying up the driveway. Luke watched impatiently as Pete slowly climbed out of his car.

"I thought you were staying with her?" Pete asked confused.

"She had told me this morning she felt it was time for me to go back to Jeff's," Luke said harshly.

"Alright, let me have a look, do you still have a key?" Pete asked Luke. Luke passed him the key and leaned against Jeff's truck as he watched Pete head inside. Five minutes later Pete reappeared in the doorway. "She's not here, but it's too soon to be panicked, could she be somewhere on the property?" Pete asked, and Luke felt like an idiot.

"She does like to run to relieve stress, but I doubt she would be running this late in the evening. Give me a few minutes let me check her usual running route." Luke didn't wait for a response as he ran full sprint in his work boots around her usual running route. The ground was muddy and his fast and heavy foot falls made the mud fly up all around him, but he didn't care. "Cristina," Luke called as he ran. It was still light enough for him to see if he came across her, but as he rounded the eastern part of her land and made his way back to where Jeff and Pete waited patiently, he was officially worried.

"Well, normally we have to wait twenty-four hours to report a missing person, but due to the incidents before; I think we can assume the worst at this point," Pete said pulling out his phone. "Yeah, Jess, get me the team. Cristina Williams is missing and we need to get a read on her ASAP." He covered the mouth piece and looked at Luke, "When did you hear from her last?"

Luke opened his phone and checked his messages. "Five-fifteen she sent me a message saying she was home safe and sound, told me her garage door wasn't working."

"Jess, yeah, call it four hours missing. Get her picture out there." Pete hung up and looked at Luke, his face unreadable. "We will get her face out there, and have this place looked over. For now, head home, and keep your phone on in case she contacts you. We could get lucky on this if the perpetrator calls for a ransom," Pete informed him, and started taking notes on his little note pad he had pulled from his pocket. Jeff climbed back into his truck and started it up.

"Keep me in the loop Pete, she doesn't have any family?" Luke asked Pete. Pete looked at Jeff's closed door and walked to Luke.

"Officially you'll hear what the public hears, unofficially, I'll let you know. Ok son." Pete placed his hand on Luke's shoulder in consolation, Luke nodded.

"Thanks."

"You love her don't you?" Pete asked.

"Well, I'm not sure if it's love yet, but I do care for her a lot sir," Luke agreed.

"Thought so. Now, go to Jeff's and stay there. Send me the address of the hotel y'all are working on so I can find you quick if I need to," Pete told him. Luke nodded again then climbed into the truck with Jeff.

"Shall we head home?" Jeff asked quietly.

"Yeah," Luke said simply and looked back at Cristina's house longingly. "I never should have agreed for her to stay alone."

"It's not your fault man. I know you want to argue with me about it, but let's be honest, I could have been bringing you back here and she still could have been taken when she did. I'm sure the guy has been waiting patiently for you to be late or unaware. The guy is smart, but they will find her," Jeff said pulling onto the main road.

"I just hope alive," Luke said and shuddered. He had finally found someone he wanted to spend time with, someone his mother would even approve of; it would kill him if they didn't find her alive, and he never would forgive himself.

*****

Jeff strummed his fingers on the steering wheel as he drove to his house. He couldn't believe after three weeks and silence from the stalker she had gotten herself somehow, missing. Jeff couldn't understand how someone could snap and decide to kidnap someone, or resolve to stalking instead of just coming out and saying that they like someone. Jeff liked Emily, yet he wouldn't fall under a spell to stalker her or take her against her will.

Jeff pulled into the driveway and Luke instantly jumped out, ran in the house while Jeff sat in his truck thinking about everything and where in the world the young woman could be. Five minutes later, Luke was out the door wearing his usual running gear. Jeff would have followed him for a run, but he knew Luke needed time alone.

"Lord, please keep her safe and alive. Bring her home, I beg you Lord," Jeff prayed and tears dropped from his eyes before he could dash them away. He pulled the keys from the ignition and stormed into the house to look through his pictures to see if he had taken one of Cristina. He found one of her smiling while she leaned into the railing of her back porch from the week before when they gathered for dinner. Her long brown hair fell across her breast and her deep chocolate eyes were bright from laughter and now Jeff couldn't remember what had made her laugh.

Jeff pulled up his email and shot the picture off to Pete so they could get the flyers up and the news report set in motion to bring her home. Jeff felt lost and helpless as he sat in his desk chair in his office. Everything was quickly falling apart, just when his dreams were tapering off and he was beginning to sleep through the night.

*****

Emily sat watching the news waiting for Alan to return from work. Dinner was ready and covered to retain the heat for when he returned. She still hadn't eaten and it was almost eleven in the evening, she knew if she were to eat, he would yell at her, so she patiently waited. A news alert rose on her screen with the face of a young woman she had seen once or twice before at the library and at church with Jeffery Parker. Her face held a light bright smile and the words "Missing" beside her name with her information and the tip line telephone number.

Emily covered her mouth with her hand and gasped as fresh tears sprang to her eyes. A thud at the door brought her up short as Alan drunkenly fell through the door. "Emily, baby," Alan slurred his words as she rushed to help him up.

"Oh Alan," Emily said calmly using what strength she had to help him to the couch.

"You're one crazy bitch, I beat the shit out you and yet you stay. Either you're super stupid or I'm one lucky bastard," Alan slurred as she settled him onto the couch. "I think it's a little of both. I love you baby," Alan said softly before dropping into a deep sleep on the couch. Emily shook her head and put their dinner in the fridge for the next day.

CHAPTER 12

Cristina opened her eyes slowly, she was groggy and confused, and the room was dimly lit and she couldn't feel anything. "That's my girl. Wake up for me sweet thing." She heard a male voice she recognized somewhere close by. She tried to move but couldn't find the motor functions to do so. Her head was still fuzzy. She tried to find her voice but all she could manage to do was blink and hear. She focused on the breathing nearby and it sounded rushed, like he was out of breath.

"You woke up just in time," he said and he came into view, blocking the little light there was. "You're mine and I love you Cristina. I've always loved you," he said and his head left her view. She looked at the ceiling and it started to bob in and out of focus, that's when she noticed the grunts from the man who had taken her, now he was taking everything off her. "You're so sweet Cris, oh how I love you," he said breathlessly.

When the ceiling stopped moving his face came into view. "Can you feel me, baby?" he asked her. She knew what he meant, and she was glad she couldn't answer. Whatever he had given her to sedate her was working really well, she still couldn't find her voice. "I take that as a no. You will soon baby, I promise. I have to leave you now. Sleep my love, I'll be back."

Cristina heard footsteps and it sounded as if he were walking over a non-carpeted floor and since the footsteps echoed, the room must either be large or pretty bare. Focusing all her energy on the ceiling she was able to make out that it was white with a popcorn design finish. She could hear drips of water somewhere nearby so she counted the drops. *"One, two, three and four....... One hundred thirty seven.*"

She was starting to feel her fingers. "*Eight hundred twenty-seven.*" She could feel her body but she didn't dare to move. She could feel something soft under her and something light laying across her, what had her worried was the tight feeling she had on her ankles and wrists, the fact she wasn't wearing anything, and she wasn't exactly laying in a proper way with her legs spread eagle the way she was. She cried herself back to sleep.

Cristina opened her eyes then clamped them shut as she heard a door open, and then close followed by the footsteps as earlier. She knew she was in trouble, but what she didn't know, was how long she was out, where she was and who this person was or if he would kill her. "Is my baby awake?" the man asked and she knew the voice, but still couldn't place it. It was a soft voice, a voice she could enjoy hearing at any other time or situation, but not here, not now. She had hoped whoever was stalking her had an annoying husky voice, raspy even, not someone girls dream about hearing over the phone.

"Come on Cristina, wake up." His hand caressed her cheek and the automatic flinch gave her away so she opened her eyes and looked up at dark eyes, surrounded by a dark face. "There's my beautiful." He smiled down at her, she recognized him, but still couldn't place him in the dark room.

"Who are you?" she rasped. Her throat was dry which told her she had at least been out for a few hours.

"Cristina, I'm hurt you don't recognize me. It's Eric. Don't you remember me?" he asked and he sounded very hurt to her. She blinked at him a few times and he shifted his face and let the light illuminate his features. Now she could clearly see his baby face, with day stubble growing around his chin, his dark eyes gazing at her and his lips parted, just how she remembered him from high school, minus the stubble.

"Why are you doing this?" she asked him.

"I love you baby, that's why." He leaned down and kissed her lips. His lips were warm and he pushed his tongue across her lips trying to get her to open to him, but she wasn't going to. He lifted away from her. "Come on baby, you know you want to," he said and tried again. She still refused him, she wouldn't give him the satisfaction of her giving in. She was a one man woman and she'll be damned if she would give in to a man who couldn't even approach her correctly. "Ok, well in time, but for now, I'll have fun with you and eventually you'll want me like I want you."

He shifted his weight and he lifted the blanket, she looked down and she was completely naked. "Please, don't do this," she begged him.

"But baby, I want you; I need to feel every inch of you. You'll want me too once I'm buried in you." he said as he shifted his body and she could see him hovering above her. He wasn't bad looking, better now than he did in high school. Not that she had ever seen him naked in high school, but if he had made himself known before now, she may have given him another chance, maybe this wouldn't have happened. Now she wanted him dead as he thrust himself into her.

Cristina closed her eyes and thought about Luke, and how worried he would be when he realized she wasn't at home. She focused on being wrapped in the safety of Luke's arms, her worst nightmare having come true and she wasn't sure when or if she would get out of this. Cristina thought about the runs she had taken with him. "Oh Cristina, respond to me baby." Eric interrupted her thoughts with a smack across the face, as his breath came out in a rush, and as she watched him she focused on not letting her body react to him. She hadn't had sex in over a year and she wasn't going to give him the satisfaction. Finally with a final rush Eric collapsed on top of her.

"One day soon, you'll not be able to resist me; I'm so looking forward to that day my love." He kissed her around her neck and chest then finally lifted himself off her and covered her back with the thin sheet. "Can't have you catching cold," he said, then he pulled out a needle and jabbed it into her arm. Something cold rushed through her shoulder and as the minutes passed her eyes grew heavy and she was no longer able to keep them open. The noises seemed to fade away and she was lost to the darkness.

*****

Luke was frantic, the search party had made their way through her property that morning, and were working with the Canadians to search the neighboring forest in their area. He and Jeff would be posting pictures in all the neighboring towns.

"Luke, come on, she's not in the woods," Jeff coaxed him back to reality. Luke had been walking all day without a break looking everywhere. They had covered a total of ten miles that day, but Pete had said there was no use in coming back the next day.

"K," Luke said simply. He had closed himself up, he didn't want to feel anything because he knew it wouldn't help her. Luke followed Jeff as they headed back to his truck and went home. When they reached Jeff's, Luke pulled out his phone and called Ray.

"Hello," Ray answered.

"Hey Ray, this is Luke. Um, I have bad news."

"What the hell happened to her Luke," Ray spat over the phone.

"She's missing."

"What the hell," Ray whispered, "Shit. I'll be out there."

"Sure man, we're doing everything we can to find her," Luke informed him.

"I'll be there in the morning," Ray said and hung up. Luke closed his phone and tucked it into his pocket and went to bed.

*****

Jeff got busy in the kitchen and concocted something for them to eat for lunch before he set to printing the flyers for Cristina. They would be headed out later to hand the pictures out and beg for information. Calls had been coming in left and right and leads were followed up on that hit dead ends at each turn. It was hard for Jeff to watch his best friend close himself off and not even feel the chill in the air from the rain they spent the whole morning in.

Jeff dropped from his chair onto the floor on his knees as he raised his hands in prayer. "Lord, please let us find Cristina, bring her home," Jeff prayed over and over begging for a sign that didn't come. She had become family to him, in the short amount of time he had known her. She was family and he didn't want to lose her, couldn't lose her.

*****

Emily heated up the leftovers from the night before as quietly as she could muster while Alan slept soundly on the couch. She knew he would be waking up soon, from all the times he had gone drinking, he always woke up hungry and angry. She was just finishing when the snoring stopped from the living room and she held her breath for the onslaught of anger that was surely to come soon.

"Emily," Alan said calmly.

"Yes honey," Emily said softly, knowing his head would be pounding.

"Get me a glass of water please," he asked and she quickly and quietly grabbed him a glass reeling from the fact he'd said please. She grabbed a bottle of Advil and went to the living room to find him slumped onto the back of the couch.

"Here you go." She handed him the water and he accepted it with a soft smile then reached for the Advil she held in her hand. He took two then chugged the water.

"Thanks. Lunch?" he asked, sitting the glass on the table.

"Coming right up," Emily replied and scurried to the kitchen to get his food, hoping to keep his mood tame. Emily brought him a plate of food and he accepted it with a smile and she excused herself to retrieve her lunch. They sat in silence as they ate before he dumped his plate in the sink and disappeared in the bedroom. The sound of the shower was the only noise from him and she set to work on cleaning the kitchen before he could comment on the mess.

***

Cristina woke every day after the injection wore off that Eric had given her, she had counted five weeks. With a shackle around her right ankle she would rise from the bed, stretch her aching muscles and use the small bathroom at the side of her bed. The chain was just long enough for her to get in the shower awkwardly and wash Eric's scent from her body. She got one meal a day and it was always the same; a turkey, ham, cheese, tomato, and mayonnaise sandwich, two pickles, an apple and a bottle of water. Cristina was beginning to lose hope with each passing day and the relentlessness of Eric trying to get her to bend to his will.

Each day after her shower and eating her lunch Eric would always enter her room from the wooden door she could never reach and he always wore a pair of jeans and nothing else. The days were all the same, he would point to the bed with the gun in his hand and she would quickly clamber into bed as he shackled her arms and left leg to restrain her while he fulfilled his needs. She watched the anger form in Eric's eyes as she resisted responding to him, each day leading to a smack across the face; today was no different.

"What is wrong with you?" he yelled after kissing her again and once more trying to get a response in his favor.

"I don't like you Eric. I may have before this, I may have even loved you if you would have approached me like a normal human being, but keeping me here against my will, forcing yourself on me; is not winning you any points here." She yelled at him and his fist came down hard on her face. If she hadn't turned to the left side he would have broken her nose for sure, as it was he may have cracked her jaw. The pain was intense and the tears that escaped were the only response she would give him.

"Why couldn't you just love me? We could be so happy together." He rubbed her stomach, "You're going to have my child." She knew he could be right, he had taken her during her normal ovulation and she hadn't been on the pill or anything. She was most likely due to have his child and she felt sickened by it. She knew she would never abort the child and since it was a part of her she would love it no matter what. It wasn't the child's fault that it's father was nuts and a sick individual, and if she was never rescued he would have a child no matter how she felt about it.

"I may have a child, but it will never be yours," she spat at him through a closed jaw, pain radiating from the punch. And he hit her again. Then he crawled on top of her and had his way with her once more. When he was finished he left her awake, no drugs this time. He slammed the door behind him and she breathed a sigh of relief to be away from him and pulled on her restraints trying to break free.

She knew she shouldn't taunt him, but she hated him so much and being strapped to a bed while he did what he wished to her most of the last five weeks was killing her. She wasn't sure what happened as she slept or for how long, but shortly after she woke and took care of her nagging needs he was always there.

Huffing, she closed her eyes and tried to let sleep claim her but she failed miserably. She turned her head at the sound of approaching footsteps and watched as Eric opened the door carrying a knife in his hand along with bandages; she knew she was in deep trouble then.

"You'll love me, and this child will be mine when it's due," he informed her with an odd crazy look on his face. Flipping the sheet off her legs and pulling a lighter out of his pocket she watched as he let the flame lick the sharpened edge of the knife. She watched as he sliced her upper thigh with the hot sharp knife, felt as the pain seared through her wishing she could pass out, but no such luck as the tears streamed down her face. She felt the blinding pain, and watched as he heated up the knife with each pass, screaming out until he stuffed a wet cloth in her mouth, which made the pain in her jaw ever present.

Ten passes later he stopped and kissed each cut and rubbed some type of cream on her thigh. "I'm sorry," he said. "You make me crazy," he told her. The pain was still ever present and tears slipped from her eyes. "I love you, please don't make me do this again. You have to know it kills me." He kissed her eyes and the cheek he had punched; which she could feel was already puffy. He pulled the cloth out of her mouth and kissed her lips.

"Tell me you love me and let me make love to you," he said to her. Her strength was leaving her rather quickly, she didn't want to feel that pain again, she couldn't. What could words hurt and what could responding to him hurt? It would feel like wind caresses compared to that agonizing pain. How anyone could be tortured for hours on end and not give in to their capturer was beyond her, she couldn't do it, she wasn't strong enough.

Finding her voice, "I love you," she told him, her voice cracking from the pain still racing within her. Her jaw hurt as she spoke and her heart broke wondering where God was during the last five weeks.

"Do you really?" he asked, a hopeful look in his eyes.

"No," she whispered, hating herself for even trying to lie to him. He quickly moved to her right leg and started the cutting process again. After ten slices she was ready to give him anything he wanted. She couldn't handle it, the pain was too much. She was starting to teeter in and out of consciousness, but with each cut she was brought back to the pain in full wakefulness.

"Can you ever love me?" he asked as he rubbed the cream on her right leg. She knew the answer he wanted and she was going to give him whatever he needed and not take it back. It had been so long, everyone had to presume she was dead. She was clinging to the hope that Luke was still looking or maybe Ray for that matter. She wondered if Eric had left some kind of clue for the police that she was dead and where ever she currently was, she would remain there until she really was dead.

"Yes."

"Really?" He sounded hopeful again, like he didn't realize that what he was doing to her was getting him the responses he longed for. Eric seemed to have lost all his senses and any form of reason as he looked upon her with a bright smile.

"Yes. I love you," she whispered and when he leaned down to kiss her, she granted him entrance and as his tongue danced and prodded for a response and she responded to him, weakly. As they kissed his hands splayed on her chest as he began to kiss down her neck. She faked a response as he did what he had done every day since he had taken her.

She pretended to find a release as he had; he didn't seem to know the difference so she felt safe in her acting. But when he sat up he just began to punch her in the face, chest, arms and legs, but avoided hitting her in the stomach, so he still had a semblance of sanity, or the baby was all he was worried about. Either way he wouldn't hurt the child, "how comforting" she thought through the pain and tears.

She felt like she would die from the pain, her eyes were swelling so badly that it was getting hard for her to see even if she wanted to. He stopped hitting her as the darkness took over. She listened and she heard a scuffle, then a loud thud, which sounded like something large hitting the floor. She was in too much pain to care about what the noise was, the blackness took over and she was no longer aware of anything as she prayed for death.

CHAPTER 13

"It has been five weeks since we last saw her," Pete told Luke. "We have no leads to go off of and the dream she had says nothing to us, unless you can remember the name, maybe we could at least make sure that person is where they are supposed to be."

"I told you I don't know. I can't remember." Luke shook his head, he felt defeated, restless, tired and completely angry with himself. Ray had come and stayed for three weeks, but when they kept hitting dead ends he went home defeated as well.

"Sorry man, we'll keep the pictures up and I'll let you know if anything changes. Remember if she contacts you let us know immediately." Pete patted Luke on the shoulder and walked back to his office leaving Luke standing in the hall of the police station. *"Dear Lord, please give us some sign that she's alive. Please,"* he prayed. Luke walked out of the police station to his truck. It was a rare sunny day and he just couldn't give up on finding her, he did love her and he knew that now.

Getting into his new white Dodge truck he headed back to Jeff's. The roads were empty, and he wished the road would open up and swallow him whole. He needed to find her, he had to. He pulled in front of Jeff's, parked and went inside. He didn't know what else to do but to watch the news, part of him waited for her to be found alive and another part waited for her to be found dead and almost unrecognizable, he really feared the day when that happened. "Damn it," he yelled to the empty house.

He and Jeff worked with search teams for two weeks investigating the forest surrounding her house. Pete had wanted to quit after one but Luke wouldn't let him, and then they searched in a ten mile radius around her house, and with the help of a Canadian search party they turned up nothing. No ransom, no note, not even a hint that she was alive, nothing. When his phone pinged with a new text message he almost ripped his pocket trying to get it out. *Check your truck* it was an unknown number but since he had only been in the house for ten minutes he ran out to his truck to find a piece of paper under his wiper blade.

"Pete, I might have something," he said "Come to Jeff's hurry." Then Luke hung up. Luke looked around but didn't see anyone around. He paced as he waited for Pete, finally the man showed up and Luke waited for him to get out of his truck.

"What is it Luke."

"I got a text to check my truck and there is a piece of paper folded under the wiper blade, the number was an unknown. But I didn't touch the note, look at it, please," Luke pleaded and watched as Pete pulled on a pair of latex gloves and unfolded the paper and read out loud:

Luke,

You'll find her near the rocks with the man that took her. Be quick about it, she needs you.

Luke didn't wait for Pete to say anything before he jumped in his truck and floored it to Cristina's house. Five weeks and she was at her house. The speedometer hit a hundred and five as he plowed through town weaving in and out of light traffic. He caught the attention of a passing cop which was perfect. When his tires hit her driveway he was still going one hundred. He slammed on his brakes, threw the truck in park and was running. The cop that was following him was now chasing him and close behind. "Call an ambulance, give me a ticket later," he yelled over his shoulder. The pursuing police officer didn't slow but was on the phone calling for back up at least.

Luke rounded the final bend and was almost to the rock formation when he saw two figures; one tossed haphazardly on the rocks, the other tenderly wrapped next to the rocks. He stopped next to that body, gently he pulled back the blanket that was covering her head as he gazed down at the woman he loved so badly beaten she looked as if she was in a boxing match hours before. He quickly felt for a pulse and found a weak one.

The police officer skidded to a stop next to him and once again had his phone out. "Is this the missing woman?" the officer asked. Luke kept his eyes focused on Cristina as if she might vanish if he looked away.

"Yes, this is Cristina Williams."

"How can you tell?" the police officer insisted.

"I just know ok. Get help here, call Pete." His phone rang and without looking he answered.

"We found her," Luke said and Pete was on the other end praising God. "We're at the rock formation on the northeast side of her property. We need an ambulance and maybe a coroner ASAP," Luke said into the phone then snapped it shut.

"Everything is alright now Cristina," he whispered into her ear over and over. He found her hand within the blanket and found that she was bare so he kept her covered, but he squeezed her hand over and over. The EMTs came and pushed him out of the way as they carefully lifted her onto a stretcher and braced her neck. Luke didn't let go of her hand as they carried her out of the woods and loaded her into the truck.

On the way to the hospital, she had tried to open her eyes a few times but the swelling kept her from doing so. He cooed into her ear over and over that she was going to be alright. He prayed she would be alright, he had her, and he wasn't ever going to let her go. He knew his feelings weren't rational or normal by today's standards, but he loved her no matter what the reason, he would only leave her if she asked him to, and not without a fight.

The ambulance reached the hospital and she was whisked away. A security guard kept him from following so he paced the waiting room after calling Jeff and telling him the news. He had no grasp on time as his thoughts were racing and hoping a doctor would come to him sooner rather than later to tell him she would be just fine. Jeff busted through the waiting room door, walked next to Luke and pulled him into an unusual hug. "She will be just fine Luke," Jeff said then pulled away from him and sat down.

"Luke," Pete said entering the waiting room.

"Pete," Luke replied dryly.

"Any word?"

"No."

"Well, we already know who the perpetrator was. His name was Eric Miller, his folks had reported him missing over a year ago when apparently he had a psychotic break or something," Pete informed Luke.

"Is he dead?" Luke asked, he sure hoped he was, otherwise he may kill him himself.

"Yeah, he'd been beaten and a knife was pushed through his heart."

"Good," Luke said and Pete nodded and took a seat near Jeff to wait word on Cristina's condition.

Luke went back to pacing the floor until a doctor came out.

"Luke?" the young male doctor asked.

"Yes, is Cristina going to be alright?" Luke asked walking to the front of him

"She will be just fine. She has a fractured jaw, a few cracked ribs, badly bruised face, arms, legs and chest, and she has burns and cuts on her legs but everything should heal with minor scarring. And she has a concussion." The doctor smiled at Luke and relief washed over Luke. "She's asking for you."

Luke followed the doctor into her room and she looked bad but he didn't care, she would heal, she was safe and she was alive. Luke walked to her bed side and saw a safe spot on her forehead, so he leaned down and kissed her.

"Luke?" Cristina's voice was raspy and low.

"Yes, I'm here. I'm not going anywhere," he said softly. She didn't try to open her eyes but he watched as the tears escaped from the corners of her eyes as he gently blotted them away with a tissue. "Are you hurting, do you want pain meds?" he asked.

"No, got 'em," she said softly. As he watched her, he noticed her breathing was labored but getting slower. After about five minutes he knew she was asleep. Luke pulled up a chair, sat next to her and held her hand. He didn't want to let her go, so he decided to sit and stay until she didn't want him anymore.

"Hey, how's she doing?" Jeff whispered. Luke had missed the fact that Jeff had entered.

"She'll be just fine," Luke whispered back.

"I brought you some grub," Jeff said sitting a paper sack and a drink next to him.

"Thanks man," Luke replied and as quietly as possible opened the bag to find a burger and fries from the root beer stand down the street. Glancing at his watch he realized it was after seven in the evening and they had been in the hospital since eight that morning. Luke devoured the food and washed it down with the Dr. Pepper that Jeff had gotten him. When Luke looked up he found that Jeff had settled into a chair on the other side of the room with his legs stretched out in front of him, arms crossed across his chest, head tipped back to the wall and eyes closed; he looked completely at ease.

Pulling his phone out he sent a quick text to Ray *We found her, she's in the hospital, she'll be just fine.*

Thanks, I'll come back for a visit in a few weeks. I'm glad she has you, I failed her.

Not a problem man.

Putting his phone back in his pocket he placed his hand back into Cristina's. He crossed his arms on the edge of the bed, laid his head down resting it in his arm and dozed off.

*****

Jeff sat relaxed in the chair with his eyes closed feeling the heavy weight that had been on his shoulders for five long excruciating weeks. He listened to the calming beeps of the equipment hooked up to Cristina, her heart rate was even and strong. Her face was so swollen it made Jeff sick to his stomach when he looked upon her sweet face in such a mess. *"No one deserves that abuse'"* he thought. He sent up a prayer thanking God they found her and that she was alive. He resolved to not take a day for granted as his body relaxed and he drifted off to sleep.

"Jeffrey." He could hear Sara's voice somewhere in the distance as he walked along the park in the dawn near his house. "Jeffrey." He heard again and this time it was closer and he turned around trying to find her but she was nowhere to be seen.

"Baby, where are you?" Jeff asked the air around him.

"Right here, always right here," she replied and he could finally see her. She wore a long white dress and her hair fell long across her shoulders and her smile was bright.

"Don't leave me," he begged.

"I'm not going anywhere but you are," Sara said softly and brushed her lips across his.

"I don't want to go," Jeff complained pulling her into his arms.

"Baby you have to, it's time for you to move on," Sara smiled sweetly at him.

"I don't understand," Jeff replied sadly.

"You will. I love you." Sara smiled at him and kissed his cheek.

"I love you too," he replied as she drifted from his arms.

"I'm always here," Sara said as she faded away and his arms fell slack to his side.

*****

Emily sat crying in the bathroom as she set up a bath to sooth her aching backside from the beating she just took from Alan. He had come home from work and was angry for no reason. The dinner was on the table and everything was perfect and she had waited patiently for him. He had come through the door throwing his things on the floor and quickly removed his belt as he made his way to her. He grabbed her by her recently freed wrist and began to hit her with the belt, fifteen licks and she was collapsing into him from the pain. She didn't know how much more she could handle, Alan was so extreme in his mood shifts she couldn't keep up. Lately even doing everything he wanted correctly still brought him to raising his fist, hand, belt or anything he could get his hands on.

*****

Cristina was aware of a beeping sound nearby; she recognized the sound as a heart rate monitor from her time in the hospital with her mother. She opened her eyes and was relieved that the movement was relatively pain free. She was bathed in a soft light from above her bed but the rest of the room was dark. She felt a very warm pressure in her left hand and reflexively flexed her hand, and a quiet grunt followed the action. She hurt too much to look towards the sound but she had an idea who it was. Glancing to the right of the room she saw Jeff relaxed against the wall, his mouth slack open and a hushed snore escaping. She smirked but the motion hurt and her hands flexed from the pain since they were the only things that didn't seem to hurt at the moment.

"Cristina?" Luke, whispered sitting up. When their eyes met she felt a calm rush through her and tears slipped from her eyes. He was there with her just like she had wanted and he was clasping her hand like he really cared. She wanted to smile but knew it would hurt so she forced out "Hi." It was a low whisper and enough for her to notice that her jaw was being held shut by something under her chin.

"Are you in pain?" Luke asked, and the look on his face would have made her laugh if she could. "Sorry, don't try and say anything, just blink twice if you want some pain meds." He smiled at her, and as much as she wanted to look at those amazing blue eyes of his, she was in pain, so she blinked twice.

"Nurse," Luke said, but she couldn't see what he was talking into.

"Yes," a female voice sounded over the intercom system.

"Ms. Williams could use some more pain medication," Luke said calmly.

"Someone will be there shortly," the voice said.

"Thank you," he said, then Luke took her hand once again but he stayed standing so she could see his wonderful, stressed out, unshaved, handsome face. "I'm so glad you're safe," he whispered. She heard movement then saw Jeff leaning over her.

"Hey sugar plum, you got the other guy good," Jeff told her with a huge, sad grin. She was confused about what he said, but she couldn't ask him about it. "The guy who had you, you beat the crap out of him, damn girl, I'm impressed you're so little and he was so big. What's the most interesting thing was…"

"Jeff, let her rest," Luke scolded Jeff for rattling on about how she was found. "After she's better she'll tell us what she wants us to know."

"Ok, sorry Cris, sugar, rest up," Jeff said then stepped aside so the nurse could get to her. She was a big lady with bright pink scrubs. She was older and her hair was graying from what she could tell in the dim light.

"How you doing sweetheart?" the lady asked her but kept on talking knowing she couldn't respond. "I'm going to give you a sedative to help you sleep through the night and place a few ice packs on your face for the swelling; your face is already looking much better dear." She continued, "Luke hand me those packs next to you." Cristina heard pops of something then watched as square packs were hovered above her face, then she felt the cold relief rush through her skin. She felt a cool numbing sensation start in her arm, then spread through her system. The sounds around her, the hushed voices began to fade as the darkness claimed her.

***

The two weeks after the rescue by the unknown individual had been long and grueling for Cristina. Her jaw was still really sore and she wore a head brace at night. Her ribs were mending slowly and the doctor had informed her that they had only been cracked and not fully broken. Her face was back to normal but her thighs were an issue. Eric had sliced her on the insides of her thighs and up high close to her panty line. With her ribs, she'd had to have help with the maintenance. She remembered the conversation she had with Luke when she was talking to the nurse about everything she needed to do:

"So, no heavy lifting, liquid meals with a straw, and apply this ointment twice daily and careful with a shower or bath."

"Sounds good," she had murmured through her teeth. It was hard for her to talk but she managed simple things.

"How will you manage the ointment with your ribs?" the nurse had asked thoughtfully. "We can have a nurse come by twice a day to assist you, but that's not covered by your insurance," the nurse told her.

"I'll take care of her," Luke said flatly. She liked that he wanted to help, but she wasn't that close with him and she still hadn't told him about the pregnancy that the doctors had confirmed yesterday. She had nightmares every night and was very jumpy, which caused searing pain to radiate from her ribs.

"Luke," she said softly and he turned and gave her a smile that almost had her giving in, but she couldn't, not this time. "Roberta already offered; she was a nurse at one point."

"You sure?" Luke asked, his eyebrows pinching in the center. She just nodded and looked back to the nurse.

"Since that is settled, please sign here and you can be on your way." Cristina signed the release form. "Thank you, oh and for the next week, walk as little as possible." The nurse smiled and stood up from her crouch next to her wheel chair.

"Ready?" Luke asked. When she nodded he wheeled her out to his waiting truck. He lifted her easily into his truck, then an orderly came and wheeled the chair away. Luke buckled her in and kissed her softly on the lips. "I'm glad you're coming home, I mean going home," he corrected himself. He closed her door and got in. "Are you sure I can't help with the cuts? It wouldn't be any trouble?" Luke said, and she knew he would ask about helping her bathe as well, but she just couldn't yet, not after everything. She really needed time to get through the whole ordeal and being naked around Luke was not something she was ready to deal with.

"Thank you, but, Roberta really wants to help." She gave him the best smile she could with her current bruising and the pain in her face; two weeks wasn't enough for that to ease.

Cristina walked slowly away from the bathroom sink sighing. Roberta was staying in the room across from hers in case she needed her during the night and morning; then

Luke was there every day after work. Often times he brought her dinner in a cup, along with a chocolate shake. She had invested in a Vita mix blender and made soups while she was alone during the day. Roberta went back full time at the library while Cristina healed and Luke had changed his hours so he was going to work earlier and getting off sooner so Cristina didn't have to be alone for long.

Currently, she was alone in the house and she was ready for a nap. Easing herself onto the bed she pulled the covers over her and closed her eyes. She still hadn't told anyone about the baby. Every night Cristina dreamed about the look on Eric's face; and every night she was jolted awake from reliving each touch, kiss, cut and the feel of his skin on hers. She no longer screamed from the dreams to alert anyone she was having them, but she knew she tossed and turned because each morning her ribs hurt and she always struggled to take the pain medication the doctor prescribed.

Relaxing into her soft bed she tried to focus on Luke, the soft smile he gave her every day, the way he kissed her forehead with such care since her jaw hurt most of the time. She focused on his bright blue eyes which looked more relaxed and relieved with each passing day. She heard the rattle of keys as she fell into a deep sleep. She wanted sleep and knew it was Luke; he always rattled his keys like that so she would know it was him.

She wasn't sure how long she had slept but when she awoke from her dreamless sleep, she felt rested. "Good evening sleepy head," Luke said. She saw him sitting in the corner of the room reading a book, but she couldn't make out the name.

"Hi," she said as she slowly pulled herself into a sitting position.

"So, Roberta called me and told me about a family emergency that she had to rush to Idaho to handle. She didn't say when she would be back but that the library was covered until either she returned or you were better." Luke got up, walked over to her and sat down next to her on the bed. "I know this changes things, but I'm here for you and I'm going to take care of you. I won't hurt you," he said softly and she knew he wouldn't hurt her.

"Luke," she said, "I know you wouldn't hurt me." She looked at him and placed her hand on his jean clad thigh.

"Good," he said and smiled then leaned in to kiss her on her forehead but she shifted so his lips landed softly on hers. "Sorry," he said quickly when he realized what he had done.

"No," he said when he went to pull away from her. She wanted him near her, he had been her life line for the five weeks Eric had her. She lifted her right hand and placed it on his jaw then lightly pulled his lips back to hers. His lips were soft and warm and felt perfect against hers. The light pain she felt from the pressure was bearable in comparison to ending the kiss. He leaned back and put his forehead against hers, "Oh Luke," she sighed.

"I'm not going anywhere until you tell me to go," he said so softly she wasn't sure she had heard him correctly. "Ready for some grub?" he asked with a smile.

"Sure," she said. He shifted off the bed and helped her to her feet. He walked in front of her as she walked slowly down the stairs, doing her best to keep from rubbing her thighs. She was wearing a dress to keep the fabric from aggravating her cuts, which were healing pretty well according to Roberta. Cristina silently worried about the bath and cut maintenance Luke would be assisting with. She still wasn't sure she was ready for him to see her naked body, she didn't even want to see it herself, but she didn't have much choice.

She drank her chicken broth then her yummy chocolate shake and was already tired. Luke never ate with her, he told her he didn't want to make her hungrier by looking at his meal since she was stuck with drinking through a straw five times a day. When she was done, she stood and made her way to the living room to watch whatever was on TV while Luke devoured his food down in record time. By the second commercial Luke was scooting next to her on the couch.

"What are we watching?" he asked.

"Looks like Bones," she said letting her left hand rest on his thigh as she restrained a painful yawn.

"Ok, time for your night time regimen," Luke said getting to his feet and gently pulling her to her feet.

She hesitated, she wasn't sure she could handle him seeing her. She knew even though she could feel her way around getting the medicine in her cuts, she would miss some. She was afraid of his response, but mostly she wasn't sure if she was ready to be naked in front of a male, Eric still had her tied up in knots.

She followed him to her bathroom and watched as he filled the bathtub with super bubbly water. If it didn't hurt so much to smile, she would have. He'd help her wash what she couldn't, but he wouldn't see because of the bubbles; she liked the thought. The cuts were going to be a different story all together. But she knew it was one battle at a time.

"Ready?" he asked. She nodded and walked to him kicking off her socks. Roberta had helped her put them on that morning, but getting out of them was rather easy. "Focus on my eyes," Luke told her. His eyes never strayed from hers as he unbuttoned the few buttons on her dress and let it fall to her feet. She hadn't bothered with anything under since it would just be a pain to deal with later. Reaching behind her he slowly and carefully unwrapped her ribs, apparently per Roberta's clear instructions. She hadn't worried about not wearing a bra since the ace bandage covered her quite well, but now she was as clad as could be.

Dropping the ace bandage to the floor, he reached his arms out and she grasped them as he helped her into the tub, still keeping his eyes focused on hers. She knew he could see her in his peripheral vision, but she wasn't going to focus on that. Slowly she lifted one leg and stepped into the tub, then her next leg. He helped her sink into the tub letting the bubbles hide her. "Bubbles suit you," Luke said as he released her when she was fully hidden by the bath. "I'll let you do what you need to. I'll be on the other side of the door, call when you need me." He smiled and picked up the ace bandage from the floor and started rolling it.

She focused on slowly washing her arms and lifting her razor to remove what little stubble she had under her arms, she gently washed everything she could reach without hurting her ribs. When she couldn't do anymore she sighed cause she hated needing help. "Ok," she said and Luke entered the room. He had changed into a pair of shorts and another t-shirt.

"Would you like me to wash your hair?" he asked and she hadn't thought about it. She was really feeling like a little kid. Roberta just did what she needed to with small talk to distract her.

"Sure," she replied and sat up straight resting her arms on the side of the garden tub. She closed her eyes and felt

Luke gently pull the clip out of her hair to let it cascade down her back. He picked up a cup Roberta had next to the tub and scooped up water to carefully wet her hair starting at the ends and moving up. She relaxed her head and allowed it to fall back, keeping her eyes closed while his fingers gently stroked her hair and dumped the water from her forehead down. She could hear him fumble with the shampoo bottles and when he lathered the shampoo into her hair it felt amazing to her. He was gentle and meticulous whereas Roberta rushed through it like she was her daughter or something. With Luke she felt relaxed and almost turned to putty in his exceptional hands. He rinsed the shampoo out then did the same process with the conditioner. When he was done he wrapped her hair in a towel that had a rubber band at the end to keep it in place.

"Ok, lean back and I'll take care of everything else." She couldn't see his face but from his voice she could see the smile in her mind. He was careful with the loofah as he washed her, taking extra care with her thighs; her heart began to race with panic. When he got to her feet he massaged them with his amazing hands and the moan that escaped her lips brought a laugh from him. She opened her eyes and he was smiling, like a kid in a candy store, at her. "You like?" he asked, restraining a laugh, but the bright smile on his face told her that he was satisfied with her response. *"So not cool,"* she thought and rolled her eyes at him; but her heart rate began to slow.

She was done with her bath, but now for the fun part. She didn't have to worry long as Luke produced one of her large fluffy beach towels and then reached in the tub and pulled the plug to let the water drain out. This was less difficult with Roberta, but she was enjoying him making a huge effort for her. She was still covered in bubbles when all the water drained out, but without looking he passed her the towel which she laid over herself and did her best to tuck it around her. He still had to get the bandage back around her ribs and put the ointment on her thighs, which only needed a few more days to heal.

He leaned down, finished tucking the towel around her, then gently lifted her out of the tub. He carried her to her room and sat her on a towel which he had laid on her bed. She was really feeling like a small child. "Thank you," she told him and he just smiled. She sat up straight and was about to let the towel drop from her chest when he crawled behind her on the bed.

"Lift your arms please," he instructed. She complied and lifted her arms slowly above her head, it was a task since her ribs hurt with any movement, but to feel his gentle hands on her she would endure it. The towel fell to her waist and he made quick work of the ace bandage placing it perfectly across her breasts first, then he worked his way around her making it tight on her ribs, giving her back a small amount of freedom. When he had completed that task he crawled back off the bed and produced her nightgown. With her arms still raised he slipped it over her head and stripped her of her towel as she tucked the gown down concealing her most private area.

"I have to look now," Luke said softly. He pulled the towels aside and shifted her so she was lying down on the bed. Doing his best to keep her gown from shifting upward she produced another towel and laid it across her lap as she closed her eyes. He shifted her leg and carefully put the ointment on her right leg followed by the nighttime bandage, and then he moved and did the same on the left leg. After covering her with the blankets he whisked the towel away and placed it on her night stand with the ointment and bandages. "That wasn't so bad was it?" he asked. He smiled down at her and once again kissed her forehead. She had hoped they were passed that so she reached up and wrapped her arms around his neck, which wasn't without it's pain, but she pulled his lips to hers and he went easily.

"Thank you," she whispered against his lips. She really wanted her jaw to heal, she really wanted to kiss him, really kiss him. He pulled away and passed her a sleep aid and pain medication. She slipped the straw between her teeth and sipped the water he offered. Taking pills was always a process, but once it was completed she felt better a few minutes later. Luke walked to the door and turned the light off.

"Good night. If you need me I'll be across the hall."

"Stay," she said although she didn't know what had come over her. She could still see his face since the hall light was on, and the smile that quickly covered his face was priceless, but he whipped it off almost as fast.

"Is that what you really want?" he asked. He paused for a moment and thought about the answer; yes she wanted him to stay.

"Yes," she answered.

"Ok, I'll be right back." He slipped from the door and before she could count to fifteen he turned the hall light off and closed the door to her room after he entered. She rotated her head to look towards the window as he climbed into bed after ridding himself of his shirt. She knew he normally slept in his boxers, but he left his shorts on to her dismay and luck.

"Good night," he whispered as he turned to face her pulling the blankets to his chin.

"Night," she whispered back and moved her hand in search of his. When her fingers caressed his, he twined his fingers with hers and she fell quickly to sleep.

CHAPTER 14

Four weeks had passed since the night she asked Luke to stay in her bed. Her cuts were fully healed, her ribs perfectly fine and her jaw was feeling pretty good; Cristina was on the moon. Luke was at work, and Roberta had come home the week before her jaw was fully healed, but wouldn't discuss the family emergency. Cristina had been driving her new Subaru and was enjoying the freedom of not needing someone for most of her needs but she still looked over her shoulder often. She knew she would never take a shower for granted again, or washing her hair; even getting dressed was a welcome change of pace and enjoyable for her.

Ray had called several times apologizing for not sticking around and keeping up the search, she had decided to forgive him, even though it was hard to. He was her best friend, she wished he hadn't given up on her being alive after only three weeks, but he was a man and a practical one at that. Her heart was softening towards him. Ray had told her how crazy Luke had been while she was missing and that he felt that Luke was a great man and he approved.

Today she was getting an ultra sound of the little one growing inside her so she was sitting in the waiting room of her Ob-Gyn. The room was stark white with baby images on every wall from different stages of pregnancy to birth.

"Cristina. Dr. Collins can see you now," the young receptionist said from behind the counter.

"Thank you," she responded and walked through the entry and found Dr. Collins standing at a tall counter.

"Cristina. How have you been feeling?" the doctor asked. She was a tall lady with short brown hair and a pretty face which was void of any make-up.

"Good morning. I've been pretty good this week."

"Well, let's get your weight, temp and check this little bugger out shall we?" Dr. Collins said, then motioned for her to step on the scale. She knew she had lost a good ten pounds from her liquid diet and the five weeks she was held captive, but when she saw the scale, Cristina gasped. She had lost eighteen pounds. "Now that your jaw is better, you need to eat well-rounded meals. Have you been taking your folic acid and prenatal vitamins?" Dr. Collins asked her.

"Yes. But I still can't eat too much since my stomach is not used to solid foods. I'm eating yogurts, mashed potatoes, fruits and steamed veggies, but as far as protein goes, that's still in liquid form," she replied.

"Ok, well I want you to eat more as you can, you need to be in a happy weight when pregnant so you'll need to gain ten pounds and then you'll be on track." She finished taking her temp and heart rate, then led Cristina to a room with an ultrasound machine and tossed a gown at her. "Put this on, get up on the bed and put your feet in the stirrups and open up."

"I thought we were doing an ultrasound today?" Cristina asked; she was a little freaked out.

"We have to do a pelvic ultrasound since you're still pretty early on, two months is still pretty small." Dr. Collins said then exited the room. Cristina pulled on the gown, got on the table and covered herself with the paper blanket Dr. Collins had left on the bed. There was a knock on the door and Dr. Collins reappeared.

"Ready to see your baby?" she asked as she dropped onto a rolling stool.

"Yeah," Cristina answered looking at the little monitor next to her. She glanced down at Dr. Collins as she slipped a condom over a long wand and put some jelly stuff on the tip. Without a word of warning the good doctor inserted the wand into her cervix and an odd shape appeared on the monitor.

"See that right there?" she was pointing to an odd shape surrounded by a lighter background.

"Yeah."

"That's your baby." The doctor said quietly. "Would you like a print out?" she asked.

"Please," Cristina replied. She felt tears forming in her eyes. She hated how the baby came to be, but she already loved the little thing. She still hadn't found a way to tell Luke about it, but she planned to do it over dinner. The doctor finished and the image was gone.

"Ok, you can get dressed now. Here is your picture. Everything looks good and the baby is growing like it should. Come back next month and I want you to have gained some weight," she instructed.

"Yes ma'am," Cristina responded and Dr. Collins left. Cristina dressed quickly and tucked the picture in her purse.

She was glowing when she left the office after setting her next appointment. She headed to the grocery store to get the ingredients for enchiladas. It was a soft food she could manage and she knew Luke loved spicy foods. She pushed the nagging fear of rejection aside as she combed the aisles for everything she needed. She was rung out and back in her car within an hour after leaving the doctor's office.

She looked at her watch and it was just after lunch time when she pulled into her garage, unloaded her groceries and started the preparations. It would take about two and a half hours to cook with about twenty minutes of prep work. Luke was getting off at three, and since it was Friday they had the weekend to themselves if he chose to stick around that is, before she went back to work.

It was three thirty when Cristina heard the sound of a truck pulling into her driveway and dinner was almost done. When Luke entered the kitchen he wrapped his arms around her and kissed her neck. "How are you doing today, my fair lady," he said.

"Not bad, how ye' be?" she laughed back.

"I feel like I'm walking on air right now. But it's time for a shower. I'll be right back." He kissed her neck again and then she heard the sound of his footsteps as he thudded up the stairs to the bathroom overhead. She breathed in deeply trying to calm her nerves; she wanted to wait until he had eaten to tell him about the baby and knew she had to tell him delicately. They had grown so close since her kidnapping, and she loved it. She felt a twinge in her heart every time she thought that he might leave, having another man's baby wasn't high on anyone's list, especially as young as they were but she had hope.

The timer went off on the stove just when the shower stopped overhead. She pulled the dish out and placed it on the table. She had already set the table and had ice water in their glasses. "Wow, something smells amazing," Luke said as he entered the kitchen. He was wearing a pair of jeans and a black t-shirt that was straining against his muscular upper body. He kissed her on the lips and went to sit, but she pulled him back and deepened the kiss. If this was the last kiss she was going to get, she wanted it to be good. "What's that about?" he asked with a confused yet pleased look on his face.

"Just wanted to kiss you is all," she said, then planted her butt in a chair across from Luke.

They ate with small talk about the day, odd people she saw in the store and the house Luke was remodeling. When they had finished she finally had to tell him.

"I have something to tell you, and before you get upset, please hear me out," she blurted and he washed away any type of emotion from his face.

"Ok," he said. She pulled out the picture of the little baby inside her and passed it to him, he looked very confused.

"I'm pregnant," she said. He sat staring at the picture for the longest time, not moving, not saying a word, and not showing any emotions on his face. "Are you alright?" she finally asked, she couldn't take the silence any longer.

"I think the better question here is, are you alright?" He rose quickly and crouched on his heels next to her and swaddled her hands with his.

"I'm good."

"This is what you want?" he looked at her, concern clear on his face.

"It's what I'm going to do. I may not have wanted this now, but here it is," she told him bracing herself for the fallout.

"You're sure?" he asked again.

"Yep. You don't have to be a part of this, that's why I'm telling you now."

"Do you want me to go?" he asked.

"Only if you want to go," she told him after a long heart wrenching pause.

"That's not what I asked," he said while squeezing her hands.

"Then, no. I don't want you to go. But I don't want you to stay for the wrong reason, or because you think I need help. I want you to stay because... because..." She couldn't finish that statement, she wanted to tell him she loved him, but she didn't want the rejection. Her emotions were starting to get the best of her as tears began to fill her eyes.

"How about I stay, because I want to then. How about I stay, because I love you," he said softly and the tears she was trying to hold at bay rushed down her cheeks.

*****

Luke couldn't look from her face as she processed what he just told her, tears streaming freely. Sure his timing was off, and maybe a little more rushed than he had intended, but it was out now and he wouldn't take it back.

"I, I love you too," she whispered and more tears fell down her cheeks. Leaning up he claimed her lips, she was his, no changing that now and they were going to have a baby. Not something he was ready for just yet, but she needed him whether she knew it now or not.

"Since Eric is dead we can keep anyone from knowing the full extent of the situation if you would like?" Luke was talking before thinking but, he loved her and wanted to protect her and the child growing inside her.

"How, I mean, the only one who knows all the details is you, the doctors and the police."

"Well, Jeff knew I was staying with you before so we could easily play off that we had sex that morning and the child is mine."

"That seems like a lot to put on you." He watched as her emotions twisted across her face and tears streamed down her face in a fury. He stood and pulled her to him, wrapping his arms around her while holding her tightly to his chest.

"I'll take it, this child never needs to know how it came to be, at least not before it knows family and love first. One day the child will find out I'm not its biological father but by that time, it won't matter."

"Luke, that's..." She sobbed.

"Shh. It's ok. Sometimes parents do what they have to in order to protect their child. I may not be the father of this child, but I'll be the best dad he or she ever has." He rubbed her back as she cried into his chest. He knew she didn't have a good standing on what a dad was, but he did and he would show the child all the love he could. "I know it will be hard, but together we can do it. I'll talk to Pete to ensure no one slips out anything about it and the child will live a normal happy life."

"How did I get so lucky?" She pulled from his chest and looked up at him, her eyes were red and her cheeks wet from tears.

"That would be my question about you." He planted a kiss on her tear swollen lips. If he hadn't hated to see her cry he would say kissing her was the best feeling in the world. The quick pull away Cristina did told him something was wrong. When he saw her face he noticed it had paled and before he could ask what was wrong she ran to the little half bath by the living room. "Morning sickness. Great timing," he mused. He grabbed a glass of ice water, wet a wash cloth with cold water and followed her into the bathroom. She was hunched over the toilet heaving her dinner.

"No, you don't need to be in here," she told him weakly. He scooped up her hair and held it for her as she tossed the remaining dinner that her body apparently didn't like. She closed the lid, flushed and leaned back on her heels while relaxing into his legs. He passed her the wash cloth, she wiped her face and then he passed her the glass of water.

"Here, sip," he ordered. She obeyed and then he lifted her to her feet. "Feeling better?" he asked, he knew his face looked amused, but he couldn't help it. For such a strong woman who had gone through such intense circumstances, morning sickness is what brings her down. But he couldn't help but laugh a little and her bewildered expression made him laugh harder.

"What?" she demanded and when she actually stomped her foot like a two year old, he laughed harder. He couldn't control himself. "What?" she asked again, but she too started laughing and before he knew it he was kissing her with such ferocity she could have been a snickers bar and he a starving man.

A knock at the door interrupted him from delving his tongue into her mouth, which with the brief interruption, he knew she would have stopped him since she had just lost her dinner. *"Moron,"* he thought. "Stay here," he said as he went to the front door to see who was calling.

"Hello," said a tall man with dark hair and deep brown eyes that he had seen before.

"Hello," Luke replied.

"I need Cristina," the man said and Luke instinctively

blocked the door with his broad body.

"Who are you and why do you need Cristina?" Luke asked hoping that Cristina had stayed in the little bathroom or went upstairs to freshen up.

"I'm her father," the man informed Luke.

"Well shit," Luke said without thinking. Looking at the man in front of him he saw her eyes, her nose and hair color. "Why now?" Luke asked.

"I saved her life, now she needs to help me."

"You saved her? Why didn't you come forward when we found her?" Luke was pissed, "Why didn't you take her to the hospital?" Luke stepped towards the man, really restraining himself from punching the dead beat.

"I knew you would save her in time and the bastard was dead, he could harm her no longer." This man was creepy, even dressed in jeans and a long t-shirt.

"What do you need from her?" Luke asked.

"She needs to marry a descendant of the tribe who rescued my forefather, and she needs to do it before the next full moon," the man said simply. Luke wasn't going to have Cristina marry some random man just for her father's sake, the man who had raped and left her mother, and the man who had left her to possibly die In the middle of the woods.

"What tribe is she supposed to marry?" Luke asked interested, trying to tame his anger.

"Lummi," the man said simply and Luke almost smiled. That was the tribe his father's family descended from.

"Would any man from that lineage do?" Luke asked.

"Yes."

"Good," Luke said then he felt a hand press on his arm.

"Who is it?" Cristina asked coming up next to him.

"Cristina, I'm your father and you need to marry a relative of the Lummi Tribe before the next full moon."

"Ok, so are you pulling some kind of star wars deal on me like "Luke I'm your father" deal. It's so not funny." Luke admired her fiery wit as she spouted off to the man that Luke could clearly see as her father, or well, sperm donor really.

"No child. What is this Star Wars you speak of?" The man didn't know Star Wars, what had he been doing, living under a rock? "Please you must marry before the next full moon. Our people need to be joined with this tribe as you're the princes of the tribe of the wolf totem."

"Huh?" she asked, snuggling up closer to Luke as he wrapped his left arm protectively around her.

"You're the first born daughter of a tribe long since lost to fever. The Lummi Tribe took in the last male child of the fallen tribe. That child was raised and cared for by the Lummi people and he married and had one male child for each generation waiting for the perfect match to have a daughter. My drunken night had created that daughter and now here you stand," the man said. Luke hated this man, but was glad he had saved her life no matter how he did it.

"You're blaming drunkenness on raping my mother, robbing her of her life and ruining everything she had built up?" Cristina all but yelled at the man in front of them.

"Yes dear, I'm, but you didn't ruin your mother's life. You have to know that." He looked concerned, how did he know she hadn't ruined her mother's life.

"How would you know?" she asked, now they were thinking alike.

"I watched after I learned what I had done. Your mother loved you very much. Please marry before the full moon."

"Why?" She asked.

"You're with child, the child will die should you not," he informed her. *"Way to strike a mothers' instinct right there bub,"* Luke thought.

"Like I believe that?" Cristina stated crossing her arms in front of her. "How do you know I'm with child as you put it?"

"I saved your life, and I just know. Your child will be great should you do this. Also you'll free your descendants to move on to the next life that they've been waiting on." The man crossed his arms across his chest and Luke could see the stubbornness clearly and now knew who to blame for Cristina's.

"What is your name?" Cristina finally asked and Luke looked at the man expectantly.

"My name is Baby Bear Running," he said simply.

"Well ok then." She said. "Who might I marry then? And why would my marrying someone help?"

"All good questions dear one, and I believe you're standing next to the man you can marry." She looked up at Luke and he smiled at her. "Also, legend said the first female will join the families. Since a man takes a woman as his bride she joins his family and since it was a male child he brought the Lummi bride to his family. It is not clear the reasoning, what is clear is that it must happen. You should also marry where you were found, making it a holy communion and one with nature."

"Um, ok."

"I must leave. You've been warned, I'll be watching." Luke watched as he turned on his heel and took off running, the man was barefoot; Luke hadn't noticed before.

"Well, that was an odd little visit."

"Are you a Lummi descendant?" She looked up at him confused.

"It is the heritage of my father's and also mine. The blood has thinned over the years, but I am."

"Interesting how fate works isn't it?" she said walking and plopping her little butt on the couch.

Luke closed the door and sat next to her then pulled her into his lap. "It is, and my mother always told me that fate works in mysterious ways."

"Smart woman," she said simply. "Do you believe it?" she asked

"For the most part I do. I have heard of the legend, but I had never connected it with you, nor the rock formation in the back. My father passed before I was old enough to learn our full history and my mother couldn't handle going around his family, it made her too sad. So I never did either, nor have I since. But I believe it to be mostly true even though I have more worldly views now."

"But the marriage thing?" She leaned into his shoulder.

"All it would be doing is joining us in a commitment that we have already made, but the commitment would be public," he stated.

"But, by the next full moon, that's next Friday?" she informed him. He had no idea it was so soon, but it really didn't matter to him. He loved her, and was more than willing to live the rest of his life with her, so why not.

"I think we can do it." He smiled at her. "Will you marry me Cristina?" he asked.

"Don't ask if you don't really want to. I'm not a damsel in distress, I don't need protecting," she said and tried to scramble off his lap, but he clamped his arms around her and wouldn't let go.

"No, you're feisty, independent, head strong, smart and an incredibly brave woman, did I mention hard headed and stubborn?" he told her and was satisfied by the laugh that escaped her lips.

"Wow, really? You think all that about me?" She smiled and laughed again.

"Sure do, and woman, It would be a pleasure to spend the rest of my years with you."

"Really?" she asked softly.

"Yes."

"Then, yes, I would be honored to make your life pleasurable," she said rubbing her hands on his chest. Luke was fascinated by the woman sitting in his lap. Her mood swings were giving him whiplash, but he didn't mind as long as she was in his arms.

"Ok then, guess we better get a pretty ring on that gorgeous hand of yours and start getting prepared for a rushed wedding which will no doubt start a few rumors and set the baby story in motion." He paused and smiled at her. "Everything will work out perfectly." He kissed and cradled her into his chest as he stood, then helped her to her feet.

*****

Jeff had gone back to work with more gusto than before, smiling as he worked, getting involved with everyone. "Hey Jeff can I talk to you?" Rick asked him as they took a break from installing a set of windows on a new addition to a set of apartments in Bellingham.

"Sure man, what's up?" Jeff replied striding up next to his foreman.

"My cousin Alan was laid off a few weeks ago due to cut backs at the factory and I was wondering if you could give him a shot? We've been working a lot and I remember you saying that you needed a few extra hands," Rick asked.

"Yeah sure, I'll give him a trial. Has he done construction before?" Jeff asked, he was always the nice guy and most of the time he wasn't coming in last, but he had an odd feeling in his stomach about this guy Rick was talking about.

"He has helped me out with a few projects around the house along with a few on his mom's house," Rick said brightly.

"So he can wield a hammer?" Jeff smirked.

"Yes, and he can paint, he's actually a really good painter. We repainted every room in my house last summer and he did the majority of it," Rick smiled.

"Have him be here tomorrow." Jeff smiled at Rick before he turned and sauntered to his trailer to pull together the hiring documents and adding another person onto his crew for insurance purposes.

*****

Emily scrubbed the whole apartment for the arrival of Alan's cousin Rick. He was coming over for dinner and Alan was grilling steaks when he got home while she prepared the vegetables that would accompany the meal. For dessert she had made her triple chocolate fudge cake per Alan's request with homemade frosting topped with perfectly sliced strawberries.

"Looks wonderful baby," Alan pulled her into a hug and kissed her cheek.

"Thank you," she replied with a soft smile. "Is there anything else you would like?" Emily asked making sure everything was done.

"Just you, come to bed with me, we got time." Alan smiled and pulled her from the kitchen and into the bedroom kicking the door closed behind him.

CHAPTER 15

Cristina was a ball of nerves as she stood in her bedroom wearing Luke's mothers' white deer hide wedding dress she wore when she married his father. He'd had it preserved in storage; Cristina loved it and was honored to wear it. It fit nicely on her curvy body with the fringes touching the tops of her ankles. The sleeves covered her to mid forearm but the fringes hung to mid-calf when she lifted her arms. The bodice had a V of fringe and peeked at her shoulders with a modest filler across her chest. She loved everything about it. She was surprised to find the white matching moccasins were only a pinch too big and was easily fixed with thick footie socks that didn't show. Cristina couldn't help but think about when Luke pulled the dress out of storage and they had a tickle fest:

Standing in front of a small storage shed behind Jeff's house, she watched as Luke dug through his belongings and produced a cardboard box that had the name "Wedding's By Destine" printed on the box. "Here, if you like, you can wear this dress. It was my mother's, and I think it will fit you. It might be a little big, but I'm sure you'll still look phenomenal, as you always do," Luke said as he passed her the box.

"Luke, are you sure?" Cristina asked him. He had just bought her a pretty solitary diamond with a white gold band and now this.

"I love you, so yes, my mother would have been proud to have you wear it." Luke smiled at her, bent down and planted a kiss on her lips.

"Oh Luke, love you as well, crazy man."

"Crazy?" Luke smiled and the twinkle in his eye made

Cristina run, she knew what was coming. She ran towards Jeff's house, bolted inside and placed the box on the kitchen counter just as Luke came running into the house, wrapped his arms around her and started tickling her ribs. "Crazy. I'll show you crazy." He laughed and she couldn't help but giggle in response although she hated being tickled.

"Stop, please stop." She was laughing so hard tears were streaming down her face. "Please, you're not crazy." He only tickled her for a few more seconds, then finally stopped, turned her around, pressed her against the island and kissed her passionately.

"I'm looking forward to spending the rest of my life with you, Cristina." Luke said breathlessly as he pressed his forehead to hers.

"I am as well, even if this seems sudden," she replied.

"Can't fight fate baby." Luke planted a soft kiss on her lips again.

"I guess you're right." She smiled then turned her attention to the dress box. The front, which she hadn't noticed, had an image of the dress. The native American white dress was breath taking and she couldn't help but gasp.

"You like?" Luke asked her.

"I love." She smiled and turned to give him a hug.

Coming back to the here and now, Cristina looked in the mirror again to make sure her hair was in place. Roberta had straightened her hair so it hung long and straight down her back. No make-up and nothing extravagant had gone into making her feel like a happy little bride. She felt bad about wearing white since she was pregnant and she was sure his mother was pure when she married his father, but Luke had told her over and over that his mother would have loved to see her in her dress so she agreed.

"You look every bit the native American princess," Roberta said as she entered the room. She was wearing a similar style dress but brown with teal beading on the fringes. Her hair was braided down her back and she looked amazing.

"Thank you for being our witness today and please thank your husband again for me for doing the service. Luke wanted to have it as traditional as we could have since our families would not be attending," Cristina said as she hugged Roberta tightly.

"Richard volunteered the moment I told him the story, he will also do a cleansing for you both and prayer for your families, but mostly it will be a very simple ceremony," Roberta assured her. She knew they would wash their hands in a large basin then join hands to complete their vows. Apparently this was of great significance about washing away the past and past lovers. Cristina had planned to wash twice since Eric was not a lover but an evil crazy person, who had a sick twisted obsession for her that she still didn't understand. "Are you ready?" Roberta asked. Cristina nodded, followed her out of the room, down the stairs and out the back door. Luke and Jeff had worked all day the day before to put in a clear path to the rock formation using flat stones that matched closely to the house.

She and Roberta had set up little torches along the path that morning and apparently she had them lit before she came to collect Cristina from her room. She and Roberta walked down the path and they came upon the rock formation and a wooden archway that Cristina hadn't seen before. It was covered in white roses and baby's breath, but what caught her eye was the man standing in front of the older gentleman who was wearing regalia a lot like

Roberta's. However, he had a chieftain headdress or something on his head with feathers and bead work like she had never seen before; it was beautiful in and of itself.

Cristina turned her focus on Luke who wore an outfit like the man next to him, but the top hung open, his bare chest giving her a pull of pride to claim a man as handsome as Luke; the fringe of his outfit had red and black beading. Looking up at his face Luke smiled brightly at her as she approached him. She hadn't noticed Jeff standing behind Luke wearing a suite, but he looked dashing as well, his normal disheveled hair was brushed and orderly.

When Cristina approached, Luke washed his hands in a large wooden basin and Cristina followed suit, but did it twice noticing the odd looks she got from everyone but Luke. Once she was done, Roberta placed a white cloth over her hands as she had done with Luke and they dried their hands. Roberta took the clothes from them and Luke and Cristina joined hands facing each other. Mr. Smith gave them the wedding vows they both repeated when prompted. "Luke you may now kiss the bride." Luke didn't hesitate when he pulled Cristina into his embrace and claimed her lips. She could feel the possessiveness as he devoured her lips. A clearing throat caused him to release her with a smile.

Mr. Smith lit something that smelled of sage and peppermint, the smoke burned light almost clear. "Congratulations Mr. and Mrs. Luke Black. You are now joined as one, may the forefathers bless you and may you forever remember your heritage." Then he started chanting something and walked around them twice then circled the rock formation that was next to them. The ceremony was completed by the time the sun set and the full moon presented itself in the evening sky. Cristina heard the sound of a howl followed by several others.

"What was that?" she asked cringing into Luke's strong chest. He wrapped his arms around her protectively, but he didn't answer her. Instead it was Roberta who had.

"Your people are free child. Once you consummate the union they will move on with their new lives," she answered simply. Cristina listened as twelve howls surrounded them, then fell silent. She wasn't sure what to make of the situation, but she was officially scared.

"Congrats you crazy kids." Jeff thumped Luke on the back and kissed Cristina on the cheek. "Can we get out of these clothes and grab some grub, this man is wasting away here." Jeff laughed.

"Sure man," Luke said leaning down and kissing her on the lips. He was hers and she wasn't going to let him go. He was, in her mind, perfect.

Roberta pulled Cristina to her for a big hug and whispered in her ear "You can have a honeymoon, but when that baby comes Grandma wants time with him or her." Cristina laughed. The poor child wouldn't have paternal grandparents, at least not from them, and she sure as heck wasn't having Eric's family involved at all, no matter how mean that might sound. No one was going to know the child wasn't Luke's.

"You got it. At least I have a job where I can bring a child with me to work, well mostly anyways," Cristina whispered back.

"Yep,." Roberta laughed and they all headed back to the house to change and head to the Little Italian restaurant to eat.

On the drive to the restaurant she kept glancing at Luke, her husband, the thought was a little unnerving since they hadn't really known each other long, but she knew she loved him. He had never tried to hurt her and he accepted her for who she was and the unborn child she carried. That week had flown by with preparations, getting the marriage license, planning things at work, and moving Luke's things into her place since he had been living with Jeff. He'd been sleeping in the room across from hers and they had only kissed or hugged that whole week. Cristina was worried about the night when they would solidify their marriage; she was still having nightmares remembering her time with Eric.

"Hey, what are you thinking about over there?" Luke interrupted her thinking. His face held a concerned look she was growing accustomed to and she could see it clearly with the lights in the parking lot, which she hadn't realized they were in.

"Just thinking about this week," she replied smiling, trying to conceal her worries.

"Hey, now none of that. What's really bothering you?" he asked and reached for her hand she had settled on her lap. The action made her smile and the electric zap left a tingling sensation in her hand.

"Just worried, you know, about later." She said looking at their twined hands instead of his wonderful face. He pulled his hand out of hers then jumped quickly out of the car. Before she could react to what he was doing he had her door open and her in his arms.

"You have nothing to worry about with me. I love you, that's all that matters," he said into her ear and she melted into his chest breathing in that magnificent cologne he wore.

"What is that cologne you wear? It smells heavenly."

"Oh." He smiled at her. "That would be an Avon Cologne called His Story. My mother loved the smell, my father wore it and now I do. I have grown quite accustomed to the smell and I have found it's not as grotesque to the senses like a lot of the newer expensive colognes out now," he informed her and she breathed in the scent.

"Oh, and I love you too." She pulled her face from his chest, grasped the back of his head and pulled him down so she could plant a kiss on those plump lips of his. "We should get inside and eat, before Jeff wastes away to nothing." She laughed and he held her lips captive, their tongues doing their own mating dance.

"Ok, let's eat. The sooner we eat, the sooner you and I can go home. Then in the morning we will head off on our honeymoon." Luke reminded her and she giggled against him. She was trying to relax, but she knew it was only temporary, when they got home that night, she would have to face everything all over again.

*****

Jeff lounged in his seat at the restaurant and smiled as Cristina and Luke snuggled into each other. Cristina looked scared to death and Luke looked like he was over the moon. Jeff went about telling a few jokes he had heard at work about couples, trying to get Cristina to smile.

"After nearly 50 years of marriage, a couple was lying in bed one evening, when the wife felt her husband, begin to massage her in ways he hadn't in quite some time. It almost tickled as his fingers started at her neck, and then began moving down past the small of her back. He then caressed her shoulders and neck, slowly worked his hand down, stopping just over her stomach. He then proceeded to place his hand on her left inner arm, working down her side, passing gently over her buttock and down her leg to her calf.

Then, he proceeded up her thigh, stopping just at the uppermost portion of her leg. He continued in the same manner on her right side, then suddenly stopped, rolled over and became silent. As she had become quite aroused by this caressing, she asked in a loving voice, "Honey that was wonderful. Why did you stop?" To which he responded: I found the remote." Jeff laughed out loud as did Mr. and Mrs. Smith.

"Oh Jeff, that was so funny," Roberta laughed hard beside him.

"Oh, here's another one. "Part way through his dinner date, my brother deduced the woman he was with was more interested in his money than in him. When the check came, he took out his credit card to pay the bill and was not surprised to hear her gush "Is that a platinum card?" Jeff rolled and Cristina started to laugh. Jeff felt he needed another one to really open her up.

"No," my brother replied dryly. "It's aluminum."

"Jeff!" Luke laughed.

"Oh, here. A dietician was once addressing a large audience in Chicago. The material we put into our stomachs is enough to have killed most of us sitting here, years ago. Red meat is awful. vegetables can be disastrous, and none of us realize the germs in our drinking water. But, there is something that is perhaps more dangerous than anything else. The dietician peered into the crowd and asked, "Can anyone here tell me what lethal product I'm referring to?" A handful of people in the audience raised their hands with possible answers. "Yes, you, sir, in the first row," said the dietician. "Please give us your idea." The man grinned and blurted, "Wedding cake!" Jeff laughed and Cristina finally joined in as their meals were brought to them.

*****

Luke loved having Cristina in his arms, he felt at home and comfortable with her there. They had just spent three long grueling hours with Mr. and Mrs. Smith and Jeff with his crazy jokes that really weren't all that funny, at least not to him since he had heard them half a dozen times. He lifted Cristina into his truck relinquishing her for now. Walking around his truck he spotted a figure at the edge of the shadows, at closer inspection he saw it was her father. He lifted his hand in response to her father's raised hand then he climbed into the truck and started for home.

"Who was that?" Cristina asked. She had witnessed the subtle hand exchange.

"That was your father."

"Oh," was all she said and reached over the center console of his truck and placed her hand on his thigh. The feeling in her hand sent a chill down his spine and a tingle of electricity in its wake. "I love you," she said softly.

"I love you too. Want to take a warm bath while I clean up a little before bed?" He wanted her comfortable and relaxed so he was going to take it very slow with her. He knew the holdup was what had happened during the time that freak held her captive. He waited for a few minutes as he drove to their house for her response.

"That sounds like a wonderful idea. Want to join me," she asked as he pulled into the driveway and parked the truck in front of the house.

"Only if you want me to." He clasped her hand in his and brought it up to his lips and kissed each of her fingers.

"I do, um, give me a few minutes first," she said shyly. He had already bathed her, felt every inch of her body and took complete care of her, yet she was still skittish, but he didn't mind. He liked the shy side.

"Not a problem, I need to check and make sure all the torches are out." He gave her a little wink. He knew she knew he was coming up with an excuse just from the look on her face, but she didn't contest it. He hopped out of the truck and ran to open the door for her. He lifted her into his arms and cradled her into his chest.

"What are you doing? I can walk," she told him laughing.

"I'm going to carry you over the threshold, again, my lady," Luke informed her. He closed the truck door, locked it with his remote and carried his blushing bride into the house. He unlocked the door with ease and carried her in, kicked the door closed and carried her all the way up stairs. When he entered their bedroom, he tossed her on the bed and listened to the laughs as he exited the room without a second glance or word. He knew if he saw her or said anything she wouldn't get her few minutes, nor would she get her bath.

He walked to the kitchen and took a steadying breath. He heard the water running upstairs so he hurried outside and did what he said he would do. He was running, checking the torches as he went. He rounded the corner where the rock formation was and stopped dead in his tracks. He could see twelve wolves standing on the rock thanks to the full moon's beams busting through the trees. When he gasped all twelve wolves turned and snarled at him. He seemed to be frozen where he stood as he looked upon the twelve wolves of varying sizes, the wolves looked from him, to the moon, to each other, then back to him. They did this about four times before they focused completely on him and growled again.

He turned and took off running. He pushed himself hard through the trail they had formed for the wedding. The house was in sight when he found Cristina standing on the porch in a robe, her hair pulled into a pony tail. "What's wrong," she called and he turned to find that the wolves had stopped pursuing him, but he could easily see all twelve of them at the edge of the trees. He ran to her pulling her into his arms and rushed them both into the house.

"Just running from a few family members of yours it seems." He laughed, catching his breath.

"What, are you ok?" she asked brushing her hands over his arms, face and chest.

"Yes. I'm fine." He pulled her flush against him and kissed her worried lips. "Time for bed my dear wife, let's send your family on their way." He whispered in her ear then nibbled her little ear lobe as he proceeded to plant kisses down her neck, up her jaw and back to her lips.

"Ok," she replied softly. He lifted her into his arms and swiftly carried her up the stairs to open the most amazing present he was ever given, which was wrapped in a delectable little package.

*****

Emily sat quietly in the dim light of the living room as she read her Bible. Alan had been sweet to her over the past few days and was enjoying his new job in construction with his cousin Rick. Jeffrey Parker had been so kind to offer him a temporary position based on performance and from what Alan came home saying, everything was going well and the pay was much better than the factory.

Alan was sleeping peacefully and allowed her to stay up to read since she wasn't really tired. She had heard from church that the Cristina woman was located and getting married to Luke Black, which was Jeffrey's best friend. Emily smiled at the happy ending that was due to that young woman who had gone through a lot.

Emily listened to the soft snores coming from behind her as she read a passage from John Chapter 3. And as Moses lifted up the serpent in the wilderness, even so must the Son of man be lifted up: [15] That whosoever believeth in him should not perish, but have eternal life. [16] For God so loved the world that he gave his only begotten Son, that whosoever believeth in him should not perish, but have everlasting life. [17] For God sent not his Son into the world to condemn the world; but that the world through him might be saved. [18] He that believeth on him is not condemned: but he that believeth not is condemned already, because he hath not believed in the name of the only begotten Son of God. [19] And this is the condemnation, that light is come into the world, and men loved darkness rather than light, because their deeds were evil.

Emily finally closed her Bible and slipped into bed next to Alan who stirred slightly, enough to pull her into his chest as his face nestled into her neck in a comforting fashion. She wondered when the storm would hit and how long it would take for everything to go back to normal.

***

Cristina woke to the sunshine streaming through the window. She had slept wonderfully curled around Luke after the blissful lovemaking they had made the night before. He was so sweet, and tender, she couldn't help but to smile.

"Good morning sleepy head," Luke said kissing her on the

head. She was nestled into his side with his arm wrapped snuggly around her. "How did you sleep?" he asked her. She couldn't help but feel shy.

"Pretty well, yourself?," she replied but didn't look up at him.

"That was the best night's sleep I've had since I was a child," Luke said, and then he pulled her up so she had to look at him with this cute little smile on his face. He pulled her lips to his, giving her a chaste kiss, then tucked her back into his side.

"Well, good," she said shyly, then tried to slip out of bed to brush her teeth and take care of her pleading bladder.

"Hey, where do you think you're going?" He held her tight to his side.

"Hey, you're not the one pregnant, I have something I need to take care of." She laughed, pulling away from him when his arm fell lax next to her. She planted a quick kiss on his lips and scurried to the bathroom scooping up her robe as she went. She was feeling very shy, but completely blissed out of her mind by the wonderful man she would get to spend the rest of her life with.

***

Luke couldn't keep his eyes off the door that Cristina had hidden herself behind. She was the most amazing woman he had ever met and he was married to her. He was a happy camper! "Love you," he called pulling himself out of bed. "Love you too," she called back. When he heard the water running in the sink he opened the bathroom door to find her brushing her teeth. He scooped up his tooth brush and followed suit, bumping her with his hip making her laugh and get toothpaste around her mouth in a very uncharacteristic way. He loved her and they were going to spend the rest of their lives together happy as clams.

CHAPTER 16

Emily Hensley sat in the emergency room yet again to get her ribs taped up. Alan was really angry that night because she had forgotten to pick up his dry cleaning. She had intended to pick it up today since he hadn't needed it until Sunday. "Ms. Hensley," a young nurse called her up to the counter. "Nurse Shields will take you back to the doctor now."

"Thank you," Emily replied and followed the tall stalky Nurse Shields to an exam room, carrying herself with as much care as she could.

"I need to ask you a question and you need to answer it honestly Ms. Hensley," Nurse Shields said sternly looking her square in the eyes. Emily knew the drill, but she also knew how to play her role, she had been since she was five.

"Ok."

"Who's hitting you? This makes the fifth time in a year that you've been in here with a broken bone of one sort or another." The nurse propped her hands on her waist. "We can't help you if you don't tell us," she said softer. Emily knew she should have done what was asked of her and she knew men had very short tempers and her sweet Alan was no different.

"I'm just clumsy, honestly. I'm surprised I haven't done more damage this time," Emily said coolly.

"Ok. Let me get you taped up then. You just have a fracture on your fourth right rib, so just take it easy and try not to fall anymore for a few weeks ok," Nurse Shields said as she helped Emily remove her shirt so she could tape her up.

"Not a problem." Emily smiled the best she could. Once the nurse finished she was released without a doctor to talk to. Emily signed her release forms, retrieved her insurance card and slowly walked to the car where Jackie waited.

"Girl, I swear I'll kill that... Ooh," Jackie blurted as Emily slowly climbed into the SUV.

"Jackie, it's ok, he didn't mean to do it." Emily was used to these conversations with Jackie, her best friend was a true miracle and was always there for her.

"Em, honey, he has a lot of accidents that involve you. I'm worried one day I'll be saying good bye to you for the last time," Jackie said shaking her head. "Why don't you leave him?" she finally asked.

"It wouldn't matter Jackie. The next guy I get with would be the same, that's how they are." Emily shook her head and looked out the passenger window.

"Not all men do this baby, don't you understand that?" Jackie turned her body and Emily could sense her eyes on the back of her head.

"Every man I have been with or around are the same Jackie, nothing's going to change." She took a breath to steady herself. "Besides, who is going to want messed up, broken me? Alan loves me and he helps with the bills. If I leave, what will happen then, besides, the apartment is in his name, everything is in his name." Emily felt a tear drop down her cheek. "I can't leave him, I would have nothing if I do." The tears streamed down her face.

"Leave him and come stay with me. I have the room, and frankly since Sam moved into the little apartment above the store, I have been awful lonely in that house," Jackie said placing a consoling hand on her shoulder.

"Thanks, maybe he will change," Emily said and started looking back out the window again. She knew he wouldn't change and she knew that Jackie didn't understand men like she did.

"Whatever girl, just be smart ok. You're a bright woman, your first graders love you and so does everyone you work with." After a few minutes she put the car in reverse and took her home. The drive was short with Jackie driving faster than she normally did. "Em, please, remember I love you, you're like a sister to me, please let me know if I can help and never feel like you can't get out of a situation because you have no place to go, you can always come live with me."

"Thanks Jackie, you're the best. See you tomorrow," said Emily as she slowly exited the car. She watched as Jackie left her apartment parking lot before she turned and headed inside, knowing she was later than she should have been. She felt her heart begin to race, as she approached the door she had just pulled out her keys when the door flew open. Alan stood there in the doorway glaring at her. His red hair a mess, his blue eyes giving her the look she feared.

"Where the hell have you been?"

"At the hospital getting my ribs taped sir." She lowered her eyes as she spoke to him.

"Get your sorry ass in this apartment now." He yelled and she shuffled in slipping off her shoes on the entry mat. When she got her shoes off she felt the hands on her back before she was sent head first into the coffee table and landing on the floor. "You stupid, lazy woman," he yelled as he kicked her in the ribs, legs and arms as she drew herself into a ball.

"I'm sorry, Jackie was driving. I'm sorry Alan, please," she cried but he didn't stop. He reached down and grabbed her by the hair and lifted her to her feet as her hands reflexed and grabbed at his hand that had her hair. His fist collided with her face twice before darkness started to creep in on her. She felt him drag her, heard the door open, and he dropped her on the stairs as she rolled down them. She tucked herself in so she wouldn't break her neck. She heard a scream before her head hit the railing on the landing and went black.

Emily came to, to the sound of hushed voices. "So what's the bastard done to her this time?" she heard Jackie ask.

"She has a concussion, several cracked ribs, busted lip, bruised arms, legs and back. She will make a full recovery." She heard a male voice reply.

"Well, good. The bastard is in jail, at least for the night. I'm going to go over there and get her things, call me when she wakes up," Jackie said. She heard a door open, then close again as the darkness took hold of her once again.

*****

Jeff adjusted his jacket as he readied himself for church. It had been a week since he drove his best friend Luke and his bride Cristina to the airport for their honeymoon and today after church he would pick them up. Jeff hadn't realized how much he enjoyed the company of his best friend and how lonely it was without him. Even Cristina made a wonderful friend through the past few months since they met and all the crazy stuff she had gone through. Jeff grabbed his keys and Bible and headed off to church. He had a spring in his step that morning since he knew Luke would be back in town. Jeff knew Luke was keeping something from him, so he was hoping to learn what it was today.

Jeff lived five minutes from his church and with little traffic in his small town it was an easy drive. He pulled in to his usual parking in the rear of church. He walked across the small parking area to the little white building that doubled as the elementary school and the church. "Good morning Pete," said Jeff as he spotted the sheriff just inside the entry with his wife.

"Morning Jeff. How are things this morning?" Pete greeted him as the men shook hands.

"Things are fine. Luke and Cristina will be home at one today."

"That is good news, I'm so glad Luke found someone as sweet as her," Pete said with a big smile. Pete was a jolly man and knew everything about everyone in town.

"Sure is, getting a little lonely though," Jeff laughed.

"How's the construction business treating you?" Pete asked as the choir began to sing in the chapel area.

"Doing really well, Pete, real well. Shall we go enjoy the day's service," Jeff answered. He was normally an usher but today he was going to enjoy his time off and focus on the sermon. As Pete, his wife and Jeff entered the chapel to find seats he saw Emily in the back with Jackie and he almost tripped over his feet. Her face was bruised and puffy. He was about to head over to see what happened when Pastor Reynolds approached the lectern.

The service started and Jeff just couldn't pay any attention and he knew his mother would have been upset at him if she were alive, but he couldn't get Emily out of his head as he wondered what had happened to her. He hadn't been able to say more than three words to her in the past few months, so if he approached her after the service he didn't know what he would say and not sound like a total blabbering idiot.

Ever since he was younger he never really could talk to girls but Stephanie was his light. She brought him out of his shell when she tripped and fell into his arms their sophomore year. He had planned to propose to her after graduation, but never got the chance. After the accident he crawled back into his shell determined not to let another woman reach him the way she had, but he was lonely.

"So ladies and gentleman remember this simple quote Tony Robbins once said, "If you do what you've always done, you'll get what you've always gotten." So let's go with what Henry Kissinger once said, "If we do what is necessary, all the odds are in our favor." So today, go out and make a change in your life for the better. Go with God." Pastor Reynolds said with a closing prayer and the minute they were released he made a beeline for where he saw Emily sitting.

When he reached the row, he noticed she had already made her exit. Snaking through the growing crowd he found her and Jackie walking out the front doors. He caught up to them outside.

"Jackie, Emily. Good morning," he managed. Jackie stopped and smiled but Emily didn't turn around, which made him wonder, but he focused on Jackie instead hoping to get some nerve.

"Jeff, good morning. How are you doing?" Jackie asked reaching her hand out for a shake.

"I'm well, how is the real estate business?" he asked her.

"You know, it has its ups and downs." She laughed.

"Emily, how are you doing this morning?" he asked,

replaying the quotes in his head from the sermon. She turned and gave him a weak smile as her hair fell across her face hiding most of the bruises.

"Morning Jeff," she said looking at the ground, then she turned and started walking towards Jackie's car leaving the two of them staring after her.

"Jeff, please forgive her, she's, um, having a hard time right now," Jackie said with a small smile.

"Sure, not a problem, if there is anything I can do, please let me know," Jeff said to Jackie but couldn't stop staring after the beautiful woman who was walking away from him. "What happened?" he asked without thinking.

"Not my story to tell." Jackie shook her head. "I better go. See you later Jeff." Jackie made her way to the car where Emily waited. Jeff glanced a t his watch and realized it was twelve-thirty and he had a forty-five minute drive ahead of him to get to the airport.

Jeff practically ran to his car just as the rain began to fall. His brown hair fell into his eyes. *"I really need to get a haircut" he thought*. Jeff clicked the remote to unlock his truck and he climbed in just as a clap of thunder roared overhead. He flipped his hair out of his eyes, turned the truck on and started his journey to the Bellingham airport. Traffic was light as he traveled.

*****

Luke pulled Cristina into a tight hug after they exited the plane. He was so happy to have her with him, and after learning why she drove all the way from Florida rather than flying, he found her fear of flying rather cute. "I love you," he whispered in her ear.

"I love you too," she replied and pulled his lips to hers.

"I hope Jeff finds someone soon, I feel bad about being so lucky finding you," Luke smiled at her. "On second thought, I don't feel bad, I'm so happy I found you. I just hope he finds someone so he won't be over at the house every day," Luke laughed.

"Yes, uncle Jeff might get a little crazy if he doesn't find someone soon," replied Cristina with a laugh. Luke couldn't get over how her mood had shifted since the night her father made an appearance. She was smiling like crazy, laughing and having fun. Hawaii had been interesting for her since the scars on her thighs were evident in a swimsuit but she found a wrap and walked the beach hand-in-hand with him.

"I wonder if he made any head way with the Emily chick he met at church." Luke pondered out loud.

"I guess we'll find out soon. Let's get our bags and head home. We got lucky not having any sickness while in flight, but I'm not feeling so hot at the moment." She pulled his arm and walked toward the exit and baggage claim area. The Bellingham airport was small, but was very well kept. Luke imagined all little airports would look this clean if he traveled more. There were big murals around the area, large quilts hung on the walls and art scattered around made a comforting welcome home.

Cristina released his hand as they walked past the ladies' room and she darted inside. He knew she wasn't feeling well since her hand had become clammy quite fast as they made their way from the gate. Luke leaned against the wall by the bathroom and waited for his wife to return; several people passed him, laughing and smiling. Luke couldn't help but be happy with the way his life was turning around. Five years ago, before he made the decision to move to LA, he held his hand gun to his head and wanted his life to be over. When he pulled the trigger, nothing happened and Luke took it as a sign; now he was glad he went for a change instead of ending his life.

"Sorry about that, I feel better now." Cristina said as she popped a piece of gum in her mouth. She had a little sweat on her forehead and Luke pulled out a handkerchief and dabbed it off before kissing her forehead. "Thank you," Cristina smiled.

"Shall we, my fair lady?" Luke asked as he held out his arm for her to take.

"We shall." She smiled tucking her arm through his. They made their way to the baggage claim and Luke collected their bag. He smiled at the memory of packing, thinking they would surely have multiple bags.

"What are all those bags for?" Cristina asked as she came out of the bathroom with a little toiletry bag.

"Well, I figure we would each need a bag for the trip, we will be gone for a week." Luke replied not seeing the small pile of clothes on the bed.

"Shoot, maybe you need a whole bag, but honey I know how to pack." She laughed and planted a kiss on the side of his mouth.

"Well my lady, teach this old dog a new trick then." He laughed and jumped on the bed and watched her work. He had told her they were going to Hawaii that morning and she gave him a weak smile but set to work.

She opened the large suitcase and worked on his clothes. She rolled five pairs of shorts, his tank tops, boxers and sandals he had laid out; she finished by rolling her few pairs of longer shorts, tank tops, undergarments, flip-flops and her bathing suit. She tossed in two towels and the toiletry bag and zipped it up. "Done." She smiled. He fell in love with her all over again, a woman who needed little was amazing."

"How about a camera?" Luke asked crawling off the bed and pulling her into his arms.

"It will be in my purse." She smiled and pulled his lips to hers.

"What are you smiling at mister?" Cristina smirked.

"Oh nothing, I'm just a happy man, that's all."

"Well, I'm hungry so let's go feed the walking incubator, shall we?" Cristina laughed.

*****

Cristina walked next to Luke with their arms interlaced as he pulled the suitcase behind them. She had a wonderful time with him, not as awkward as she had thought. He had gone out of his way to make sure she was comfortable, even buying her a beautiful wrap that matched her swim suit to hide her scars.

They walked out of the airport and found Jeff just pulling up; Jeff hopped out of his truck and gave Cristina a big hug then thumped Luke on the back after stealing the suitcase from him. "So glad y'all are back. I have been having too many parties at your place, I'm going broke," Jeff joked as he put the bag in the back seat then helped her inside.

"Well, as long as you cleaned everything up, I'm glad you had fun." Cristina responded with a laugh as she slid her seat belt on. Jeff didn't know about the baby yet, but he would very soon. Luke kissed her then closed the door as Jeff laughed and walked to his side of the truck. Luke climbed in the front and directed Jeff to head straight for Little Italy before he dropped them home.

CHAPTER 17

Emily snuggled into the bed in Jackie's spare bedroom. It had been a week since Alan had put her in the hospital, and Jackie had brought her to her place the night before to stay after she was released. Jackie had Alan arrested and during the twenty-four hours of lock up, Jackie had gone to their apartment and brought all of her things to her home. Alan was released on bail the next day and a court proceeding would be held, pending date. Jackie had taken tons of pictures of Emily as proof of the abuse; some pictures Emily didn't know she had from the previous incidents.

"Hey girl, how are you doing?" Jackie said, peeking her head through the door. After church they had eaten a light lunch and Emily turned in while Jackie went to see her son Sam.

"I'm doing alright," Emily said softly. It was still hard to talk since the muscles in her face and jaw were badly bruised.

"Can I get you anything?" Jackie asked entering the room.

"You're doing plenty Jackie. Thank you again for all of your help. I should have." Jackie cut her off.

"No shoulda, coulda, woulda's ok. It is done, you're safe and the bastard will rot for what he did to you." Jackie placed her hands on her hips. "The school has a substitute in place for the next two weeks so you'll rest, take it easy then you can get back to those amazing children who love you dearly and think you were in a car accident." Jackie smiled.

"Yes ma'am," Emily said trying not to laugh at her best friend who always seemed to know what she needed to hear.

"Now get some rest, I'll come get you for dinner, I'm making homemade ravioli tonight." Jackie smiled and left Emily to her thinking. She couldn't stop thinking about Jeff and his beautiful blue eyes that actually looked concerned for her. He was such a sweet guy and did seem different from all the rest, but she knew the truth about men and she wasn't going through that pain again.

Closing her eyes and focusing on her calm breathing, she let the darkness claim her as her pain medication finally kicked in.

"I'm sorry, please forgive me daddy." Emily cowered in the corner of the small home she shared with her mom, dad, brother and sister. Her father kicked her again, mindful of what could be hidden by her clothes, as he always was. Tears streamed down her face.

"Daddy please, I'm sorry. I won't do it again." Emily had spilled her milk when she sneezed, her little hands curled around the glass her mother had given her to set on the table, but her hands were tiny at age seven.

"You damn right you won't do it again. Now go to your room without supper." He yelled and let her quickly crawl past him to her room where she curled into the bed she shared with her sister as her stomach growled in protest.

Emily's eyes opened wide as she remembered the horrid childhood that still haunted her. The smell of tomatoes drifted through the air as her stomach growled in hunger. Carefully she clambered out of the bed and slowly pulled her wayward hair into a pony tail that she only wore when her and Jackie were alone since the bruises on her face were still pretty evident. Emily slowly descended the stairs and entered the kitchen as silently as she could. She watched as Jackie stirred her wonderful pasta sauce and lightly manipulated the ravioli. Jackie was a great cook, and her handmade pastas were to die for, metaphorically speaking of course.

"Wow, that smells wonderful," Emily said pulling up a stool at the island. Jackie spun around and clenched her chest and Emily tried not to laugh, but failed painfully.

"You scared the dickens out of me," Jackie scolded then laughed.

"Sorry about that. Can I help with anything?" Emily asked, she hated being helpless or not doing anything to assist.

"No, you can sit your happy butt right there and just talk to me. It will be done in about, oh, ten more minutes," Jackie said pointedly.

"You say it as if it were a science project." Emily smirked, again painfully.

"Well, it's not an exact science, but the sauce has to be just right. Otherwise it won't taste that great with the spicy beef ravioli." Jackie went back to stirring the sauce. "How are you feeling?" she asked.

"I could be better but the pain is considerably less than it was," said Emily. Her ribs still hurt like the dickens and her face was stiff.

"Well, good. Do you want to play a little piano after dinner? We could work on the Fur Elsie by Beethoven a little more," Jackie asked as she slowly drained the ravioli. "You've been doing remarkably well with the few lessons you've had when Alan was working late the last few months." Jackie stated. Emily loved playing the piano since she had never been given the chance growing up, but she wasn't in the mood.

"I think I'll pass tonight," Emily replied. She knew she sounded depressed, and well she was, how could she not be. The reality of her future was sinking in like someone had slammed a door in her face. She would never get married, have children and live a happy life growing old with someone like she watched in the movies; that life didn't exist for her.

"Hey, did you want to go to a movie Friday night? I think Despicable Me 2 is finally coming to our little theater. I know it's a children's film, but everyone keeps raving about how funny it is, might be fun," Jackie asked as she moved the sauce and ravioli into a large bowl and set it on the dining room table that was already set.

"Sure, a distraction might be fun," Emily replied as she slowly climbed off her stool and took a seat.

"Hey, what do you think of Jeff?" Jackie asked as she spooned a few raviolis onto her plate.

"He seems nice. Why?" Emily looked at her quizzically.

"Well, he's single, owns his own business and he's a complete sweetheart if you ask me," Jackie replied.

"Are you looking to go out with him or something?" Emily asked stabbing a ravioli and tossing it in her mouth, the taste was phenomenal. The zippy tang of the tomatoes with the perfect mix of seasonings, followed by the spice in the meat made the ravioli blue ribbon perfect.

"Ha, um, no way, he's too young for me. I was thinking about for you," Jackie said taking her seat and spearing a ravioli and devouring it.

"I'm swearing off men from here on out; it always ends badly for me." Emily responded coldly, "It's not that I don't think he seems nice or that he's not attractive, I mean who wouldn't find that gorgeous hunk of a man attractive, you would have to be blind not to notice him; but men are all the same and I always end up looking like this." Emily replied harshly.

"Well, maybe after some time you'll reconsider and give him a try. You never know, he could be the perfect one, and the one man who doesn't ever strike you." Jackie shrugged. Emily knew her friend was trying to be nice and thinking about her, but Jackie didn't understand men like she did. Emily refused to give her a response so she focused on eating.

*****

Jeff sat across from Luke and Cristina at Little Italy as they prattled on and on about their honeymoon in Hawaii. "So did you take lots of pictures?" Jeff asked sipping his Pepsi.

"We sure did." Cristina smiled and took a big gulp of her ice water, he hadn't seen her order her usual Dr. Pepper the last few times they went out to eat.

"Jeff, we have some news for you," Luke interrupted his little thinking.

"What's that."

"Well," Luke smiled at Cristina. "We are going to have a baby." Luke replied with a smile and Jeff started counting back in his mind, they had been married for a little over a week, Luke never said they had had any type of physical relationship prior, so Jeff was really confused.

"What, how, I mean congrats, but how would you know so soon?" Jeff asked with a dumbfounded look on his face.

"Well, um, before she was taken we had connected before she kicked me to the curb." Luke replied and Jeff was still

233

confused, but it would have made sense with how crazy Luke had been when she was taken, so he didn't question it further. He had to be happy for his best friend, even if he felt it would never happen for him.

"Well, then congratulations. I get to be an uncle." Jeff smiled and squeezed Cristina's hand that was resting on the table. She smiled at him with her chocolate eyes, but he could see something was off with the statement his best friend had made. There was something they weren't telling him, and it bothered him greatly; he decided to corner Luke at a later date and find out what was really going on.

"Thanks man, and yes you get to be an uncle." Luke smiled back just as the waitress brought them their dinner.

"So, have you approached this Emily person from church yet?" Luke asked as he cut up his chicken.

"I tried but she avoided me like I was the plague or something, and it seems she was in some kind of accident," Jeff replied thinking about how Emily had avoided him and raced off to Jackie's car after church, only getting a few simple words from her. He had finally gotten up the guts to approach her and she'd made herself scarce.

"Wow, really, do you know what happened?" Cristina asked concern written all over her face.

"No, but I hadn't heard of any major car accidents this week either, just a few rear-ending's, that's all," Jeff replied spearing a ravioli into his mouth. The spicy mushroom ravioli was his favorite.

"Wow, maybe she was, never mind. She will tell you when she's ready," Cristina said and twisted some pasta on her fork with a distracted look on her face.

"Maybe she was what? What are you thinking Cris?" Jeff

asked making her look up at him.

"Well, does she have a boyfriend? Maybe they got into a fight." Cristina stated and it dawned on him that Emily did have a boyfriend that never came to church. Jackie hated the guy and there was an arrest last Saturday.

"I'll call Jackie tomorrow," Jeff said and focused on eating his dinner.

"Probably not a bad Idea," Luke said after a few beats.

They ate with little conversation, other than gender of the baby, names they were considering and the plan to paint the babies' room soon in a Noah's Ark theme because it was unisex.

*****

Sitting across from his best friend, Luke couldn't help but see the sad expression Jeff tried so hard to hide. Luke ate in silence and he listened to Cristina as she finished telling a story from their honeymoon.

"So this guy was all like, Aloha, and I was like, Aloha, then the guy said it again, then I looked at him and asked what they say when they want to say goodbye. You know what he tells me?" Cristina laughed, "He says Aloha. So I asked, what do you do if you're on the phone with someone who you really want to hang up with, if you only say Aloha wouldn't that person start talking all over again?" She laughed and Jeff joined in. It was kind of funny, and a good point, but Luke was pretty sure the good bye was Aloha.

"Wow, crazy. You sure he just didn't know English and that was the only word he really knew since he was in Hawaii?" Jeff asked.

"Well, sure it is possible, but then that kills the story."

Cristina pouted, Luke loved seeing her pout, she was so darn cute when she did it too. Luke watched as Jeff went back to eating and he turned to look at Cristina who's face flushed.

"Excuse me." Cristina said as she pushed away from the table and hurried to the lady's room. Jeff watched her leave then gave Luke a stern stare.

"Explain," Jeff said coldly.

"About?" Luke was confused by Jeff's sudden anger.

"Dude, you and I both know that if you would have had sex with her that day, you wouldn't have been kicked to the curb," Jeff said in a hushed voice.

"I know." Looking towards the bathrooms. "But you have to understand, this is to protect the baby, ok."

"But it's not yours," Jeff said calmly.

"Yes, it's mine, and I'm going to make sure it knows love and what a dad is. It doesn't have to know all the other scary stuff, nor does the town. Please don't say anything," Luke pleaded with Jeff.

"No worries man, next time warn me, alright. I won't say anything," Jeff said finishing up his dinner. By the time Luke finished his Chicken Parmesan, he looked up to see Cristina making her way back to the table. Her cheeks were flushed and he could see the moisture on her forehead as she took a seat.

"Well, um, I'm ready when y'all are, I know it's been a long day and you both look plum tuckered out." Jeff said waving at the waitress and giving the universal sign for the check. "Dinner is my treat. Welcome home, and again congrats, I'll look at the schedule and see when we can paint that youngin's room." Jeff smiled at Luke and then Cristina. Luke looked over at his wife and found that she really wasn't looking so good.

"Wanna step outside to get a little fresh air?" Luke whispered in her ear. She nodded and stood grabbing her purse. "We are going to step outside for some air before we head back home, ok." Luke said to Jeff who nodded as he and Cristina left the restaurant.

"I'm so sorry." Cristina cried as soon as they were outside. She looked so miserable when he wrapped his arms around her.

"It's ok, just a few more weeks then maybe it will go away." Luke cooed and rubbed his hands up and down her back.

"I'm sorry about being sick, but I was talking about how you had to lie to Jeff, I feel awful. I think you should tell him the truth, I'm sure he'll keep it a secret." Cristina cried and Luke relaxed and laughed a little.

"My emotional wife, I love you and if you want me to tell Jeff, I will." Luke replied trying not to laugh too hard, but failing miserably.

"I love you too, now stop laughing at me." She leaned away from him and pouted again. He leaned down and pulled her lower lips between his and she giggled.

"Uh, hmm, we ready to go?" Jeff interrupted and they started laughing.

"Yeah man, let's get my wife home to rest," Luke replied.

*****

Cristina was seated in the front seat in case she needed to toss her cookies on the short drive. She could feel her temperature rising as they made their way through town. She focused on breathing slowly and relaxing in the plush seat. Jeff cracked the window next to her and she felt the cool evening air brush across her face which instantly made her feel a little better.

"So Luke, will you be at work in the morning?" Jeff asked as they finally turned into their driveway.

"Bright and early. It will be nice to be building a house this time instead of some business." Luke laughed.

"Yep. I'm glad that this will be a multi-million dollar house. Quite the commission and perfect for the new little family," Jeff laughed. Cristina knew Luke was excited about the payout of this project, but the fact that they were going to be building it three towns over and had a rush on getting it done, had her worried.

"Thanks for coming to pick us up Jeff. See you in the morning," Luke said as Cristina scooted out of the car and almost tripped over her weak legs. She couldn't get used to the odd weak feeling since the morning sickness had reared its ugly head. Cristina caught herself on the door then felt the lurch and bolted to the door, quickly unlocking it and rushing to the half bath off of the living room.

After tossing the last bit of marinara sauce and pasta Cristina felt two strong hands on her shoulders followed by a cool cloth. "How are you doing my lovely as ever wife?" Luke said as she flushed the horrendous reminder of her dinner.

"Better, I think," she replied as he helped her to her feet. She had never felt so much love in her life, her mother loved her, but this was a different love.

"I turned on the AC already and I'll pull a fan out and set it up on your side of the bed," Luke informed her as he kissed the top of her head.

"I love you, have I told you that recently," Cristina turned and snuggled into Luke's chest as he wrapped his arms around her.

"I do love hearing it, but I love you as well." Luke replied and they headed out of the bathroom and to their bedroom. She pulled out a silk nightgown and pulled it on as Luke hunted down and situated the fan on her new side of the bed. She now had to sleep on the window side of the room away from the door. Cristina still smiled at the memory of the debate.

"I sleep next to the door." Cristina pouted when Luke moved her pillow to the other side of the bed.

"My dear wife, the man sleeps by the door to stop the danger from getting to his beloved wife," Luke said with a stern look on his face.

"But I have always slept near the door" she quipped before Luke wrapped his strong arms around her.

"I want to protect my wife, will you deny me that?" Luke asked and it was a very good question, and no she didn't want to.

"No, dear husband of mine, I'll not deny you that. Doesn't mean I have to like it." She laughed and lightly slapped Luke in the chest. He lifted her up and plopped her on the bed and began to tickle her relentlessly.

"Ready for bed?" Luke asked pulling her onto his bare chest and kissing her bare shoulder.

"Yep," she replied as his hands roamed across her body stopping to rest on her firm stomach. She wasn't showing yet, but you could feel the firmness where the baby grew in the safety of her womb.

CHAPTER 18

Emily clambered out of bed determined to make her first day back to school a good one. The three weeks away from her first graders were challenging but she understood she needed the time to heal. Her face was back to normal and she only had slight pain in her ribs, but she knew she would be fine as long as she didn't lift any of the children.

Emily pulled on a pair of black slacks and a short sleeved purple blouse, wrapped her hair into a bun and pulled on her black slack socks. She pulled on a light jacket and threw her messenger bag over her shoulder. She made her way to the kitchen where she heard Jackie whipping up breakfast. "Good morning," Emily said cheerfully when she entered the kitchen, it was six-thirty in the morning and she could tell that Jackie hated being up that early.

"Morning. Coffee?" Jackie said taking a sip of her coffee then focusing on the pancakes.

"Yep." Emily walked over and poured herself a cup and dumped in a little creamer and sugar. "Can I help this morning?"

"Nope, sit, relax. How are you feeling?" Jackie replied as she flipped the last pancake on to the stack next to the stove.

"I'm feeling pretty good so far." Emily smiled as Jackie pulled up a stool next to her putting the warm syrup between them.

"Well good, now eat up. This will be the last breakfast you get at this hour," Jackie stated and dropped a few pancakes on her plate.

"Yes ma'am." Emily tried to restrain a laugh but failed.

Jackie was a sight in the morning. If Emily didn't have to be at the school by seven, she wouldn't be up either. They ate breakfast, cleaned up and made their way to the school.

It was still dark out, but there was no sign of rain in the early hours. Jackie dropped her at the front door, "I'll see you at three thirty." Jackie said with a smile.

"Sounds good. Thanks again for driving, when I'm good and healed I'll ride my bike again," Emily told her dearest friend.

"Not a problem, have a good day and remember no lifting the kiddos." Jackie smiled and pulled away from the curb. She was heading to Bellingham to pick up her cousin who was staying with her for a week. Emily was excited about meeting Jackie's cousin, she had seen the photos of him, and he was rather a good looking fellow, but she couldn't remember his name.

Emily walked into the school and was greeted by Principal Greely, she was a small older lady with gray hair, bright green eyes and thick glasses. Emily loved Ms. Greely, she was always friendly and the kids adored her.

"Good morning Emily, so glad you're back," Ms. Greely said pulling Emily into an awkward hug.

"It's good to be back," Emily replied with a smile. Ms. Greely was the only one who knew the truth about the accident.

"I never trusted the bastard to begin with, pardon my bluntness dear." Ms. Greely smiled, she was a fiery old coot.

"It's alright, I should have seen it before this incident to be honest, I was a little hard headed." Emily shrugged.

"It's alright dearie, you're young, you'll find the perfect man soon," she said and patted Emily on the arm.

"I'm swearing off men for a while, so maybe not so soon." Emily smiled.

"Well, when the right one comes along, you'll feel it in your heart dear," Ms. Greely said then sauntered off to greet a few other teachers that had come in.

Emily made her way down the eastern hall to her classroom. She had it done in bright colors with cartoon characters all over the room. Each student picked a character at the start of the year to help with their reading, it had become a fun way for the kids to learn. Emily set her things down and started rearranging the desks into groups of fours. She had planned a group activity before everything happened so she let the substitute cover her next lesson instead of the activity.

When she finished moving the desks, she could already feel the pain in her ribs. She hadn't thought about shifting desks when she got up that morning, and she forgot just how heavy the little things could be. Emily settled into her desk and waited for her students to join her and begin the tortoise and the hair project.

*****

Jeff was ready to go that Monday morning, the week before they had leveled everything out. They had also dug the basement out and cemented it in along with the doors and windows. The progress was going to be slower than the standard hotel, but he already had everything planned and with Luke's help they were going to have the home done in no time. Jeff pulled into the parking area and found Luke leaning against the trailer talking with Alan, one of the new workers. When Jeff approached, Alan nodded and left the two men to talk. Jeff unlocked the trailer and entered followed by Luke who pulled the door closed.

"Hey, did you know that Alan guy had been arrested and is pending trial?" Luke blurted.

"Well, not really; he's Rick's cousin, so I told Rick I would give him a chance," Jeff replied. Rick had worked for Jeff for four years and was a hard worker who Jeff would have appointed second, if Luke hadn't come back.

"I know Rick is an awesome guy, but this Alan dude seems a little off to me, something isn't sitting well," Luke said plopping into the chair in front of Jeff's desk.

"Well, would you mind working near him today, see if you can get anything out of him that would make me worry? I trust your gut man, but I can't fire a guy off of a gut feeling," Jeff said leaning his elbows on his desk.

"Sure man, not a problem," Luke said getting to his feet.

"Great, thanks, and hey, when do we learn the sex of the baby?" Jeff asked skimming over the plans one more time before they set to work.

"When the baby is born," Luke said then exited the trailer with Jeff on his heels.

"What, really? You're going to wait? What about buying clothes, and decorations, how will you know what colors to buy?" Jeff called after him. He was confused, he thought all new parents wanted to know the sex of the child so they weren't surprised or anything, not to mention they had the right colors to go along with the child.

"We are going with Noah's Ark, unisex man, it won't matter, besides everything Cristina will have on the registry will be greens, browns and yellows. No worries man, we want to be surprised," Luke replied as he grabbed his tool belt from the back of his truck. "I'm going to work now, so if you want to join us." Luke chided and made his way to the basement where they were going to finish laying the I-beams and mark off the rest of the main floor area. The house was going to be a large U shape curving to the back of the house with an enclosed heated pool in the center.

Jeff watched as Luke made his way to the basement and started working alongside Alan. The man looked familiar to Jeff, but he couldn't place him. Setting to work they held steady as they shouted out orders, a few watch outs, lunch time and that's a wrap for the day. They had gotten the basement enclosed and concrete poured for the remainder of the main floor.

After quitting time Luke and Jeff remained but everyone else left. Jeff wondered why his best friend had stayed knowing his wife was at home making dinner. "Hey man, what are you still doing here?" Jeff asked as Luke approached him.

"Alan has a girl friend named Emily, says she's an elementary teacher. Said she's staying with her friend Jackie to recuperate from a bike versus tree accident. Said she had been drinking and struck a tree on her way home a few weeks ago." Luke looked doubtful. "Who would let the best friend of their girlfriend take care of them after an accident like that, I mean come on." Luke was getting upset, he could tell.

"Well, we don't know for sure what happened, but I doubt what he said was true, after all, he just met you. I think he might be painting a bad picture of his girlfriend to be saying that stuff, but it does sound like the Emily from church," Jeff said thoughtfully, he really needed to talk with her now. If this Alan guy did those things to her, he was going to fire his sorry ass.

"Ok, well thought you should know, I need to head home now. See you in the morning man." Luke thumped him on the back and ran to his truck to head home to his waiting wife. Jeff made a final walk through to ensure everything was secure for the night and all tools were put up, then he headed for his lonely empty house.

*****

Cristina paced the floor, it was after seven and Luke was nowhere, no phone call, nothing. She was worried. She knew Jeff always cut them loose at five o'clock sharp since they started working so early, and it was unlike Luke to be late. She knew she needed to calm down, they had only been married a month, but still everything was blissful and perfect and he was very good at communicating to her when he was going to be late.

The dinner sat untouched and covered on the stove when ten o'clock approached, she had already called Jeff who didn't know anything, when a knock came at the front door. He heart stopped and she was frozen in place. "Cristina, it's Sheriff Pete." She took a deep breath and opened the door.

"Pete, what can I do for you at this hour?" she asked trying not to be alarmed even though she knew something was wrong, very wrong.

"Your husband has been in an accident," Pete said removing his hat. Cristina crumpled to the floor, tears streaming down her face. "Damn, he's going to be alright," Pete said crouching beside her. She felt relief in her chest but the tears didn't stop flowing.

"Sorry, can you take me to him?" she asked wiping her eyes and clambering to her feet.

"Sure," Pete said so she pulled on a jacket, grabbed her purse and locked the door behind them, the dinner completely forgotten. Cristina climbed into the passenger seat of Pete's patrol car and they headed for the hospital, where she spent so much time a few months before, the reminder still caused her to shiver.

"What happened?" Cristina asked.

"Well, some car was driving on the wrong side of the road from the looks of it, Luke tried to miss the car but was a bit too late, the car was totaled and the truck slipped on the wet pavement. The other driver perished in the accident and Luke, well, he seems to be pretty banged up, broken leg, wrist but the thing that has us all worried, and I should let the doctor tell you but, he's in a coma. It seems he hit his head pretty hard on the window, he had some minor swelling, but the doctors say he should come to within the next day or so," Pete said and Cristina started crying softly. "He's strong and healthy Cristina, he will be just fine." Pete continued. Cristina nodded but she knew Pete couldn't see her in the darkness of the car.

Coming to her senses she pulled out her phone and called Jeff. "Hello," Jeff answered.

"Hey Jeff, it's Cris. Luke was in an accident, Pete and I are headed to the hospital now."

"I'll meet you there," Jeff said then she heard the phone disconnect. Jeff was Luke's only family as far as she knew just like Ray was hers, until Luke and Jeff came along. Cristina sent up a silent prayer willing her husband to make a full recovery. The few months she had known Luke, were the best and the worst, but mostly the best of her life. With the minor five weeks of her abduction and torture, her and Luke had their ups and downs, but since Eric had taken her, he and her were like two peas in a pod.

Pete rounded the bend to the ER and let Cristina get out of the car. She ran inside to the receptionist desk, "Luke

Black," she asked.

"Are you family?" A young woman asked appraising her frantic look.

"I'm his wife," Cristina said quickly through her tears.

"Right this way." The young lady got up and Cristina followed her through the double doors, into an elevator, up to the second floor where the critical patients were held.

"I thought he wasn't critical?" she stammered.

"I'll let the doctor talk to you." She led her to a room where he was the lone patient. His body was hooked up to many machines, a steady beep alerted that his heart rate was fine. She had to force her legs forward since they seemed to be incased in cement. His face was pale, he had cuts and bruises everywhere his skin was visible.

"Oh Luke. My sweet wonderful husband," she cried leaning into his shoulder that looked mostly perfect. "I love you, please come back to me." She cried harder. She lost track of time and how long she'd been crying when two strong hands gripped her shoulders and turned her into a vast chest.

"Shh, everything is going to be fine," Jeff soothed and squeezed her tightly. "He's a fighter," Jeff whispered in her ear. She cried into his chest until her eyes were dry.

"Thanks for coming Jeff," she choked as she pulled away from him.

"Nothing could keep me away from my brother," Jeff said as he passed her a cup of water. She took a big gulp trying to calm the churning of her stomach, she hadn't eaten since lunch but she didn't want to be sick when Luke could wake up at any time. She pulled a chair up next to Luke and leaned her head on his arm as she squeezed his big hand. He looked like a small child and completely at peace, she began to cry again.

When Cristina opened her eyes again, light was streaming through the window and she heard soft snores from the corner of the room. It looked almost the same as when she awoke in the hospital a few months before but Luke was where she had lain, his eyes began to flutter. She stood and kissed his lips, "I love you, please come back to me," she whispered in his ear over and over.

"Shh, trying to sleep." She heard him whisper back. And she cried so hard.

"Oh Luke." She choked as his eyes fluttered open. "I love you," she cried into the crook of his neck.

"Shh baby, love you too," Luke whispered back.

"Hey man, welcome to the land of the living dude," Jeff said sleepily.

"Yeah. Hey drink man," Luke said in a whisper. Jeff poured him a cup of water and Cristina placed a hand gently under his head and lifted it enough for Jeff to give him water. They were a team.

"Thanks. Can I go home now?" Luke said with a clearer voice.

"Let me get the doctor eager beaver," Jeff said and left the room.

"Elvis has left the building," Luke said under his breath and Cristina couldn't help but laugh at his light demeanor.

"I love you," Cristina said again, reassuring her husband her love was still strong as he lay helpless in the hospital bed.

"Love you too darling wife. I expect sponge baths from some hot babe named Cristina when I get out of here." Luke smiled.

"Oh you'll get sponge baths, but not sure if they will be given by a hot babe or Jeff." Cristina laughed and winked at him. The doctor walked in with a smile on his face but Jeff didn't follow.

"How are you feeling Luke?" the doctor asked after checking all the vitals and pupil reaction.

"A little banged up, but good," Luke replied. "When can I go home?"

"Well, we need to do a scan to make sure the swelling is gone in your head, but I would say by the end of the week." The doctor smiled and patted his arm.

"So what's wrong with me?" Luke asked.

"Well now that you no longer seem to be in a coma that takes one thing off the list. Your left leg is broken along with your right wrist. You're pretty banged up and have minor cuts across your face, arms and neck area. Other than that you're perfect. Your leg only needed to be set but lucky for you, you were out for that part and your wrist was just fractured, no setting necessary. You'll be in casts for six weeks, so let this pretty lady tend to you without arguments." The doctor smiled.

"Not a problem, other than getting upstairs and into bed." Luke was thinking hard, Cristina knew that look.

"Well, you could always be like a small child and crawl up the stairs." Cristina was trying to make a joke, but apparently Luke took her serious.

"Sounds good," he said and she watched as the doctor just shook his head in clear amusement.

"Stubborn man," she whispered in his ear and he smiled.

"So we'll run the scans in the morning, meanwhile you need to rest up. Cristina you may stay, Jeff, you'll need to head on home." The doctor instructed, she was sure the doctor wanted her to leave as well, but that wasn't happening. The doctor left without further instructions and Jeff said good bye to Luke and patted her arm with a small smile.

"Sleep up my dear husband, I'll be here when you wake up." She kissed his lips then applied a little chap stick since they were a little dry. "I love you."

"I love you too, maybe you should head home and get some rest, you look beat," Luke said softly.

"Not going to happen mister, I'm not leaving your side until you tell me to go," she replied using his own words against him.

"Pain." He smiled softy.

"Back at you. Now rest, do you need any pain medication to help you sleep?" she asked him, she remembered how she'd felt. Although from what the doctor said she'd had it a little worse with the fractured jaw and ribs, but he looked pitiful.

"Sure, would love something to kill this pain in my head, wrist and leg," he replied sheepishly.

"I'll be right back." Cristina kissed his forehead and walked out of his room to flag down a nurse. "Hi, can my husband get something for the pain?" she asked a nurse passing by wearing bright pink scrubs.

"Sure ma'am, someone will be in there in a moment," the

young woman replied and scurried off in the direction she had come from. Cristina walked back into the room and looked down at her sleepy husband.

"You know staring at a man while he's trying to sleep is not cool," Luke murmured and she giggled. "I love that sound," he informed her. She leaned down and planted a soft kiss on his warm lips.

"I love you," she told him.

"Love you too," he replied. A nurse came in wearing black and purple scrubs and gave him an injection in the IV he had running into his arm.

"There, rest up Mr. Black," the nurse said giving him and Cristina a smile before departing the room.

"Good night my dear, I'll be here when you wake." Cristina kissed his forehead and looked down on his amazing face.

"Good night," he said softly as the medication took over his body and she watched as he drifted to sleep. She watched him sleep for so long the sun began to rise in the sky. She listened to the beeps of the monitors and watched the steady rise and fall of his chest. His eyes moved rapidly through the night and soft smiles played on his lips occasionally. "Don't leave." He had whispered sleepily. "Cris, stay." "Can't lose you." "Sweet baby." Cristina was in awe as he spoke in his sleep. All the nights they had spent together and she never noticed he talked in his sleep. "Bring her home" "Let her be ok" "Kill the bastard" "She's here." Cristina began to cry when she realized that he was dreaming about when she was taken, she wondered how often he thought about it. She couldn't get it out of her mind, maybe it was the same. "My life." "Everything."

When the nurses began their rounds Cristina felt

completely drained and drifted to sleep cradling his hand in hers and leaning on the side of the bed.

CHAPTER 19

Emily was excited to be leaving for the last day of school before it let out for the summer. She had only been back for three weeks, but felt elated for break. Emily pulled on her black slacks, a polo shirt and then pulled her hair into a pony-tail. Since her ribs were fully healed she was ready to get back on her bike and ride to work for the last time for a few weeks. Jackie was still sleeping when Emily slipped out of the house and jumped on her bike for the two mile ride to work. It was still dark out that morning when she left at five-thirty but she had the safety lights on, her helmet and all of her reflectors.

She reached Main Street just as a large white truck turned from the street and stopped. A young man jumped out of the truck as she passed. "Emily." He called and she hit the brakes and turned to look who it was that was calling her. Jeff stood on the sidewalk and waved at her, she got off her bike and walked back to where he was parked.

"Good morning Jeff."

"Morning, where are you headed this early in the morning?" he asked her, his sweet handsome face was a welcome site this early in the morning.

"Off for the last day of school and yourself?"

"Off to work, I'm having to work longer hours since my man Luke was in an accident."

"That sucks, is he alright?"

"Yeah, he'll be fine, he has a broken leg and wrist but his wife is tending to him, I think he's driving her nuts to be honest." Jeff chuckled and Emily was amazed by the sound;

it was deep yet sexy as hell.

"Probably," she smiled.

"Hey, I didn't have a working number for you, would you, um. Would you like to go to dinner with me Friday night, say at seven?" Jeff stammered and she thought it was so sweet and cute, she had never heard a man stammer when asking her out on a date. She had been feeling pretty good not being beaten up for a few weeks, it was a nice break for her face and body.

"Um, sure. I'm staying at Jackie's, do you need the address?" Emily gave in, he was nice, and dinner couldn't hurt. It was always a few weeks later that the hits came, she could enjoy a little time before she broke it off with him, surely.

"Oh I have the address. Would you like a lift to the school? I can put your bike in the back?" Jeff asked just as it started to rain down on them. She couldn't help but laugh at how fate always seemed to intervene.

"Sure, that would be great." She smiled and he leaned down and took her bike and gently placed it in the bed of his truck. His t-shirt rose over his biceps and she couldn't take her eyes off of how ripped he was. She hadn't noticed before how sweet his smile was. She climbed into the passenger seat of his truck and buckled in. She still had another mile to go before she would have gotten to the school and just as Jeff jumped into the truck the rain started falling harder.

His dark hair was wet and hung in a messy skater-boy way into his eyes and he brushed it out of his eyes as he started the truck. Soft music began to play through the cab and she couldn't place it but it was beautiful classical music she often listened to, to relax. He didn't say anything as he turned his truck around and headed to the school. She watched him drive carefully as the rain began to fall so hard it was hard to see through the windshield.

He pulled up at the front of the school beneath the large carport that covered the area for school buses. She watched as he climbed out of the truck in a flash and had her door open before she could get out of her seatbelt. When he smiled at her, his blue eyes twinkled in the lights of the school; he was handsome, sweet, and chivalrous. She jumped out of the truck and he lifted her bike out with ease and stood it next to her.

"Thank you for the ride, I would look like a wet dog had you not stopped." She smiled up at him, she was tall but he was about six two compared to her five eight.

"You would look like an angel no matter what," Jeff said softly giving her a look that made her blush. "But um, you're welcome. Pick you up Friday. Have a good day Emily." Jeff hung his head and walked around to his side of the truck before she could say another word and drove off. Emily was left standing in awe of the one man who could leave her speechless let alone leave her longing for the quiet demeanor he presented.

Emily gave herself a little shake as she made her way into the school and got settled for the day's events that would surely be fun They were going to have relay races in the gym, ice cream, pizza, face paint and tons of pictures. Emily would be sad to see her students head off to second grade, but she was happy to be getting a whole new group the next year.

*****

Jeff drove to the multi-million dollar house almost in a daze. He couldn't believe the words he spoke to Emily, she was a mystery to him and one he would enjoy solving. The fact that he was able to talk to her and get her number, even set up a date, was amazing to him. He cranked up the music when Beethoven's Symphony number seven began to play. He loved the calmness of the music and the happy sounds, it was like children playing to him and he enjoyed every second of it.

Jeff pulled into the main drive of the house they were working on and luckily for him the rain stopped just in time for him to set to work. He spotted another truck in the parking area and saw that Alan was sitting reading a magazine inside as he approached the truck Alan looked up, waved to him and climbed out to greet him.

"Good morning Jeff," Alan greeted closing the truck door.

"Morning Alan, what are you doing here so early?" Jeff asked, he didn't like the guy nor did he trust him. He had spoken with Jackie about Emily and Alan and sure enough it was the same guy. Jeff wanted to fire him on the spot but thought better of it, he could easily take his anger out on her again and that wouldn't be very good for her. He didn't like him, but keeping that man busy kept Emily low on his radar, or so Jeff hoped.

"Thought since Luke's been out and will be for another few weeks, I assumed you would need more help," Alan replied cheerily.

"Well, mighty kind of you to consider me, let's get to work shall we." The wall and roof was up, the insides still needed to be wired but the exterior was wired and they would be putting brick up in the next week or so, which took time. The house would be fully completed in the next six weeks if everything went according to plan.

Jeff set to work in the kitchen as Alan was in some other part of the house laying more of the floors. Jeff focused on his task at hand trying not to get distracted by the memory of Emily sitting in his truck that morning. As the other men began to drift in, the calming sounds of hammers and chatter relaxed Jeff into his normal work mode. He could now focus on directions, orders, and inspecting work as he helped some of the young men with a few tasks they hadn't done before.

Lunch time came and he situated himself in his trailer giving a quick call to Cristina to check on Luke. "Hello," Cristina answered.

"Hey girl, how's that friend of mine?" he asked. It was so easy for him to talk with Cristina.

"Oh, you know grumbling about this and that, trying to care for me and hopping around the house like a big kid," she laughed.

"That's Luke. How are you holding up?" Jeff asked.

"I'm doing alright, the baby is making it hard to eat, I can't seem to keep anything down, and with helping Luke do certain things I'm starting to feel the strain," she said softly. He knew she didn't like to complain about anything but it wasn't just her anymore.

"How about I swing by after work and pick him up, we'll go for dinner and you take a nice long bubble bath." Jeff smiled at his offer.

"Yes, yes, please." She laughed. He knew his friend could get cranky being cooped up in the house and it was hard for her to maneuver him around even with him being able to hop and stuff, he couldn't get down the stairs.

"Ok, we'll go to Bob's. I'll have him home before ten since I have to work, but maybe he won't be so cranky," Jeff laughed. Pizza and beer sounded great to him.

"You're the greatest Jeff." She laughed and he joined in.

"Hey, I have a date with Emily on Friday," Jeff started the gossip like a little school girl.

"That's great, like I told you, just relax like you're around me and you'll be fine," Cristina reminded him. He loved her like a sister, and really that's what she had become to him.

"Will do, see you later Cris," Jeff said

"Bye Jeff, thanks again," Cristina replied and hung up.

*****

Luke sat on the couch in the living room and he was restless. Cristina had been hovering over him since the accident and as much as he loved her, he wanted her to spend more time at work. His bruises had healed, but his leg and wrist were still bound by the annoying and itchy blue casts. Luke watched the NCIS marathon that was on while trying to relax as he sipped on his Dr. Pepper Cristina had brought him a few minutes before.

"Can I get you anything else?" Cristina called from the kitchen. She was working on their lunch since she wasn't tossing her cookies in the bathroom at the moment.

"I'm good. When are you going back to work?" he asked.

"I'm going back Monday, now stop grumbling." She laughed at him, he didn't know she was going back. They had argued earlier and she said she wasn't going back until he was back on his feet. He loved her but the way she fussed over him was driving him mad. He now understood how she'd felt, but yikes, he hated to feel weak in his woman's eyes. The way she jumped every time he said something, or tried to help every time he hopped his way to the bathroom, or tried to get comfortable. It was starting to wear on him and the fact that the casts were making him itch like crazy was bugging him to no end.

"Ok," he grumbled back while sticking a finger into the opening of his cast on his leg. He was wishing it had been his ribs instead of his wrist and leg since he would be able to take the wraps off at least for a few minutes to shower. Instead he had to let Cristina cover his casts with garbage bags and help lower him into the tub so she could bathe him. He felt like a child and he hated it.

"Are you still grumbling in there?" Cristina called, she was picking on him for how much he complained, he knew he shouldn't but he couldn't help it. He was itching to play some ball, go running, or something other than sit around watching boring television all day.

"Oh honey, you only have three more weeks left, hang in there. Ok." She came into the room and kissed his forehead. He wrapped his good arm around her waist and planted a soft kiss on the stomach that was now showing signs of a child growing.

"I know baby, I'm sorry." He apologized and she kissed his lips.

"It's ok, I'm sure I was no picnic myself." She laughed, and she really was good. She hadn't complained, she was just nervous when it came to her cuts, but he understood that. She'd been quiet the whole time while he was loud and annoying.

"Nah, you were great and so quiet," he replied as she playfully slapped his shoulder. "Now if I could have that again." He laughed and pulled her into his chest.

"You're such a pain sometimes." She laughed against his neck.

"I know you are but what am I?" He laughed and she nibbled on his neck sending shivers down his spine. Oh how he loved the woman in his arms.

"Lunch is almost ready." She wiggled away from him. Getting to his foot, he hopped his way into the kitchen and pulled up a seat. He watched as she finished making the sandwiches and potato salad, then placed them on the table.

"Looks good Cris," Luke said as he dug into his turkey sub. She had layered the meat, tomatoes, lettuce, bacon, and mayo just the way he liked it.

*****

Cristina watched as Luke fumbled with his sandwich trying to get his semi-restrained fingers to cooperate. Over the past three weeks, he had complained about everything and she was at the end of her patience with her dear husband. She was feeling drained more and more by the day. The pregnancy was keeping her sick most of the time. She wasn't able to put on nearly enough weight as she had been instructed to and she was getting lightheaded often.

She took a few bites out of her food before she leaped from the table to relieve her upset stomach. She heard the thumps before she felt the strong hand on her back, "How are you doing?" Luke asked.

"Eh, you know, kid doesn't want anything I try and give it, we have a picky eater on our hands already." She laughed and wiped her mouth, flushed and stood leaning into the man in front of her.

"Oh well, the doctor said the morning sickness should let up soon." He cooed in her ear.

"I know, I just hope it's soon. Every smell is making me

sick. Even the smell of my beloved books at the library make me queasy," Cristina replied drinking in the only scent that didn't make her stomach ache, the scent of her amazing husband.

"Come, let's finish eating, well, um. Have some crackers." He kidded as he released her and started his awkward hopping to the kitchen. He looked really odd with his height hopping through the house. When he goes up the stairs he crawls, which really made her laugh.

They settled back at the table and Cristina remembered her call with Jeff earlier, "Hey guess what?" she said as Luke stuffed his face with the rest of his sandwich. He hated eating in front of her when she couldn't stomach food, so he inhaled it like a high school jock trying to impress his friends.

"What?" he asked covering his full mouth with his good hand.

"Jeff will be here after work to take you to dinner." Cristina smiled as she watched Luke digest the information she gave him, he swallowed and grinned.

"You not coming?" he asked.

"Nope, I'm going to take a much needed relaxing bubble bath, and you need out of this house," Cristina said as she sipped her water.

"You sure?" he asked.

"Yep, you're going and that's it." Cristina got up and planted a soft kiss on his lips. He wrapped his arm around her, pulled her into his lap and deepened the kiss.

"I love you, you know that right?" Luke asked.

"Yes, and I love you too," she replied, kissing the side of his mouth.

*****

Emily sat in her classroom and began to cry softly. Her students had all gone home for the summer. She was just informed that due to cut backs, and the fact that she was the most recent hire, she was out of a job. Emily loved her students and loved teaching, she wasn't sure what she was going to do now.

"Hey girl." Jackie said carrying a few boxes into the classroom. She had called Jackie when she heard the news.

"Hey," Emily replied softly.

"How you holding up?" Jackie asked her.

"I feel like no matter what I do, no matter how hard I try, nothing ever goes right. Every man in my life has beaten me, the school I love is getting rid of me, and I'm living with one of my best friends and trying to wrap my head around a date with Jeff," Emily blurted. She was broken and had no fight left.

"You're going on a date with Jeff?" Jackie asked, of course that's all she heard.

"Yeah, Friday at seven."

"That's great news."

"Do you remember I just lost my job, my only income? I'm going to have to start the job hunt." Emily started to cry again.

"No, you won't. I need an assistant, the pay is decent and the hours are reasonable," Jackie said and patted Emily's arm. "Now, Jeff, he's a wonderful man. He has gone through a lot in his life, but he's a great man. He's honest, sweet, works hard and knows how to treat a lady. You'll have fun with him."

"However, let's get packed up so we can head home, I'm beat," Emily said and they started packing up her things. Jackie headed out to the car with the final box leaving Emily to collect herself.

Emily sat at her desk one last time when she heard someone clear their throat. Emily jerked her head up to see Alan standing in the doorway holding a dozen red roses. Panic rose within her and her heart began to race. She was terrified of the man before her with good reason.

"Alan, what, what are you doing here?" she stammered rising to her feet.

"I wanted to come and apologize, I don't know what came over me. I was such an ass, please, will your forgive me? I swear to never do anything like that again and I just can't see my life without you." Alan stepped toward her, his face was somber and he looked sincere.

"Alan, I." Emily paused when he pulled her into a soft hug, "I need time Alan," Emily said softly pulling from his grasp, trying not to upset the man that almost beat her to death and praying that Jackie would come back in. Alan let her go, smiled and handed her the roses.

"Sure, sorry. Take all the time you need, you know where I'll be," Alan said in a tight composed voice with a forced smile on his face. He turned and exited the room without even a glance back in her direction. She listened as his footsteps faded down the hall before she collapsed in her chair and began to cry.

*****

Jeff pulled into Luke's driveway and exited his truck. He
had showered and cleaned up at his house before swinging
by to pick him up. He hadn't been by since the day he
brought them home from the hospital. As he got out of the
car, Cristina came out to greet him. She had dark circles
under her eyes, was really pale and thinner than the last
time he saw her.

"Hey girl, you look like hell," Jeff laughed as he pulled her
into a hug. She was tiny compared to him.

"Yeah, I feel like hell. Come on in, he's waiting and excited
to be leaving the house. Have fun and please bring him
home safely." She poked him in the ribs.

"Not a problem there sweet cheeks." He pulled her into his
side and squeezed her. If he had a little sister he figured
she would be like Cristina.

"You're such a twit." Cristina laughed and he had to agree
with her, when it came to her and Luke, he was a twit and
protective, how could he not, they were his family. He
followed Cristina into the house and saw Luke almost
bouncing in his seat like a small child, he looked so excited
and Jeff couldn't help but laugh.

"Are you ready?" Jeff asked still laughing. He watched as
Luke hopped up on one leg and over to him, he doubled
over laughing so hard. Luke was such a big guy and looking
like a child was hilarious.

"Oh stop laughing at me you big jerk." Luke punched him
in the shoulder with his good hand and Jeff laughed
harder, he couldn't help it. His friend looked good, like a big
kid, but he was ok. His sense of humor was back.

"Sorry man, let's get some grub while your wife gets some

much needed rest." He glanced at Cristina as she swayed back and forth, he figured she wouldn't make it in the bubble bath before she crashed in their bed for the night. "Call if you need anything Cris," Jeff said and he followed the hopping Luke outside to help him down the stairs and into the truck. Cristina quickly followed with the wheel chair they would need and Jeff tossed it in the back. He watched as she kissed Luke and headed back in the house. Before he left the driveway every light in the house went out.

"She looks like hell man," Jeff said to Luke as he turned onto the main road leading into town.

"Yeah, I know. I'm worried about her. I've noticed her almost tumble over so many times these last three weeks, and she isn't able to keep anything down. She keeps assuring me that she's alright, but I think she's trying to be strong." Luke shook his head. "Not to mention she's trying to cater to me for everything like a mother hen, but she doesn't need to."

"Maybe she feels responsible, and you did hover over her when you weren't at work when she went through her ordeal," Jeff commented.

"Yeah, I know," Luke replied in a solemn voice.

"We're going to get pizza and beer, talk about the women in our lives and relax. Cristina just needs some rest, maybe in the morning you can sleep in and hold her in bed," Jeff recommended.

"She hasn't been able to eat anything, she drinks plenty of water with lemon and tea without sugar. But everything seems to come back up. She said that her doctor said it's normal for some women with their first pregnancy, but she looks like she's dying. She's all skin and bones other than her stomach which has grown quite a bit the past few weeks," Luke yammered on. "I'm worried about her Jeff, now that I'm on the slow end what if she really needs me?" Luke sounded pitiful to him.

"Luke, relax, ok. Let's eat, drink and I'll have you back home to cuddle with your beautiful wife in no time, ok," Jeff said pulling into a parking space near the door and the ramp.

"You're right." Luke agreed opening his door and hopping out of the truck and almost face planting onto the pavement.

Jeff hopped out, set the wheel chair up and helped Luke lower himself to the seat. He could see how tired his friend was and the worry about Cristina was clearly written on his face.

Jeff wheeled his friend into the bar and they were quickly greeted by many single women in the bar asking what had happened. Luke paid them no mind really, other than to tell them he was in a car accident and how his wife had been caring for him. The girls immediately backed off. Jeff wheeled Luke to a table in the corner near the window and ordered a large meat lovers pizza and fat tires.

"So, how are you doing Jeff?" Luke asked propping his broken wrist up onto the table.

"Not bad, I have a date with Emily on Friday." Jeff smiled.

"Really, that's awesome dude." Luke smiled back and kicked him under the table with his good leg.

"Yeah, I'm excited," Jeff said, thinking about Emily's smile in response. Since the day he got to drive her to work her strawberry scent still clung to his seat. The waitress brought their dinner and beer. They chatted away about his future date with Emily, the progress of the house he was working on and the plans for the home he was looking to build soon, should he find a wife. Living in his parents' home was great but it was only two bedrooms and not fit for a family.

"So have you found a property?" Luke asked. Jeff wanted to wait until the paperwork was finalized to inform his best friend that the ten acre lot next to his property went up for sale and he'd snagged it thanks to Jackie.

"Well, if you keep it hush-hush, I'm working to buy a piece of land close by, the paperwork won't be finalized for another week or so," Jeff said softly.

"Wow, man, that's awesome. Make sure I'm up and running when you start to build, I'd definitely want to be in on that." Luke smiled and started to relax, he had already downed two beers before they got their pizza, which was odd for him, but Jeff knew the man needed to unwind while he just sipped his beer.

After they'd chatted awhile and ate, Jeff drove Luke home. Luke was in a drunken stupor when Jeff carried him up the stairs to his room and as quietly as possible slid him into bed next to the curled up Cristina. Luke grunted when he was settled and started snoring right off the bat. Jeff quietly pulled the bedroom door closed, locked up the front door and headed home for the night sending off a silent prayer for his friends to get through the tough times and for Cristina to feel better soon.

CHAPTER 20

Luke rolled over in the bed as the bright sunshine began to glow throughout the room. His head was pounding but he wanted to pull his wife close and sleep a little longer. Luke pulled her into his arms and noticed she was burning up. His eyes sprung open to see his wife covered in sweat and her face flushed. "Cristina, honey." Luke tried to shake her awake but all she did was grunt and cough.

Luke let her settle back into the bed as he swung himself out of bed putting all of his weight on his broken leg. He leaned down, ignoring the pain that shot from his shin clear up to his hip, and picked his small wife up and carried her down to the car gently settling her into the front seat and buckling her in.

Luke turned the car on, backed out of the garage and floored it to the hospital. He swung into a parking spot near the door, clipped the keys onto his shirt and carried his wife into the building. "I need a doctor." He was straining from the pain not only in his body, but in his heart for his wife who hadn't opened her eyes once.

"Lay her down." A nurse had pushed a gurney in front of him, he laid her on the bed gently and the doctors whisked her away. As he began to fall over, a large doctor grabbed him and pulled him to a wheel chair then pushed him after his wife.

"Thank you." He looked up at the tall man pushing him through the corridor, he was black, with a shaved head and a calm expression on his face but didn't say anything. Luke noticed the man's name was John and he was wearing green scrubs.

The young man wheeled him to a waiting area and left him. Luke's head was pounding from his stupidity from last night, his leg was throbbing and his wrist was starting to hurt a little. Luke pulled the cell phone out of his pocket that Jeff had failed to remove the night before and called him.

"Hello," Jeff answered and Luke could hear the hammering in the background.

"At the hospital, come when you can." Luke said simply, he knew his voice sounded bleak, he never should have left his wife last night, not with how bad she looked.

"What the hell happened Luke?" Jeff yelled into the phone.

"It's Cris." Luke lost all his strength and let the phone drop into his lap and for the second time since he met the woman he felt broken, lost and helpless. Luke sat with his head in his hands for so long that he fell asleep until he was shaken awake.

"Luke, have you heard anything yet?" Jeff asked squatting down in front of him.

"No, what time is it?" Luke asked.

"Just after ten, you only called an hour ago," Jeff assure him and passed Luke a Dr. Pepper.

"Excuse me sir, I was instructed to bring you this medication." A young blond nurse passed him a small cup with a few pills. "We will need to do an x-ray on your leg and wrist once you hear from the doctor ok." Her smile was sweet and he took the medication that was offered and the nurse turned and walked away.

"Well, maybe we won't have to wait so long. What happened Luke?" Jeff persisted, plopping into a chair across from him.

"I woke up and pulled her onto my chest and felt how warm she was. I couldn't even wake her up and she was flushed so I carried her to the car, drove here, brought her inside and that's pretty much it. She didn't look good Jeff, she was so pale and so hot in my arms." Luke dropped his head into his hands again and tried to breath.

"You did good by bringing her here Luke, you did what you could." Jeff tried to calm his raging emotions and fear that he was going to lose her, but he was ineffective.

He sat for a long time feeling the relief from the medication slip through his veins. His leg and wrist began feeling much better, but now he was starting to feel a little loopy.

"Luke." A male doctor approached him and squatted down in front of his wheel chair. "You got her to us just in time. She and the babies are going to be fine."

"What's wrong with her?" Luke asked.

"She has the flu which she didn't realize because of the morning sickness, she was dehydrated and weak from the lack of food since her body was rejecting it all. We have her sedated with an IV and her fever is already going down. She'll be just fine," the doctor reassured him.

"Did you say babies?" he heard Jeff ask.

"Oh yeah, twins, didn't you know?" The doctor looked at Luke with raised eyebrows.

"No, I don't think she knew yet," Luke replied.

"Well, she does now. I'm surprised her doctor didn't get a second ultrasound with how sick she's been." The doctor stood and got behind Luke's chair and started pushing him.

"Shall we go see your wife then get your x-rays to make sure you didn't hinder any of your healing?" the doctor asked. Luke saw Jeff get up and follow them out of the waiting room.

"Man, we are spending a lot of time here this year," Jeff observed.

"Yeah, seems that way," Luke replied with a shudder. The doctor wheeled him into the room where Cristina was lying. From his vantage point she looked better and wasn't as pale but she had an IV in her arm and looked to be sleeping.

"I'll leave you for a few minutes then a nurse will come to take you to get your x-rays, ok?" the doctor said and shuffled out of the door. Luke saw Jeff take a seat in the corner of the room and he placed his hand into her small one.

"Luke?" Cristina said and turned her head towards him.

"Yes baby, I'm here," he replied. He wanted to get up, but he wasn't feeling his lower half at the moment.

"I'm sorry, I didn't realize how bad I was," she cried softly.

"Now, none of that. You're a tough woman and stubborn too. Everything is going to be alright, you and the babies are fine." Luke assured her rubbing his thumb on her hand.

"Are you ok with the idea of twins, I can't believe it." Tears streamed down her face but he wasn't sure if it was pain or from happiness.

"Yeah, it's cool." He smiled at her. He hadn't had time to wrap his mind around the idea of twins, but it couldn't be that bad. He loved her, loved the one baby now two. He just hoped it wasn't three; that might be a little much for him.

"I love you."

"I love you too, now stop being stubborn. You have two other lives to think about and I'm here for you ok," Luke said.

"Yeah, me as well," Jeff interjected.

"So you'll be taking it easy from here on out and we're going to get a few tricks from some other moms to get some food in you." Luke informed her with as stern a voice as he could muster. The medication was starting to make him drowsy and he wasn't able to feel the hand he was clasping.

"Not a problem. They told me you carried me in, are you ok?" she asked.

"Yeah, I um, they gave me medication, I'm starting to feel odd, I uh, think I need some sleep." Luke stammered over his words, leaned his head against her bed and let his eyes close. He heard Jeff and Cristina chuckle in unison.

*****

Jeff lifted Luke out of his wheel chair and laid him in the empty bed next to Cristina. He knew a nurse would be in to get him, but he doubted they had any idea what the medication was going to do to him considering all the alcohol he'd ingested the night before and the adrenaline from getting his wife to the hospital.

"Thank you," Cristina said softly when he came and leaned against the side of her bed.

"Not a problem, but the nurses will have to move him next time. He's not a light dude!" Jeff laughed and looked over at Luke who looked peaceful in sleep. "How are you feeling?" he asked, her eyes still had dark circles under them but she didn't look as pale.

"I'm feeling better, well, other than being in this place for the third time in less than six months and having my husband all worried and conked out from pain medication because he had to bring my sick butt in here; I'm right as rain." She laughed weakly.

The door to the room opened and a pretty red head walked in wearing blue scrubs. She looked up at Jeff and smiled, her bright blue eyes were striking and Jeff forgot how to speak for a minute. "I'm here to bring Mr. Black to x-ray," she said as he watched her eyes fall on Luke's sleeping figure. "They gave him a sedative I see." She shook her head.

"Let me get him back in his chair for you." Jeff offered, he hadn't intended to help, but she was cute.

"That is so kind of you, but I'll just wheel the bed out, otherwise we'll have to put him up on another table anyways." She laughed and Jeff opened the door for her to push the unconscious Luke out the door.

"Wow, Jeff a pretty woman comes in to take my husband off and you jump at the chance to help her, here I thought you were going to make them do all the work," Cristina chided him with a smile.

"Well, she didn't need my help after all so it's a moot point." Jeff plopped into the chair he'd been occupying, crossed his arms over his chest and focused on the memory of Emily's soft smile when he dropped her off at the school; the nurse faded from his memory.

*****

Emily sat in the office of Jackie Blake reviewing her first real estate contract and couldn't help but notice the name. Jeffrey Parker, was purchasing a parcel of land to the west of the Black residence. Emily studied the name and wondered if it was the same Jeff she would be going to dinner with that night. She finished the paperwork the way Jackie had instructed the day before and she had everything in the file for her review. She discovered that Jackie had OCD when it came to her contracts, files, clients and office. Everything had its place and everyone had a file in a different cabinet.

Emily had learned how to use the client list from the online company called Top Producer and she loved it. Each contact had the house they had for sale, purchased or were leasing through Jackie along with descriptions and pictures of the properties. The program could sort between buyers, sellers and owners that were leasing their homes. Emily was in awe and felt a little in over her head as Jackie eased her into the real estate business.

She had already learned quickly on outdated software that held contracts for anything she needed for Jackie. She was scheduled for a class on Wednesday to learn about the online database called eContracts. Apparently, that system held the same contracts and information as Real Fast but, allowed for people to sign in on the computer. It saved and locked the documents so no one could alter them. Jackie had showed her a little bit of the program that morning. Emily was glad she had taken a typing class in college since Jackie had already dictated a few letters to her and she had to type as Jackie spoke.

After two days of working with her best friend she wasn't sure how the woman did it. She was always running around from town to town, getting clients left and right. Jackie was a fun person to talk to and she knew her business better than anyone Emily had ever spoken to. She was enthralled by the woman.

When Jackie offered her the position she had informed her that she would have to invest in more business attire and then took her shopping. She was sporting a black pencil skirt, a blue ruffle blouse that was tucked in with a nice black belt, black pumps and nylons, which she hated. Emily had pulled her hair into a French twist letting her curls fall loose at the back of her neck. She was beginning to think maybe she would wear the outfit on her date, or at least leave her hair up.

"Hey girl, you ready for lunch?" Jackie came into the office and almost made Emily jump out of her skin.

"Oh my goodness, you scared me half to death." Emily placed a hand on her chest and felt her heart as it began to slow down.

"Sorry, I forget I walk like a cat." Jackie laughed, grabbing her purse from the chair. She had been at a house closing all morning.

"Yeah, let's eat." Emily glanced at the clock on her computer and found it was one o'clock and the thought of food made her stomach grumble.

"What sounds good?" Jackie asked as they locked up the office and headed for her car.

"Well, doesn't really matter to me, you're the boss." Emily laughed and gave Jackie a squeeze around the shoulders.

"Yeah, and don't you forget it little missy." Jackie laughed back and bumped her with her hip almost sending Emily into a car they were walking past. Luckily for Emily, Jackie had quick reflexes and caught her.

"How ever did we become friends Jackie," Emily laughed.

"What, don't you remember me almost running you over on

your bike?" Jackie laughed. There was a large age gap between Emily and Jackie but it never seemed to matter to them.

"Ha, yeah after I was swooning over your son, who seems to be happy as a clam with, what's her name?" Emily asked.

"Anna, and he does seem happy," Jackie replied thoughtfully. They climbed into her Escape.

"Anna is beautiful. Blond hair, good height and she has beautiful blue eyes not to mention how smart she is. I think we might have a wedding soon enough." Emily smiled at her friend as she backed the SUV up then slammed on the breaks and looked at Emily, *if looks could kill.*

"Don't say things like that, he's my baby and I don't need to think about him getting married off so soon." Emily watched as her friends' eyes reddened and she could see the unshed tears the woman had fought to keep at bay. Sam was twenty-two, had graduated high school early, started the coffee shop when he was sixteen and was doing pretty good for himself.

"Sorry Jackie, just saying. They're young, they'll probably wait a few years." Emily patted her friend on the knee and watched as she finished backing out of the spot.

"So, have you spoken to Alan? He keeps calling," Jackie said as she turned onto the main street towards a small shopping center near the office.

"He scares me," Emily admitted.

"Alan scares the hell out of me too," Jackie agreed.

"He seemed sincere, but I don't believe it for a minute. Part of me wants to go back because it's all I have ever known and maybe he could change," she knew she was lying to herself so she continued before Jackie could comment, "but after meeting Jeff I want to explore what a calm relationship would be like," Emily said as she stared out the window at the few passing cars.

"Well, each message he has left has gotten worse, have you let Pete know about everything?" Jackie asked as she turned into the KFC.

"Yes, I told him about the roses, each recording, letter and email," Emily said.

"I still can't believe he was begging, but the anger is evident with each communication," Jackie commented and Emily silently shuddered.

"Yeah, he seems very agitated, I'm worried about my date with Jeff tonight," Emily admitted.

"Now don't you go borrowing trouble. Pete has all this information and I'm sure he's keeping Alan in his sights." Jackie reassured her.

"I hope you're right," Emily replied unbuckling her seatbelt and stepping out of the car. She couldn't help feeling like someone was watching her and it made her skin crawl.

*****

Jeff was freshly showered, had on a pair of clean jeans, a black t-shirt tucked in with a black belt and his leather jacket. He brushed his hair back but didn't use gel to restrain it. He knew he needed a haircut but he didn't want people thinking he and Luke were really brothers. Not that it would have been a bad thing, but he liked having his own life. Jeff slipped on some thick socks and pulled on his cowboy boots he had worn for years. "Well." Jeff said to his bathroom mirror, he couldn't help but be nervous.

Grabbing his keys, he switched off the kitchen light, climbed into his truck which he had cleaned earlier and made his way to Jackie's home. To his surprise, it hadn't rained all day. The roads were nice and dry and there were plenty of people out gallivanting through town on this wonderful Friday evening. Jeff pulled into Jackie's drive way, turned off the engine, walked to the front door and rang the bell. His father had drilled into his head that if he's to take a woman out, he needed to get out of his car, knock on the door like a gentleman and always open doors for the ladies and cover the bill.

The door swung open and Jackie stood there with a big smile. "Please come in Jeff," she said, her cheeks were pink and she still wore her usual business attire.

"Thank you." Jeff said stepping inside. Her home was beautiful, hardwood floors, large entry, something he would build for himself.

"She's almost ready, you know us ladies, we like to take our time." Jackie laughed and Jeff joined in. He knew he would wait all night for Emily; he didn't know what it was about her, but he wanted to take her and run away. That smile, those brown eyes, that wavy long hair of hers, she was a knock out, not to mention the fact that she was tall. "Can I get you something to drink?" Jackie asked, she was always so sweet to everyone.

"No thank you ma'am," Jeff replied.

"Now, don't you go doing that ma'am thing on me again." Jackie playfully slapped him in the shoulder just as he heard someone coming down the stairs.

Emily walked from behind the wall that shielded the stairs from the front door. She was wearing a teal dress with cream hearts and a cream knit sweater on top with light brown cowboy boots; her hair was pulled up in the back, waves still cascaded to her shoulders. Jeff couldn't take his eyes off the beautiful woman in front of him.

"Wow, you look…" Jeff started, getting cut off by Emily.

"Silly, I know. It was Jackie's Idea," Emily said shyly.

"Girl you look good now stop it," Jackie encouraged.

"…Beautiful." Jeff finished still in awe. He wasn't familiar with the new styles, but he loved the cowboy boots on her showing off her long legs since the dress stopped at her knees. He looked at her beautiful face that had a light dusting of make-up which, he wasn't a fan of, but it played up her beautiful eyes.

"Well, isn't that sweet," Jackie said, interrupting his appreciation of the beauty that stood before him.

"Shall we go eat?" he asked as Emily blushed but walked forward. She was a stunning creature and he was in awe of her.

"Sure." Emily agreed and walked out the front door but not before Jeff caught the pointed look she shot at Jackie; he almost laughed but decided to restrain it.

Jeff hurried and opened the door to his truck for Emily and watched as she climbed in, then closed the door behind her. "Drive safe Jeff, have fun," Jackie said and waved at them. Jeff walked around to his side of the truck and took a deep breath, then climbed in.

"How do you feel about Italian?" Jeff asked, he hadn't thought about a place to go, but he wanted her to choose. Jeff looked over at Emily, who was focused on her hands and simply nodded. He leaned over and placed his hand gently on her shoulder and she jumped. "Emily, I'm not going to hurt you," Jeff said in a soft voice.

"No, no sorry you just... um, startled me is all," Emily stammered, her calm demeanor gone.

"So we can do Italian." He paused gauging her reaction but she didn't move, "Or, I know of this great Mexican place." He saw her eyes turn to meet his quickly then dart back to her hands. "Do you like Mexican?" he asked softly.

"I do," she replied in a voice that was barely audible.

"Sounds perfect, I know just the place." Jeff smiled, he would take her to La Casa Fiesta, he loved that place and it had great food and was fun and relaxing.

"So Jeff, how do you like the construction business?" Emily asked, her sweet voice carried through the cab over the light piano music he had on.

"I love it, well I enjoy the design process much more, but to watch my creations come to life is pure joy," Jeff replied. He did love his profession, how could he not.

"Wow, that is good to hear," Emily replied.

"So, how is teaching, I know you're officially on summer break," Jeff asked.

"Well, um it was great," Emily replied and the sad soft voice had him a bit worried.

"Was?" Jeff asked.

"Well, due to the economic issues, the school had to lay off a few teachers and since I was the most recent hire, I got let go first. I'm now working with Jackie in real estate," Emily replied and Jeff froze. He knew Emily saw the contract that was being worked on for him to purchase the ten acres next to Luke and Cristina but he didn't want to say anything until everything was finalized; he had told Luke, but that was all.

"Wow, what a shame, I'm sure you were a great teacher, their loss and now Jackie's gain." Jeff smiled at her when he reached a red light. He was almost to the restaurant and starting to get hungry.

"Yeah, I was informed that should the economy come back around, I would get a second shot, but I'm not sure. I love the kids and all, but I'm enjoying working under Jackie's overbearing and brilliant thumb." Emily laughed a little, it was a nervous laugh, but Jeff still enjoyed the sound nonetheless. Jeff turned into the parking lot a few minutes later and leapt out of the truck to get her door, but he was a bit slow for his feisty woman. "Oh sorry," Emily said and looked down to her feet when she saw him at her door.

"Hey, it's all good. I'll have to be faster next time." Jeff laughed and closed the door and held his arm out for her. She clasped it and Jeff reached across and patted her arm. "No fears Emily, not with me." Jeff said softly and she turned and gave him a smile that made his heart melt.

"Why did you say that?" She stopped and looked at him.

"Well, I figured out what happened from little pieces here and there and the fact that I currently have Alan working for me, it wasn't hard to figure out. If nothing else, I'm here as a friend and I would never do anything intentionally to hurt you. I was raised to treat every woman how I would want my mother treated, and that my beautiful lady, is always with the most respect and care," Jeff replied, surprised that he spilled so much information without a pause or stammer.

"Really." Emily asked, she didn't look convinced and it

broke his heart, he wondered what she had gone through her whole life and he intended to find out.

"Well, yeah. My father was really good to my mom, they argued sure, but he was the kind that would stand and let my mom get it all out, then he would ask if she was done then he would say his peace. A lot of the time, their arguments ended in the bedroom and me sneaking out to play ball with Luke because that was not something a teenager should be hearing." Jeff laughed, "My father never laid a hand on my mother or me; actually it was my mother who doled out the punishments in our house."

"So your father never struck you or your mother?" Emily asked.

"Never."

"Wow, you had such a great life," Emily said softly.

"Something I hope to show you as long as you let me." Jeff smiled and her bright blushing smile was what he needed to hold his ground. He would show her how a man should treat a woman, whether he would be that man, or just a friend, he wouldn't let her get struck in anger again.

"Emily." He heard an angered yell from behind them and they both turned to find Alan approaching them. "Where the hell have you been?" Jeff pulled Emily behind him as Alan approached, "Jeff get your hands off my woman."

"Emily, are you his woman as he puts it?" Jeff asked her keeping his eyes on the very angry man in front of them.

"Um, not anymore," she whispered." He could feel her shuddering behind him.

"Alan, you need to leave, you have no reason to be here." Jeff tried to calm the man in front of them.

"Jeff, I have no issue with you man, but that bitch behind you and I have a few things to clear up."

"Don't speak ill of the lady Alan, and you'll calm yourself before I move," Jeff said. He could see a few spectators near the building watching the situation. "Alan, you should go home and refresh yourself, then call me and we'll work something out."

"Jeff." Emily cried behind him. "I'll go with him, I don't want you hurt," she whispered and moved to walk around him but he caught her.

"No, you're not going through that anymore." Jeff tried to calm her. His heart was racing but he wasn't letting him beat her again. Jeff knew Alan would probably kill her in his current state of mind.

"Last chance Jeff." Alan yelled and Jeff shook his head, then everything happened in slow motion. Alan pulled out a gun, aimed it right at them and Jeff turned and pulled Emily into his chest to shield her just as the sharp pain coursed right through his back. He fell forward taking Emily with him, cupping her head with his large hands. He heard another shot, and shouting, but his eyes focused on the crying and pleading of Emily who was tucked beneath him. He couldn't feel anything but the intense pain. "Jeff," Emily cried.

"Shh, you're ok," Jeff cooed and felt a pressure on his back and the pain intensified.

"The ambulance is on the way." Someone said from behind him. He could already hear the alarms in the distance but he could only focus on the woman, who could have died, crying in his arms. He was glad he didn't see blood on her. It wasn't a through and through shot so he'd stopped it from hurting her.

"I'm so sorry Jeff," she cried. He couldn't believe she thought it was her fault.

"Not your fault babe," he told her softly. He heard the ambulance approach and felt the hands on his back press harder as he began to feel light headed. His head began to drop and he felt the darkness creep up on him just as he saw the paramedics in his peripheral vision come up to him. He could no longer hear what was going on, the blackness was calling to him. The last thing he saw was Emily crying and saying something he couldn't hear.

CHAPTER 21

Emily paced back and forth in the waiting room as she waited to hear news about Jeff, she was informed since she wasn't family she had to wait for the next of kin. She had called Jackie and left her a message, had already given her statement to the police and was informed that a bystander shot Alan and he was gone. She was beginning to feel light headed as the doors burst open with a woman pushing a man in a wheel chair, if Emily hadn't known better she would have thought it was Jeff at first glance, but she knew better.

"Emily I take it." The young woman asked.

"Yeah."

"I'm Cristina and this is my husband Luke. What happened." She looked down at Luke and he looked half out of it.

"My ex showed up at the restaurant while we were talking outside and Jeff got in the way of the bullet aimed for me." Emily collapsed into a chair. She started to shake, dropped her head in her hands and cried like she hadn't in years.

She felt the petite arms wrap around her trembling shoulders but Cristina didn't say anything, she just let Emily cry. She heard the doors open and close again but didn't look up until the man started talking.

"Luke."

"Yes doctor," Luke replied in a sleepy daze.

"Please forgive my husband, he'd taken his medication before we got the call, I was lucky to get him in the car."

Cristina interjected quickly.

"Well, Jeff is going to be just fine. The bullet didn't hit anything vital. He'll be really sore for a while, out of work for a few weeks and will need physical therapy since it struck the muscle on his right shoulder. He did lose a lot of blood, but he's stable and out of surgery. We'll keep him here for a few days and right now we have him sedated, so he won't be awake until morning at least." The doctor informed Cristina and Luke with a few glances her way. She felt helpless.

"May we go see him?" Emily asked stepping up next to Cristina.

"Family only." The doctor informed her.

"This is Jeff's girlfriend, he was protecting her when he was shot," Cristina informed the doctor. Emily hadn't thought of using the term girlfriend with the doctors around, but she wasn't sure she was ready for that.

"In that case, yes you may see him, but for a few minutes." The doctor gestured for her to follow him.

"It's ok, go. We'll be here." Cristina nodded and pulled a seat up next to Luke placing her head on his as they gripped hands.

"Thank you," Emily said as she followed the doctor out of the waiting area and through the double doors and down the hall. She glanced at a clock that hung on the wall and was shocked to see that it was one in the morning.

"Here we are Emily." The doctor opened the door and she was frozen at the sight before her. Jeff looked so small, like a child lying in the bed. He was wearing the customary hospital gown and was covered with a light blue knit blanket. She made her feet move towards the man that saved her life. She looked down on his handsome face and was scared by how pale he looked. He had a light pink, red color around his mouth which looked more like a rust color than anything else.

"What's around his mouth doctor?" Emily asked.

"Oh, that is just a little blood, but I assure you, he'll be just fine," the doctor said.

Emily looked back to the sleeping man and she leaned down and kissed him softly on the lips. "You're one of a kind Jeff," she whispered in his ear. She kissed his forehead and squeezed his hand. She was falling for the big burly sweetheart of a man who risked his life for hers, she didn't know anyone who would have done that for her.

"Let's leave him to sleep," the doctor said, she gave Jeff one last glance, turned and left his room. She was determined to be there in the morning when he woke up.

*****

Cristina pushed Luke's chair into Jeff's room and parked him to one side, then she pulled up a chair on the other side. The doctor waited for Emily to leave in the cab she had called before letting them into the room. This doctor had been her and Luke's doctor and had no issues with the two of them hanging in his room for the night. Not that Luke would have had it any other way, even in his drugged state.

"She seems like a nice woman Jeff," Cristina talked softly to him. "Really concerned about you. Rest up big guy." She kissed his forehead and settled into the chair next to her husband after propping his legs up. She rested her head on his shoulder and he rested his head on hers.

The rare sun broke through the window and right into

Cristina's eyes. She could hear the soft conversation between Luke and Jeff so she kept her eyes closed.

"What compelled you to do it man?" Luke asked.

"Something in me wanted to protect her more than my own life. There's something about her, I can't put my finger on," Jeff replied hoarsely.

"Love at first shooting," Luke kidded.

"Yeah man." Jeff laughed lightly. "You fell in love at first hand shake man, you can't talk."

"Yeah, that was one hell of a hand shake though," Luke replied softly. Cristina wanted to laugh but she would be given away and she knew the men needed to talk.

"Ain't that the truth." Jeff laughed and she couldn't stay in her uncomfortable position any longer. She had just been released from that place the morning before, and the hospital was starting to feel like a second home.

"Good morning sunshine," Luke said as she lifted her head from his shoulder and kissed her.

"Morning. Jeff, how are you feeling?" she asked standing and stretching out her sore back.

"Like I've been shot." Jeff laughed. "Could feel worse I suppose, the medication they have me on is pretty good. I was seeing a few extra of you two when I opened my eyes this morning, it was frightening." Jeff laughed.

"Yeah, seeing more than one of this big guy would have anyone cowering in the corner." Cristina laughed.

"So, do you know what happened after I was shot, where is Alan?" Jeff asked.

"A bystander killed him." They all turned to the sound of Emily as she entered the room. Cristina watched the smile spread across Jeff's face and turned to see the softening of the one Emily gave him.

"Good, how are you, I didn't hurt you when I fell on you did I?" Jeff asked, he sounded so concerned.

"No, I'm fine thanks to you. How are you feeling?" Emily asked but before Jeff could answer Cristina interjected.

"Luke come with me to the cafeteria, let's get some breakfast." She didn't wait for a response but lowered the legs on his chair, unlocked the wheels and wheeled him through the door giving one last look at Jeff as he smiled at Emily with such warmth.

Cristina scurried out the door letting it close behind them before she started walking to the cafeteria. "What was that about Cris?" Luke asked.

"Well, I wanted to give them some privacy, and I really need something to eat." She laughed.

"Ok," Luke agreed and it looked to Cristina that he was enjoying the ride.

*****

Jeff stared at Emily for the longest time. Her hair was down and framed her face before hanging to her hips; she wore jeans and a pink t-shirt and looked as if she hadn't slept all night. "I'm feeling pretty good knowing you're alright."

"Why did you do it Jeff, he could have killed you." Emily squeezed his hand as tears streamed down her face.

"Honestly, I couldn't live with myself if something had happened to you," Jeff replied.

"But you don't even know me," she replied with a shaky voice.

"I know enough to care for your safety, I have liked you since I met you weeks ago at church."

"You never said anything," she said softly. Jeff took a deep breath before he replied, gathering his thoughts.

"I knew you were with someone and I'm a pretty shy person." He smiled at her.

"Oh sure, I'm seeing how shy you are." Emily smiled a little, then suddenly leaned down and planted a soft kiss on his lips. She moved to stand back up but he clasped his arms around her and deepened the kiss. She felt heavenly in his arms, so soft and the smell of strawberries clung to her hair as it fell around his face. He released her and she stood with a red crimson blush to her cheeks.

"Ok then." She laughed. "I'm so glad you're going to be ok. If I can help with anything don't hesitate to ask," she told him.

"Oh, I intend to." He smiled, winked and raised an eyebrow at her making her blush even more.

"You're such a tease." She laughed.

"But I plan to deliver Emily," Jeff replied.

"I look forward to it." Emily smiled shyly at him.

"Good." Jeff smiled, "Well, we'll need to go to dinner when I get released."

"Oh Jeff, I'm so sorry." Emily began to cry and he pulled on the hand he held and gently tugged her into his chest.

"Em, you did nothing wrong." Jeff rubbed her back and she

gingerly leaned into his chest.

"I did, I never should have left him, I knew he was starting to lose it, it would have ended with me and you never would have gotten hurt, it's all my fault," she cried.

"Emily look at me." Jeff ordered softly and she lifted her eyes to meet his. "I say again, you did nothing wrong, he was losing it but you wouldn't have been the end of it. He would have gotten to another woman. I'm glad you left him and I would gladly take another bullet for you if it meant you were safe." Jeff told her firmly and as scary as it was to get shot, and how much pain he was in, he would gladly take another bullet for her.

"You're crazy Jeff. I'm nothing, not worth all of this pain you're in." Emily cried and pressed her face in the crook of his neck as he held her tightly to him.

"You're everything Emily, everything. You're worth everything to me, you just have no idea." He whispered in her ear. He knew it was too soon to tell her this but, he was running out of time and after losing one woman he loved, and his parents, he wasn't letting her go so easily.

"Oh Jeff, no one has ever said anything like that to me, not even my folks." Emily cried.

"Everything will be just fine Emily, I promise." Leaving his right arm to rest, he squeezed her tight to his chest as the pain started to make itself known.

*****

Luke and Cristina drove Jeff to their place to stay for a few days after he was released four days later. Jeff was mostly drugged up and half loopy with his arm in a sling that Luke couldn't help but laugh at. Luke knew Cristina was going to have her hands full for a few days with two crippled men under one roof, but they all agreed that he needed rest, care, and good meals. Cristina was more than capable as long as Luke stopped his whining.

"I'm making meatloaf for dinner, any objections?" Cristina asked as they pulled into the garage.

"Nope," they said in unison. Cristina jumped out of the car and opened Jeff's door since he sat behind her then she walked over to Luke who was clambering out of the car awkwardly.

"Good." Cristina laughed and wrapped her arms around Luke's waist to help him hop up the stairs and inside to the couch while Jeff followed behind closing the doors. Cristina let him drop into the couch and helped Jeff lower himself into the recliner.

"Thanks Cris, have I told you how awesome you are?" Jeff asked as he relaxed into the couch.

"Nope, but keep it up. You two relax a while and I'll get dinner started in a couple hours then we can all crash." Cristina smiled and left them sitting in the living room. Luke heard her walk upstairs and start a bath, she had been doing better about taking it easy and learning to relax. She was also starting to keep a few foods down, like meatloaf which they'd had already on the night Jeff got shot.

"So, I hope you don't mind, I gave Emily the address," Jeff said sheepishly.

"Not a problem, will she be here for dinner?" Luke asked knowing if she was they needed to let Cristina know so she would make enough.

"No, she did say she would swing by after work tomorrow and then we have a date for Friday at the same restaurant,"

Jeff smiled at him. Luke was so excited that Jeff was starting to look happier even though he had to get shot for it to work out. Emily had been to the hospital every day and was there the morning he and Cristina brought him home.

"Well, I called Rick and let him know what happened so he'll cover for you the rest of the week. Cristina said she'll drive you to and from the location on her way to work every day. So you just take it easy." Luke informed Jeff of the plan he and Cristina figured out on the way to bring Jeff home. "Oh, and you're only allowed to supervise, no lifting or Rick will call Cristina to come pick you up."

"What, I'm not five here; and it sounds like a great plan. So I'll go back on Monday, sounds perfect," Jeff replied sleepily. Luke laughed as Jeff's eyes fluttered closed and a soft snore escaped. Luke flipped his legs up on the couch and relaxed for a nap himself. He only had two more weeks until the casts came off, but he was still feeling a little pain from his wrist. He was a little tired from staying up with his cookie-tossing wife the night before.

Luke woke with a jolt when he heard a pan clatter to the floor in the kitchen. He jumped up and hopped to where his wife stood staring at the pan. Then he watched as she doubled over with laughter and Luke was so confused. He knew her emotions were going haywire, but this was off the charts.

"What's wrong?" Luke asked as the tears started streaming down her face.

"I, um, my hands were wet when I picked up the hot pan that had been sitting on the stove and apparently on the burner I turned on for the potatoes. I turned on the wrong burner, burned my hand and it's sadly funny." Cristina laughed harder and he noticed her clutching her hand. Luke hopped over to her and put her hand underneath the cold water. When he checked her hand it looked a little pink but nothing bad. She had been forgetful at times, and would have odd little emotional snaps which always worried Luke.

"How's your hand?" Luke asked concerned.

"Fine, fine, it's ok." She stopped laughing and pulled Luke into a tight embrace and pulled his lips to hers. Her kiss was like fire through his body, it had been a while since they had really kissed and now he couldn't stop himself. He pulled her flush to his chest and she clung tightly to his neck as they deepened the kiss. He was about to scoot them to their room when Jeff interrupted with his impeccable timing.

"What's all the laughing about," Jeff said, "Oh man, get a room."

"Intended to Jeff, go away." Luke growled.

"No, sorry, dinner will be ready in about twenty minutes, go watch something." Cristina laughed, her face red from embarrassment. "Now scram," she insisted, apparently getting hold of herself.

Luke kissed her on the forehead and hopped out of the kitchen to leave his wife to make dinner. Jeff followed behind and they settled back into their chairs. "What's with your wife man?" Jeff whispered as Luke heard Cristina clinking away in the kitchen.

"Well, she's carrying twins so her emotions are twice as wonky as most pregnant women, not to mention they have odd emotional spurts," Luke replied.

"Ah, well in that case, I can't wait to have a wife and get her pregnant then, because that was pretty funny." Jeff laughed.

"You're such a nerd Jeff."

"Takes one to know one," Jeff said mockingly.

"You're such a child." Luke threw a small pillow at him nailing him in the head.

"Me a child, you're the one that just threw a pillow at me." Jeff laughed and Luke ignored him and flipped on the TV to see the movie The Cowboys on AMC with John Wayne. It was at the part where one of the boys gets killed and they were dealing with the funeral.

"Such a good but sad movie," Jeff said softly. He and Jeff had grown up with a lot of westerns but most were with John Wayne.

"Dinner's ready." Cristina called from the kitchen and Luke flipped the TV off and hopped his way to the kitchen to take his seat. Cristina pulled the chair out for Jeff and took her seat next to Luke. They said grace and began to eat the meatloaf, mashed potatoes, green beans and corn she had made them.

CHAPTER 22

Emily paced the bedroom wearing a pair of jeans, a fitted blue t-shirt and a light jacket. She would be picking Jeff up this time and going back to the Mexican restaurant where everything took place the week before. She had visited him most every day since and was falling in love with his sweet demeanor. He was always sweet to Cristina and Luke, and the soft sweet smiles he always managed to pass to her made her feel like a school girl all over again with her first crush.

"Emily, you almost ready?" Jackie asked as she slipped her head into the room.

"Yeah, just trying to calm myself," Emily replied still pacing as Jackie came in the room and took a seat on the bed.

"Park it." Jackie instructed her pointing at the bed. Emily complied and planted her behind where Jackie pointed and crossed her arms in front of her chest like an angry teenager.

"Do you like him?" Jackie asked softly.

"Yes."

"Then why are you pacing like you're about to have spikes shoved under your nails?" Jackie asked scrunching her eyebrows together, showing her age.

"Well, I'm worried he will end up being like all the rest but I'm falling hard for him." Emily admitted.

"Do you ever see Cristina shy away from him? Have I worried about him being with you? Have you heard anything but nice things through town about the man?"

Jackie rambled.

"Well," Emily said shyly.

"Of course not. He goes to church most every Sunday, owns his own business, will be an "Adopted" Uncle within a few months of twins, he has already set up two savings accounts for the little buggers., And the way he shielded you from the bullet that was obviously meant for you should tell you he's not like the rest. He's not like any other man that has been in your life sweetheart. Jeff is a prime catch, trust me, had I been any younger that man would be mine. But he's only a few years older than Sam, and that would just feel way odd." Jackie spouted.

"Ok, I see what you mean," Emily huffed. She never felt scared around Jeff, and really that's what scared her the most. She felt completely at peace when she was with him; he made her smile, laugh and feel protected. She was in awe of the shy reserved happy, handsome man.

"Well good. Now you go pick up that award winning man and feed him. Don't be afraid of your feelings, he's not the type to laugh at you but you may mind he feels the same way." Jackie stood and ushered her out the door. Emily knew that Jeff had taken a liking to her since they had first met, but she was with Alan and knew the consequences for looking at another man, now she knew the consequences of leaving Alan. She shuddered at the thought of what could have happened if she would have gone back with the man after she was released from the hospital.

Emily said good bye to Jackie, carefully backed Jackie's SUV out of the garage and made her way across town to pick Jeff up from Cristina and Luke's place. It was six-thirty and the roads were pretty clear, the sky was cast with beautiful pinks and blues as the sun set and cast its lingering rays across the   scattered clouds.

She pulled up in front of the house and got out taking deep breaths, it was oddly normal for her to pick the man up. That was always how she had done things, but with Jeff, it seemed very odd. He was nothing like her father or any of her exes. She figured her brother, whom she didn't think about often, would have been an abuser if he hadn't got himself thrown in jail just to get away from their family. She hated him for leaving her, she hadn't spoken to him since last Christmas and she was starting to feel pretty bad about that fact.

She hated her family, she couldn't help it, but watching Cristina, Luke, Jeff, and Jackie, she was starting to get a feel for a normal family. She was getting addicted to them all and finding herself thinking about them often and smiling. Her and Cristina had somewhat become friends, Luke had already started picking at her about how crazy tall she was and how shy she seemed to be.

"Good evening Emily, please come in and have a seat, Jeff will be down in a minute," Cristina said answering the door before she could knock. She took a seat on the lush couch and watched as Cristina darted upstairs. Luke was nowhere to be seen but she heard the boisterous laughter from above along with conversation.

"Jeff, stop squirming, I can't get your shirt on you if you keep moving," Cristina said.

"Damn woman, I'm not a stuffed animal, my arms don't move that way," Jeff called back to her.

"You sure ain't, they don't talk back," Emily heard Cristina huff loudly.

"Jeff relax and let my wife dress you, it's killing me seeing her hands all over you," Luke yelled.

"You know Emily is downstairs and she can hear you pouting Jeff," Cristina said.

"Crap woman, why didn't you say something," Jeff said and Cristina and Luke started laughing and Emily tried not to but covered her mouth to muffle it.

"There, you look stunning for you Jeff," Cristina laughed.

"Why thank you, learn how to put a shirt on someone else before those two come along. Geez, I thought you were going to take my arm off. Next time I wouldn't have worn a shirt had I known what a crazy person you are." Jeff huffed and Cristina and Luke busted out laughing as Jeff stomped down the stairs. Emily jumped to her feet as he came into view and he looked amazing even with the sling his right arm rested in. He wore jeans, which he hoped Cristina hadn't help him get into but she knew she probably had, and a blue button up shirt with long sleeves, the left sleeve was rolled up and left unbuttoned with a white t-shirt underneath. He was mouthwatering and she was now wishing he hadn't wore a shirt at that moment seeing how the white t-shirt stretched over his vast muscles.

"Hey." Jeff smiled. He was so handsome Emily thought she was going to combust with the yearning to touch him.

"Hi." She smiled at him and she was pretty sure her eyes were not concealing her current emotions because he smiled even wider. "Ready to eat?" she asked him trying to change the current situation. He walked over to her and pulled her into his chest with his left arm, which was a little uncomfortable with his right arm in the way, but the heat radiating off of him was amazing. She leaned up and kissed his lips and tried to pull away but was stopped by the force of his grip around her as he deepened the kiss. When he finally released her they were breathless.

"Yes, I'm famished, lets, um go eat," Jeff finally replied.

*****

Jeff followed Emily out to Jackie's SUV pulling the door closed behind him. He watched as her hips swayed in the tight jeans that ended at her hips, the plain blue t-shirt looked mouthwatering on her playing up her simple curves. Her strawberry scent clung to him and he was awfully glad he loved the taste and smell of strawberries already, otherwise he would quickly change his mind.

Emily had the passenger door open for him, which he would normally protest, but he smiled and climbed into the car. She leaned over and buckled him in, "I could get used to you being strapped down." Emily laughed.

"Really, that can be arranged you know." Jeff kidded but the look in her eyes told him she didn't find it funny, but something she had been considering already. She leaned down and planted a chaste kiss on his lips and quickly pulled away and closed the door. He watched as she walked around the SUV and jumped in buckling herself in. "I think I could get used to you being strapped down," Jeff said softly and Emily gave him a sideways smile that warmed his heart. He was not a dominating person, but the idea of playing made him smile. What kind of man would he be not to think about his woman in a good way.

"Shall we try La Casa Fiesta again?" she asked. They hadn't spoken about it, but it was a good idea to recapture their first date, hopefully this time without a visit to the ER.

"Sounds amazing," Jeff replied. He looked out at the sky with all the different colors and he was happy, how could he not be, he was in a car with a woman who had made him do an emotional three-sixty. She was shy, funny, smart, attractive, tall, a pretty good driver so far, tentative and seemed to like him. Jeff did worry that she was just being nice to him since he had taken a bullet for her, but he hoped that wasn't the case.

"Well, good. So what kind of music do you like, other than the classical I've heard twice so far playing in your truck?" Emily asked.

"I love Christian Rock, the band Skillet is amazing and can't forget about Seventh Day Slumber. But I also enjoy country, bluegrass and jazz." Jeff laughed. "How about you?"

"I have never heard Bluegrass, but sounds interesting. I love most music with the exception of rap; the hard core cursing and vulgarity of the lyrics bother me." Emily admitted and Jeff had to agree with her. He had gone through a rebellious stage when he was in high school after his girlfriend was killed. He had listened to all sorts of crazy rap, but he wasn't a real fan, he just did it to drive his parents nuts and drown out his own pain.

"Nice," Jeff commented and he was surprised that they were already pulling into the parking lot of the restaurant. Jeff reached down and unbuckled his seatbelt and held it as he let it slide into place as Emily pulled into a spot. She killed the engine and quickly climbed out to come and open his door which, try as he might, he couldn't reach the handle. "Thank you ma'am," Jeff said as he wiggled himself out of the SUV trying not to jostle his shoulder. It was already starting to hurt even with the medication he had taken before he left.

"You're most welcome sir." Emily smiled and took his proffered arm as they headed inside.

"Did I tell you how stunning you look?" Jeff asked as they walked through the propped open door.

"In these jeans? I think you're blind man." Emily laughed, but he could see the blush forming on her cheeks. Jeff couldn't help but notice how relaxed she seemed, she was smiling, and actually talking without too many reservations. He was completely spell bound by the woman he walked next to.

"Yes and yes, I see only you, the most beautiful woman on the planet." Jeff said softly leaning into her ear.

"Back at you," Emily smiled.

"You think I'm a beautiful woman, oh dear, we are in trouble." Jeff laughed and Emily joined him.

"Table for two?" the young hostess asked as they reached the desk.

"Please," Jeff answered. "Do you have a spot near the corner so, um, no one can walk behind me by chance?" Jeff asked softly.

"Oh my God, are you the couple from last week, oh my God you are. Wow, man you're brave, and you my dear are one lucky woman." The young lady gushed and lead them to a corner table in the bar.

"I know I'm one lucky woman," Emily replied to the hostess as she pulled out Jeff's chair so he could sit.

"Thank you Miss." Jeff replied and looked back to Emily who was taking her seat with a fresh blush on her cheeks.

"You're one strong man," Emily said meeting his gaze.

"And you my dear Emily, are a strong woman," Jeff replied and smiled. The waiter came by and took their drinks and orders since they had both eaten there many times before.

"So, when you're not taking bullets for women, what do you like to do for fun?" Emily asked.

"I don't know, the bullet was pretty fun, and look at how I get women swooning over me, helping me out." Jeff laughed, "But really, I enjoy basketball, swimming, hiking, and the occasional bike ride, when it's not raining of course. How about you?"

"Well, I enjoy photography, hiking, biking of course, and swimming most of the time. I wanted to be on the swim team in high school, but," she paused and he watched as she took a deep breath before she continued, "I was usually covered in bruises so, I couldn't." Emily replied revealing parts of her past to Jeff.

"What do you mean, if you don't mind me asking?" Jeff asked sipping on his long island iced tea.

"Well, my father had a short temper and my siblings and I were always the brunt of the impact if our mother wasn't around or conscience enough to deal with it; my mother was, is an alcoholic. My sister committed suicide when she was a freshman and my brother got himself thrown in jail when he was a senior. I was the baby and I stayed around until I could move out and go to college to study to be a teacher." She paused again, closed her eyes again and continued, "After that I had one abusive boyfriend after the next. That was my life." Emily spouted off her life and Jeff was utterly saddened by the life this beautiful woman had.

"So, why aren't you already married Jeff?" Emily asked softly, confusion clear on her face.

"Well, I lost my girlfriend in a car wreck in high school, I was driving and we were hit by a drunk driver. Ever since then I have been withdrawn into myself and focused on my studies. Both of my parents died when I was in my first year of college and now Luke is all I have, or well Cristina now you can say, and soon two little babies to steal my attention." Jeff smiled. The idea of babies was such a happy thought. He had wanted a family but it had been proving impossible.

"Wow, that is crazy." Emily sighed. "What happened to the other driver?"

"He was killed on impact and since he had smacked into the passenger side, my girlfriend died instantly as well, or that's what the doctors told me at least." Jeff still hurt from the thought of the accident, but he was healing.

"That is so sad. I'm sorry Jeff." Emily reached across the table and placed her right hand in his left.

"It's ok. I'm ready to start over," Jeff admitted.

"Yeah, me too. Jackie told me that men are not what I was raised to believe and after meeting you, I'm starting to agree with her." Emily smiled at him and he squeezed her hand.

"I hope that you'll give me the chance to keep proving her right then." Jeff smiled and pulled her hand to his lips and kissed the top.

"No worries," Emily said softly.

The waiter came, brought their meals and they ate in silence. Jeff was completely enthralled by the woman sitting across from him. She had such a hard life yet she was still smiling and still worked hard to better her life. Jeff wanted so much, to give her the wonderful life that he had grown accustomed to and not let her feel the pain of her past as much as he could. He wasn't going to let her go without a fight, and she was worth fighting over whether she believed it or not.

*****

"Hey, are you, alright?" Luke asked sitting on the tub in their bathroom. Cristina had been tossing her cookies since Jeff and Emily left for dinner and he was starting to worry.

"Yeah, dinner stayed a little longer than it had been, maybe soon I'll be able to keep my food down completely," Cristina said softly pulling herself to her feet. Luke passed her a glass of water and watched her take tentative sips. "At least it seems to be bothering me only at night now, granted it is cutting into my sleep."

"Yeah, you're starting to get those circles around your eyes again," Luke commented and opened his arms to embrace his wife. She had started to show ever so slightly and her form fitting jeans no longer fit, but she made a few knit bands to help hold her jeans up so she wouldn't have to purchase new clothes other than a few knit skirts she had bought.

"I love you," Cristina said into his neck then pulled away to brush her teeth.

"I love you too, my sweet wife." He hopped next to her and brushed his teeth, then he tucked her under his arm and planted a kiss on the top of her head. "Come to bed with me," he said and started for the bedroom.

"You know I have to stay up for when Jeff gets home." Cristina pouted and Luke glanced at the clock and relaxed since she wouldn't have to fight too much longer to stay awake.

"Good thing Jeff should be coming home soon." Luke informed her and she smiled. "Still, come lay with me until he gets home." He burrowed into the bed and Cristina followed behind him snuggling into his side, using his shoulder as her pillow; she was his perfect fit.

Luke stayed awake relishing the feel of his wife's light steady breathing, finally sleeping. Luke heard the door open on the first floor then close followed by light footsteps. Luke saw Jeff stumble into the room across from theirs and remove his sling, "Let her sleep, I'll be fine until morning," Jeff said and pulled their door closed. Luke could hear him fumbling around but he wasn't worried about his friend tonight, he was home safe. He looked a little tipsy but Luke knew it wouldn't be uncomfortable for him to sleep in his clothes one night; Cristina needed sleep and she was his priority now. Luke pulled a blanket over the two of them and let sleep claim him.

Luke woke to the sound of a shower and humming, a sound he hadn't heard in a while. Luke scrambled out of bed and hopped into the bathroom and leaned against the door frame just as Cristina was stepping out. She was such a beautiful woman, her hair fell in wet locks down her back, her curves were mouthwatering.

"What are you doing?" Cristina pouted reaching for her towel.

"Admiring the view," Luke admitted and she smiled and blushed.

"You're like a boy in high school sneaking into the ladies locker room to get a peek," Cristina scolded him with a smile.

"Yep." He smiled at her.

"I'm glad you're awake, I could still hear Jeff snoring when I woke up about fifteen minutes ago, I think we need to talk." Cristina said pulling a brush through her wet hair to tame it in a hair tie with her towel snuggly wrapped around her.

"What's up?" Jeff asked hopping to the sink to brush his teeth.

"Let's get dressed, then we'll talk." She smiled, "Nothing bad." Luke nodded as Cristina walked into the adjoining walk-in closet. Luke finished brushing his teeth, took care of his bladder , washed his hands and hopped into the closet to take a seat.

"Here, let's get you into a pair of shorts shall we, the boxers are a bit distracting," Cristina laughed and Luke smiled flirtatiously.

"I wouldn't mind a good distraction this morning," Luke smirked.

"Yeah, well, we do need to talk, make breakfast then I have to get to work before eleven today, for a few hours," Cristina said pushing the legs of his shorts over his feet. She pulled him to his feet and pulled the shorts up around his waist as he pulled on a t-shirt. "You're still sexy as sin." Cristina laughed and he pulled her into his chest. She had pulled on a dress for the day and it hung loosely on her.

"You, my dear beautiful wife, are sexy as sin." Luke smiled at her and planted a soft kiss on her lips. "Shall we talk in here or would you like to take this conversation to bed." Luke wiggled his eyebrows at her and she laughed then slapped him playfully on the chest.

"Oh you," Cristina laughed and walked out of the closet, he hopped after her and was amazed to find her taking a seat on the bed. Luke hopped on the bed next to her and pulled her into his lap, she looked so distraught, he didn't understand why.

"What's on your mind?" Luke asked lightly running a finger up and down her arm trying not to catch her with his cast.

"We need to talk about what happened?" Cristina said calmly, but he could hear a slight tremor in her voice that told him it wasn't about his accident, but about what happened to her.

"Not if you aren't ready," Luke said trying to avoid the conversation that had been haunting him since he got her back. He had endured her silent tears most nights, calmed her racing heart and held her to his chest when her body began to shake from the tremors that rocked through her when he knew she was dreaming about those five weeks.

"Well, I'm not ready to talk about everything, but I'm still wondering what happened when I was rescued," she admitted.

"What do you want to know?" Luke asked.

"I keep wondering why me? Why would an ex-boyfriend be so driven to kidnap me, it makes no sense whatsoever. Then there is this whole rescue thing by my father. I'm wondering how he did it, how long had he known where I was and then why didn't he take me straight to the hospital? I just don't understand why all of this happened and now I have twins growing inside of me and neither one of us have twins in or family." Cristina started to cry, and Luke knew it wasn't something she reveled in, she wasn't a cry baby but her emotions were a constant torment for her.

"Well as far as Eric and the obsession, you're one fine looking woman, funny, smart who wouldn't want you all to their selves, as for the twins, no one should question it. People have twins all the time and they could have come from your father's side, who knows." Luke took a deep breath as Cristina nodded. "As far as the rescue and your father, we know nothing other than what he told us that night along with the crazy family story."

"Yeah, I'm thinking that crazy wolf pack had just made a home in my woods is all, and the rocks were actually deposited in that spot to get them out of the way," Cristina said.

"Yeah I agree, that was just way too odd, but I can't not be grateful that your father was there that day, I don't know what I would have done if I had lost you," Luke admitted and kissed her forehead.

"But, we hadn't really known each other that long." Cristina looked up at him, her eyes red from crying and her lips plump. He leaned down and planted a kiss on her soft lips.

"I already knew we were meant to be together that Sunday when I stole that kiss," Luke smiled at her and rested his forehead on hers.

"You're such a tease," Cristina laughed.

"I always plan to deliver my fair lady." Luke planted a kiss on her forehead. "If we see your father again, we will try and get him to answer those questions that are gnawing at you and I." Luke replied hoping that would ease her mind a little. He really wished he had the answers for her.

"Sounds like a plan. Shall we go eat and see if Jeff is awake?" Cristina asked clambering out of his lap and to her feet.

"I'm getting pretty hungry and since one hunger won't be fed for a little while longer, I'll settle for food." Luke laughed, winked at her and then gently pulled her back onto the bed and kissed her neck up to her jaw and planted several light kisses on her lips, then helped her back to her feet.

"One of these days Luke, one of these days," Cristina scolded him with a bright   smile and left the bedroom.

*****

Cristina poked her head into Jeff's room and found him sound asleep still wearing the clothes her wore for his date. She felt kind of bad about falling asleep last night, but with how good she felt this morning, she wasn't going to let it bother her. She proceeded down the stairs to make oatmeal and toast for breakfast. Toast seemed to stay pretty well on her stomach, so it was safe for her to eat and she smiled to herself.

She heard Luke thumping into the kitchen as she set the water to boil and placed a few slices of bread in the toaster. "Wow, you're a total babe in that dress," Luke complimented her and she could feel the blush rush to her cheeks.

"You're blind, man." Cristina turned to look at her amazing husband, she still couldn't figure out how she got so lucky.

"Blind to the rest of the world maybe, but not to you wife of mine." Luke hopped to her and pulled her into his arms. "You know, my right leg is going to be so much stronger than my left after I get this darn cast off."

"Yep and I'll get to pick on you and your pogo leg." She smirked at him and pulled him into a deep kiss as she waited for the water to boil.

"You two really need to keep it in the bedroom," Jeff cleared his throat.

"Maybe you need to make more noise before you come into another man's kitchen," Luke snapped back pulling from her embrace and hopping to the table.

"Stop grumbling you two, you sound like children. Now sit down and play nice, breakfast will be done really soon." The water had started to boil so she dumped in the oatmeal and mixed it up. Once it was soft and all the water evaporated she added in a little butter and sugar and plopped it into three bowls, placed them on the table then set to work on the toast.

They sat in silence as they ate breakfast, Cristina was still thinking about everything that had happened; the accident with Luke and how she could have lost him, how sick she let herself get and not realizing that it could have risked the lives of her unborn children. And then Jeff's standoff with a crazy obsessed abusive man to protect Emily, who she hoped was planning to stick around. Cristina liked Emily for the most part, she didn't really know her all that well but she figured once she did she would like her since she was only a few years older than her.

Cristina cleaned up the kitchen then helped Jeff get out of his shirts so he could get in the shower. Luke helped him get in and out of his lower clothes and she got the fresh Jeff into a new t-shirt after cleaning his wound. She redressed it with clean bandages according to the doctor's instructions. It was already looking better, she knew one more week and he would start the arm moving process which was bound to be painful for the man. Cristina climbed into her Subaru and headed off to work on that beautiful sunny Saturday morning, pushing her thoughts into a box to handle at a later date.

CHAPTER 23

Emily walked through the small apartment above Jackie's garage that she had built; it had two bedrooms, a bathroom, small kitchen and a small living room. The walls were painted white with a wooden chair rail around the rooms, and Jeff and Luke had done all the work. It had been three months since she and Jeff went on their first date and he had used his body to protect her from her crazed ex-boyfriend. Emily was falling in love, hard and fast, but she wasn't afraid. She had watched how Jeff responded to Cristina over the three months and watched how sweet he was to her as her belly grew larger with the twins she carried. He was such a sweet family oriented man and she was hooked.

"So, what do you think?" Jackie asked as she entered the small apartment.

"It's lovely," Emily answered walking to the window in the living room that looked out into a wooded area behind Jackie's home.

"Glad you like it. So, you and Jeff are getting pretty serious, huh." Jackie prodded elbowing her in the ribs.

"We'll see, I'm not sure how he feels about me, but I think I'm falling in love with the man," Emily replied. She crossed her arms as the chill of fall zipped through the open door.

"Well, if I know the look as well as I think I do, I would say he's pretty smitten with you as well dear," Jackie said placing an arm around her shoulders.

"You really think so?" Emily pleadingly looked at her friend . She wanted it to be true, more than anything.

"Oh, most definitely," Jackie assured her and smiled. "Shall we go pick out some furniture?" Jackie smiled playfully, the woman loved to shop.

"Sure, with the wonderful new job I've had for the past three months, I seem to have a fatter bank account." Emily laughed and they headed out of the garage apartment. She pulled her jacket tight around her as the rain began to fall. It was mid-August and Fall was always fast to approach in their small neck of the woods, and the rain always made it feel colder.

"So, are we headed to Bellingham to Ashley Furniture or the American Furniture Warehouse?" Emily asked as Jackie backed out of the garage.

"I was thinking both, and then Wal-Mart. I think you need curtains, sheets, a TV, DVD player, and kitchen stuff. I wish you would let me help you get a car," Jackie spilled.

"You know, I could've always gotten everything from Alan's apartment, Pete said I could since he had no family," Emily informed her friend.

"No, you're starting fresh, nothing crazy from the past when you have such a hot looking future in front of you." Jackie turned quickly and winked at Emily.

"Fine. I'm hoping to find a canopy bed in black, with matching dressers. I'm thinking a futon for the living room, with a vintage looking coffee table, oh, and a glass entertainment center." Emily laughed, she had never gone furniture shopping before and she was getting excited. "I'm thinking I'll do red in the kitchen or red and black, that would look pretty retro, what do you think?"

"I think you're on fire and we'll have that place looking livable in no time," Jackie laughed. It was a forty-five minute drive to Bellingham, but they joked, laughed, sang along with the radio and before she knew it, they were pulling into the parking lot of American Furniture Warehouse.

They spent hours browsing the large collection of furniture before Emily decided on a bedroom set, living room set with a futon that slides in on itself to make a full size bed and a coffee table to match. She was the proud owner of a few bright rugs and a small oval dining room table with two matching chairs. She had chosen neutral colors that would go with anything.

"Wow, I don't even think we need to go to Ashley Furniture, unless you want to for fun," Jackie laughed as the cashier rung up her purchases and Emily almost had a heart attack from the cost of everything.

"I think, um, I think I'm good," Emily stammered as she passed her new credit card to the sales clerk.

"Hey, you aren't going to be out of a job for a while so you can afford this, besides, it's not like you're paying a bunch in rent," Jackie said putting a comforting arm around her shoulders as she signed her name for the thirty-six hundred dollar bill. She had tried not to go overboard with her purchases but Jackie was insistent.

"I'll hold you to that woman," Emily laughed as she tucked the receipt into her purse. Everything she bought today would be delivered on Monday after three so Jackie had already approved her to go home at two-thirty for the delivery.

"You do that, but tonight we're going out to Bob's Bar and having us a good 'ol time." Jackie reminded her of the impending drunken night she was going to partake in at the "Drink to Fall" fest.

*****

Cristina walked slowly down the stairs, her feet and ankles were swollen. She could no longer see her feet since her midsection had expanded to make room for the growing babies. She still had a little over a month to go, but the doctor thought they would need to do a cesarean at thirty-six weeks because of how small her frame was. And the fact that her blood pressure was starting to get high and she still wasn't able to eat as much as she needed to. The babies' heart beats were perfect and they were growing as expected, according to the doctor she just needed to take it easy.

It was Saturday, and she had the house all to herself. Luke had gone back to work after only a week of physical therapy with his wrist and leg. According to Jeff he was doing just fine and building his strength back rather fast. Luke and Jeff were at a hotel they were remodeling and Jeff was back to his old self. Cristina picked up her phone, feeling the need to talk with someone so she called Ray.

"Hello," Ray answered.

"Hey, it's Cristina."

"Oh girl, I know it's you. Silly, how are you doing?" he asked.

"I'm doing alright, the town is about to issue me my own zip code," She laughed.

"Well, from the pictures you keep sending me, I would say so. You're raising their town population up pretty rapidly," Ray laughed. They had been laughing at how it was a population of three hundred before she moved which made it three hundred one. Then when Luke moved back, and now the twins made for three hundred and four people, four of whom were going to be a family.

"Have you seen your father since the wedding?" Ray asked.

"No, and I really wanted to talk to him about what he knew about everything," she replied.

"Are you still having the nightmares?" Ray asked. She had confided in him about her crazy dreams that only seemed to haunt her when she napped and Luke was not with her.

"Yeah, but I'm getting to the point where they don't really bother me as much," Cristina replied softly. They bothered her, but she didn't want anyone to think anything less of her, and she had two little lives depending on her strength.

"Well, you know I'm here for you and when those little buggers are born, I'll get some time off and come visit, no need to stress you out beforehand," Ray laughed. "Besides, since you're not getting the gender of the children until you give birth uncle Ray can't buy anything for them until then," Ray chided. He had given her a hard time about not getting the gender of the babies before she gave birth so he could buy things for them, but she wasn't caving and neither was Luke.

"Come on, you know it will be a grand surprise, and you also know that sometimes the doctors are wrong about the gender anyway, so if I was told I was having girls and you went out and bought a bunch of pink things and we were blessed with boys, wouldn't that be such a pain," She laughed.

"Valid point, but I still have to give you a hard time, now go take a nap or sit down with a big 'ol glass of ice water, prop your feet up and watch a movie. Take it easy and no stressing, Luke would have my head if I got you all worked up," Ray laughed.

"Ain't that the truth," Cristina laughed with him. "Alright, have a great rest of your day and I'll talk to you later."

"You too, bye."

"Bye" she replied and hung up." While heading for the kitchen a knock came from the living room. She paused and clutched the phone tightly in her hand, she couldn't help the panic that still encroached her chest when she was alone. She walked softly to the door and peeked through the peep hole to see Pete standing on her porch. She took a deep breath and opened the door wide for the very familiar police sheriff.

"Pete, how can I help you today?" Cristina asked motioning him to enter. He stepped in and removed his hat, which she had grown accustomed to the men in that town doing upon entering a building or residence.

"How are you feeling Cristina?" he asked softly.

"I'm doing ok, and yourself?" She replied doing the niceties' because she was sure by the sullen look on his face that he had some bad news and she wasn't going to like it.

"Not bad." She watched as he took a deep breath. "The Miller family has requested paternity test for the children and they are making a claim should the test come back conclusive to being their son's." Cristina felt her world stop, how did those people even know who she was, what she looked like and most importantly, how did they know she was pregnant. She felt her knees give out and Pete grabbed her just before she dropped to the floor.

"Can they, can they do that?" she asked as he settled her on to the couch. The tears were streaming down her face. "I mean, what right do they have?" she asked.

"None, but they would be their grandchildren so they've

318

petitioned the court. The judge has not made a final decision on this matter as of yet but he wanted me to warn you. He's reviewing his books to see what grounds they might have to fight any decision he makes," Pete said softly sitting on the chair at the other end of the couch.

"I need, I need to call Luke." Before Pete could say anything Cristina was dialing his number with the phone she still clung to.

"Hey, is everything alright?" Luke answered.

"You need to come home, I'm fine, the babies are fine, you need to come home, Pete is here." She informed him. He was silent for a few moments.

"I'm on my way," he finally answered and the line went dead.

"He's on his way, can I get you anything to drink?" Cristina asked even though she was pretty sure her legs wouldn't work for her yet.

"I'm ok, but I think the better question is, can I get you anything, you're pale as snow." Pete leaned onto his knees toward her with the concerned look of a father.

"I'm ok," Cristina said softly and waited in silence for Luke to come home. He was only working about ten minutes from home, so he would be home very soon. She took deep breaths and focused on slowing her heartbeat. She couldn't handle it if the judge decided to do a paternity test, they had Eric's DNA on file from all the samples they had taken from him and her, but she never thought that his family could have any right to her children.

She heard a truck pull into the drive way, the engine dying, followed by a slamming door and fast footsteps. Her amazing husband bust through the door and dropped to his knees in front of her. Seeing the concerned look on his face broke all resolve she was trying to maintain. He pulled her into a hug as the flood gates broke again. No one said anything as she cried from what Pete had said and the feeling of all the pain she was trying to hide from since she was rescued. Luke rubbed light circles on her back until the violent shudders stopped.

"What's going on?" Luke asked, and she wasn't ready to talk yet, but Pete was there so he could inform him.

"The Miller family has petitioned the courts for a paternity test and they're looking for rights to the children," Pete said softly.

"Can they do that?" Luke asked.

"Well, the judge has the final say, but he's going through all of his law books to see if they have any rights at all since their son was a monster and caused all these problems," Pete said angrily. Cristina felt the tears lessen; having Luke holding her was bringing her strength back. She took a steadying breath and gently sat up and Luke let her as he settled into the couch next to her, but pulled her back to his side.

"We'll have to wait and see," Pete admitted. "You might want to look into lawyers, they might know more."

"Yeah, we'll do that," Luke looked down at her, she knew she looked a mess and she just noticed the sweat and wood smell of her husband. He was covered in wood shavings but was still as handsome as ever.

*****

Luke looked down at Cristina, her eyes were blood red from crying and she felt cold to him. "Are you cold, want the blanket?" Luke asked as he pulled the blanket from the back of the couch. She nodded and he wrapped the blanket around her shivering shoulders. Luke looked at his wife as a few tears escaped from her closed eyes before he turned and looked at Pete.

"Is there anything we can do?" Luke asked, his heart racing. He had chosen to care for the woman next to him, vowed to love and protect her and the unborn children she carried but everything seemed to be crumbling around him and he felt like he was suffocating. That year had been intense and full of changes, heartache and pain, but the last two and a half months had been relatively peaceful.

"Not sure this time. I wanted to come by and let y'all know what has been brought to the judge, he has the final say in everything but we will not know until he decides. Now we get to play the game of "hurry up and wait," you'll have to be patient," Pete said then collected himself and stood.

"Thanks for the heads up Pete," Luke stood and shook the man's hand.

"Yes, thank you," Cristina said, but she made no attempt to stand.

"You two take it easy and I'll let you know what I find out alright," Pete said, Luke nodded and Pete took his leave pulling the door closed behind him.

"What will we do?" Cristina started to cry again and he sat down next to her and pulled her onto his lap.

"We'll get through this together, but don't go borrowing trouble worrying about all of this. Ok, you need to keep calm, let me worry ok, I'm not carrying two beautiful children inside me nor is my blood pressure higher than normal." His kissed her forehead and held her as close as he could with her ever growing belly.

"I love you," Cristina whispered.

"I love you too. I feel like a nap, how about you?" he asked.

"Sure." She laughed and pulled his shirt out from his chest and they watched as it sucked back to his skin from the sweat.

"I'll shower first. Join me?" He pulled her up and cradled her against his chest.

"Sure," she smiled up at him and he carried her up the stairs to the shower.

*****

Jeff locked everything up for the weekend and decided he would check on Luke and Cristina after he got a shower. Then he would head to Bob's Bar and have a drink.

Jeff was showered and back on the road within twenty minutes of leaving the hotel they were remodeling. He pulled into the driveway of his best friend's home and jumped out. The living room light was on and he could see movement so he knew he was good to come calling. He knocked on the door and a minute later Luke opened the door.

"Hey man, what's up?" Luke asked ushering him inside.

"Came to see how y'all were doing and see if you guys wanted to come to Bob's for some pizza?" Jeff replied as he spotted Cristina sitting on the couch.

"Yeah, I think that's what we need." Luke turned to face Cristina. "What do you think? Let's get away for a few hours and try and relax a bit?"

"Yeah, sure, help me up so I can get dressed," Cristina

smiled. Luke walked over and lifted her to her feet, Jeff still couldn't get over how big she looked. He knew twins made the woman look larger but it was like the woman was carrying triplets with her small frame. Luke planted a kiss on Cristina's lips and Jeff watched as she waddled up the stairs.

"How is she doing?" Jeff whispered when he heard the door close upstairs.

"She's tired but doing better," Luke said solemnly.

"What happened today?" Jeff asked crossing his arms."

"Pete came by, the bastard's parents want claim to the children."

"What, that's ridiculous." Jeff's hushed anger was apparent.

"I know, Pete's not sure how the judge will rule, but we're hoping no one needs to know other than us four," Luke replied.

"I'll be praying man," Jeff said and the door upstairs opened again.

"Thanks man," Luke replied patting him on the shoulder. "Let me grab my wallet," Luke said and walked into the kitchen. He was back before Cristina made her way down the stairs.

"Girl, you're looking good," Jeff commented. She had pulled on a pair of jeans, a very large t-shirt and ballet slippers.

"Oh you," Cristina swatted at him as she walked to the door.

"You're such a ray of sunshine Cristina, honest," Jeff said with a big smile and he watched as the corners turned up into a bright smile. "There she is, dimples and all."

"Hey, no flirting with my wife," Luke thumped him on the back and Cristina laughed and walked out the door. Luke lightly pushed Jeff out the door so he could lock up. Jeff watched as Luke lifted Cristina into the front seat carefully and then pulled himself into the back and pulled the doors closed.

Jeff drove the few minutes to Bob's Bar and helped get Cristina out of his large truck that he regretted taking instead of their car. Jeff took note of all the people that were there on a Saturday night, and of black Ford Escape that was parked near the entrance as they walked in. Jeff held the door open for Cristina and Luke and he noticed how careful Luke was with her and smiled. Jeff knew how much Luke loved Cristina and it made him so happy to see his friend finally find his perfect match.

They walked in and was immediately assaulted by hello's and how are you's.

"Jeff." He knew that voice, he turned to the right and saw Emily approaching him.

"Hey," he replied and gave her a chaste kiss on the lips when she hugged him. "How are you doing?" he asked her. He couldn't help but take notice of the tight jeans she wore and the bright red halter top that gave him a perfect view of her strong, amazingly soft shoulders. He wondered how she could handle wearing such a thing in the weather they kept having.

"I'm doing pretty well, Jackie and I went shopping for furniture today to go into that garage apartment you and Luke helped complete." Emily smiled up at him, she was pretty tall and he noticed she was wearing heels but still wasn't as tall as him.

"I'm glad, did you like how everything came together?" he asked tucking her into his side while making his way to the tables that Jackie, Luke and Cristina were sitting at. He noticed that Cristina looked like she was ready to drop but was enjoying her conversation with Jackie.

"I loved it, I swear you're a genius," Emily smiled up at him and his heart pounded in his chest.

"Surely not, but I'm good at what I do," he smiled and tickled her in the ribs lightly, as she giggled and took a seat by Jackie as he settled himself in one next to her. She was radiant, her wavy hair was pulled up into a clip and looked wild yet very sexy.

"So has everything settled with our soon to be new neighbor? Do we know who it will be yet?" Cristina was talking with Jackie, Luke hadn't told Cristina that Jeff was and had finished the process of purchasing.

"Oh yeah, everything is taken care of, I think you'll like your new neighbor but I could be wrong," Jackie smiled at Cristina then looked at Jeff quickly.

"Well, who is it?" Cristina asked, dropping her hand on the table then winced from the slap it made. Luke pulled her palm to his lips, kissed it and she blushed. Jeff clasped Emily's hand under the table and she smiled at him.

"Me," Jeff said and smiled at Cristina who turned in shock.

"You, hey did you know about this?" She turned to Luke who had this look of pure shame, bright red cheeks and a big smile on his face. "You could have told me," Cristina pouted but smiled at Jeff. Luke waved for the waitress and ordered a round for everyone and a water for Cristina. The waitress brought the drinks and Luke stood.

"Ladies, oh and you to Jeff," Luke smiled and laughed. "To

my best friend, congrats on the new land and may you be a quiet neighbor because I'll have wee babies sleeping here soon." Luke laughed and they all toasted.

"When are you going to start building?" Cristina asked.

"What makes you think I'm going to rebuild?" Jeff asked with a smirk.

"Oh Jeff, I know you want to build that house you've been talking about." Jeff glanced quickly at Emily who was engrossed in conversation with Jackie. "Oh, sorry, I would forget my head if it weren't attached," she said softly.

"It's ok," Jeff smiled and left the question hanging in the air for a later date.

They all chatted, laughed and ate lots of pizza. Jeff was surprised at how much Cristina was able to eat, especially since she still hadn't been able to eat all that much. By the end of the night Cristina was dozing in Luke's arms and Emily was resting her head on his shoulder but in her drunken state her hands were lightly stroking up and down his leg. Which was making it really hard to concentrate on the conversation he was having with Jackie, but he finally placed a gentle hand on hers to stop her torment, since they weren't married, he wasn't going there yet.

"I think it's time we call it a night," Jeff said standing slowly, helping Emily to her feet.

"I think you're right," Luke said and carefully helped Cristina to her feet. The bar had died down and most of the patrons had gone home.

"Yeah, so glad we didn't drink much, but I think poor Emily here has had a few too many, I have never seen her so relaxed to drink like that," Jackie said. "Can you help me get her to the car?" she asked and he nodded and passed his keys to Luke so he could get Cristina in the truck.

Jeff walked Emily to the SUV and Jackie climbed in quickly. Jeff waited for the woman to unlock the door and held Emily tight in his arms. "Jeff," Emily said.

"Yes."

"I love you," Emily informed him and looked up at him in her drunken daze.

"I'm falling in love with you too," Jeff said softly as he heard the doors unlock. He opened the door, helped her into her seat and buckled her in.

"Really?" she asked him and smiled.

"Really," he smiled back and planted a kiss on her lips. He told the ladies good night and closed the door to the SUV. Jeff watched as they drove off, turned to his truck and took his best friends home. Then went home himself to crash and think about what he had just admitted to Emily. He wasn't just falling in love with her, he was in love with her, but he wasn't ready to admit that just yet, but he knew soon he would be.

As Jeff laid awake that night he smiled at how comfortable Emily was around him and she had more of a spark that he ever noticed, but she was a very light drinker which made Jeff laugh. They had grown so close in the past few months, he had already gone to the local jewelry store and purchased a beautiful ring that he hoped to place on her beautiful hand when the time was right. Jeff kept the ring tucked in his pocket everywhere he went as a reminder of the wonderful woman who held his heart. He just hoped she felt the same way about him, he knew she still had a few reservations about some things in her past and all, but he hoped that with time, she would accept his proposal.

Chapter 24

Luke was up late, he couldn't sleep with the due date quickly approaching. Cristina was fast asleep in their bed while he was pacing in the kitchen. He had a duffle packed for her, the car was kept full of gas and the two infant carriers were ready. The nursery was all set up in a Noah's Ark theme with two cribs that would also double as toddler beds and twin beds as they grew; but Luke was relieved by the conversation he, Cristina, and Pete had the week before.

"Luke, Cristina, how are you two holding up?" Pete asked taking a seat at their dining room table.

"Fine, Pete, and yourself?" Luke asked. They had waited a month to hear about the verdict from the judge, but they were getting antsy.

"The judge has been working with other neighboring judges to find a solution for this case," Pete replied.

"Well," Cristina said, her face was a little puffy but she was radiant.

"Well, the judge has decided in favor of you, he felt it was inconsiderate for the family to try what they did when they raised the monster, so to speak. So the judge declined their motion for paternity testing and the other judges ruled with him on it so you two will be fine with your story and these children will grow up as happy as they can," Pete said and stood. Luke was relieved and he watched Cristina slump in her seat, she had been so worried that something would happen and they would take the children from them.

"Thank you for the wonderful news Pete," Luke stood and shook the officers' hand.

"Any time. The secret is safe with me, so no worries. The doctors all believe you two interacted beforehand so they are none the wiser, and that goes double for everyone else I work with, so it is just us who knows the truth and it shall die with me." Pete assured them and placed a comforting hand on Cristina's shoulder. *"Take it easy and I'll come by again to see the little ones after the birth,"* Pete smiled and walked out of the kitchen.

"Can you believe it?" Cristina asked, tears streaming down her face that he hadn't noticed she was trying to restrain.

"I know, God works in mysterious ways to be sure." Luke pulled her into his arms and kissed her forehead.

Luke was reading over the calendar with the days marked off, the doctors had said if she didn't go into labor within the next two days she would need to come in. They had decided she could deliver naturally since she had gotten her blood pressure under control and was taking it easy, with the exception of walking a lot the past two days.

Luke had just sat down with a glass of water when he heard a faint moan, then a subtle whimper. He bolted up the stairs to find Cristina hunched over herself, her hair a mess and soaking wet from sweat. "My, he he, water, he he, just, woo, broke, and ah, contraction, yikes." He clasped her outreached hand and breathed with her through what seemed like the longest contraction of his life. When it had passed he had her in his arms and down the stairs to the car.

After getting her settled in the car, he ran back in to grab the bag and his wallet and keys before heading to the hospital. "How are you doing?" Luke asked as he focused on driving on the wet, winding, empty streets. He looked at the clock which read three-thirty and his wife who was focused completely on breathing.

"Fine," she rasped and he drove faster.

He pulled into a parking space for the maternity wing, jumped out and ran to pull her into his arms to run inside out of the rain that was coming down harder. He walked into the hospital and was quickly greeted by a nurse with a wheel chair and a smile. "So glad I'm here tonight," the young nurse said as she wheeled them into a bright pink room down the hall. "Dr. Collins will be in soon," the nurse said as Luke lifted Cristina onto the bed and the nurse started working with a few monitors and two bands which she wrapped around Cristina's stomach. Luke quickly covered his wife's lower half, thanking his lucky stars she wore a gown to bed. "Here comes another contraction," the nurse said and Cristina's face pinched as she leaned forward clutching Luke's hand so hard he almost winced.

"Almost done, and you're good." The nurse calmed them as Cristina dropped into the bed. "I'll be back," the nurse said and she disappeared out the door. Luke was focused on Cristina who looked pretty pale, but the sweat was soaking her clothes. He reached for the hospital gown and quickly got her out of her wet night gown and into the clean dry hospital gown that was as pink as the room they were in.

"How are you doing, love?" he asked as he kissed her forehead.

"Ok, already really tired, but I'm ok, ready for this to be over," she replied softly and closed her eyes. The doctor zipped in quietly and checked her out.

"She's at seven centimeters, she's doing well, I would say just a few hours longer and we will have these babies out," Dr. Collins assured them with a bright smile. She was a tall woman with short brown hair and she looked like she was jerked from her sleep to be here for the birth.

"Thank you," Cristina said and closed her eyes again.

"Yes, thank you for being here," Luke said to the woman as she stood and removed her gloves. Another contraction rang through Cristina and she clutched his hand once again. When it passed she slumped to the bed.

"I'll have the anesthesiologist in soon with the epidural." Dr. Collins smiled and walked form the room. Luke sat next to his wife listening to the steady fast heart beats of the babies and almost drifted to sleep when she was hit with yet another contraction. He knew it was going to be a long day. After the contraction subsided, he pulled out his phone and sent a text to Jeff who would no doubt be waking up soon to head off to work that Friday morning.

*****

Jeff had just silenced his alarm when his phone alerted him of a new message. He unlocked his phone and saw the message was from Luke, no doubt that the babies were coming. He opened the text and read *she went into labor, we are at the hospital keep the prayers coming.*

Jeff texted him back; *on the prayers, I'll be there soon, I'll bring food.* Jeff got out of bed and pulled on his clothes. It was four in the morning and he sent Rick a message to let him know to take over for the day and headed to the local McDonalds to grab a few breakfast sandwiches.

The drive was light and wet because it was still early and parking was easy since it was a small hospital. Jeff hopped out of his truck and made a run for the door with the food and practically walked head long into a pretty little nurse with bright blue scrubs and the brightest blue eyes he had ever seen. "Oh, sorry about that," Jeff said pulling the hood off his head.

"It's alright, can I help you find someone?" she asked him. She didn't look even twenty yet.

"Sure, yes, Black, Cristina and Luke Black," Jeff said and the nurse nodded and motioned him down the hall. She knocked on the door and Luke answered, he was wearing a t-shirt and jeans but looked super tired.

"Hey man, that was fast," Luke said as Jeff entered the room and took a look at Cristina's small form on the hospital bed wearing a bright pink gown that oddly matched the paint in the room. Her head was turned to face the window and she made no effort to move.

"Yeah, light traffic this time of morning, breakfast?" he asked and took a seat at the head of the bed from Cristina, he didn't want to see any of that going on, and he was starting to wonder if he should even be there. "You sure I should be here?" Jeff looked at Luke anxiously.

"Yeah, but not when we go to delivery and no thank you on the breakfast, too nervous to eat," Luke said taking a seat right next to Cristina and clutching her hand just as she wrenched up. Jeff watched as she and Luke breathed with each other through the contraction and she collapsed back on the bed. She glanced his way with a soft smile but her eyes quickly closed.

A half hour later Jeff was kicked out of the room so that she could get an epidural that he hoped would ease some of her pain. While he sat in the waiting room he sent a text to Emily and then one to Jackie since the women had become close the past few months. Jeff took a seat and started flipping through one of the magazines on the counter, which was about parenting. Jeff was twenty-seven and Emily was twenty-eight and had had one hell of a life, but the diamond ring that was tucked in his pocket was feeling awful heavy at the moment.

They had held off on building the house since Cristina was due so soon and Luke really wanted to help build. He had wanted to wait until the house was built to propose to Emily, he only hoped it wasn't too soon. "Jeff, you can come back in now," Luke called from the room so Jeff got up and entered the bright pink room.

They sat for about three hours, contraction after contraction, and getting kicked out of the room six more times, but Cristina wasn't progressing any and she was looking really pale. He watched as Luke kept an eye out on his wife and the monitors. When Luke froze Jeff followed his gaze. "Call the nurse," Luke shouted then he tried to raise Cristina from her rest, but it wasn't working. The monitors began beeping rapidly as Jeff ran from the room to find the nurse and a doctor while yelling for them to help his friends.

Jeff was kicked out of the room after that and he paced the waiting room as more people began to flood the area. He watched as they rushed Cristina from the room and Luke trailed quickly after them as he was passed a pair of blue scrubs.

Jeff looked at his watch and it was almost nine in the morning when his phone rang.

"Hello," he answered.

"Hey Jeff, it's Emily, how is she doing?" Emily asked. He could hear the sound of an engine in the back ground.

"They rushed her into another room, she wouldn't rise and she had started bleeding, so I, I don't know," Jeff stammered. He wanted to sound strong, but what would he do if something happened to Cristina, or the babies. She had become so dear to him and he knew it would destroy his best friend.

"We're on our way," Emily said soothingly. "Keep praying Jeff, that's all we can do," Emily reminded him. "See you soon," she said and hung up the phone. Jeff closed his eyes, bowed his head and started sending up prayers to keep her and the babies safe. Not fifteen minutes later Emily and Jackie entered the waiting room, Jeff quickly rose and pulled Emily into a tight hug.

"Everything will be fine Jeff," Jackie assured him. He knew she was a mother and that she knew more about what was going on than him. He wasn't feeling very assured at the moment, not until he saw Luke smiling again and Cristina holding their beautiful babies.

"Have you heard anything yet?" Emily pulled from his tight hug and looked up at him.

"Nothing yet," Jeff said and he plopped himself back into the seat he had vacated when they arrived.

"Let's just keep praying shall we," Emily said as she took the seat next to him and rested her head on his shoulder when he wrapped his arm around her. Jackie took a seat across from them and they all bowed their heads for silent prayers.

*****

Emily was moved by the man she was sitting next too, he was genuinely concerned for his best friend's wife and the babies. How could any woman not be moved by such a tender hearted man. She remembered a few weeks before, in her drunken stupor, she had admitted to him that she loved him and he told her he was falling in love with her, but nothing had been said since. She didn't feel a strain on their relationship because of it or anything, but seeing him like he was now, only made her love him even more.

Emily sent up her prayers to protect the small family and to keep Jeff strong during this whole ordeal. Emily looked up at Jeff to see his head was still bowed in prayer and as she kissed his cheek he looked up and planted a soft kiss on her lips. "I do love you, you know that, right?" Jeff said softly and Emily's eyes filled with tears with the admission of his feelings.

"I love you too," she whispered, choking back the tears that threatened to spill over. He pulled her into a tight hug and dropped down in front of her on one knee. Emily's eyes widened as she watched Jeff fumble with his pocket and withdraw a little black velvet box. She glanced at Jackie who was staring with a bright smile and Emily looked back to Jeff who was staring at her so intently that tears flooded her face.

"Emily, I know this is bad timing but I love you and I have never loved anyone more and I can't imagine my life without you in it. Will you do me the honor of becoming my wife?" Jeff said and popped the little box open to reveal a pretty diamond shaped like a heart and two more diamonds on each side of the band.

"Oh Jeff," she stammered, she wasn't sure she was ready for marriage, but she did love the man and it wasn't like she was getting any younger. She was twenty-eight and wanted children and a husband to love and care for, but she feared all of those things. She feared she would be a horrid wife and a worse mother, she feared she would be just like her parents. "I, I, don't know what to say." She slipped and caught Jackie nodding yes in her peripheral view. "Yes, yes, I would love to marry you," she finally admitted. He knew everything about her past and if he still loved her after all of that, how could she pass him by?

He slipped the ring on her finger and stood pulling her with him into a tight hug and planting multiple kisses on her lips, cheeks and forehead. "I love you so much and I swear I'll take care of you," Jeff whispered in her ear.

"Ditto," Emily replied between tears of joy. She felt Jackie squeeze them both just as the door to the waiting room opened. Emily saw Luke and pulled from their embrace as Jackie and Jeff turned to look upon his best friend. Luke was wearing a pair of blue scrubs and he was holding a pink and blue bundle in his arms that she hadn't noticed while hugging Jeff.

"How, how is she doing?" Jeff asked rushing to his friend's side, glancing down at the babies while towing Emily with him.

"She's perfectly fine," Luke smiled.

"And who are these two little ones?" Emily asked squeezing Jeff's arm.

"This is Skylar and Braxton, they each weighed in at six pounds even and are twenty inches long and perfectly healthy." Luke said proudly. Emily watched the little ones squirm in his arms and when they opened their eyes they were a blue color and Emily wondered what the color would be as they got older. She had learned in school that when infants are born, they all have blue eyes, but as they grow the brown color could present itself.

"They're beautiful," Jackie said next to them. "When can we pay a visit to Cristina?"

"We can do one at a time, but from the rock I see on Emily's hand I think both of you could go in together and give her the happy news," Luke said brightly. Emily looked at Jeff then Luke and saw the odd look the two usually gave each other. Then Luke looked at her and gave her the sweetest smile she had ever seen on him and she felt reassured by her answer to Jeff. She would have a family, a real family and not one that hit any time they got angry.

*****

Cristina lay in her bed waiting patiently for Luke to return with her sweet little ones. She had just woke up long enough to see them as Luke was carrying them out so she could rest. She'd told him she was alright and to bring them back as soon as he showed them off. Apparently she had started to hemorrhage after the epidural or something, she was only vaguely aware of Dr. Collins as she had spoken to her when she woke. She had lost a lot of blood and they had to do an emergency C-section to deliver the babies. But according to Dr. Collins, she was going to be just fine, and the babies were perfect.

The door opened and Jeff entered with a bright smile followed by an even bigger smile from Emily. They walked right next to her and were both glowing with happiness. "I know I'm awesome and all, but you two can't be this happy over seeing me." Cristina tried her attempt at humor even with all the pain meds the doctor had given her, she felt the daze coming on.

"Oh you, I'm so glad you're alright and the babies look so amazing and beautiful, just like their momma," Jeff admitted, leaned down and kissed her on the forehead.

"Oh, giving birth, almost dying according to the Doc, was nothing," Cristina smiled weakly, She had seen the worried looks when she was coming in and out of consciousness, but all she was worried about were her babies.

"You really are funny," Jeff said.

"So really, what is with all the happy going on other than

the cutest babies in the world being born?" Cristina asked. Jeff lifted Emily's hand and showed her the ring and smiled. Cristina was speechless but extremely happy for them. "Congratulations. Seems this day keeps getting better and better," Cristina smiled as brightly as she could.

"The great thing is that she said yes," Jeff smiled broadly and Emily's cheeks reddened.

"Did you really? Are you sure you want to marry this crazy man?" Cristina asked laughingly.

"I'm positive," Emily smiled. "We better let you rest, Luke said a quick visit, we'll get together when you get home and I'll come help with the babies," Emily smiled.

"Thank you and I'm happy for you both, now shoo let this woman rest," Cristina smiled. Jeff kissed her on the forehead again and they left her to be alone. Cristina looked towards the two empty baby hospital beds and hoped Luke would return with her beautiful babies soon. The doctor informed her that she wouldn't be able to nurse with all the medications she was on, but she was ok with that. She knew the benefits of nursing, but she couldn't risk their lives or hers at this point.

Luke walked in the room carefully holding her precious babies with a big smile. "They are the most beautiful babies in the world," he said. She couldn't help the swell of love for the man who loved the babies he held that weren't even his biologically; she was feeling truly blessed.

"They sure are," Cristina said sleepily.

"You need to rest love," Luke said as he settled Skylar and Braxton into their little beds. He pulled up a seat next to her after planting a soft kiss on her lips.

"Not tired yet. Did you see how happy Jeff looked?" she

asked him.

"They are great for each other," Luke smiled.

"I'm so happy for him, he seemed so sad there for a while," she admitted. She had noticed his sad eyes even when he had been kidding with her and it made her sad as well.

"I love you so much," Luke told her yet again He'd been saying that he loved her from the day they got married as often as he could, which made her feel more loved than she ever thought possible.

"I love you as well," Cristina smiled at him and reached for his hand, which he took in his and lightly squeezed it.

"I'm the luckiest man alive right now," Luke said softly squeezing her hand and looking at the sleeping infants at the foot of her bed.

"I would say we are the luckiest family around," Cristina said.

"Those two will have so much love they will hate us with love," Luke laughed softly.

"Hate us with love? That's a bit odd saying," Cristina looked at him with raised eyebrows.

"My mother used to say that to me all the time, "you'll have so much love son, you'll hate us with love." She was a wonderful mother, I so wish you could have met her. She would have loved not only you, but these two beautiful grandchildren," Luke looked at her and she could see his eyes had reddened from the unshed tears.

"I'm sure we'll all meet one day when the time is right," Cristina said softly as she watched a lone tear drop down his face. She had never seen a man cry, but she thought it was the sweetest thing she had ever seen. For a man to let down his "Tough Man" shield and show his true feeling for someone or something, it was a true sign of love if she had ever seen one.

"Woman, you're the best thing that has ever happened to me," Luke responded.

"Man, you're the greatest thing that has ever happened to me, well the children are blessings but I'm the happiest woman in the world right now," Cristina said as her eyes began to get heavy from the medication.

"I love you."

"I love you as well my dear sweet husband."

"Sleep my love, we are going to be the happiest little family." Luke stood and kissed her again as her eyes began to close. He sat back down and clasped her hand once more as her eyes closed letting the sweet darkness take her over.

EPILOGUE

It had been a year since Jeff proposed and Emily was as happy as a puppy with a new toy. She stood in front of the floor length mirror in the dressing room of the church. Her white wedding gown had a heart shape bodice and flowed down in gossamer silks and lace that ballooned out from her hips. The train was five feet long and her heels were three inches giving her more height to stand next to her soon to be husband.

A knock on the door pulled her attention from her dress and the thought of Jeff standing at the altar wearing a black tux with tails and bright blue cummerbund and tie.

"You ready?" Jackie asked as she entered the room pulling the door closed behind her.

"Can't wait," Emily smiled and pulled her veil over her face, she felt awful for wearing white but Jackie was adamant that it was just a color and she looked amazing so she bought the dress. Jackie was wearing a bright blue dress with spaghetti straps that hung to her ankles topped with matching blue shoes. She looked amazing.

Emily took steadying breaths as Jackie straightened the veil over her face and lead her out the door to where Luke waited. He looked stunning in his tux and Cristina looked radiant in a matching dress like Jackie's. Emily glanced at Skylar and Braxton in the stroller they had decorated to match the wedding; Braxton wore a tiny tux like his father and Skylar wore a tiny blue dress with frills and flowers, and they were fast asleep. Braxton had retained his bright blue eyes like his father, but Skylar's eyes were a dark chocolate color like her mother's. Emily was a little sad about missing the chance to look into them before she walked down the aisle.

"You look amazing Em," Cristina said as she gently hugged her.

"Thanks, I'm sure Luke is having a hard time keeping his hands off you in that dress," Emily winked at Cristina and they all laughed.

"Very true, I'm trying not to look at my extremely hot wife," Luke smiled and then winked at Cristina. Emily was so happy to be joining such a wonderful family. She had had a very hard life with an alcoholic mother, abusive father, a sister that committed suicide and a brother sitting in prison. She was feeling truly blessed to have opened up to find such an amazing family, blood related or not. They all cared for each other, loved each other and for the first time in her life she felt free to be herself.

The music started and Emily took a deep breath as everyone got ready to begin the wedding. Her heart was racing, but she was so happy she was afraid she might cry. She contained herself and looked ahead so she could see the look on Jeff's face when she entered the room.

*****

Jeff stood at the altar waiting anxiously for the doors to open at the end of the aisle. He and Luke had finished the house four months ago, taking their time to make sure everything was perfect. The weather had been relatively good and that summer had been pretty dry to his shock and amazement. He watched as Luke's babies grew and Emily was completely taken by the sweet children. His heart was ready to explode with love that he had for the woman.

The music began to play and his heart began to race as the

doors opened and Luke began to walk down the aisle with Jackie followed by Cristina pushing the flower girl and ring bearer down the aisle in the stroller they had covered in white satin fabric and blue flowers. Emily had insisted that Braxton and Skylar be a part of the wedding and Jeff didn't object, he loved those kids.

Finally the wedding march began and Jeff focused on the doors where Emily would enter. He couldn't help the smile that spread across his face when she stepped through the door and he was finally looking upon her. The dress she wore looked fantastic with her figure, he couldn't see her face through the veil she wore, but he knew she looked amazing. She walked up the aisle with such grace; he was in awe of the woman he was going to marry today.

*****

Luke watched as Jeff took Emily's hand, listened as they gave their vows and smiled happily when Jeff finally lifted the veil to kiss his bride. Luke was so happy for his best friend, how could he not be. Luke felt so happy in his life with a wonderful wife and two amazing children, he wanted the same joy for Jeff and he knew Emily was that person.

Luke shook Jeff's hand before the bride and groom took their leave then he took Jackie's arm as they followed suit with Cristina and his children behind them. They would go into a dressing room off from the chapel until the room cleared out. Then they would do pictures, head to the reception, toss the garter and bouquet, cut the cake and have the first dance.

*****

Cristina loaded the children into their respective car seats after the reception, they were already asleep and Cristina was starting to feel the need for sleep too. "Hey, how are you doing?" Luke came up behind her. She couldn't help but still be awed by the man she was happy to call her husband. The black tux and the tails took her breath away and the blues brought out the beautiful color of his eyes.

"I'm a little tired, how about you?" she asked, turning and planting a kiss on his lips.

"Much better to have you in my arms again, we got the Bride and Groom off to their honeymoon and Jackie is taking care of everything else inside like the cool maid of honor she is, and we can go home." Luke smiled and pulled her close into a tight hug.

"I love you so much," Cristina said as she inhaled the wonderful aroma of his cologne.

"I love you too, let's go home and put these two in bed so we can get some sleep ourselves," Luke said pulling her from the hug and kissing her on the forehead.

"Sounds good to me, I'm beat, and these heels, are really starting to hurt," Cristina laughed.

"But you look amazing in this dress," Luke smiled and dropped a kiss on her lips. They were so happy together, and Emily loved how good he was with the children. Their first words were da' and to Cristina, that was amazing.

Luke held the door open for her as she got into the car, she watched as he checked the buckles of the car seats to ensure they were tight enough, and he climbed into the driver's seat to take them home. Cristina couldn't believe how happy everyone around her was, Ray had even called to let her know he was seeing someone and they were both going to fly out for Thanksgiving.

Cristina couldn't get over how hard her life had been, the challenges she had faced and the many times she almost threw it all away. The past two years made everything feel worth it. She had a husband who loved her, two amazing children and a surprise for Luke when they got home since she was pregnant again, but this time it really was Luke's. She was overwhelmed with joy. Since she'd moved to Cobblestone she found love and family like no other; Jeff was like a brother, Emily a sister and Jackie was a lot like a mother to the group. There are always trials in life, hardships around every turn, but when you have love, everything works itself out. Without love, no matter if it's from a blood relative or someone you choose to love, Cristina knew love was all you needed to be happy, and she had so much love she was soaring.

ABOUT THE AUTHOR

B.M. Griese grew up in Knox County, KY. In her teen years she and her mother moved to Rochester, NY, where she met her high school sweet heart and husband. School was never her strong suit with her struggles with dyslexia. After working hard and not allowing her learning disability to stop her she started college and is working hard to obtain her degree in psychology.

Writing is her passion and one of her favorite past times along with quilting.